PATRIOTS

Book One of
THE 2ND CONTINENTAL
LIGHT DRAGOONS

SANDRA CHEN

Dedicated to Jessica – never stop inspiring

CONTENTS

TO THE READER

Some of the names mentioned in this story will be spelled differently than some sourced documents and books. A concentrated effort was put in to ensure that the characters are true to their real-life counterparts. No defamation is intended.

Regarding the dialogue in this story; most of it is not couched in the language of the time period as it would have been a difficult read. Nonetheless, I have tried to keep to the period's mannerisms and formality instead and, when it was prudent, use the language of the time in the context of conversations and happenstance.

"I only regret that I have but one life to lose for my country."

Quote attributed to Captain Nathan Hale
before his execution on Sept. 22, 1776

1

August 30th, 1776

Benjamin Tallmadge thought death smelled like rancid onions mixed with the decay of rotting fish. It was his first thought when he arrived shortly after the Battle for Bunker Hill had concluded; he had wandered through the blood-slicked fields, inspecting the troop lines, and listening to survivor stories of how they had made the British pay inch by inch until the lobsterbacks had no more heart to fight and soon left Boston. He did not know why he had associated onions, the main export of his current home, Wethersfield, with the smell of death. But now he could not help feeling that rancid onions should be present in wake alongside the absolutely putrid stink of rotting fish in Brooklyn Harbor.

"Sir, ready to push off," one of the men said and he pulled himself out of his thoughts. He looked around to see that, indeed, they were one of the last boats to push off from Brooklyn to York City.

"Push off," he ordered and the oarsmen obeyed as the echoes of others calling the same command to their troops filled the air. He could hardly see the men of his troop in the other boats through the thick soup of fog that roiled over the bay. The shore from which they had evacuated was empty, but as Tallmadge looked back, he imagined that in only a short while there would be familiar red coats of British troops lining it.

His troop, in the battalion commanded by Colonel John Chester and attached to Brigadier General James Wadsworth's brigade from Connecticut, had been assigned to the rear guard after General Washington ordered the evacuation of the army from Brooklyn Heights back to York City proper. Word had passed that the British were advancing slowly and steadily, with more caution and less reckless abandon that had been employed during Bunker Hill. Tallmadge supposed that the British had learned their lesson, but he had hoped to further bloody their noses before they evacuated. During the skirmish along Brooklyn Heights, his troop had been part of the fierce fight as they retreated to the redoubts that dotted the shores. The battalion as a whole would have been routed had it not been for Tallmadge and his troop. He had spotted the incoming British troops that tried to flank them and warned the commanding officer of his troop, Captain Wells, who sent hasty word to Colonel Chester himself. They had immediately pulled back along with the other troops, an organized retreat that made him proud of the discipline he had managed to instill in his men earlier in the summer. He had not gotten a count of his lost men, but he had seen at least three shot dead from British musket fire near him. Losses were heavier in the other battalions and he supposed it was why Chester wanted his troop to be one of the last to evacuate.

Tallmadge was proud of the steadiness his men displayed. He and his fellow lieutenant, Bulkley, had spent the summer drilling them. Though the men had initially wavered under British fire, when it came time to retreat, they had done so without breaking their lines. As he trained them, he had studied some of the latest techniques and had even asked Colonel Chester for advice on making sure that his troop was in tip-top shape. Chester had directed him to some of the other more experienced commanders and had even put in a good word for him. Those officers had apparently taken Chester at his word and taught Tallmadge their own techniques which he brought back and used to drill his men.

When the orders came down to his troop that they were to be the rear guard, Tallmadge had been excited. He had hoped that the British would advance faster so that the men would be able to give them another fight before leaving with the ships – but looking back at the empty docks and lack of red uniformed British colors, it was not to be.

His only regret was that he had to leave his favorite horse, a gift from one of the ladies with whom he had been in correspondence before he had deployed from Wethersfield. The beast had a steady foot and was unafraid when muskets and cannons had shelled their initial position in Brooklyn. The option to requisition a new horse after the loss of this one would be available to him, but Tallmadge did not want to spend the time breaking in his new mount.

"Steady," he quietly called out at the sound of one of the oarsmen slapping his oar against the water. "Steady man."

"Sir," the oarsman apologized with a hoarseness in his voice as he continued to row. Tallmadge looked around him as the fog rolled and ebbed from the movement of the boat. He occasionally caught a glimpse of the rest of the his troop in other boats rowing alongside him. He thought he also caught sight of Captain Wells and Lieutenant Bulkley in their boats, but for the most part, it felt like his boat was the only one rowing to York City. After several minutes of rowing, the sound of water hitting the shoreline grew louder, and he knew they were fast approaching the opposite shore. Tallmadge turned, cupping his hands to his mouth as he peered through the thick gloom.

"Ho there!" he called out.

"Ho back!" someone called out. Not even a second later, "Identify yourself!"

"Lieutenant Benjamin Tallmadge, 3rd Troop under Captain Wells of the 6th Battalion, Wadsworth Brigade," he called back.

"Tallmadge, that you?" he heard another voice speak up in the murky fog that surrounded the docks. He saw the faint glow of a lantern waving as the docks seemingly emerged from the fog. The mist parted enough for him to discern a sizable crowd of soldiers. Their shouts and commands of other troops that had been last to evacuate Brooklyn Harbor echoed across the area. Some were disembarking and mustering at various points along the docks that his boat was approaching. Oarsmen were already pulling the rest of their boats back to make way for them.

"Oars back, oars back!" He realized they were approaching

the docks at a too-fast pace and grabbed onto the sides of the boat as the oarsmen immediately pulled in the opposite direction that they had been rowing in, trying to slow the boat. The boat docked with a rough splintering sound, but it had slowed enough that Tallmadge knew there was only surface damage to the vessel.

"Tallmadge, you grew up where? Along the coastline?" the same voice spoke up, this time above him. He looked up, shaking his head in exasperation.

"Never said I was a whaler, Hale," he commented as he accepted the hand that was offered to him and pulled himself up to the docks. Finding his feet back on steady ground, Tallmadge tightened his grip on Hale's hand and pulled him into a back-slapping embrace. "Good to see you again Nathan," he greeted his best friend before releasing him, a wide smile on his face.

"I did not realize you were posted as rear guard until I saw Colonel Chester and a couple of others I recognized when he evacuated," Nathan Hale had a similarly glad expression on his face.

"Aye," Tallmadge nodded as he looked around the docks, the fog thinning so close to the coastline. "The rest of my troop should be coming in." No sooner than he said the words, he saw several boats carrying the rest of his troop docking at various points. "Excuse me." He wanted to talk more with Nathan, having not seen him in the last few of weeks, but he needed to report to Captain Wells on the success of the evacuation.

"Sir," he called out to Wells, who was at the head of one of the boats. He heard Nathan following him, his boots echoing sharply on the docks. The rest of his men filed out of the boat, young Ensign James Hecox gathering them into a semblance of rank and file as he made his report. The young man had a good steady head on his shoulders and it was Tallmadge who had recommended him to Wells for his appointment as ensign. Tallmadge had been teaching him in Wethersfield when the call to muster went out and Tallmadge along with some of his friends, Hecox included, and fellow students had answered the call.

"Sir," Tallmadge called out again as he reached over to help Wells out of the boat, the older man wobbling a bit on the docks before finding his legs. Wells had clearly never been on any body of water, not even the Connecticut River that ran right through Wethersfield. He dared not comment on the paleness of the man's face as he briefly saluted him and stepped to the side to allow the men on his boat to disembark.

"Handsomely, now, handsomely!" the booming voice of Edward Bulkley sounded near them as his boat docked. He was clearly used to the water, having been part of a merchant family that operated trade all the way down to New Haven where several cousins of the family resided. Tallmadge knew that Bulkely's family plied trade-wares all along the coastline of America and across the ocean.

"Sir," Tallmadge started again, addressing Wells. "We were the last boat to push off and I saw no sign of the enemy."

"Good," Wells nodded. "Muster your men a few blocks north and east of here and join the rest of the battalion. I will join the lines with you after I meet with the Colonel."

"Sir," Tallmadge threw a quick salute, and hurried to the other dock where Bulkley was guiding the men off the boat. "We're mustering a few blocks away," he said quietly to Bulkley who nodded before his eyes widened and he stiffened.

"S-Sir, sorry sir, didn't see you there," Bulkley stammered, and Tallmadge turned to see Nathan with an mild expression on his face. It was also then that he finally noticed the single epaulette on his uniform's shoulder that denoted his rank – captain.

"...Sir." Tallmadge had to admit, it felt unusual to be saluting his best friend, but he did so with respect to his friend's rank. He had been too caught up in seeing Nathan again to realize that his friend now deserved his respect and salute. Tallmadge wondered why he had not noted his friend's rank the last time they had met.

"Lieutenants," Nathan returned the salute with a flick of his fingers. He hid a smile at his sudden discomfort at the discovery of his rank. "Continue. I am here just simply observing."

"Yes sir," Bulkley shot Tallmadge an odd look that he knew he would have to address later in a more private setting. His fellow lieutenant was not only of similar rank, but they both shared the same passions for rhetoric and politics. He, Bulkley, and several others who served in the troop had both gone up to see what happened after the Battle of Bunker Hill and had talked to their military friends at Cambridge. Afterwards, when the declaration came from the Continental Congress to call upon the militia of each state, the two of them had enlisted at the same time. Bulkley was a good friend, but Tallmadge thought of him as a bit thick-headed – perhaps from the amount of sun he received on his family's boats each day.

He turned and headed back to his boat, where Hecox had gotten a majority of the men to stand to attention. He could hear Bulkley calling for Sergeant-Major Davenport, who led the men in the fourth boat that carried the last of 3rd Troop over. Davenport was another friend who had gone with them to enlist, but had not had the money to purchase a commission. Bulkley had purchased his appointment before Colonel Chester had personally appointed Tallmadge to his commission. It technically made Bulkley a 1st Lieutenant while he was, a 2nd Lieutenant. There was little to no pay difference, but in terms of opportunities, any sort of promotion would be given to Bulkley first by virtue of his enlistment date. The odd thing was that Bulkley was not as aggressive as Tallmadge would have thought he'd be with his commission, seeking out opportunities to drill or train the troop. Instead, Tallmadge had taken the initiative to seek out training opportunities to drill the rest of the troop and also to ensure that every single man in the army evacuated Brooklyn Heights successfully.

"A fine troop, Lieutenant." There was a teasing note to Nathan's comment as he inspected the troops. Tallmadge nodded. He knew Nathan's comments were to tease him about his initial discomfort at his rank and the same camaraderie he had felt during their school days started an idea brewing in his mind.

"Sir, if you would be so kind," Tallmadge gestured a little more grandly than protocol dictated for Nathan to lead the procession. "Unless you are needed elsewhere?"

"On special detachment from the 19th," Nathan replied offhandedly, as the drummer beat the march. Tallmadge took the lead with Nathan next to him, Ensign Hecox behind them. Another one of his Wethersfield friends, Sergeant Andrew Adamson, followed next to Hecox, setting the pace for the rest of the troop that fell behind them. Tallmadge could hear Bulkley and Davenport organizing the rest of the troop. The sound of marching boots soon echoed across the cobblestone and dirt as the men followed him and Nathan.

"Special detachment?" Tallmadge was curious as he turned his head a little to acknowledge Bulkley, who had joined them after he finished dealing with the rear.

"Sir," Bulkley tipped his hat towards Nathan, who nodded in return.

"Lieutenant Colonel Knowlton just received a dispensation to raise a regiment of Rangers to help scout out the area here and potentially take Long Island back," Nathan sounded proud and Tallmadge nodded.

"Congratulations on your posting, sir." He remembered to add the respectful 'sir' this time.

"Captain Bacon and his regiment were asked to join and I was hoping to recruit some of your men to join in this offensive." Nathan looked earnest and Tallmadge instantly knew his friend had greeted him in deliberate fashion at the docks. He wanted him to join him in Knowlton's Rangers.

"I am honored," he replied, but shook his head, "but I must decline the offer."

"Ben-"

"Colonel Chester was kind enough to appoint me as lieutenant to the 6th Battalion he raised," he explained, and saw Nathan's eyes soften in understanding. Appointments were not taken lightly, especially when offered by friends or those in high places. Rarely were they declined, and those who did were shunned to some extent. Most of the commissions in the Continental Army had to be brought with a good amount of coin, or were appointed by those with influence.

"Colonel Webb gave me my first commission," his friend replied and Tallmadge knew his friend understood his meaning. They had both been appointed, and he knew his friend must have felt an intense loyalty of sorts to Colonel Charles Webb and had made the decision to join Knowlton's Rangers on special detachment after considerable thought.

"I will ask Chester when he returns, but for now, I must decline your offer," he compromised, and saw Nathan nod, an agreeable smile gracing his youthful features. It was the only thing he could really say without outright declining his best friend's invitation.

Tallmadge would ask, but he had the feeling he already knew the answer from Colonel Chester. With Captain Asa Bacon and more than likely the rest of 6th Troop recruited into Knowlton's Rangers, Chester would hesitate to allow others to join from his battalion. It would deprive him of the needed men to hold whatever line General Washington or any of the other commanders were to order them to next.

An amicable silence fell between them as they marched their way to the muster point where Tallmadge saw the rest of General Wadsworth's Brigade. He could see small artillery being unloaded from the boats that had not been used to ferry the troops across the river. They had been salvaged in the hasty evacuation from Brooklyn Heights. The snorting and neighing of the horses helping to carry the artillery to position prompted a sudden pang of nostalgia for the mount he had left behind. It had been a magnificent beast, well broken in and cared for, and it had taken him from Wethersfield down to his father's homestead in Setauket, Long Island, then back to the main action in Brooklyn.

"Still, I dare say we will see action soon, but let me know of your offer by week's end, all right?" Nathan suddenly spoke up and Tallmadge absently nodded as he continued to stare at what was happening before him. He managed to remember to give Nathan a brief salute as he left them, headed towards what looked like 4th Troop who were also stationed in the mustering area. Captain Marcy of the 4th and his two lieutenants, Holmes and Samuel Marcy – the captain's son – had managed to save their horses when they crossed with the salvaged artillery. Tallmadge supposed his friend was making the same offer he had made to him to Marcy and his troop. Colonel Chester must have approved of such an order since it seemed that the commission for Knowlton's Rangers came from General Washington himself.

Tallmadge could not help the sudden surge of jealousy at the sight of the 4th Troop officers' horses. He, Bulkley and Captain Wells had to abandon theirs because all the ferries had been taken for artillery use, and they were rear guard. He pressed his lips together as an idea started to form. It was foolhardy and foolish, the rational part of him protested, but the part that had been overjoyed to see his friend Nathan knew it was one of his greatest ideas – bold, daring, and much like the mischief he and Nathan had hatched at Yale before they graduated. If it worked, it would irritate the British.

"Ensign, deploy the men along the docks here. Rations and water and to get some rest," he ordered Hecox who nodded, "Bulkley, I'm going to find Captain Wells."

"You planning something, Tallmadge?" Bulkley stared at him with a hint of suspicion and narrowed eyes. Tallmadge shrugged. Bulkley was far more cautious than Nathan, but Tallmadge had cajoled him on more than one occasion to have a little fun.

"Perhaps," he replied as he broke away from the bustle of men and beast, and the acrid smell of artillery being unloaded. Battalion headquarters had been established a few blocks north of the mustering point for most of the Connecticut 6th Brigade, along the intersection of Post Road and Bloomingdale Avenue. It was north of his troop's position, but not as far south as where General Knox and Putnam's forces were. Wadsworth's 1st Battalion under the command of Colonel Gold Selleck Silliman, had been deployed to General Putnam's forces to guard the tip of York City itself in case General Howe decided to move his forces back to Staten Island and attack from the south. The rest of Wadsworth's brigade – which included Colonel Chester's battalion – were currently mustering and lining the south-eastern tip of York Island.

Tallmadge pushed his way past the men, some of whom were milling about while they waited for further orders while others sat down and rested. They all looked a little weary from the recent battle and two days straight without sleep. To Tallmadge's concern, he saw that some had open looks of fear, and were whispering prayers with eyes wide and unseeing, while others simple shook. He made a note that after he talked to Captain Wells about his idea, he would talk to some of the sergeants he knew from the regiments about calming the men down. He had already learned quickly that panic did no one good. Panicked men were worse than idle men. His own troop was thankfully disciplined enough not to show panic when they had retreated and were ordered to rear guard. But he had seen it when the lines had initially broken down; men fleeing at the advance of the red coats of British troops.

It did not take long for Tallmadge to find his captain. He saw him emerging from a small inn of sorts in close discussion with Colonel Chester and the other captains of the 6th Battalion. The meeting must have just ended as he approached the small group.

"Tallmadge," Wells greeted and he saluted him, receiving acknowledgments from Chester and some of the other captains who were not in deep discussion.

"Sir, if I may propose a plan of action." He dared not turn his attention directly to Wells as he slowly walked back with them.

"Plan of action?" Colonel Chester turned to him and he nodded.

"Yes sir," he gestured towards the direction of Brooklyn Heights, "3rd Troop was unable to move their horses over due to the lack of ferries. Since they have finished moving the artillery, I respectfully request leave to retrieve Captain Wells, Lieutenant Bulkley, and my own mounts."

Silence fell among the group and Tallmadge kept his expression as neutral as possible. He could see the disbelief in the faces of some of the other captains who had overheard his proposal while Wells stared at him with an expression he could not quite understand. From Colonel Chester, he received no indication of his thoughts.

"Have you been taken ill?" he heard one of the captains whisper into the silence. A glare from Wells quieted the speaker.

"Explain yourself, Tallmadge," Wells turned back to face him.

"We would not be able to effectively command the men if we are not visible to the men, sir," he said and saw Wells' expression grow pinched. "I doubt that we would be able to find horses so quickly if we are to be deployed in the next few hours to repel a potential attack by the British. And if we did, the urgency in which we have evacuated here would be known to those who wish to sell us their mounts at a much steeper cost. Such high of a price should brand them as Tories."

Out of the corner of his eye, he saw Chester rub his chin, and knew that there was some hope and merit to his plan. "We evacuated under the cover of fog, Lieutenant," Chester said slowly and Tallmadge nodded.

"We did sir, and we still have the element of surprise. Neither myself nor my men saw the British advancing when we pushed off. If I go now, we would have time to take one of the ferries and bring back the horses."

"And if the fog lifts?"

"It will not, for divine providence wills it so." Tallmadge forced his voice not to waver and hoped it sounded convincing. He saw Chester's gaze sliding to the side and knew the other man was thinking, before he pinned him with a look that he steadily held.

"Volunteers, Lieutenant. Do you understand the consequences of your actions?" Chester asked and Tallmadge nodded, forcing himself not to smile at his success. He understood that if he was caught by the British, there would be no quarter for him – for a mere lieutenant. His rank, especially since he was militia instead of Continental Army, did not warrant any courtesy of a prisoner transfer and he would more than likely be confined to a jail for the duration of the war.

"Yes sir," he replied and saw the ghost of a smile appear on Chester's face. He saluted the small group. They returned his salute with varying degrees of crispness – some openly showing their disbelief at his audacious plan and Colonel Chester's agreement to it. Turning on his heel, he left them, heading back to where the rest of the 3rd had mustered.

It was time to find volunteers.

Colonel John Chester did not need to look around him at the assembled captains of his troops nor did he need to look to where his second, Lieutenant Colonel Solomon Wills, and his third, Major John Ripley, were standing next to him. Disbelief and wonder radiated through the small group after he had called them for a debriefing following General Wadsworth's meeting a half hour before. He had been one of the last commanders under Wadsworth's brigade to attend the meeting, due to the fact that his battalion had been ordered to rear guard.

"The boy is touched in the head," he heard Wills mutter mostly under his breath, and did not comment as Ripley and

Captain Israel Seymour of 1st Troop both nodded in agreement.

"It is a rather bold plan." Instead, it was Captain Chester Wells, Tallmadge's own direct commander, that defended the young man.

"It's a plan that will get him and others killed," Reuben Marcy, captain of his 4th Troop said, his voice gruff with disapproval.

"I take my leave, gentlemen," he suddenly cut into the conversation, temporarily halting the rise of tempers he could see building between his subordinates over Tallmadge's actions. He was certain the young man did not know what he had touched off between his subordinates. He was well aware that those under his command were fiercely competitive, men all from the same region, some of whom were friends or familiar with each other. Tallmadge was no exception, but during the early summer months after they had deployed to New York, it had been 3rd Troop out of the whole of the 6th that was praised by General Wadsworth as the best drilled troop. Each of the battalions had their own best drilled, but that had apparently sparked a jealousy and rivalry among his captains to win such accolades and praise.

Chester knew it did not help matters that it was he who had directed Tallmadge – who had expressed interest in drilling his men – to those in Wadsworth's Brigade who had experience drilling and fighting. He, himself had fought since Lexington, but he knew he could not show overt favoritism for the young man. Personally appointing him as a lieutenant over some of the other bids for appointments he had received had soured some of the goodwill he had with a few families that wanted their sons to have rank and position in the brigade. But there had been a fire, a fervor in Tallmadge since the young man had come up to visit after Bunker Hill. He had readily talked to him about patriotism and service against the injustices that the British had heaped upon them.

"Sir," they saluted him and he tipped his hat towards them before leaving. He heard Wills and Ripley follow behind him. He also knew there was a reason for some of the resentment among the captains towards Tallmadge. Besides appointing him as one of his lieutenants, he had given the young man the position of regimental adjutant. It was a staff position, one that

Tallmadge had fulfilled to great expectation before fighting had broken out in Brooklyn Heights, but it was also a position where one was relied upon to pass messages to and from the rest of his command staff to his commanders. It was the chief reason why he had directed 3rd Troop to be the last of the companies in his battalion to push off from the docks.

And now, whether Tallmadge knew it or not, he was his eyes and ears to the advancement of British troops in Brooklyn Heights with his bold plan. The 3rd was the last to push off, and therefore the last to vouchsafe whether or not the British were pursuing them with haste. There was danger for Tallmadge should he be captured, but since he was in his uniform instead of military scouting, he would at least have the protection of being thrown into jail instead of hung like a spy.

"Sir, do you really think-"

He held up a hand to stop whatever other complaint Wills had against Tallmadge's plan. "It has been done, Solomon." Wills had served along side him since Lexington, as had Major Ripley. When he was given the 6th by General Wadsworth, he had immediately appointed them to the available positions of lieutenant colonel and major as was his given choice. He knew caution and their own actions at Lexington and later at Bunker Hill, had instilled in them a healthy respect and fear for British lines, but he had wondered lately if Wills' caution was motivated by fear. Something had changed in his long-time friend – gone was the spark of boldness that had urged the three of them to recklessly charge the British lines in an attempt to draw a few of them into a flanking maneuver during Bunker Hill. Ripley had stayed silent, but he also knew his other friend tended to agree with Wills more often than not.

He could see Wills' expression flatten. "Yes sir."

"If I may ask, where are we going?" Ripley spoke up.

"To where General Wadsworth is," he replied as he turned the corner, nodding to two militiamen who were stationed as guards outside the general command post. As they entered, the sheer amount of noise that emanated from the open doors might have been mistaken for that of a rowdy tavern.

The hearty roaring laughter of General Israel Putnam might have been heard from miles away. Chester silently shook his head at its sound. He could also smell the cigar that Putnam had taken to smoking every time he had seen the esteemed general. Putnam must have stayed to discuss line options, as he and General Henry Knox were stationed at the southern tip of York Island to repel any attempt from Howe to launch his forces from Staten Island. Knox commanded a majority of the army's artillery forces and Putnam and the regiments under his command had been deployed go safeguard their artillery.

"Sir." He heard the echoing statements of respect from Wills and Ripley as they waited in the foyer.

They knew they would not be welcomed as he ventured deeper into the tavern, which had been converted in General Washington's temporary command post. Washington had another command post that was situated in the naturally fortified Harlem Heights north of the city in the hilly woodlands, but in order to facilitate faster communications with his generals and commanders, he had set up a temporary one here. Chester knew that his immediate commander, James Wadsworth would not have left since giving him and the other colonels of the brigade their briefing, the planning of retaking Brooklyn starting in earnest. The initial briefing was for deployments along the east coast of York Island and then the real planning would begin. When they had received their orders to be the rear guard, it had been initially couched in the fashion that the men were to retire to York Island where fresh soldiers would replace them. Chester knew that it had been done to prevent a mass rush of soldiers to the ferry boats as well as to give a semblance of order, but he had quickly surmised that rear guard meant they were doing a full evacuation. He had told his own captains as much, trusting their instincts as soldiers to hold the line for their fellow comrades.

He slipped past two aide-de-camps of a couple of the other commanders who were running to notify their regiments of fresh orders and the like. The tavern was crowded, but Chester saw Wadsworth, standing at the far edges of a circle that included Washington himself. The other generals were crowded around as were their seconds, and Chester saw Putnam with the ghost of a smile still on his lips from whatever he was laughing about earlier. It seemed that Washington was in quiet discussion with

Knox about artillery placements along the eastern shores and Wadsworth studied the battle map in silence.

"Sir," he stopped respectfully at Wadsworth's elbow. He and James Wadsworth had known each other for a while now. They both fought together at Bunker Hill and also came from the same region of Connecticut – the Wethersfield and Hartford area. It was Wadsworth who put in for his commission as a colonel, a two rank promotion he would have never gotten on the battlefield and gave him a chance to lead his men into battle. He knew his friend had other ambitions, hoping to rise up from the rank of brigadier general to perhaps one of Washington's trusted commanders or even part of his command staff, but Chester had no such ambitions himself. He was content with his station and if he had to admit it to himself – the recent action in Brooklyn Heights had brought back memories of Bunker Hill he'd rather not relive.

But he would not let that deter him from his duty and service to drive the British out of Long Island and so waited until Wadsworth looked at him to speak. "John," his friend addressed him in a congenial manner.

"Lieutenant Tallmadge requested leave to retrieve his horse from the shores of Brooklyn Heights since he and his troop were the last to evacuate," he said quietly and saw one of Wadsworth's eyebrows rise up in surprise.

"The boy surprises me yet again," Wadsworth commented, a wry smile forming on his lips. "Why? If he was the last-"

"He and Captain Wells reported that there was no sign of enemy advancement when they left the docks, sir," Chester explained. "I thought it prudent for him to perhaps see if any of Clinton's or Howe's forces have arrived from where we had evacuated."

Wadsworth pursed his lips for a moment and nodded, "Good plan, Colonel." Chester could clearly see that he understood the implicit meaning in his statement. If Tallmadge did not report back within the hour, it meant the British had overrun their evacuation point and would be preparing to move soon.

"How long ago was this, Colonel?" The last voice either one of them expected to hear was General Washington himself. Chester stiffened.

"Chester, sir. Colonel John Chester," he hastily introduced himself with a rigid salute as he turned to face the esteemed Commander-in-Chief of the Continental Army across the table. "And sir, my lieutenant left in the time I walked here to find you. I expect he has found his volunteers and is crossing back to Brooklyn at the moment."

Washington nodded before gesturing to someone that Chester could not see. A few seconds later, that gesture was answered by the appearance of Lieutenant Colonel Thomas Knowlton. Everyone knew Knowlton was a favorite of the general and had been recently given his own specialized regiment called the Knowlton Rangers. None of the commanders under Washington had been happy to have some of their men plucked away to serve under special detachment, but they could not voice their complaints about it. Resources and able-bodied men were scarce and those that had some specialized skill or training were put to use wherever they were useful.

"General Wadsworth, Colonel Chester, you may know of Lieutenant Colonel Knowlton I presume?"

"Yes sir." He shook hands with the man across the table as did Wadsworth.

"Colonel, if you could point out young Tallmadge to Mr. Knowlton here after he returns, I'm sure any knowledge he may have regarding any deployments he may have spotted in Brooklyn would be of great help to his men."

"Yes, sir, by your leave sirs." He respectfully inclined his head at them before gesturing for Knowlton to follow him even though he was a junior officer. "This way sir."

"Chester, we'll talk later. Bring Tallmadge with you," Wadsworth called as he and Knowlton left.

"Yes sir," he called back before he saw Wills and Ripley detach themselves from where they had been resting against the wall and approach them.

"Lieutenant Colonel," the two greeted one after another as Knowlton shook hands with them.

"Good to see you again," Knowlton had a friendly look on his face. Chester knew it was because when Knowlton was pleased to have been granted his request of Captain Bacon of 6th Troop and the men following him as part of his small detachment.

Chester had left most of the details to Wells and Ripley to sort out along with Knowlton requesting permission to take his cousin, a young Ensign Daniel Knowlton from Ashford out of 4th Troop. After Chester agreed to Knowlton's request, the officer had informed him that he had sent one of his men, a Captain Hale if he remembered correctly, to retrieve him after they had successfully evacuated Brooklyn Heights.

"Come for more apples on our fruitful trees?"

"No," Knowlton smiled, "just for information one of your men can provide me after he returns."

"If," he heard Ripley mutter, trying to cover it with a hand to his mouth. Chester gave the man a sharp look. He would brook no such talk from one of his officers, even if Ripley was a friend. "My apologies sir." Ripley said staring down at the ground, shame coloring his pale features.

"Sir, I will have to see to my battalion for a moment, but we can make our way to the docks afterwards to receive Tallmadge and whatever information he may provide." He turned and saw Knowlton nod. There was no expression on his face after Ripley's comment, but he did not dare put it past Knowlton to file such discontent away in his mind for future use. "I also ask for you to strike what Major Ripley has said from your mind, sir."

"Consider it done. It was, after all, a stressful affair with the British breaking our lines." The lieutenant colonel gave an amicable smile and Chester found himself warming a little to the junior officer. He could see why Washington had picked Knowlton himself to form a Ranger regiment. The man reserved his judgment and was not so quick to make decisions based on offhand comments. He also seemed fair-minded and optimistic about tactical information, instead of despairing of their evacuation as Chester knew some of the other commanders were wont to do. He knew that the injuries and death that occurred in some of his companies during the evacuation had made them bitter and afraid of the British – their lines broken so easily – but Knowlton seemed to have brushed aside or used it as armor, bolstering himself in the Patriotic cause.

It reminded him a little of Tallmadge's wide-eyed idealism and courage, and if Chester had to observe some more, he could almost see his young friend in Knowlton if he survived into the next year or so with this war.

They arrived shortly to where his battalion was posted, stretched across the south-eastern tip of York Island. They overlapped with some of Knox's forces, but that could not be helped. Washington wanted all soldiers to stay near the shores in case the British decided to cross the East River. It was crowded, dank and reeked of a sour smell that Chester recognized as death. The surgeons were operating in a makeshift infirmary off one of the larger docks and the screams mixed with the braying and snorting of animals could have made some of the newer recruits green in the face. Chester was not surprised to see several of the new recruits he had mustered in Connecticut a mere three months ago throwing up into the river at the sights, smells and sounds.

Those that had served at Lexington, Concord and Bunker Hill were steadfast, but even they had weary looks about their countenances. Some of them had a far away gaze that he knew all too well, while others resolutely ignored what was happening. A frown suddenly appeared on Chester's face as he saw the last thing he wanted to see among his men.

"Ripley, Wills, get these prostitutes out of here. Tell them to ply their wares elsewhere. I will not have the men fall into such disorder," he growled out, angry that the vermin of the city had already decided to come out and offer their 'comfort' to the men. They were still watching for the enemy and he would brook no man to fall into such lax discipline.

"Sir," he could see the stoniness in both Ripley and Wills' faces as they too had spotted the prostitutes whirling in and out of the mass of soldiers. In fact, more than one had already led a few of them into nearby alleyways. He watched as they moved quickly past them, shouting and pushing the whores away from some of the men with the butts of their rifles while calling for the Captains of the companies to instill some order. Some of the men reacted with disdain, but they were soon quickly put into place with harsh words and punishment meted out in immediate fashion.

More than one seemed to have noticed him watching and realized the error of their ways as they immediately stood at attention. The prostitutes themselves fled, fear clouding their heavily painted features as the captains rallied themselves to Wells and Ripley and helped reorganize the men into a semblance of an army. More than one pointed their rifles at the bolder prostitutes who tried to stay, and in the face of a loaded musket, even the hardiest of whores fled back into the bowels of the city.

"Sir, Lieutenant Colonel Knowlton, sir," a young pitched voice suddenly spoke up beside them.

Chester pulled himself away from Ripley and Wills, who were moving down the battalion line to clear the area of undesirables, and saw Captain Marcy of the 4th Troop approaching them. The younger man had a head full of dark curly hair that always seemed completely untamed no matter how short it was. Chester knew the young man as a foot soldier from Lexington who had been wounded and did not fight in Bunker Hill. After his recovery, he had given him his appointment to captain for his service. The man seemed to have a good head leading 4th Troop so far in this campaign.

Marcy saluted them and turned a little to address Knowlton. "Sir, begging your pardon, but Captain Hale wished me to convey to you that he has successfully sent Ensign Knowlton to your regiment's current posting. He apologizes for not being able to return at the moment, having undertaken a volunteer excursion to Brooklyn Heights."

"With Tallmadge?" Knowlton asked and Chester raised an eyebrow.

"Y-Yes sir," Marcy looked confused. "The lieutenant was asking for volunteers for a mission he said had your approval Colonel Chester, sir-"

"I approved of it," he confirmed.

"Yes sir, but I told him that none of my men were to go with him, and the good captain told me he was going to go with the lieutenant and for me to convey to you if he did not return the success of his mission to find Ensign Knowlton," Marcy explained, the initial nervousness at making his report lessening with the knowledge that Chester had approved of Tallmadge's excursion to Brooklyn Heights.

"Thank you for your report, Captain," Knowlton replied and

the young man saluted crisply and turned to return to his post.

"Hale never ceases to surprises me," Knowlton commented absently as they turned to walk to the docks.

"Captain Hale?"

"Yes, Nathan Hale. Good young lad from Coventry," Knowlton mused, rubbing his chin. "Graduated Yale, was working as a schoolmaster before he joined the cause last year. He's serving in Colonel Webb's regiment, but I requested him for special service into my rangers. He was the one who stole the provisions sloop from under the *HMS Asia's* nose. He has an enthusiasm that rallies men to the cause and to the battlefield. A good strong head on his shoulders – perhaps a bit reckless, and is passionate about our fight. Personable, which is why I think Webb made him into a captain. He can relate to the men and perhaps found Tallmadge's request to be intriguing."

"Ah, the *Asia* affair. Good man to do that. Tallmadge graduated from Yale too," Chester commented and shrugged. "Perhaps they knew each other?"

"Perhaps. When they return, I shall interview my captain. He would know a little more of what my rangers would be sent out to do. I still wish to meet Lieutenant Tallmadge though. This seems as reckless as something I think Hale would do," Knowlton smiled and Chester could not help but mirror it. It was reckless, foolhardy, and had a high risk of capture. They would find out within the hour if Tallmadge's gamble paid off or not. Chester hoped that it would – he would hate to lose a good friend and someone whom he knew would grow into a fine officer if given more time.

The fog had not lifted much as Tallmadge steered the boat in the direction the docks they had pushed off from at Brooklyn Heights. He could hear no distant sound of marching boots save for that of those behind him that grew steadily fainter with each stroke. "Nathan, what do you see?" he called out in a harsh whisper as the fog enveloped them.

"Nothing yet," his best friend called back quietly, his finger on his flintlock that was raised, but still at half-cock.

Next to him was young Ensign Hecox who, to Tallmadge's

surprise, had volunteered to go back across with him. Hecox was alert and looking about, his rifle pointed towards the direction they were rowing in. Bulkley had also volunteered, but Tallmadge had told him to stay behind since they needed at least one ranking officer besides Captain Wells to lead the troop. He had seen his friend's crestfallen face, but his reluctant nod told Tallmadge that Bulkley understood why he needed to stay.

"Hold," Nathan called out, raising his hand up Tallmadge saw the rest of the volunteers, four soldiers who did the duties of oarsmen, lift their oars up as Nathan strained to hear what was happening in the fog. The other two held their muskets at the ready. After a minute or so of silence, Tallmadge also canting his head to try to hear if they were approaching any British presence, Nathan waved his hand for the men to get back to rowing.

They did so with the vigor and excitement of the chance of bloodying the British nose while rescuing what each man perceived as needed supplies – namely the three horses left behind. Tallmadge knew the men depended on their fortitude and strength to lead them into battle, and he was pleased that the four oarsmen and two riflemen that had accompanied him were eager to prove themselves. When they returned to the friendlier shores, he would have to put in for an extra ration of rum for them.

"Steady..." he heard Nathan call out after a few minutes of hard rowing and Tallmadge could see the fog thinning a little; enough for him to make out the docks that lined Brooklyn Heights. "Easy men, easy...feather oars..." he saw Nathan gesture with his free hand. Tallmadge steered the ferry boat they had commandeered accordingly as they pulled along side one of the docks.

"No sign, sir," Sergeant-Major Henry Davenport, one of the two riflemen that had volunteered, called out hoarsely. The other was his friend Sergeant Andrew Adamson, also of Wethersfield. Adamson was a couple of years older than Hecox and had just finished his first year at Yale and returned home when he joined Tallmadge and a few others to head to Bunker Hill and Cambridge to see the aftermath. Immediately afterwards, when the call came to muster a militia force from Connecticut, Adamson had volunteered. He had recommended his former student to the rank of sergeant after Davenport's promotion to sergeant-major.

"Silas, William, James wait here with the ferry. Abner, Daniel, Lieutenant Bulkley's horse was left on one of the docks south of here. Nathan, Andrew, Captain Wells horse was by the farmhouse," he directed the others, ignoring the slightly surprised looks his men gave at his familiar address to Nathan. But it seemed that Nathan did not mind the familiar address as he clapped Adamson on the shoulder and pulled him in the direction of the farmhouse that was situated next to the docks.

"Sir?" That left Davenport who shouldered his rifle.

"Shadow should be somewhere here..." he looked around, trying to get his bearings in relation to where he had left his horse. The dock they had landed at was not the exact dock where he had left his horse when they had initially pushed off, but Tallmadge was familiar with the area. It was a little more south than the initial launch point, but not too far away. He turned and walked to the edges of where the dock met the port and started to turn north.

The fog was murky and did not part easily and Tallmadge gripped his pistol a little tighter as he looked around him. He dared not light any torch for fear of alerting the British to their presence, but the faint moonlight that shone through lit his path. His ears were alert to any sounds of boots or of musket fire that would indicate that they had been spotted, but could not sense anything amiss. He took a few steps and heard the faint familiar snorting sound further up ahead and smiled. Shadow was right where he had left him, standing at the post he had tied him, absently chewing on fluttering bits of hay he had found.

"Hello beastie," he greeted his horse with some affection, patting him gently on the nose, and leaning in to receive an equally affectionate nudge. Shadow was a beautiful dapple grey gelding, a dark to light coloring of mane that showed his mixed breeding, but he was sturdy, steady, and a brave horse that never fled in the face of musket fire in recent days.

"Sir." Davenport had taken a look out post and Tallmadge turned to see him cupping one of his ears, seemingly straining with his eyes closed. "I think I hear the sounds of marching."

Tallmadge nodded, breaking from the brief spell he had fallen under upon seeing his favorite horse again. He quickly untied

Shadow from his post and led the horse back to the ferry. The others had not arrived and he could feel a sense of worry rise up in him. Davenport might have been skittish enough to falsely report any sign of the enemy, but he also knew that his friend would not lead him astray. If he heard something, Tallmadge was inclined to believe him. The men of 3rd Troop were all brave souls, all of them had known what it was to be the rear guard and knew that if the British had set upon them, they would have been the first to give their lives so that the rest of the army could flee to safety and fight again.

His worry was mitigated not even a few seconds later as he heard the distinct snort and half-neigh of a horse followed by the sight of Nathan riding upon Captain Wells' horse with Adamson running behind him. Wells' horse was another dapple grey that was part of the same stock as Shadow. They shared the same dame and both beasts had been gifted to him and Captain Wells by the same family that owned them. It was quickly followed by the sounds of men running and the clip-clop of horseshoes upon the ground – the other two men, Privates Abner and Daniel Butler came back with Lieutenant Bulkley's horse.

"We saw a few lobsterbacks by the farmhouse, Ben, better get moving," Nathan commented. Tallmadge nodded as his friend dismounted Wells' horse and led him onto the ferry. The horse protested a little, but with some forceful shoving on his flanks by Silas and Hecox, the horse settled and Tallmadge nodded for the two privates to bring Bulkley's horse aboard. Bulkley's horse was completely white save for a few mottled dots here and there. He knew his friend had such luxuries afforded to him due to his mercantile family, but it was a horse that Tallmadge felt was more for show than for fights. Still, he did not deny that Bulkley was easily spotted among the men whenever they fought.

With Bulkley's mount settled, Tallmadge started to lead Shadow onto the ferry. The beast snorted a little in protest, but seemed to calm down when he smelled and recognized the other two horses already standing languidly at the small post on the ferry. Tallmadge could hear the sounds of a drum beat now, somewhere in the murky fog that still enveloped Brooklyn Heights. He knew that he had to hurry. He tugged on Shadow's reins, pulling with some effort before his horse responded and moved towards the crowded post. Patting him on the nose as he tied him to the post along with the other three, he saw that his men had moved onto the ferry without even his order. Nathan started to go around to give each man an oar. It would take all of their might to transport the three beasts back without having the usual four oarsmen.

"Hecox, rear guard," he ordered the young ensign and saw him nod and set his rifle, checking the pan and ensuring he had a ball inside as he held it at the ready. "Push off!" he called out, taking his station as steersman. Nathan joined Hecox, taking one of the rifles that had been placed on the ground since the other men were busy with the oars.

His men shoved off the docks with a great heave and three of them rowed on one side to turn the ferry while the other three feathered their oars on the other. Tallmadge watched until he was sure that their orientation was towards York Island. "And...row!" he ordered, and all six men dipped their oars into the water and pulled with all of their might.

He saw Nathan and Hecox move from the bow of the ferry back towards him as they took up their position with the muskets. The sounds of marching and drums were louder, but as he glanced back, he could not discern any sign of the enemy within the fog. However, they were perhaps only four or five great heaving strokes and a few yards away from the docks when the sudden discharge of Nathan's rifle made him jump a little. He turned back to hear a wounded scream render the nearly silent air before the body of a soldier fell from the docks into the waters.

"Row, damn you, row!" he called back to the men who responded with a stroke so powerful that Tallmadge could feel the ferry lurch under his footing. He grinned as he turned back to see Nathan pick up another rifle just as the sight of a multitude of British soldiers emerged from the murky fog.

"Make ready!" he could hear their commander call from where the lone soldier felled by Nathan's musket ball had fallen. The soldiers were clearly not organized to form lines, but he saw them hastily make ready and braced himself for a hail of musket balls to come their way. "Aim! Fire!"

Tallmadge saw Nathan and Hecox duck away from the

sudden barrage of musket fire, but nothing seemed to indicate that they were hit and to his great pleasure and humor, he saw that a majority of the balls had fallen into the water a few feet before him while some had managed to splinter the bottom of the wood. They were too far for the British to hit.

An impulse overtook him and he waved, a grand exaggerated gesture, towards them. "Thank you good sirs!" he called out. The British commanding officer frowned, his hands tightening on the reins of his horse as the beast danced around, sensing the agitation and anger his rider must have been feeling.

"Yes, thank you and fare thee well!" Nathan called out and Tallmadge glanced down at him at the same time his best friend glanced up. The two of them burst into laughter at the closeness of their escape and the British's misfortune. Their laughs abruptly died as the distinct whistle of cannonades rendered the air.

"Row! Row!" Tallmadge turned and shouted at his men who in turn gave it all they had as the first shell landed not far from them with a giant splash. Tallmadge could not help the instinctive reaction to duck as the next cannonade whistled through the air. This one landed not too far from the first shot, but judging by how fast they were rowing, the initial danger had passed. "Ease up, men, ease up," he called back. The fear slowly died from their expressions as the initial rush of danger passed. They were well out of range of the British musketry and cannons. A nervous twitter of laughter ran through the men and Tallmadge could not help the rush of nervousness that suddenly overcame him as he too laughed with them.

"Well, Benji-boy, that was a spot of fun." He turned and caught Nathan's bright smile and nodded.

"Felt like we were back at school," he replied in kind and his friend chuckled as he sat down on the ferry's edge, shouldering his rifle. Tallmadge glanced towards the bow of the ferry to ensure that they were headed to York Island proper and adjusted his steering. Hecox moved around the two of them with a polite 'sir' and took up position on the bow, a little more relaxed, but still alert. The horses snorted as Wells' beast pawed the wooden deck in annoyance.

"Did you get a chance to visit?" his best friend suddenly

asked, still staring out at the bay. The fog had enveloped the Brooklyn docks once more.

"My father was surprised, but understood why I had to fight," he replied. When General Wadsworth had marched them all down to New York, Tallmadge had asked permission to take a quick leave to visit his father and the rest of his family in the sprawling village of Brookhaven, the small hamlet of Setauket. The sleepy little port town was situated near the middle of Long Island and had been a nestled haven to grow up in. His younger siblings had been speechless when he arrived, in awe of his uniform, but his father had been quiet when he had presented himself to him.

He knew that his father had reservations about him joining, but since he had officially left his house and protection when he enrolled in Yale, he was considered his own man. He carried the proud name of Tallmadge, and was the third son of the family to join, but he knew his father had hoped he would not. Still, the visit had been pleasant and his father had given him his blessing and even prayed with him – not out of his obligation as Reverend, but as a father to a son.

"William, Samuel?" Nathan asked and Tallmadge shook his head.

"I saw them when we first arrived, but they did not come with me to visit our father." He forced himself to smile briefly as the thoughts he had pushed out his mind since the evacuation started to creep back. Truth be told, he had not seen either one of his older brothers since the attack had started. He knew under whom they had served, but did not know what the status of their troops or numbers were. It was his hope that when they were across in safe ground, he would be granted some leave to find his brothers and ensure that they were well.

He knew from his initial visit that both of his brothers served in the Long Island Militia that had been raised per Congressional call earlier in the year. However, they both served with different troops. Both served under General Nathaniel Woodhull, a cousin of one of his childhood friends, Abraham whom he had visited when he paid his respects to his father. Setauket itself was staunchly Whig, with several of the men and boys of the town rising to the call for arms under Woodhull, but there were those who wanted no part in taking up arms. Abraham was one of them and Tallmadge respected that.

"They are fine," Nathan reassured him.

"They are," he agreed, "and yourself?"

"My family is doing well," he answered. "Like your father, they understood the need to join the cause."

"Anything come of...Elizabeth, was her name?" he asked, trying to remember the lady that Nathan had taken a liking to the year after they had graduated Yale.

"Nothing," his friend shook his head, "though her company was quite enjoyable. She found herself engaged to a merchant who has ties with the tobacco trade in the South."

"Pity," he replied and saw Nathan shrug a little.

"It is what it is, my friend." He did not seem disconsolate about the loss and Tallmadge knew that his friend would perhaps soon find another woman to set his affections for. "Though I must say, my heart is currently occupied with this fight, so in a way, I do have a lady to pine for."

"I admire your grace in such matters." He let a hint of teasing color his words and saw Nathan smile. "For war is a harsh mistress in bloodshed and in the sharp silver blades of bayonets."

"Musket balls and the dance of rank and file. The slow steps of the waltz that is retreat, forward, flank," his friend continued in a slight rhyme. The two of them finished in quiet laughter just as Ensign Hecox spoke up.

"Sir, I think we're approaching the other side," the younger man said.

Tallmadge pushed himself up, the last two days of exertions hitting him as he stifled a yawn. Behind him, the quiet clatter of boots and shuffling told him Nathan had also stood up. He listened for a moment. Hecox had heard correctly; the soft tolling bells of buoys and sounds of the army on the opposite shore were starting to grow once more.

"Steady, men," he called out as the fog parted to reveal the docks on the opposite side.

"Hey," he felt Nathan clap him on the shoulder as he moved past him, "try not to run the boat aground, all right?"

"Yes sir," he replied with a straight face and saw Nathan's shoulders shake with silent laughter as he moved to join Hecox at the bow of the ferry. "Ease up, men, ease up," he called out the docks came fully into view. "Feather oars, feather..." He gently steered the ferry towards the docks and it coasted the last few feet before sliding up against them in a near-perfect maneuver that made him smile.

"Not bad, Lieutenant," Nathan called out, stepping onto the docks and grabbing the ropes to help tie the ferry to its moorings. He handed one to Hecox who looped it around. "Looks like you do know how to dock a boat," his friend commented as he finished his work and stepped back onto the ferry to help untie the horses from their posts.

Tallmadge stepped forward and rubbed Shadow along his nose as his horse snorted into his palm, "Safe and sound," he murmured. He turned to address the six others who had accompanied him. "Thank you men, for your efforts. Report back to the muster point and let the quartermaster know that I've ordered an additional ration of spirits for you."

The men cheered and more than one knuckled their foreheads as they left the ferry. "Hecox, get Captain Wells and let Lieutenant Bulkley know we've their horses," he said, but the order was unnecessary as he saw Captain Wells move from a crowd of soldiers that had been curiously watching them as they docked. Behind him was Colonel Chester himself and another man he did not recognize. He immediately saluted the three, recognizing the rank on the unknown-man as a lieutenant colonel.

"Uh, sir!" Nathan stiffened beside him, and saluted the other man as the three of them came to a halt, peering down at them from the docks. "Lieutenant Colonel Knowlton, sir."

"Captain," Knowlton nodded once.

So this was Nathan's commanding officer. He seemed no older than either one of them, but there was an personable air about him that begat discipline, but also demanded respect.

"Sir, I hope Captain Marcy of Colonel Chester's 4th was able to convey the urgency of my request to join in this endeavor," Nathan said, his face utterly still and not even a hint of nervousness about him. When Tallmadge asked for volunteers, he had been surprised that Nathan had decided to go with him, and his friend had waved off the matter of not asking his own commanding officer for permission with an absent air. Tallmadge had believed Nathan until now; now he was hoping that his friend would not be punished for what was a successful mission.

"He was," Knowlton acknowledged, "and I see the efforts were a success."

"Yes sir," Nathan replied, "the lieutenant here was most persuasive in asking for volunteers to help recover these fine horses."

"Gilded tongue?" Knowlton looked at Tallmadge who shook his head.

"No sir," he replied. "Just a distaste for wasted resources."

He saw Colonel Chester duck his head as if he had suddenly had a coughing fit, but no sound issued from his commanding officer. Captain Wells gave an exasperated look while, Knowlton's face broke into a wide smile.

"Resources, indeed," Knowlton replied before turning to Nathan, "Captain, please walk with me. I wish for some information from you."

"Sir." Tallmadge watched as his friend handed the bridle of Wells' horse to its owner, who had walked down from the docks with a brief thanks. "Lieutenant," his friend bid him goodbye in a crisp manner and Tallmadge obliged by saluting him.

"Captain," he said before Nathan turned and hurried off the ferry and up to the docks where Knowlton and Chester were waiting. He watched as the two disappeared into the crowds of soldiers milling about. He hoped that his friend would not be punished for his actions, but it seemed like Knowlton was a fair man.

"Tallmadge, walk with me." Chester's words were like cold water thrown on him as turned back to look at his commanding officer, but he nodded.

"Sir," made to tie his horse back up to the post on the ferry when Wells took the reins from him with a shake of his head.

"I'll see to your mount, Tallmadge," his captain said, and Tallmadge nodded gratefully.

"Thank you sir." He stepped off of the ferry, his legs buckling once from the uneven footing as the boat swayed gently back and forth. But he managed to catch himself and straightened as he walked onto the docks. "Sir," he greeted Chester who gestured for him to follow. He did so, a little nervous about the manner in which Chester was leading him through the throng of men and deeper into the streets of York Island. Chester had agreed to his proposal, so Tallmadge feared no punishment, but the fact that Nathan had joined him and was from another regiment; that worried him. He knew he could excuse Nathan's presence as just another officer being there when he asked for volunteers, but he ran his commanding officer's previous words through his head: Had Chester asked for volunteers only from his troop or had he been allowed to recruit from others?

"Sir, if I may inquire as to where we are headed?" he asked as the crowds of soldiers thinned and the alleyway became more residential with civilians hurrying through the streets, more than likely headed home considering the lateness of the hour. Tallmadge managed to stifle another yawn, his body feeling heavier than it had been. The rush of alertness was fading away quickly and with two nights and days of no sleep, fighting, and evacuating, it started to feel like one of his ill-advised benders from his first year at Yale with Nathan.

"General Wadsworth requested to see you after you've returned," Chester replied and though Tallmadge followed behind his friend, he could not discern the nature or intention of his words. They had been spoken without serious inflection or any tone that would betray his state of mind. The only thing that was telling was that Wadsworth knew of his undertaking.

And that worried Tallmadge. He had first met James Wadsworth back during his days at Yale when the man served as town clerk in New Haven and was also a practicing lawyer. During his last year at Yale, Wadsworth had been appointed judge of the New Haven County Court before he had enlisted at the initial call to arms for Lexington and Concord and had been commissioned a colonel. Tallmadge had met him again after Chester had given him his lieutenant's commission and had been happy to see his friend promoted to brigadier general of the Connecticut militia that had been raised a few months ago. They had been on cordial terms, but Tallmadge knew that a gulf had opened between them since they were of rank and officers in the militia – he, a mere lieutenant, Wadsworth, a brigadier general.

There were strict protocols and etiquette that needed to be followed. For Wadsworth to request his presence made Tallmadge a little more than nervous.

"Sir..." he started, but he did not know what to say. He knew from his time at Yale that saying more than what should be said could be used in counter arguments later – especially since he and Nathan had spent so much time debating various subjects, alongside and against each other to the delight of the crowds that joined them. They had other friends who joined them in their lively debates, but all of them knew the power that their words had against the subjects they were debating about.

"Here we are." Chester had not made any comment regarding his attempt to speak up as they approached a tavern that was guarded by two Continentals. It sounded as rowdy as some of the taverns he and Nathan had frequented during their years of study, but as Chester opened the door, Tallmadge knew that was not the case.

For one thing, he immediately saw a lot of epaulettes that denoted high ranks along with dress uniforms made from bolts of cloth more expensive than the uniform he wore. His friend and fellow merchant James Lockwood had procured the linen used to make his uniform, but it was not the most expensive one he knew many of the other uniforms were made from. Another was that he recognized some of the generals that were scattered through the tavern. Putnam was the most distinctive, having a cigar in his mouth that had already burned almost completely through – giving the tavern a distinctive tobacco smell. He seemed to be concentrating on a map to the side with some of his junior staff officers crowded around.

Tallmadge swallowed a little, his throat feeling suddenly dry as he tugged absently at his cravat. He was definitely the most junior officer in the tavern, the adjutants, aide-de-camps, messengers, and servants not withstanding. He hurriedly shadowed Chester's steps as his friend led them deeper into the tavern. They passed through one room to another, then Chester finally stopped. Tallmadge nearly ran into his friend's back.

"General Wadsworth sir, I've brought Tallmadge." Chester cleared his throat and Tallmadge caught wind of the quiet tremor in his friend's voice. He felt oddly relieved that he was not the only one who was a little nervous in such a setting.

"Ah, Tallmadge," Wadsworth said. He was perhaps just a few inches taller than Tallmadge, with a fashionable greying powdered wig that gave his craggy features a gravitas he had not seen until just recently on the battlefield. The general stepped away from the main body of officers who were pouring over various maps and Tallmadge thought he caught another pair of sharp eyes staring at him, but could not quite discern who it was.

"Sir," he saluted smartly and lowered his arm when it was returned by Wadsworth.

"How was your foray into Brooklyn Heights?"

"Without incident, sir," Tallmadge replied. "The British were upon us when we were casting off, but they had no time to bring their musketry and cannonades to bear, sir. None of my men were wounded in the attempt and all three horses have been recovered."

"Very good, very good," Wadsworth nodded congenially. "Cannonades you say?"

"Yes sir. I am sorry to say that I did not get a good count, but there were at least two twelve-pounders that fired at us. They were not in range and it is my educated guess that they had not time to form and prepare." He was aware of the different types of whistling sounds the cannons produced; he had become well acquainted with the ones fired at him and towards the enemy less than a day ago. He was sure the ones fired at him were twelve-pounders. Relatively small, but able to do far more damage to their rank and file due to the lessened reloading time. Their range was not as versatile as some of the larger ones, but the fact that the British had been able to get them to bear on him and the ferry was telling.

Wadsworth rubbed his chin for a moment, his eyes staring to the side before returning to him. He had a feeling that the general was evaluating him with a critical eye and sought to stand at full attention. "Tallmadge, you were part of the rear guard, were you not?"

"Yes sir," he replied. "Captain Wells and the rest of the 3rd were rear guard per Colonel Chester's orders, sir."

Wadsworth made a humming noise before nodding again. "Pass along my compliments to Captain Wells for a job well done and that the 3rd may stand down for now. John, a word with you?"

"Sir," Tallmadge saluted once more and stepped back a few paces, but Chester held up a hand for him to wait as he and Wadsworth bent their heads together. He took the opportunity to discreetly look around him, noting that several of the higher ranked officers were staring at him in open wonderment and simultaneously ignoring him. He supposed that his uniform was a rather dirtied and reeked from the fighting and seawater that had splashed upon it; compared to the pristine cleanliness many of them displayed. But perhaps that was not the case he he saw some of the generals and even their lieutenants who had participated in some of the battles during the retreat look much like himself. It was more than likely the fact that he only had the epaulette denoting him to be a mere lieutenant. Tallmadge resisted the urge to brush himself down as he waited for Chester and Wadsworth to finished with their conversation.

He took the time to study the tavern itself, its heat a little stifling and the smell of ale and food making his mouth water. He had nibbled on the hard bread, cheese and pork that each soldier had been rationed for two days, but the wonderful smell now made him aware that he had not had good food for the last twelve hours. Combined with the lack of sleep, the warmth and humidity of the tavern and the raucous joy that seemed to promote well-being among heady company was starting to make him feel sleepy. He forced himself to shift his feet and blink, moving his head a little to stare at the comings and goings of those who served the officers at the tavern.

He would not say he felt uncomfortable in such a room full of illustrious figures. but neither was he comfortable. Wadsworth and Chester he knew as friends, but he could not address them as such – they were his commanding officers and protocol demanded respect due to their rank. The others knew he would never warrant such an introduction to them without a significant amount of influence. But Tallmadge could not help but bathe in the knowledge that these were good men who were of the same mind, of American independence from British rule. That thought buoyed him and a slight smile appeared on his face. He forced himself to blink again, quickly shaking his head to keep himself awake.

However, his movement caught the attention of his commanding officers and they turned their heads from their conversation to glance over at him before turning back to talk. But in that moment, Tallmadge caught a glimpse of someone beyond Wadsworth that he would recognize anywhere. Wadsworth had been in a meeting with General Washington. He belatedly realized to whom the sharp eyes had belonged; Washington himself. He realized that he had not noticed the Commander-in-Chief of the Continental Army earlier due to the fact that the general was bent over a map, his recognizable towering height level with the others. Washington looked like he was conferring with a few other generals who had not taken up seats in the tavern. Tallmadge was almost beside himself at how *close* he was to the head of the Continental Army. However, he steeled himself to remain at attention and to stay awake. Now that he knew that Washington was in the room, he could not afford to show any sign of fatigue or disrespect.

Not even a few seconds later, he saw Wadsworth and Chester lift their heads up from conferring, the former of the two extending his hand out to shake before Chester turned and headed towards him.

"Sir," he greeted, discreetly glancing beyond the colonel to see that Washington had looked up at Wadsworth's approach and was nodding his head a little to what the general of the Connecticut militia was saying.

"Let's be off, Tallmadge," Chester placed his arm around him and guided him through the throng of officers.

"Sir?" Tallmadge was not quite used to the gesture, finding it more as one would do for a friend than the protocol that guided the conduct of officers and gentlemen. However, Chester did not answer his inquiry until they were outside of the tavern the raucous noise muffled by the doors closing behind them. "Sir?"

Chester walked a few steps forward, still guiding him before he stopped and lifted his hand from his shoulder. "A letter was already sent to your father in Long Island, Benjamin," his friend started in a grave tone, eyes serious, "but it is better if you hear this sooner rather than later. General Wadsworth made inquiries as to the health and welfare of your brothers whom you said were serving in the Long Island regiments when you first enlisted."

"Yes sir." Tallmadge did not like where this was going. "Samuel and William are both with the New York militia, under General Woodhull."

"General Woodhull was captured by British forces when Jamaica Pass fell," Chester explained and Tallmadge suddenly found it hard to hear, as if he was listening to a conversation from very far away. "Your brother William was also taken prisoner and we do not have the whereabouts of your other brother Samuel. His regiment did not report in and it is feared that they had either deserted or were captured-"

"Samuel would never desert," Tallmadge cut in, his voice heated. "He's a Patriot through and through!"

"I know that son, I know." Chester's arm on his shoulder again, followed by a squeeze of reassurance, snapped him out of the tunnel-like state he had fallen into and he belatedly realized he had interrupted his commander.

"Sir, I apologize-"

"No need Tallmadge," Chester stared at him, his expression kind and understanding.

He nodded and swallowed a painful lump forming in his throat. His father would be beside himself to find out that William had been captured and that Samuel was missing. And in light of that, his own recent actions in rescuing his horse...when he could have easily been captured. Tallmadge shook his head – he could not think such thoughts. It was a gamble that paid off and it was something that apparently had brought value to whatever General Washington was planning; otherwise, General Wadsworth would never had summoned him.

"Sir, will William be imprisoned or transferred? He is only but a sergeant..."

"Unfortunately at this moment, imprisoned. We can only hope for his release at a later date, but he is not of rank to be given parole until a prisoner transfer, Benjamin." Chester lifted his hand once more and Tallmadge nodded.

"I understand," he replied as a thought occurred to him. "Sir, if I may, may I write the letter to my father informing him of the circumstances that have befallen two of his sons. Since General

Woodhull has been captured, and the state of the Long Island militia is in dire straits, I wish to reassure my father of the goodwill and health that finds him."

"Of course," Chester replied. "Report back to the 3rd and do so. Also, please let Captain Wells know of General Wadsworth's orders to stand down for now."

"Yes sir, thank you sir," he nodded and saluted before taking his leave. It was easy to find his way back to where the 3rd were posted and he found Captain Wells brushing down his horse while Bulkley attended to his own. Shadow had already been cared for and was absently grazing away, tied to a post with water and feed readily available.

"Sir," he greeted Wells with a nod and his immediate commanding officer nodded back, occupied with brushing his horse down. "Orders from General Wadsworth. We are to stand down for the moment. I wish to take leave to write a letter to my father, sir, if you do not mind?"

"Go right ahead. I have some spare paper and quill in my roll if you wish to use it. Let the men know that they may rest for the moment before you attend to that, will you?" Wells seemed pleased and patted his horse's neck a little.

"Yes sir," Tallmadge rubbed Shadow's nose before leaving the area and flagged down Sergeant-Major Davenport and Ensign Hecox. Relaying the orders that he had been given, he saw the relief in their eyes as they went to pass along the order to the rest of the company. The men would be able to rest, enjoy themselves, and the six that had accompanied him would get their extra ration of rum to enjoy.

Task done, Tallmadge headed to where he saw an officer's tent had been set up by Bulkley in his absence on the corner of an alleyway. Another officer's tent was set up a little further into the alleyway and he knew that it was more than likely Wells' own tent. He opened the flap to the one Bulkley had made and smiled as he saw that his fellow lieutenant had used a crate as a makeshift desk while three more were stacked next to each other to make a bed of sorts. There was enough room for at least two to fit in there, but even with their orders to stand down, Tallmadge knew that one of them would always be on rotating duty.

Three bedrolls, each tied with their own haversack and knapsack were piled in the corner and Tallmadge pulled the one he knew was his own. He unpacked his knapsack and pulled out a used candlestick which he lit up after two strikes with his flint. Setting the candle gingerly on the desk, he reached back into his knapsack and pulled out a large piece of paper, ripping it into a quarter piece before rolling the rest back up and putting it back into his knapsack. He pulled out his quill and inkwell, setting the implements on his desk before gingerly seating himself in the cramped quarters.

His eyes itched from the tiredness he was feeling, but Tallmadge wanted to finish and seal his letter before getting any rest. His father needed to know before anything else happened. He quickly scratched out his letter, giving his father the barest of details and the knowledge he had garnered from Chester's words. In addition, he made sure to mention that he was in good health and spirits and that God would watch over his brothers and give them the health and strength to see their father once more. It was not much as comforts could go, but Tallmadge knew that it would have to do.

Finished with his missive, he blew on it several times, drying the ink. He reached over to the small candle and poured some of the wax that had pooled at the top, letting it drip before blowing the candle out. He then pulled out the small dagger he carried with him and pressed its hilt into the wax, sealing it against the paper. Flipping it over, he scrawled the address to his father. He looked out through the open flaps of the tent and saw the early dawn light starting to brighten the sky. Tallmadge sighed softly and reached over once more, pulling down the flap that would at least give him a semblance of darkness to sleep against. It would not be much, but it was enough for now as he crossed his arms and leaned against the crates, closing his eyes. He was soon fast asleep.

INTERLUDE

Early September, 1776

He would have normally carried his diploma upon his person, but considering the nature of war and the loss of luggage from evacuations or sudden retreat, it was not prudent. His orderly would have taken care of most of it, but losses were expected. He did, however, carry letters of recommendation to vouchsafe his integrity and the truth of his graduation from Yale College, class of 1773. In this, Nathan Hale walked with a purpose in his step towards the tavern in which he knew to be General George Washington's temporary headquarters. His commanding officer, Lieutenant Colonel Thomas Knowlton, had pressed upon the urgency of this meeting and said he would already be waiting for him at the tavern.

Nathan did not know what it was about, but he understood the urgency of it. The Rangers had been stationed close to the headquarters for the last few days, Knowlton preparing his regiment for departure to ascertain the British and their latest movements. In the closeness of their station, he had seen several prominent Congressional officials move through the area, headed south to where Knox and Putnam had been stationed. Rumor had it that they were sent to talk terms of sorts with General Howe of the British, but nothing came of it. There had also been reports filtering in that it seemed like the British were massing in

Brooklyn Heights and Queens County instead of all staying fixed on Staten Island. But they could not discern the truth in those rumors – at least not yet.

He supposed that this meeting was more than likely a chance for him to receive his orders and move his small troop out for reconnaissance purposes. Nathan hoped that it was a chance to go back into Long Island and scout the British numbers as he had it in mind to also find out where the British were keeping a particular Sergeant William Tallmadge and perhaps also General Woodhull. He had overheard the news from Knowlton in a chance conversation just mere days ago – recounting the story of Benjamin's daring rescue of his troops' horses. His best friend's actions had put some life and morale into the army after the disaster of evacuating Brooklyn Heights. Nathan did not know if Benjamin was aware of how much his actions were being talked about, by both higher-ranked officers and the militiamen. But what he had learned from the chance conversation was that one of Benjamin's older brothers had been captured while the eldest of the family, Samuel, had been found safe albeit serving under Putnam's command after his militia was absorbed following the evacuation.

His own older brother Enoch declined to join when the initial call had gone out, but Nathan himself understood the fear that Benjamin had for his brother. Four of Nathan's other brothers were serving in various regiments and he had sought them out after the evacuation. They were safe and he had written to Enoch and the rest of his family and friends of the Hale brothers' health and safety. British warships were always patrolling Long Island Sound, occasionally reaching New London and farther down the Connecticut coastline. His brother had taken up his posting as schoolmaster in Union School after he had joined. He had also heard that his brother had decided to minister at the church on Sundays. He would have thought his brother would have returned straight to Coventry, but sometimes Enoch surprised him. But even in the pleasant surprise at finding his brother taking up his duties, there was always the constant fear that his brother would have to fight, and perhaps die as a civilian casualty. Though the British operated at least somewhat honorably, Nathan knew from experience that the Tory cowboys were not so kind to civilians. Tories were apt to burn and pillage and Nathan feared for Enoch's safety in that regard. It is why he hoped that this meeting Knowlton had called would give him a chance to find William and relay the information to Benjamin so that he at least knew his brother was safe.

Nathan opened the door to the tavern, stepping in and taking off his hat. He tipped it towards the proprietor who looked like he was closing up for the evening. "Sir," he greeted, clearing his slightly sore throat, before heading to the back rooms of the tavern where he knew Washington's offices were. He had been feeling ill for the last couple of weeks since he had accompanied Ben to fetch his horse; with a mild fever that waxed and waned along with sneezes and an occasional cough. He missed a few meetings with Knowlton and the others officers, but this one had been spoken of with such urgency that he knew he could not miss.

He opened the door and stepped in, mildly surprised to see his fellow captains, Brown, Grosvenor, Holmes, and a few of the lieutenants there. He absently clapped Lieutenant Jesse Grant's shoulder as he moved past him to stand next to the other captains of the Rangers. Grant nudged him with an elbow in return and he shot the other man a quick smile of acknowledgment. He and Grant along with Ensign Shipman and Fosdick, the two ensigns not present in the room, had been recruited by Knowlton himself to join the Rangers. They brought their own troops with them, but it was a shared camaraderie that they had for being picked to join such an illustrious regiment.

The room was rather large and Nathan supposed it was for a more private dining selection. There were three other doors that more than likely led to even smaller rooms, but they were all closed.

"Any idea what we're here for?" Grant spoke up behind him as they waited.

"No idea," he replied back, sniffling a little, looking around the assembled officers. Most of them seemed content to wait, but there was one who had a frown on his face, "Sprague?"

Lieutenant James Sprague had a heartily dapper, but rough and wild look about him, and reputedly a temper to match the look. Nathan knew that the man had served Knowlton since the

French and Indian War and was well-disciplined, but suspected that the man's temper was more than likely why he was still a lieutenant instead of a higher-ranked officer.

The lieutenant opened his mouth to reply, but did not get a chance as one of the doors opened and all of them straightened to attention at the appearance of their commanding officer. Nathan watched as Knowlton closed the door behind him and resisted the urge to frown at what he had glimpsed – the Commander-in-Chief himself in the room that Knowlton had exited from. He straightened some more – whatever General Washington and Lieutenant Colonel Knowlton had been talking about – it was of the utmost importance for the Rangers.

"At ease, men," Knowlton waved them to parade rest and Nathan relaxed a little as Knowlton stepped in front of the slowly dying fireplace. Its embers gave off little heat, but it did make the room stuffier than the lingering late-summer heat outside. "I have gathered you here to ask one of you to undertake a mission of utmost importance-"

"I will sir," Nathan immediately spoke up, catching Knowlton's glance at him before his commander smiled and shook his head.

"Please hear me out, Captain, before you offer your services," he chided him gently and Nathan pressed his lips together, chagrined that he had done such a thing. He nodded and took a small step back in apology. Out of the corner of his eyes, he could see the others assembled hiding their smiles or rolling their eyes in derision. He ignored their looks – they all knew that he had gone with Tallmadge on his excursion back to Brooklyn Heights and he had made his succinct report to Knowlton regarding what he had witnessed as to the British forces before they had crossed back to the other side. He knew it was information that Knowlton and by extension, Washington, wanted from this special regiment.

"We require the service of espionage for a predetermined time in the near future," Knowlton announced and an audible hush fell over the assembled officers of the regiment. Even Nathan drew in a sharp breath at his pronouncement.

Espionage. Spying. For which if a person was ever caught, especially an officer of either the Continentals or the British, they would be treated with the utmost disdain and given an dishonorable death. There would be no exchange, not even a moment of reprieve. It was dirty business, and shady too as money could be exchanged without any information procured. It was ungentlemanly and only the lowest forms of life resorted to being paid in coin for the information they were willing to impart. There was no other way to verify such information unless it was through thorough military scouting. As a military scout, one did not have to linger as long among the enemy, able to get in and get out of enemy territory and report back. As a spy...well, one had to stay and gather as much intelligence as possible.

And if a spy was caught, the only death afforded to them was a hangman's noose. Disgraceful. And it was a request that one did not decide so lightly, especially since they were all officers and gentlemen in a war that was fought in a gentlemanly way. Spying was not such gentlemanly pursuit in a war.

"One of you will go be among the enemy and find out their movements-"

Yet, Nathan found himself oddly compelled. He did not know what possessed him to take a step forward again and speak, but he did. "I will undertake it," he said solemnly, interrupting Knowlton once more.

This time, instead of a chiding smile on the colonel's face, it was flat and serious. Nathan met Knowlton's piercing gaze with a steady one of his own. "I will undertake this mission, sir," he repeated. He could feel the eyes of the rest on him, but kept his eyes forward and expression resolute. He knew what he had just volunteered for, to become a spy; to be the lowest form of life and to shed the exterior of gentlemanly form that he had worked so hard to adopt.

He could feel the gazes of his fellow officers on him, but kept firm to his statement without moving. The silence was broken not a second later and Nathan heard, more than saw, his fellow officers step towards him, their voices a cacophony of noise and pleas. He could hear their words, pleading for him not to undertake such a mission, saying that his love of home should not preclude his honor, family ties, all of the fame on the battlefield he would not have by undertaking such a lowly occupation. That he was throwing away his rising career. He heard mutterings about his exploits with the sloop against the Asia that he would not have the chance to do something like that again. He even heard some say that if was caught, he would die like a dog.

But through all of his fellow officers' protests, Nathan did not say a single word and instead, kept his gaze steady on Knowlton.

"All of you are dismissed. Not a word to the others who are not present," Knowlton suddenly interrupted, not even looking at the rest of his officers. Nathan heard the others bid their commanding officer farewell with a scattering of sirs before the sound of their footsteps faded away. The last one to leave closed the door behind him, leaving Nathan and Knowlton alone in the room. The room now seemed far more cavernous without the others here, but Nathan kept himself steady.

"Captain Hale," Knowlton addressed him formally and Nathan stiffened.

"Sir."

"You understand the nature of what you have volunteered to do, twice no less?"

"Yes sir. To become a spy among the enemy at a predetermined time and place," Nathan replied. "To gather intelligence that would be beneficial to the cause."

"Why?"

"Why would it be beneficial, sir?"

"No, why are you willing to volunteer for such a duty?"

"Because it is needed." Nathan was a little confused. "Sir, I know what needs to be done."

"It is a dirty business, spying. The only punishment for a spy if caught is hanging. There will be no quarter given, not even a sentencing on a prisoner ship nor an exchange. Your rank will mean nothing if you are caught behind enemy lines, Hale." Knowlton stared at him before tilting his head a little. "It may be the right thing to do, but you will receive no glory from this unlike your excursion with Lieutenant Tallmadge to Brooklyn Heights or your procurement of the provisioned sloop-of-war from the Asia."

"I understand sir," Nathan replied, "and it was not for glory that I accompanied Lieutenant Tallmadge, sir. He and I are good friends, both from Yale, and I only wished to help him in his endeavor. I so happened to garner a little more information since he sent me to search for Captain Wells' horse by the farmhouse."

"First Bushnell, then you and Tallmadge," Knowlton muttered mostly under his breath, but Nathan had a feeling the comment was not exactly directed at him.

The only common thing he could think of that linked his name, Benjamin's and David Bushnell's was that they all went to Yale. He knew of Bushnell's creation, the Turtle which had attempted to blow up Admiral Richard Howe's flagship the HMS Eagle just mere days ago with little to no success. Sergeant Ezra Lee had been hailed as a hero upon his return to York Island's shores even though he was not successful in his mission. Nathan remembered back in his college days, Bushnell would experiment with explosives down the Quinnipiac River and into New Haven harbor.

Nathan decided to not comment on Knowlton's mutterings and instead, continued to hold himself at attention.

"Are you certain, Hale?" Knowlton sighed and looked at him once more.

"Yes, sir," he replied before Knowlton nodded mostly to himself and gestured for him to follow.

He did so with a sureness in his steps as he was led to the room that Knowlton had come out of to make his announcement. His commanding officer knocked once on the door and the muffled command of 'enter' called back before Knowlton opened the door and Nathan saw that it was indeed General Washington himself standing in the room. Papers, maps, reports, and tokens that more than likely denoted enemy troops and Continental Army forces were scattered across the table, but the esteemed general himself had taken to pacing by one of the windows, holding a report in his hand.

"Sir, this is Captain Nathan Hale," Knowlton introduced him. Nathan snapped off a crisp salute as Washington set his paper down and clasped his hands behind him.

"Captain," the general nodded once and Nathan held himself at parade rest.

"Sir," he greeted.

"Has Lieutenant Colonel Knowlton explained your duties to

you?" Washington asked and Nathan nodded.

"Yes, sir. I am to go behind enemy lines and gather intelligence at a required date and time that has yet to be determined," he replied, "I understand these duties and consequences of my capture."

Washington nodded, staring at him with sharp eyes that Nathan found rather fascinating. Those were eyes that dissected so much and led the army from Bunker Hill to here. Those were eyes that hungered for information. He had seen such eyes before. They reminded him of his time with Ben at Yale, once his friend had gotten over his habit of being a little lazy during his first couple of years. The two of them had hungered after the knowledge Yale provided, and were further inflamed by the increase of British taxation and acts passed. They both wanted to find ways of circumventing such acts and to help the growing Patriot sentiment back then.

However, in the span of less than a second, the hunger for knowledge was seemingly shuttered away and instead, Washington gestured to him. "Tell me a little about yourself, Captain."

"My family is originally from Coventry, Connecticut, sir," Nathan started, "and my older brother Enoch returned there after we both graduated from Yale. I decided to become a schoolmaster at Union School in New London before I joined the cause, sir."

"And how did you come about to join us-"

"During the Siege of Boston, sir," Nathan replied, "my teaching contract did not expire until July last year, sir, and I must confess, I was unsure of my zeal to the cause."

"Oh?" one of Washington's eyebrows rose up in fascination.

"My friend, Lieutenant Tallmadge who just joined us a few months ago serving in General Wadsworth's Regiment, sir, had urged me to join when he could not at that time and his fervor ignited my own. I am glad because I was able to serve and help liberate Boston itself."

"Schoolmaster, you say?"

"Yes sir," Nathan nodded.

"And how well would you say you know Long Island?" Washington asked.

"Not well, except for the areas Lieutenant Tallmadge described to me during our Yale days. He is from the coastal town of Setauket on the Sound side, sir. He and I talked about visiting his family some day and he described some of the roads that used to get to Setauket from York Island," Nathan replied. "I am sure these roads would be easy to find, sir as to my knowledge, they are main roads in and out of the city."

Washington nodded, seemingly lost in thought as he started to pace around the small room. "Then the army would be along there..." he seemingly moved a token on a map before looking up at him, "I would like you to reconnoiter the area, Captain. Find out what resources General Howe has and what they plan to do with those resources. Troop numbers, artillery, cavalry, and any foreign aids."

"Sir," Nathan gave a sharp nod.

"You will pose as a Dutch schoolmaster-"

"Sir, I will need a copy of my diploma from Yale if I am to use this as my cover," he said and saw Washington frown a little, the small flare of annoyance and anger appearing on his face as he glanced down at his maps. He moved a few things to the side and pointed at a section of the Connecticut coastline that Nathan recognized as Stamford.

"You will sail on the four-gun sloop Schuyler from Stamford once you get your diploma and land here at Huntington. Her captain will be informed about your arrival. How soon can you get to New Haven and back to Stamford?"

"Three and half days at most, sir," Nathan replied. Yale had the only copy of his diploma, but Nathan was pretty sure he was entitled to it since he certainly could not go all the way back to Coventry for it nor all the way out to New London and be back within a reasonable time.

"Good," the General seemed more agreeable with his answer. "Make your preparations and leave for New Haven tonight. I will write you a pass to get you to New Haven and back to Stamford unhindered. The Schuyler will be ready to sail when you arrive. Once you do, the Schuyler will meet you in two weeks time to retrieve you, Captain."

"Sir," Nathan nodded, an indescribable feeling running through him. It was as if he was excited, but at the same time fearful with anticipation of what he was able to do for General Washington personally. If he could get the needed information, it would help them strike such a blow to the British that they would certainly take Long Island back. They would be able to drive General Howe out of New York like they had driven the British forces out of Boston if he was successful.

"You understand the consequences, do you not, Captain Hale?" Washington asked again, his voice quiet and serious. This time Nathan nodded solemnly.

"Yes sir. I think I owe it to my country. The accomplishment of an object so important, and so much desired by you – and I know no other mode of obtaining the information, than by assuming a disguise and passing into the enemy's camp." He took a breath and continued, "I am fully sensible of the consequences of discovery and capture in such a situation, but for a year I have been attached to the army and have not rendered any material services while receiving compensation for which I make no return."

Washington was silent after he finished speaking, staring at him for a long moment before he seemed to accept his explanation with a graceful inclination of his head; his previous anger and annoyance abated.

"You may take your leave, Captain. Good luck and godspeed," Washington said and Nathan saluted.

His Commander-in-Chief returned the salute before Nathan spun on his heel and headed out of the small room. He heard Knowlton follow behind him, his footsteps echoing across the wooden floors before he pulled the door closed behind him.

"Are you well enough, Captain?" Knowlton asked and Nathan nodded.

"Yes sir. It will pass. I have been feeling stronger in recent days."

"See to whatever preparations you wish to make, Hale. I will retrieve your pass and meet you at our encampment in three hours," Knowlton replied.

"Thank you sir," Nathan said, then bowed his head once and left the tavern altogether. As soon as he was outside, he let go of a breath he did not know he had been holding. He had three hours to get his affairs in order before meeting Knowlton. Three hours to write whatever letters he wished to be delivered, three hours to find friends and get drunk with, or even three hours to find a woman to warm his bed. Nathan easily discarded the last idea; finding a good woman, not one of the prostitutes that had been making the rounds up and down the East River warming every soldier's bed, was not easily accomplished in three hours. That left the first two options.

Glancing up at the waning afternoon sun, he decided to write his letters first using the natural sunlight instead of completely relying on candlelight. Nathan made his way to the Rangers' camp and ducked into his tent, avoiding the other officers who had been at the meeting. He could sense their gazes on his tent, but he ignored them and instead, dug around for parchment and quill. Finding them in his knapsack, he struck a small candle light and started to write. His first letter was addressed to his family in Coventry, wishing them well, reassuring them of his health and updating them on how the battles fared. He made mention of his posting to Knowlton's Rangers and of the importance of the Rangers to General Washington himself. He also made mention of meeting Benjamin and his exploits in retrieving his horse as he was sure that the local gazettes would be publishing that story soon and wanted his family to hear from him first. It was a bit of daring that he knew would send the women of his family into fits, but he supposed he could have a small bit of humor at their expense. Finishing his letter, he made sure to ask after the health of everyone and reassured them that whatever news they heard from New York, no matter how dire, the cause was still strong.

Nathan set the letter aside to let the ink dry before he started on another, this one to his brother in New London. He started by thanking him again for taking over his posting as schoolmaster even though Enoch had no interest in teaching the children of the town. He supposed that his brother would probably have finished his teaching contract if he had not already. He also thanked his brother for his ministerial duties since the children would need a guiding hand to ensure they were not led astray from God's will. The new school year had already started, but the last letter Nathan received from his brother dated in early August seemed to have spoken that his brother was staying in New London for at least the winter before returning to Coventry to continue ministering to the parishioners there. Nathan wished him well and hoped for his safety against the Tories and raiders that happened along the coast. He also jotted down the name of an apothecary he knew in case Enoch was not familiar with him to help with injuries or any sickness he may feel. Finished with that letter, Nathan set it aside and took to folding the first one, sealing it with a small bit of wax he had before addressing it to his family in Coventry. Letter done, he blew on Enoch's a couple of times, accidentally spreading some of the ink at the bottom that had not completely dried, then shook it a little to make it dry faster. He sealed that one and addressed it to Enoch in New London.

Setting both letters on his small desk, he peered outside and saw that the afternoon sun had waned a little. He decided to change in case he had to use his remaining time to search for a few friends he wanted to talk to before he left. He found a pair of slightly worn, but still good brown breeches, an off-white shirt, a dark vest and stockings, along with plain black shoes and pewter buckles – the clothes he had worn before joining the Continentals. A simple jacket kept him warm, though he deigned to leave it in his tent for now along with the two letters he had written. The lingering humidity was still too great to wear the jacket at the moment. As an afterthought, he pulled out several of the books he had taken with him when he had first joined – books he thought he could read whenever he had spare time. He had not touched those in recent days, too busy acclimating to his new regiment as well as fielding requests per his rank of captain.

He finished changing and re-tied his queue before ducking out of his tent. Nodding to a couple of the lieutenants that had been at the meeting, he headed out of the small encampment and towards where he knew Benjamin's troop was stationed at the moment. Turtle Bay was a little far from where the Rangers were posted, but it could not be helped. Judging by what he saw on Washington's map, there were regiments stationed as far as Westchester all the way down to where Putnam and Knox had placed both their troops and artillery at the southern tip of York Island. The Commander-in-Chief simply did not know where Howe was going to strike from and Nathan was bolstered in this fact that his mission was of vital importance. His information would save a lot of lives and give the needed information to Washington himself.

"Hale?" the sound of his name made him pause and glance to his left.

"William!" he greeted, happy to see one of his long time friends and fellow Yale classmate, William Hull, rise up from the small fire pit he had been sitting at and approach him. The last he had seen of William was a couple of weeks before they had evacuated.

"It is you," William extended a hand and Nathan shook it eagerly.

He and William had both been a part of Colonel Webb's regiment, both promoted to captains at roughly the same time in their respective troops. They had been as thick as thieves during their stay in Boston before moving down to Long Island. The last he had heard of William and the rest of his old regiment, they had been stationed in Brooklyn, but had not engaged the enemy much and had evacuated successfully. He had meant to seek out William, but his bout with the flu had kept him from seeking him.

William stared openly at his clothing. "What...?"

"Intelligence gathering," he said. "The general himself picked me for such a mission."

He saw a bit of confusion spread across William's face before a hesitant smile appeared, "But Nathan...you?"

Nathan frowned. It sounded almost as if William doubted his abilities. "William, you know me-"

"Aye, that I do," his friend nodded. "Nathan, lying and spying on the enemy, I...you..."

"I will befriend them," Nathan shook his head, waving his hand a little. "There are other ways of deceit and befriending the enemy is one of them."

"Befriending, I can see, but Nathan, this is the enemy," William stressed. "They will give you no quarter if there is none to be had. The enemy that deceives us and kills us with a smile on their face. Who thinks we are nothing more than rabble, than rebels who should submit under the rule of authority bestowed upon King George himself!"

"We are not rabble and my mission will convince them of that. I owe it to my country the accomplishment of an object so important." Nathan did not understand why William was being so obstinate. His friend was saying the same words that he had felt for a long time now, inflamed by the actions the British had heaped upon the colonies, forcing them to declare independence. Why did his friend not understand that he wanted to do this. That he was sure of his actions. "There is no other way other than disguising myself."

He arched an eyebrow at his friend who considered him before shaking his head. "It's an action which has serious consequences, Nathan. You're not required to perform it. Who would wish success at that price? The price of your life, Nathan. Do you have to denigrate yourself in such a fashion to advance our interests? Nathan, you will receive no respect if you do take on this mission. Your actions in training the men, against the Asia-"

"I don't want a promotion out of this, William. I want to be useful. And this, spying. This is necessary to the public good and becomes honorable by being necessary. I've made my decision, William," Nathan gave him the same resolute look that he had given to Knowlton and to General Washington. He knew the consequences and was prepared to accept them. He knew that his friend was trying to talk him out of it and while he had ignored the arguments of his fellow officers during the briefing, he could not easily brush off William's concerns without at least giving him some explanation. He owed William at least that much, if not more. His friend had been with him since the beginning.

William sighed, "You will not be convinced otherwise."

"I will not," he replied. "General Washington has given me this mission himself. I will see it to the very end and will return with great success."

"I understand." William pursed his lips for a moment before clapping him on the shoulder and releasing it just as quickly. "Be careful, Nathan. Not every friend is a foe and foes may look like friends."

"You could never be my foe, William," Nathan smiled a little and shook his friend's hand, "always my friend." He had a feeling that it would be rather easy to identify those who were

Tories and those who were Patriots on Long Island. All he had to do was say some choice words to see whom they supported and he would be able to differentiate those he needed to make friends with and those who were foes. He would be able to gather the needed information in no time.

"And mine as well. Good luck, Nathan." William started to move away and Nathan bid him farewell with a quick wave before he turned to continue on his way.

He arrived at 3rd Troop, 6th Battalion's posting a few minutes later and found Ben inspecting the state of his troops' weaponry and provisions. His friend seemed so absorbed into duties that Nathan was able to quietly step up behind his friend and stand there. He could see some of Ben's men looking wide-eyed at him, but shook his head a little to stop them from saying anything. It seemed that they recognized him even without his uniform as they grew quiet and nodded. Next to him was Ensign James Hecox, the young man that had diligently volunteered and went with them to pick up the horses. Even he quieted after Nathan put a finger to his lips. The young officer desperately tried to hide a smile as he realized what Nathan was trying to do.

Nathan cleared his throat.

"Captain Wells' tent is at the far end," Ben pointed southward without looking at him and Nathan frowned a little. Hecox stifled a laugh by making it sound like a cough and he gave the younger man a look.

He cleared his throat again.

"Captain Wells-"

Nathan interrupted Ben's statement again with a definitive clearing of his throat and saw his friend turn around, annoyance crossing his face at being interrupted from his inspection. The annoyance turned into puzzlement, then wide-eyed amazement and Nathan could see the exact moment Ben recognized him underneath his civilian garb.

"Nathan, er, Captain Hale?"

Nathan laughed, grabbing Ben in a bear hug before releasing him as his friend stared at him in bewilderment. "It's me. Do you have a few minutes to talk or is this inspection you are pressing upon your men so terribly important?"

"No sir." He saw a slight twitch of annoyance in Ben's

expression at his sarcasm regarding the inspection he was doing. It seemed Ben truly enjoyed making sure his troops were well stocked and equipped to fight.

"Come on, let Hecox try his hand," he gestured to the young ensign and saw Ben sigh before giving him the papers he was holding.

"I'll be back in a few minutes James. Just finish up with this lot," Ben said before Nathan gestured for him to follow.

They stepped to the side, far enough that they were not near the troops, but close enough that at least Ben could keep an eye on Hecox and the troop inspection. He could see that his friend wanted to return to his duties. "Ben, they're fine."

"Some of them don't even have the requisite amount of powder and musket ball is required after evacuating. I've taken to inquiring the quartermaster of our brigade about being re-supplied, but it seems some of the provisions were lost during the evacuation and that they can't resupply us. There's also the matter that some of them have not been maintaining their weapons to the standard in which they should. They're disciplined enough to know, but I fear for them after the evacuation from Flatbush Pass. 4th Troop who was holding our flanking lines fled. One of their lieutenants, Holmes, I saw him shot straight through the throat. Did not even have a chance to cry out." Benjamin shook his head, and for the first time since Nathan had found his friend among the Connecticut militia line, he could see the worry and toll the recent fighting had taken on him.

"You've trained the men as best as you could with whatever resources you had, Ben." He had heard that Wadsworth had been very pleased with the 6th Battalion overall. The rumor was that he had cited them as the sturdiest, most disciplined, and it seemed likely; otherwise he would not have posted 6th Battalion as the rear guard during their evacuation to York Island. But neither was Nathan unsympathetic to Benjamin's plight. His friend was going through what every single soldier, every single commander went through the first time they entered combat.

It only seemed to affect Ben now, with the constant worry of when Howe would strike and where he would strike. His friend cared for the men under his command and only wanted to ensure their survival. Nathan did not really have much advice to give to his friend, but patted him gently on his shoulder. "Your men are fine," he repeated. "They will adhere to their training. They will flee when there is much blood, but you will find the words to rally them and they will reward you with their loyalty."

It sounded a little empty in his mind, considering that he had tried to rally his own troops from time to time, sometimes with success, sometimes without. He had sworn at them, had harried them, had cajoled them back into the firing lines, but he knew that they did not have the discipline that the British had when marched upon. There was only so much one could do with men who were not professional soldiers, but he had tried to make the best of circumstances. It was a harsh lesson, but one that had to be learned directly on the battlefield. It seemed Ben was starting to learn this lesson. Nathan patted him again on the shoulder; he would push through it, with the sheer stubbornness and determination that sent them on adventures throughout Yale and to finish their studies well enough for Ben to be given the honor of address his graduating class.

Ben smiled, one that did not reach his eyes before he gestured to him. "Have you been discharged?"

"Scouting mission," Nathan replied and saw consternation in his friend's expression. "And before you speak, I've already heard it from William Hull. Ran into him before I found you."

"Hull's here?" Ben asked. William had graduated a year ahead of them, but they along with a few others currently serving in other posts had been good friends back in their college days. Nathan realized on the occasion that he had met Ben while they were posted in Long Island, he had not mentioned Hull. It had not occurred to him then, but there was always a time and place for such matters.

"Aye, a captain with Colonel Webb's regiment."

"So, military scouting," Ben stated, still staring at him. Nathan shook his head before gesturing to his friend to come a little closer.

"Direct orders from General Washington himself. I am to go to Long Island and ascertain the movements of the enemy. I'll see if I can find any information about William-"

Ben immediately drew back a half-step and shook his head.

"Nathan, I...I found out that William died, about two days ago..."

Nathan blinked, shock coursing through him. "I...I am sorry for your loss Ben," he said, and his friend nodded tightly. He could not describe the expression on his friend's face at telling him the news. It was partly a melancholic sadness, but his eyes were full of terrible anger, a furious one that spoke of revenge. It certainly explained why Ben was conducting such an inspection and had gotten heated about it when interrupted.

"His name came through on a dispatch regarding General Woodhull. It seems that Woodhull was ill-treated during his captivity and died. My brother's name was on the list of others who had died, no cause of death, but considering the general's fate..."

"Damn lobsterbacks to all of hell and back," Nathan swore and saw his friend give another tight nod in agreement. There were protocols for treating prisoners of war, especially officers. Despite the fact that William was just a mere sergeant, he still held rank and should have been treated in a better manner. But for the British to outright mistreat General Woodhull. That was despicable.

They fell silent for a moment before Ben sighed and scratched the back of his neck. "I need to see to my men."

Nathan realized that the sun had set a little more, and pulled out his pocket watch. It was nearly time. "I should too," he said and saw his friend give him a small smile.

"I wish you the best of luck on your mission and for you to stay safe, my friend," Ben extended his hand and Nathan shook it.

"You as well. I should be back in two weeks time if all goes well. By then we will know where and when to strike so get your men in order by then, all right lieutenant?" He could not resist teasing Ben about his junior rank when it had been Ben who led them on all of their adventures and pranks during their Yale days. That drunken escapade that ended with smashed windows at the quad and dorms was all Ben's idea, though he would not deny the fact that he started the bar fight. No one punched his friend and got away with it.

"Yes, sir, Captain Hale." It seemed his teasing did its work; his best friend looked to be in better spirits as he released his hand. He tapped his head in a casual salute to Ben before heading away.

He pushed his way through the crowds of civilians who had turned out en masse a day after the army had evacuated to York Island. Most of them were peddling their wares or going about their business, but some were just observing the soldiers who littered the streets or had camped out on the docks. Most of the officers had been placed in the nearby inns and taverns and some of the enlisted men had also found those willing to quarter them, but a lot of the army was camped along the edges of York Island.

Now that he had received his mission from Washington, he understood why – they needed to know where Howe would strike from. His mission was of vital importance and his resolve hardened by the knowledge that the information he would gather would prevent more cruelties from being inflicted upon his friends and their families. As he walked back, his determination became his armor and he soon arrived back where the rest of the Rangers were stationed.

"Sir," he greeted Knowlton with a crisp salute that was returned.

"Are your affairs in order, Captain?" Knowlton asked.

"Yes sir." He reached into his pocket and pulled out the two letters he had written to his family and to Enoch. "If these could be sent to my family?"

"Of course. I will put it into my personal post," he replied as he took the envelopes and stuffed them into the inside pocket of his jacket. At the same time, he pulled out a smaller sealed letter and handed it to him. "Burn this before you cross, Captain."

"Yes sir," Nathan took the missive knowing it was the pass that would allow him to move unhindered to New Haven and then back to Stamford.

"You have your orders and your horse is waiting for you at its usual spot. Godspeed captain and good luck." Knowlton looked at him solemnly before extending his hand out.

"And to you and the rest of the rangers, sir," Nathan replied, shaking his commander's hand. He released his hand and took one more look around at his fellow brothers, some of whom had gathered to see him off. He nodded to them and they nodded back, some with smiles on their faces, others with solemn looks about them. These were the ones who knew what he was doing and the risk he was about to under take. They understood and silently wished him well.

A few minutes later, Nathan galloped out of the city.

2

For the last two weeks, 3rd Troop had been stationed at Turtle Bay with a group of artillery salvaged and evacuated by ferry. Tallmadge found himself standing next to one of the large cannons, watching the distant specks of red that he knew to be the British. They were running to and fro across the docks on the other side of the East River. The fog that had generously given them cover a couple of weeks ago had given way to summer's last stifling heat and storms had raged on and off for the last few days. Rain had forced many of them to shelter in the alleyways, but most of them had endured the constant downpour with little to no complaint.

"Look at 'em, scurrying like rats lookin' for cheese," one of the artillerymen commented, spitting out a wad of dark tobacco.

He did not bother to answer such a comment as he stared at the distant red forms. It had only been a few days since he had found out William's fate and the grief had turned into anger. William's cause of death had not been listed, but Tallmadge had a feeling that his brother had suffered wounds and they had not been treated properly. That angered him the most as he knew his brother was as strong as an ox. A childhood fall from a tree that gashed William's arm had healed with little to no issue after proper care was invested in it. Ill-treatment was the only explanation Tallmadge could think of; that the British had put him on one of their deathly prison ships and let him rot to death without even a doctor or surgeon to see to his wounds.

Tallmadge flexed one of his hands as he stared out at the scurrying British soldiers. He was sure that Samuel knew of the news, but due to his posting and orders to watch for any movements across the river, he could not visit his brother and commiserate together on William's fate. The only thing he had been able to do was to send another letter to his father, reassuring him that he was safe and that he too, mourned the loss of William. He hoped the rest of his family would be able to help his father through their time of grief and finished his letter with a prayer to God for William's soul.

"Sir, what do you make of that?" Sergeant Adamson spoke up at his elbow and he turned to see the other man pointing down river.

Tallmadge frowned, his anger momentarily diverted as he stared at the two British warships that were moving up river. He counted at least twelve guns on one side of the the larger ship, making it at twenty-four-gun frigate. The other had about nine-guns if his count was accurate; eighteen-gun sloop-of-war. Both of them were under half-sail, moving slowly up river. He pulled out his spyglass and peered through it, staring at the flags that were raised before focusing on the crew running back and forth. He saw the British marines, standing at parade rest, but the fact that they were on deck instead of below, as was usual for transportation purposes worried Tallmadge.

"Adamson, find Captain Wells. See if he has orders." He was sure that the sight of the ships moving up river was already being reported to Washington and the others.

"Sir," Adamson saluted before hurrying away.

"I don't like this..." he heard one of the artillerymen mutter, and glared at the small group manning the cannon.

"Quiet," he said sternly. They obeyed, looking a little disconcerted that they had been overheard. He did not need dissent or negativity from the men his troops were stationed with. It was one of the early lessons he had learned when drilling his troops in the summer. One word of dissent or malcontent spread like wildfire among the enlisted men. It was also then that he had witnessed his first execution after one of the men of another battalion had been caught trying to desert. The deserter had been summarily hanged as a warning to the men who had joined the militia. Tallmadge had taken the opportunity to instill better discipline among his own men.

He continued to stare at the warships that were coming closer. A majority of Admiral Howe's ships had been reported near Staten Island, but the fact that two of his smaller ships were coming up the East River worried him. Since the army had evacuated to York Island, they had been moved from their initial posting near General Knox' artillery to Turtle Bay – ostensibly to give cover to the artillerymen here. But Tallmadge knew that there were several other artillery troops, like the well-renowned Hearts of Oak division who were set up near the Hell's Gate area in the northern section of York Island. From his current vantage point, he could see a line of Continental soldiers spread along the edges of the island, ready to repel any manner of attack from the British.

"Sir," Adamson's voice behind him made him turn and set his spyglass down. The sergeant shook his head a negative. "No orders from Wells. He says to keep an eye on the passage of the ships and to report to him, if possible where they anchor."

"Thank you," he replied and saw Adamson knuckle his forehead before resuming his post a few steps away from him. Tallmadge handed Adamson his spyglass. "What do you make of the ships, Andrew?"

Adamson took the spyglass and held it to his eyes for a few moments before handing it back to him. "Not sure, sir," he said.

Of all of his friends who had joined as enlisted personnel, Andrew Adamson was one of the only ones who maintained the protocol of an officer-enlisted relationship. Sergeant-Major Henry Davenport tended to forget that he was a non-commissioned officer and that there were protocol and boundaries. James Hecox tended to just 'sir' everyone, even the enlisted men, forgetting that he technically outranked them as ensign. Another one of their mutual friends, William Pullings, did not even hold a rank, and had from time to time, wandered over and thought that rank had no meaning between friends. It had taken Captain Wells sternly talking to Pullings to stop that nonsense, especially when they were all on duty.

Tallmadge made a noise of agreement as he held the spyglass up to his eye again, this time focusing on the troops across the river. They still scurried, but what was curious was that some were starting to form lines and such. Did they mean to board one of the ships? What was equally puzzling was that as he watched the lines being formed, some had marched off, not to other docks, but rather farther inland.

"Sergeant," he called to Adamson, "tell Captain Wells that the troops' movement across the river are forming lines and possibly marching inland."

"Sir," he heard his friend reply before the sound of his booted feet on the cobblestone ground was lost among the soldiers and civilians walking the main road alongside the docks.

"Sir," another one of his men suddenly tapped him on the shoulder. He pulled his eyes away to see the man pointing towards the smaller sloop.

Tallmadge frowned and pointed his spyglass towards the sloop. He could see some of the sailors swinging from mast to mast and his frown grew even more pronounced as he saw some of the sail being taken in. The sloop was to anchor soon if his guess was correct. Though he grew up along the coastline of Long Island, his main body of water was the Sound, which serviced much smaller ships than warships. Sloops or larger warships appeared from time to time, but Tallmadge never really studied them, as he was far more interested in the whaleboats and smaller sailing vessels used by his community. One of his childhood friends had taken a liking to the whaleboats and the sailors' stories and dedicated his life to that. He did not know what became of his friend, but the last time Tallmadge had seen him, his friend had regaled him with outlandish stories about icebergs the size of mountains. During his college days in New Haven, he barely paid attention to what was happening with the shipyards; his pursuits far more feminine in nature alongside the pranks he played with Nathan and their group of mutual friends.

When he took up his schoolmaster duties in Wethersfield, Nathan wrote to him from time to time about the number of frigates, sloops, sail boats, and other manner of sailing vessels that happened to dock in New London. It had been interesting to read, but they provided no context to Tallmadge until now. This was his chance to study some of the ships that were anchored off the bay and along the river front, all part of Admiral Howe's fleet.

"Get Captain Wells, Private," he ordered curtly and heard the clatter of the man's feet and gun as he ran to find Captain Wells. If the ship was to anchor near them, or even across from them, what was it doing? Were the troops to be loaded onto the ship where it would deposit them into the coastal borders of Connecticut, or perhaps they were sailing to ports farther north? Perhaps they were to head up river to intercept the northern army commanded by Major General Horatio Gates.

A few minutes later, he heard the sounds of booted feet and turned, extending his spyglass to Captain Wells, who looked like he had been in the middle of grooming himself. Sergeant Adamson and the private he had sent were behind Wells, both out of breath from running. There was still a little bit of shaving soap on the sides of Wells' face, but Tallmadge did not comment on it. "Sir, it seems the sloop that made its way up river is to anchor across from us."

Wells made a noise of agreement as he peered through his spyglass and raked it back and forth from the docks to where the sloop was definitely making maneuvers to anchor at the docks across from them. "I do not see a contingent of marines aboard the sloop..."

"Yes sir," Tallmadge agreed with him, "I have also seen troops in parade, but some of them stayed while others marched inland."

"Curious." Wells rubbed his chin with one hand as he continued to study what was happening across the river as well as the sloop-of-war. "Ports are not opened. They do not mean to fire on us, but..." His mutterings devolved into something unintelligible before he pulled the spyglass from his eye. "Tallmadge, report to Chester at regimental headquarters on your findings. Where are Bulkley and Hecox?"

"Farther down the line, sir. Shall I request their presence?"

"Yes. Just one of them in case I need to relay a message. Report back any orders we may receive," Wells ordered and Tallmadge touched his forehead.

"Sir," he said, and left his captain to continue to peer through his spyglass. Tallmadge pushed through the crowds with ease as he made his way to where Hecox and Bulkley were stationed. His role as Colonel Chester's adjutant had been greatly utilized since the battalion's posting to Turtle Bay to deliver messages or orders from troop to troop. He had been complimented a few times on his efficiency and it was something in which he took pride.

"Hecox!" he called out and the younger man immediately stood up from where he was sitting on a half-broken dock. There were a bunch of splashes in the water and Tallmadge resisted the urge to sigh at the fact that Hecox had decided to let discipline slide and throw rocks instead. He gave him a pointed look and the young man at least had the sense to look ashamed.

"Report to my station. Captain Wells wants to utilize you as a messenger in case of further orders or movement from the enemy," he said and the ensign nodded quickly, scampering away just as fast seeing that he was not to receive a lecture.

"I told him he was going to get into trouble," Bulkley's voice called out from Tallmadge's left. He turned to see his friend walking towards him, wincing a little. Bulkley had apparently received a little too much sun in recent days, and had turned as bright red as the British uniforms. He could sympathize with his friend's predicament, having done the same thing one summer with his brothers as they swam up Little Bay in Setauket.

The retort that Bulkley could have intervened was on the tip of his tongue, but Tallmadge held back. He recognized the method in which Bulkley was trying to teach Hecox. It was one of training methods he had utilized when they had first mustered, a little inefficient considering that some of the men did not understand the lesson behind it – but he would have thought Hecox would have understood it well. It was one of his own teaching methods and he *had* used it on Hecox to help him advance his studies. He supposed that it never worked on Hecox considering his actions, but there was still hope judging by how shamed he was at being caught in such a manner.

"I'm sending him to Wells in case there are to be more reports or orders," he explained and Bulkley nodded.

"I saw the sloop make its way up." He nodded towards the

sloop that was now north of their position. "I'll make sure the men here are ready for any action the enemy might make against us."

"Thank you," Tallmadge nodded before heading towards regimental headquarters.

Captain Wells had his own makeshift headquarters a couple of blocks away from them, a shared command post that he had with Captain Marcy of the 4th. Marcy's troop was stationed farther north of 3rd troops, thus extending the line. Regimental headquarters for Colonel Chester and his command staff was a few blocks west of that, closer to general headquarters that General Washington had made for all of his officers including General Wadsworth.

He wound his way through the cobblestone streets, ducking and avoiding the street urchins who ran around like wild animals, laughing, jeering, and generally making a mess of things. Some of them were cut purses, but Tallmadge had gotten deft at avoiding them and their known habitations. He had warned his own troop whenever they had a brief furlough into the city to watch their pockets and bags of coins. But that still did not deter the urchins and some of the more ruthless dredges of society from accosting his men or himself. Thankfully, he had avoided being accosted, more than likely due to the fact that he kept his hand on his sabre at all times and made sure that his pistol was visible on his belt. But he had heard from Bulkley that it was only by the grace of God that he had not been shanked while on short furlough in the city about five days ago. The cutthroats had made off with his money but left him alive after a Continental patrol happened by and chased them off.

Tallmadge arrived in short order at regimental headquarters, a small inn with one of the side rooms converted into an office of sorts for Colonel Chester. A lone Continental was guarding the entrance, and Tallmadge saw the other one that was supposed to be on duty in the nearby alleyway relieving himself. He nodded to the lone Continental and entered, pushing the heavy oak door open. It stuck on the hinge for a moment before letting him in.

"Ah, good day sir, are you here to-"

Tallmadge waved away the proprietor's greeting with a tip of his hat and pointed it towards the room that he knew Chester had taken as his office. "Apologies sir, but not today."

"Ah, that is fine," said the proprietor, a portly middle-aged man with greying hair and fine tailored clothing that told Tallmadge he had done well for himself with his inn. He did not miss the look of disappointment on the proprietor's face at what he was more than likely hoping was a customer.

"Excuse me," Tallmadge said, keeping his voice polite as he moved past the desk and headed towards the back room. He knocked on the door.

"Enter," a muffled voice came through and he entered, giving Chester a crisp salute. He noted that only Major Ripley was present.

"Sir, report from the artillery front," he said, "an eighteen-gun sloop-of-war has been spotted moving up river and anchoring across from our position. The twenty-four-gun frigate accompanying her has not made anchor yet. Troops have been observed at parade formation, but not preparing to board the ship. Some of the troops have been seen moving eastward and inland."

"That corroborates the information Solomon got from Wadsworth," said Chester, standing up from his desk and moving to another table where books and other sundry heavy objects were flattening a map of sorts. It took a moment for Tallmadge to realize that the miscellaneous objects were Chester's equivalent of tokens to denote troop positions and movement.

"John, relay what Tallmadge just said to Wadsworth and have Solomon return. Stay for further orders." Chester moved a few of the makeshift tokens around the map as he frowned and studied it.

"Sir," Ripley dropped put his quill down and capped his ink well before heading out from behind his desk and out the door.

From his vantage, Tallmadge could not see what movements were made on the map, but he could see bits and pieces of the map itself, outlining York Island and its surrounding land masses. Chester fell silent, his attention solely devoted to the map to the point where Tallmadge cleared his throat a little. "Sir."

Chester made a noise before glancing up, a little surprised to still see him standing there at attention. "Oh," his commander said, "no orders. Return to your post for now. Inform Captain Wells that there will be a general meeting tonight at eight o'clock."

"Sir," Tallmadge saluted again and left. He made his way back and found Captain Wells resting against the cannon, a contemplative look on his face.

"No new orders, sir. Colonel Chester requests a general meeting with the captains of the troops at eight o'clock," he reported and his captain nodded before handing him his spyglass back.

"I believe this belongs to you, Tallmadge," Wells said. "Let me know if the situation changes."

"Yes sir."

As Wells left Tallmadge turned back to watching the activity across the river. He noted that the twenty-four-gun frigate that had been escorting the sloop-of-war had begun maneuvers to anchor a little north of their current point. Whatever battalion or division was stationed there was more than likely giving the same report to the commanders and that information was being relayed to the generals and ultimately to Washington. A brief extraneous thought occurred to him – had Nathan discovered something about the British plans? He could imagine that his friend had relayed information in some manner and that General Washington was preparing a counter attack to the strange British maneuvers. He could only hope that his friend was still safe behind enemy lines, and that whatever information he had gathered thus far would strike a decisive blow to the British.

He was awakened with a shake of his shoulder and snapped his eyes open. His hand automatically went to the knife sheathed in his boot, but did not draw it as he recognized who had awakened him. Hecox looked rather solemn as he stepped back to let him get his bearings in the small tent that shared between himself, Hecox, and Bulkley.

"Sir, captain's called for us, says that there might be an attack of sorts," Hecox whispered. That was when he became fully awake.

He reached over and threw on his jacket, hunching over in the tight confines of the makeshift tent. He grabbed his sabre and pistol belt and tied it on his waist as he ducked out of the tent. Hecox scurried quickly out ahead of him. "What's the time?"

"About eleven twenty, sir," Hecox replied.

Tallmadge silently cursed. He blinked his eyes several times to clear away the gummed feeling of lack of sleep. He had only gone off duty for the last two and half hours, right after Captain Wells had gone to the general officers meeting that Colonel Chester had called for. He had considered attending, but it seemed that it was only captains that attended judging by whom he saw walking to the command post, and so he stayed behind. He had thought the meeting would inform the respective troop commanders of a plan of action tomorrow, but what had Hecox just said – this was to be an immediate night action?

He gestured silently for Hecox to lead the way as he adjusted his belt. They found Captain Wells standing by one of the large brick buildings by the waterfront. Bulkley joined them a few seconds later, having run from his post farther down.

"Colonel Chester wants us to fire on the sloop-of-war identified as the *Amaranthine* attached to Admiral Howe's fleet. This will be done at morning's light," Wells explained. "Get your men rested, provisioned, rotational watch with the last one commencing two hours before morning light."

"Yes sir," they replied as one and Wells nodded, leaving them to their efforts.

Tallmadge immediately turned to Bulkley and Hecox, "Hecox, get some rest, Bulkley, relieve him in three hours-"

"Tallmadge, you're supposed to be sleeping now-"

"I'm fine," he shook his head, the prospect of seeing action invigorating him and removing the remnants of tiredness from him. "Hecox, also see that our rolls are packed before you sleep so we can move them before the fighting commences."

"Sir." Hecox did not even need to say anything else as he hurried away, more than likely eager to rest. Since Hecox was the most junior of the three of them, he was the one stuck with long shifts and little chance to rest before movement or even drills. Tallmadge had little sympathy for him, but did not deny the fact that Hecox relished any opportunity to rest or be the first to rest.

"I'll find Davenport," Bulkley offered and Tallmadge nodded before his friend left to find the sergeant-major. It was good division of labor – since Davenport was the ranking non-commissioned officer of half the men, numbering about twenty-five, while Adamson directed the other half, bringing the total to nearly fifty enlisted. Their numbers were roughly sixty-seven when they first came into Long Island, but attrition and a few desertions in the beginning of the summer had whittled down that number. There were one or two who were shot dead during their initial hold at Flatbush Pass in Brooklyn, but otherwise, no one from the 3rd Troop had been injured or had deserted since then.

Davenport also worked well with Bulkley, whereas Tallmadge knew that Adamson disliked Bulkley due to his supposed wealth and the off-hand comments he had made before they entered service. He knew that Adamson would never disobey a direct order from Bulkley if things got heated, but he knew his friends well enough to understand that Adamson would carry a grudge against Bulkley. It was why when he and Bulkley received their commissions, they had parted the 3rd Troop into a manageable level and worked with the non-commissioned officers in that sense.

He found Sergeant Adamson among the men, sitting by a small fire they had struck near a couple of buildings. The men involuntarily straightened as he approached and he smiled at them with pride. "Sergeant, pass the word to the men that they are to be provisioned and ready for action come morning light. Rotate current watch into three-hour shifts."

"Sir." Adamson's smile was wide with delight as the men who currently had the watch with him quietly cheered. It meant that the current watch was to stand down and the ones who had gone to sleep about four hours ago were to be awakened for the next three before Adamson's watch came back.

The men around the fire immediately stood up and headed in different directions, some towards the small stores of ammunition and powder to take their share and distribute it among their fellow soldiers, while others passed the word to those who were watching from the edges of the docks. The half-moonlight that peeked through the clouds did not give much in the way of visibility, but Tallmadge watched with some pride as his men walked to and fro, using lanterns to guide themselves. Seeing that his men were competently preparing on their own, he moved towards the cannon he had taken to leaning against to watch what was happening across the river.

He knew the British were more than likely watching them from their positions across the river, but Tallmadge was also astute enough to know that the movements he had his troops make were part of normal procedures. The British were more than likely well aware that they had rotating watches and this one, perhaps considered. early, was no different. At least that was what he hoped the British were thinking. He settled into his usual watch position and stared out at the looming sloop-of-war now anchored across from them. In the half-moon, the warship looked far larger than when it first made anchor off the river and Tallmadge found himself imagining it on the high seas, chasing down American privateers and other ships before being destroyed itself.

"Sir," Adamson's voice behind him pulled him out of his musings. "Provisions are set and watches have been rotated. I bid you good night until it is my time to take up post again."

"Good night," he nodded to his friend, who left. Tallmadge was pleased with Adamson's efficiency and turned back to stare out at the inky night. In about six hours, they would be attacking the British once more.

The six hours passed quickly, especially since into the second watch, Hecox came with some steeped tea and hard tin of crackers and salted meats that Tallmadge ate with some gusto. He had not realized how hungry or thirsty he was until the young ensign presented him with the food. Hecox also reported that their rolls were packed and on their way along with the rest of the baggage that was exiting the city. It made for a very uncomfortable sleep for Bulkley, but it could not be helped. He then ordered Hecox to prepare his and Bulkley's horses and the young man did so with far more professionalism than he had displayed earlier yesterday. His reprimand must have frightened

Hecox, but it produced the result that Tallmadge wanted from the young officer in the making.

Hecox needed to understand that he was to be looked at as an officer, not as one of the enlisted men even though he felt a kinship and kindred feelings for them. They were the troops' leaders if Captain Wells or any of them should fall in battle.

By Tallmadge's reckoning, it was nearing morning light, the deep blue-black of the sky slowly giving way to lighter blues when the sounds of hooves made him turn to see Captain Wells approaching on his horse.

"Sir," he saluted his captain.

"Bulkley and Hecox?" Wells asked, and Tallmadge was about to answer when he spotted Bulkley on his own mount while Hecox led Shadow towards them. They greeted Wells with respective 'sirs' and Tallmadge reached over to take Shadow's reins from Hecox, rubbing his horse's nose. His horse seemed delighted upon seeing him, nibbling a greeting into his hand, but it seemed to strain towards Hecox who immediately procured a carrot and fed it to him.

Tallmadge resisted the urge to smile at the display. He knew the younger man had always taken a liking to the horses and would feed them treats from time to time. He did not mind that Hecox doted on the animals, seeing as he grew up in a farming family, and thus knew how to care for them.

"Get your men and artillery ready," Wells ordered and Tallmadge nodded, swinging onto his horse before turning the beast towards his division.

Though it was only a few paces away, he technically commanded at least three artillery pieces to the six others that lined the area where 3rd and 4th Troops were stationed. Captain Marcy had seven others along where his troop was stationed north of them, bringing it to a total of sixteen artillery pieces all stationed in Turtle Bay. For the last couple of weeks, the cannons had been bolstered by earthen works that were dug using the materials at hand. They all hoped it was enough to withstand a barrage from artillery or ship cannon.

He glanced back to see Hecox assume his post next to Captain Wells, designated as the messenger between the three of them. They would use hand signals once the firing commenced, but Hecox was there in case Captain Wells needed to relay information to Colonel Chester or any of the other regiments.

"Nothing like morning cannon fire to wake you up, eh, Tallmadge?" He glanced over to see Lieutenant Samuel Marcy, Captain Marcy's brother, trotting over to where he would command at least three of the seven cannons the 4th were in charge of.

"Good morning to you too, Marcy." He smiled a little as his fellow lieutenant wheeled his horse around, making it prance a little bit as he returned to his post. He turned back to his own men who were standing at attention by their cannons. "Artillery, prepare for fire," he ordered. "Sergeant Adamson, draw your men back into two lines."

"Sir," Adamson nodded, and Tallmadge watched as the militiamen formed their lines a few paces behind the artillery. Musketry was ineffective next to cannon fire, but Tallmadge wanted his men to be prepared in case the *Amaranthine* decided to send over boats.

He heard Marcy echo his command to his left while Captain Wells directed his group to do the same and farther down he heard Bulkley's booming voice giving similar commands. The 4th had their work cut out for them as they had recently lost their lieutenant, John Holmes to an advance scout for the incoming British. Tallmadge had seen Nathan recruit young Ensign Daniel Knowlton for Lieutenant Colonel Knowlton and that only left both Marcys as their officers in the 4th.

"Sir!" Adamson called out, echoed a few seconds later by the sergeant of the artillery, indicating that they were all set, but Tallmadge did not acknowledge his call and instead turned to Captain Wells, waiting for his order to fire.

Wells seemingly turned to his left to stare at him, but Tallmadge caught his gaze moving beyond him and turned also to see Captain Marcy glancing over, the two captains conferring with silent looks before Marcy jerked his head once.

"Fire!" Wells shouted and Tallmadge echoed his command, turning back to his own small group.

He saw the burst of smoke from the cannons before the thunderous roar ripped across the air. Shadow tensed and danced from the sudden noise and Tallmadge gripped his reins tight, fighting his horse's urge to bolt from such terrible racket. He could feel the air and ground shake above him as all sixteen cannons blasted their shots towards the *Amaranthine*. The smell of sulfur and gunpowder wafted into the air and Tallmadge watched as the artillery crews began to reload, some of them cheering at the fact that some of their cannon shots had hit the docked ship.

The distant tolling of an alarm bell across the river told him that their fire had woken up the crew of the *Amaranthine,* and he smiled. "Gentlemen!" he called down to the artillerymen, "let us bid them a fair good morning some more!" The men laughed and doubled their efforts.

"Not if we bid them a good morning first Tallmadge!" he heard Marcy shout from his position and glanced over to see the 4th's lieutenant smiling sharply at him.

"You hear that men?!" Tallmadge mock glared at Marcy as he addressed his men.

"Yes sir!" the artillerymen replied back heartily and he heard ragged cheers behind him from Adamson and the rest of the soldiers. The cheer was drowned out by Wells' artillery crew firing another burst before his men responded with their own.

This time, Tallmadge was able to see through the thick smoke. Some of the shots fell into the water while others hit the *Amaranthine's* side and deck. Splinters of wood and distant cries of men who were injured rendered the air, but they were drowned out with a barrage of staggered fire from where Bulkley and Captain Marcy's four cannons were. As the men continued to reload, Tallmadge saw movement on-board the *Amaranthine* as the enemy scrambled to their own cannons. "Get ready men," he warned, "they are preparing-"

The sudden barrage of cannon fire splintering wood and shattering against the earthen mounds followed by horrific screams cut Tallmadge off. He turned to see Captain Marcy thrown to the ground as his horse reared and fell to the side. The beast's neighs and whinnies were silenced as a cannon ball ripped through the animal, cutting it into pieces before it slammed into a nearby building.

"Incoming!" Lieutenant Marcy screamed as the thunderous sounds of cannon fire exploded towards him. Tallmadge's eyes widened at the sight of the twenty-four gun frigate that had escorted the *Amaranthine* emerging from the smoke that had clouded the area. The frigate was clearly at half-sail already, moving down river. It was clear that the British had sent it to assist the sloop-of-war in rendering their artillery from firing at them. It was only by the grace of God that they had struck first before the *Amaranthine* had been prepared.

"Lieutenant! They've got their ports opened!" he heard Adamson say behind him as he pulled on Shadow's reins, fighting his horse's urge to dance away from another broadside that hit all four of Captain Marcy's artillery. He could barely see Samuel Marcy leap off his horse to check on his brother, two of his men running to control his steed as the artillerymen fled from their positions.

Tallmadge turned away from the chaos to see the first white smoke emerge from the barrel of the sloop's gunports followed by the familiar whistling sounds of cannonades. He gritted his teeth and pulled hard on Shadow's reins, turning his horse from the incoming fire as it slammed into the earthen works. He could feel his horse dance from the flying debris and caught one or two pieces of shrapnel across his uniform. A sharp pain lanced across his cheek and he swiped at it, noting at small draw of blood but nothing more.

"Steady men! Brace!" he shouted over the sounds of both the *Amaranthine* and her escort frigate firing an unending barrage. The artillerymen pushed themselves against the earthen works, seemingly hiding instead of moving the pieces to respond.

"Sir!" he barely heard Adamson shout as another round blasted towards them, and he turned to see his men looking nervous at the fact that they had no cover.

"Hold your lines!" he shouted at them, drawing his sabre to emphasize his command, "hold your lines-"

A cannon ball ripped through the left flank of his line, cutting two men down before the ball lodged itself against the wall of a building. The others stared, wide-eyed and frightened and Tallmadge spurred Shadow hard in their direction. Shadow reared, kicking his forelegs out. "Hold!" he shouted as some of them looked nervously about.

"Sir! Look out!" The shout almost came too late, but

Tallmadge wheeled around in time to see one of the cannons flying through the air, tumbling end over end. He made to pull Shadow out of the way, but somehow when one of the ends landed, it slid to the side coming to a stop near his horse's still dancing feet. Shadow snorted, whinnying in fright. Tallmadge could not help but stare at the still smoking barrel of the cannon that had nearly felled him, the sudden surge of horror at what had almost happened rendering him still.

"Sir, sir!" It was Adamson, shaking his arm to snap him out of his fugue. He looked up to see the sergeant pointing towards Captain Wells.

Wells made a motion with his hands in regards to the cannons, and Tallmadge realized that his captain wanted him to salvage ones that were not destroyed and to move from their position. He nodded sharply and glanced at the artillerymen who still cowered behind the earthen mounds. He spurred Shadow again, moving his horse a few steps forward. "Dismount the guns! Move, damn you men, move!"

The artillerymen looked at him with wide frightened eyes, but he gestured for them to keep moving, forcing himself not to wince or start in fright at the continued onslaught. He grimaced as two cannon balls slammed into the second of the three artillery pieces he had been commanding, dismounting it in spectacular fashion. One man screamed, a dying ragged sound as he was suddenly pinned by the dismounted gun. That seemed to spur his artillerymen to move. Some tried to help the pinned injured man, while others surged to save the other two cannons.

"Retreat! Retreat!" he heard Wells shout and turned to see that Bulkley's crew was already moving their salvaged pieces, only numbering two while Wells had just one.

"Come on men!" he shouted, waving his sword in the air. He saw some of the men help the wounded to rejoin the line led by Adamson who began to bark orders for his small group to form lines and march. The artillery crew threw up a ragged cheer as they managed to dismount the last cannon and began hastily rolling it away. Several of the artillerymen carried kegs of powder. "Forget the cannon balls! Fall into formation!" he called out, as he saw two move towards a cart that was promptly shattered by cannon fire. They nodded and ran to join their fellow soldiers as Wells directed them inland, away from the docks.

Tallmadge ducked as Shadow skittered across the cobblestone, the seemingly unending barrage of cannon fire from the ships slamming into the dirt. He could not risk to see what Marcy's 4th Troop was doing as he herded the men towards a mass of other soldiers making their way to the Post Road, the main road leading out of the city.

"Tallmadge!" Wells called out from in front of him and waved for him to keep rear guard.

"Sir!" he acknowledged as he slowed Shadow down, hoping that the next round of fire would not send a house down on him. He forced his horse to walk along side the rolling artillery pieces that had been saved, moving through the alleyways and following behind the main column of 3rd Troop.

As they slowly wound their way to the Post Road, he could hear the distant sounds of more cannonades rendering the air, north of them. Tallmadge wondered if he was hearing their battery that had been setup near Hell's Gate or perhaps it was the result of the odd movements from the British. But he did not think much more of it as they arrived at the intersection of the Post Road. He was taken aback at the sheer number of soldiers marching up the road, some of them with no emotion on their faces, others looking surly. More than one looked wounded and Tallmadge realized that the British warships had pushed all their lines away from the docks. He turned and joined the wave of soldiers moving up the road, passing small farmhouses and fields where crops looked to be completely picked clean or were trampled.

Another roar of cannonades sounded, this time closer, and it reoccupied his attention as he stared in the south-easterly direction from which it came. "That's Kip's Bay," he heard someone in the crowd of soldiers mutter. The murmur rolled like a ripple in a pond around the men.

"Quiet!" he called out, glaring at them. He could practically feel their fear at what had just happened and he paced Shadow behind the artillerymen to keep them from fleeing. He could sense the men staring up at him, but did not acknowledge it. It was no time for pleasantries or hat waving. The men needed to focus and so he kept his focus on Wells' orders. He could see the back of his captain's head a few feet in front of him, and could barely make out of the form of Bulkley as they led the rest of 3rd Troop and the artillery pieces to safety. He imagined Hecox somewhere in that mass of soldiers; the ensign did not have a horse of his own. It was more than likely that Hecox had been sent to Colonel Chester's command post to report on the situation.

The cannon fire sounded like it was getting closer, rolling in from the south as they marched northward. Tallmadge could not help but glance behind him, imagining the shaking and thunderous roar of cannonades that seemingly hit the area at Kip's Bay. He knew that Colonel Douglas' 5th Battalion was stationed there; the troops had barely seen any action on Long Island during their retreat. The 5th had been stationed right along the line of works and entrenchment, but pulled back early to help guide the other militiamen towards the boats.

Tallmadge heard yet another staccato of cannon fire – almost as if it was ceasing – but this time he felt his jaw drop in sheer incredulity at what was happening around him.

Men, hundreds of them, were streaming into the Post Road from the south-easterly direction of Kip's Bay. All of them had terrified faces, blood streaming from wounds. Many others limped or were suddenly dropped to the ground by their fellow man as they ran right into the lines. He saw some of the soldiers that had been marching in an orderly fashion get shoved to the side by the frantic blind fleeing of the soldiers of the 5th Battalion. The murmurs that had started before became whispers of agitation and nervousness.

"Steady, men, steady!" he called out, his command echoed by Bulkley and Wells. He felt Shadow skitter and step to the side as a man ran right into the horse's flank. He pulled on Shadow's reins to stop his horse from reacting and he saw the soldier stare uncomprehendingly up at him before being swallowed up by the surge of men.

"Flee, we must flee!" He heard the hushed frightened whispers behind him and twisted in his saddle to see who had spoken them.

"Who said that?!" Tallmadge demanded, but his voice

sounded too sharp, even in his ears, and he realized that the dismay that he had seen on the faces of the fleeing men had affected him. He gritted his teeth and tried to tamp down the nervous burst of fear. But the rumbling cannonades – this time sounding much closer – and the sudden sound of splintering wood made him jump a little.

Tallmadge squeezed the reins and gripped his drawn sabre tightly as he glared at the men behind and around him. "Keep moving!" He forced himself to keep his voice steady.

"They're coming! They're coming! We're going to die!" one man suddenly wailed and Tallmadge turned in his saddle, but it was too late. The fear that had only been a pervasive wraith above them dove down and fastened its ugly grip on the soldiers behind him. He saw the moment in which terror for their lives had taken a hold of them. They surged, like a wave that could not be outrun, running past the other soldiers, knocking them to the ground in a mad scramble to get away from the Post Road, to stop marching at the current pace.

It took all of Tallmadge's strength and horsemanship to control Shadow as he bucked and reared in fright against the slamming of bodies and movement around him. He wheeled Shadow about, trying to find a way to calm his horse down. Out of the corner of his eye, he saw his artillerymen suddenly drop their cannons and join the flight up the Post Road. "No!" he shouted as he spurred his horse to chase them down, but he could not move far against the uneven tide.

"Return to your posts! Return!" he heard Wells shout and at least one company of his artillerymen returned, dragging one of the cannons, but Bulkley looked like he too was having problems with his men.

"Captain!" Tallmadge managed to pull his horse next to Captain Wells as some of the 3rd Troop fled. He did not spot Adamson or Davenport, but could at least hear the cries of others trying to rally the men. Their voices were inefficient against the terror that had gripped the men.

"We have to follow them!" Wells looked angry as he pointed his sabre downward at the six men that had returned to their artillery and were slowly pushing it along. They were pale, frightened and soot-covered. More than one was bleeding from small cuts while another limped but managed to keep pushing. "You men, if you get this cannon to the mustering point, I will personally reward you with a bounty of ten dollars apiece."

Tallmadge blinked, stunned at the amount Wells was willing to part with, but it seemed to have done the trick. The men pushed with renewed vigor, fear still evident by the way they glanced back on occasion, but their greed for reward overriding their terror. They crested the hill where the well-known Murray estate was – the Murray family known for their Loyalist ties. He could see two riders dashing down the crossroad between the Murray estate known as Bloomingdale Road. One was vaguely familiar, portly with a balding head. He caught the brief glimpse of epaulettes that denoted a general and realized that it was General Putnam riding alongside someone he did not recognize. The two were hurrying down the road back towards the city.

Tallmadge wondered why the general would be headed back *into* the city before he realized with some dread that while he and the rest of the 6th had retreated, Knox and Putnam's forces were stationed at the tip of York Island. They must have not received such orders. He swallowed heavily as he stared at their dwindling forms. If the British had overrun Kip's Bay and if Putnam and Knox's forces could not come up Bloomingdale Road before the British cut them off by going across the whole of York Island... They would lose a lot of men and most of their artillery.

"Sir, General Wadsworth!" he heard Wells suddenly call out and turned towards a small hill to see Wadsworth riding down towards them. Beyond him, Tallmadge could see the imposing form of General Washington himself – his face a thunderous mask of anger. Washington's sabre was drawn, but it looked like one of his aides and a fellow staff member were holding his horse back. The number of soldiers that had panicked and fled had thinned considerably. Tallmadge saw Colonel Chester and a few other ranking officers of the battalions that made up the Connecticut militia, guiding those who had slowed down from sheer exhaustion to safety.

"Sir, we have one cannon that has fallen behind!" Adamson suddenly appeared against the tide of soldiers and Tallmadge wheeled his horse around to see that indeed, one of his own crew had decided to go back for a cannon and was slowly rolling it up the hill. Beyond, a troop of British soldiers slowly advanced on them.

"Men, on me!" he called out, pointing his sabre towards the advancing soldiers. His men looked up at his command and streamed towards him as he kicked Shadow into a trot. Adamson helped sort them into the semblance of a line. Some came from the hillside where Washington and the rest of the officers were guiding the men to safety while others streamed from the side, having fled before they found their courage and rallied to his call.

The artillerymen hurried their efforts as he moved past them, halting just a few feet away. "Form lines," he called out, ignoring the praises of thanks from the still-frightened, but determined artillerymen. His men, still far too little to be all of 3rd Troop, but enough to at least number twenty or so formed into two lines of ten men each. Tallmadge gave a tight smile as he spotted Hecox among the soldiers, musket held at the ready.

"Make ready," he called out, wheeling his horse about, his sabre pointed straight at the slow but steady advance of the British soldiers following their route up the Post Road. It looked to be a small scouting party, he could only count about a troop of men – but that did not discount the fact that one small scouting party could potentially overwhelm his artillerymen and take the cannon as their own. They had already left the others and he would be damned if they would lose this one.

The first line of soldiers knelt down, and pointed their muskets at the advancing British. Their arms trembled in fear, but he counted on them to draw strength from his presence. He heard the distant calls of the commanding officer of the British troop ready his own men. "Aim!" he countered, judging the distance to the slope of the hill they were on versus the advancing British, "Fire!"

Ten muskets roared in answer and Tallmadge saw a few of the soldiers fall to the ground, but the British kept advancing.

"Second line, make ready!" he called out; Hecox and the second line stepped forward while Adamson and the first line fell back to reload. "Aim! Fire!"

Ten more muskets roared in answer and Tallmadge saw a few

more fall to the ground. They stepped over the fallen bodies of their comrades and ignored their wounded calls as they advanced. He glanced back to see that the artillerymen had received extra help from the troops that had lagged behind. They were already nearing the place where it had been deemed safe.

"Shoulder flintlocks!" Tallmadge called out and saw the second line rise up as his men shouldered their muskets. "Fall back on me," he continued as he heard the British commander call for his men to make ready to fire. He wheeled Shadow around and kicked his flanks, sending his horse back to the safety of the lines while his men fell in behind him. Just in time, as he flinched at the sound of musket fire roar behind him. A couple of the men cried out as the balls hit them, and Tallmadge flinched as he heard the snap and pop of the balls hitting the ground or tree branches near him. A few seconds later he heard the distant order of the British officer calling for the troop to fall back and breathed a ragged sigh of relief.

"A fine job, Lieutenant, fine job." He had not realized that he had nearly ridden into the safety zone when General Wadsworth's voice spoke up near him. He blinked, startled to see the general with a grim smile on his face. Soot darkened parts of his uniform and Tallmadge surmised that the general himself had been close to a ship's barrage.

"Sir," he saluted as he pulled Shadow to a stop. He turned to see the twenty men that had followed him to stop the British advance make their way up the rest of the hill and into the safety Harlem Heights. A frown appeared on his face as he saw two of his men limping, helped up the hill by their fellow soldiers. They had caught the fire that had been shot at them. Colonel Chester directed the two wounded men to the left, near a church that had been set up as a surgeon's station. There were other wounded men there, and numerous soldiers sat outside, blank looks upon their faces. It was a sight he wished he could erase from his mind.

"I would offer you reprieve, but we need the cannons 3rd Troop managed to salvage at the battery at Hell's Gate. Captain Wells is already on his way there and will coordinate with Captain Hamilton of the Hearts of Oak as to the defensive placement," Wadsworth said, and Tallmadge nodded.

"Sir," he knuckled his forehead and moved to join the rest of his men, who were making their way to the right of the Post Road. They branched off onto a side road that would lead them to the battery near Hell's Gate. As he rode past the line he saw Colonel Chester nodding in approval at his actions before reaching out to pat him on his leg in acknowledgment. He smiled grimly in return before turning to join his artillerymen that had managed to save the last cannon.

They soon arrived as the sun beat its warm rays down upon them in the early afternoon. Tallmadge found himself a little more than exhausted as he lifted a hand in greeting to Bulkley and Wells. To his surprise, a cheer went up as the rest of the Troop saw them crest a small hill and come down towards them. The artillerymen were greeted with back-slapping hugs and cheers from their fellow troops while the eighteen, minus the two that had been diverted to the church due to injuries, were greeted by the rest of the troop with equal enthusiasm.

Tallmadge spotted Bulkley cantering towards him and heeled his horse in an abrupt stop before him. "You are mad, Tallmadge, just mad," Bulkley grinned, and Tallmadge shrugged.

"It was the least I could do for the artillery pieces." Truth be told, he was very proud that at least one company of his artillerymen had mustered up the courage to go back and retrieve the piece, all the while knowing that they had to move much slower than the advancing British forces.

"Come, Captain Hamilton is discussing placements and assignments." Bulkley gestured for him to follow and he did.

He rode the short distance to where a large tent was set up behind the battery overlooking the area where the East River met the Harlem River and the inlet that eventually emptied out of Long Island Sound. Hell's Gate was not exactly an island, or a particular point in the land, but rather the convergence of all three bodies of water that churned and made for a treacherous landing point for any ship looking to navigate through the area. If one made it past Hell's Gate to the north, then there was the spit of peninsula known as Throg's Neck or beyond that, Pell's Point. No British warship could pass Hell's Gate without falling prey to the churning waters, but if they had gathered enough flat-bottom boats, Tallmadge knew that they could try to navigate the natural Scylla and Charybdis that made up Hell's Gate.

It was of utmost importance that this battery and whatever remained of the artillery salvaged from Turtle Bay be put to good use overlooking Hell's Gate. They would be able to fire upon any British boats looking to bypass them and head farther north. Unfortunately, as Tallmadge glanced to his right off the hill side, he could see that the British had a strong presence there and what looked like heavy artillery.

He pulled Shadow to a halt and dismounted, handing the reins over to a young boy who looked no older than fourteen, while Bulkley handed his to another. They were not dressed in any semblance of uniform that denoted militia or Continental colors, and he supposed that they were local boys from a nearby farm who wanted to help out in any way. He followed Bulkley into the tent and the two of them stopped, giving the officers in the room a crisp salute.

"Sir, Lieutenant Bulkley and Tallmadge reporting." Bulkley addressed Wells and the other officer who had a captain epaulet on his green uniform with red trim.

"Welcome gentlemen," the captain greeted. "Alexander Hamilton at your service."

Tallmadge shook hands with the young man, surprised at how youthful he sounded. But he could not deny the fact that there was a fire of sorts in Hamilton's eyes, a fervor that he found himself agreeing with – Hamilton was a true Patriot, one who fought for the cause as much as he felt for it.

"This is Captain-Lieutenant James Moore," he said, introducing the other man in the room, and Tallmadge also shook hands with him. "How many more cannons did we get?"

"I escorted the last one, sir," Tallmadge replied and Hamilton nodded before gesturing to a junior lieutenant who had not been introduced.

"Sir," the other man left the tent, more than likely to deal with the placement of the final salvaged cannon.

"The eighteen-pounders won't make a dent in the British battery, but we can use them to cut off any ships below that try to pass through Hell's Gate and get caught up in its currents," Hamilton explained. "I've positioned the cannons here, here, and here. My crew will fire upon the battery itself as a distraction while your three take care of the boats."

"A sound plan. When will this commence?" Wells asked.

"I've not received word from any of the generals as of troop movements so far. The report you brought relayed from Washington to Wadsworth is that the British have not made any advancement aside from their landing at Kip's Bay," Hamilton stared at the map, his lips pursed in thought. "We'll be on alert and I will send word down to Washington's command post later tonight as to our actions. It is about two in the afternoon and I think the British are currently more concerned about the landing at Kip's Bay than moving their troops northward, but I expect rotational watches to be set up."

"Understood." There was something in Wells' voice that Tallmadge picked up on. To him it sounded strained, but he could not quite discern what it meant. He glanced back in time to see Captain Hamilton give a look to Wells before looking back down at his map.

It occurred to him that while Wells and Hamilton were of the same rank, Hamilton had been treating Wells in a far different manner than others of equal rank were. He realized that Hamilton considered himself in command of both the battery set up here and of the cannons that had joined him – he thus considered Captain Wells under his command. And it seemed Wells was not too pleased by this judging by the strain he heard in his captain's voice.

Silence reigned in the tent for a few minutes before Hamilton looked up at them, a frown on his face. "Where are my manners, gentlemen? Please, do take this moment of reprieve to get yourselves sorted. I will send for you when we have our orders."

"Sir," Tallmadge saluted as did Bulkley and after a moment's hesitation so did Wells before he left the tent, Bulkley following quickly behind him. He had no doubt that his friend had sensed the growing tension between Wells and Hamilton. He and Bulkley quickly walked away and headed towards where their horses had been stabled by the two young boys. They were tied under a large oak tree, munching on hay with pails of water by their legs. The boys were brushing other horses and Tallmadge waved to them.

"Thank you for your kindness," he said as he pulled out two coins from inside his jacket, and flipped them towards them.

"Yes sir, any time sir." The boys seemed pleased with their bounty as Tallmadge reached Shadow and rubbed his nose. His horse whickered a greeting as it resumed munching on bits of hay. He reached over to his pack at the back of his saddle. He pulled out his water canteen and drank deeply from it, not realizing how thirsty he was since the bombardment had started.

"Ben, get some rest. I'll keep watch," Bulkley suddenly said and Tallmadge looked up to see his friend staring at him, eyes earnest.

"But-"

"You have not slept since last night and only then for two hours," Bulkley shook his head, and held up a hand. "I will pull rank and tell Captain Wells and make it an order, Tallmadge."

He frowned, "Bulkley. Edward-"

"We are safe for now. We have reprieve. Use it." His friend shook his head and Tallmadge sighed before reluctantly corking his canteen and stuffing it back into his traveling pack. "Wake me in three hours, Bulkley. Three."

"I will," his friend promised before moving away, leaving him alone.

He sighed and ran a hand through his hair before glancing up at the large oak tree. There were several branches that dipped low, and he supposed that he could find respite up there instead of sleeping on the ground, where he knew Shadow was more than likely to nibble on his hair or uniform. If there was one vice his horse had, it was that he loved to nibble on everything near him. He climbed up the tree and found a branch that he was able to settle himself into and also be visible enough for Bulkley or anyone else to find. Crossing his arms, he settled himself into the crook of the branch and closed his eyes, hoping for sleep to come.

September 21st, 1776

The order to fire upon the British heavy battery set up across Long Island never came the next day like Tallmadge and the rest of 3rd Troop had expected. Instead, it seemed Captain Hamilton had abruptly received orders later in the day to move a few of his artillery to a bluff of hills around Harlem Heights. Hamilton's artillery had been stolen from the *HMS Asia* in a daring raid led by the man himself. The move to Harlem Heights was to reinforce a counter attack against reports that spoke of British soldiers trying to flank up the western section of York Island. The counter attack had launched the very next day with Knowlton's Rangers involved in the attempted ambush along with two hundred riflemen from three troops. According to the report, after two hours of skirmishing and fighting, the British had withdrawn, giving the Patriot forces a badly needed victory.

Tallmadge and the others who had heard about the report cheered at that fact, their spirits and fervor renewed. Captain Wells, who was left in charge of the rest of the artillery left on the bluffs overlooking Hell's Gate, also delivered some sobering news with the victory. There had been casualties, one of which was Lieutenant Colonel Knowlton. The initial elation Tallmadge felt died quickly with that report. He had only met Knowlton at the docks, but the fact that Nathan had seemed to hold him in high regard made him sad on his friend's behalf. In an effort to cheer the men's spirits, Wells had also announced that Generals Greene, Knox and Putnam and their forces had successfully escaped along the Bloomingdale Road along with their troops. 1st Battalion of Wadsworth's Brigade had been with Knox's forces and he was glad to hear most of them had not been captured and had lived to fight another day.

Now, a week since the retreat from Kip's Bay and victory over Harlem Heights, they waited on the bluffs overlooking Hell's Gate. Tallmadge sat on top of Shadow once more, peering through his spyglass at the British heavy battery on Long Island. The British had been making odd movements for the last hour or so and he'd already had Captain Wells look, but Wells dismissed it out of hand.

He could hear Ensign Hecox near him, examining one of the larger artillery pieces that had been left behind. Hecox had taken a shine to Captain Hamilton in the brief time he was here and had decided after his six-month bounty was up, he would apply for a position in the artillery corps. He had spent the past week learning from the artillerymen their duties and how he could help them as an officer. The artillerymen had in turn, taken Hecox under their wing. It was good to see Hecox being accepted by a group of men that he would eventually lead.

Tallmadge pursed his lips a little as he noted the movements of the artillerymen across the river. What were they doing?

"Get to cover men!" He pulled the spyglass from his eyes just as the whistle of artillery pierced the air. He realized that the British had been setting up their cannons the whole time. The British must have prepared their powder and balls in the dead of night in the dim moonlight, hoping to catch them off guard.

"Hecox, get away from there!" he shouted to the young ensign who had ducked next to the cannon, pushing himself along with the other artillerymen against the earthen mounds. "Hecox-"

His only glimpse was of Hecox's wide fearful eyes before, the young officer simply disappeared into a fine mist of red and blackened dirt, utterly disintegrated by an incoming cannon ball that pierced the earthen mound. Tallmadge stared, his mouth agape in shock; the hazy cries of artillery exploding all around them, throwing dirt, body parts, blood, and men into the air. The thunderous rumble split the air and Tallmadge was snapped out of his stupor at the sudden explosion of dirt hitting his face. Shadow bucked, throwing his hind legs wildly into the air and Tallmadge automatically grabbed his reins and pulled him down to control him.

He danced his horse back, horror filling him at the sight of the men reaching out to him with bloodied hands or with half-ripped arms and legs, begging him to take them along just as a horrendous crack filled the air-

"Tallmadge! Run!" he heard Bulkley's roar across the haze of cannon fire and, to his shock, he saw that the ground before him was crumbling. The barrage of cannon fire from had softened the earth underneath where their artillery was stationed.

He pulled on Shadow's reins and spurred him to gallop away, turning to see the men who had survived the barrage running with him, but most of them suddenly fell away as the earth collapsed around them. They were sent down the hilly cliff side into the river. He heard more screams as the British battery responded by firing more shots, the smoke creating hazy-looking white clouds. Tallmadge could not tame the horror in him at what had just happened.

"Tallmadge! Ben! Ben!" It took him a moment to see Bulkley waving frantically at him. They were in full retreat from the bluffs that overlooked Hell's Gate.

"H-Hecox," he managed to stammer out before coughing, "Hecox...Bulkley, Hecox-"

"I know, I saw," Bulkley shook his head. "There is nothing we can do, Ben. Captain Wells called for a full retreat to the main body of the army."

Tallmadge nodded numbly as he took several deep breaths and pulled himself together. He could not let his horror and fear show, for the sake of the men who had witnessed the same thing he had. He needed to show them strength. After what seemed like several breaths, he managed to focus himself. "How many-"

"Look around you, Tallmadge." Bulkley gestured and Tallmadge looked to see that only one full company and maybe a half company of artillerymen had made it. The rest...the rest had fallen into the river, crushed by the cannonades that fell along with them, or had been killed by the barrage that caught them all off guard.

He swallowed thickly, refusing to let the despair fill him. He needed to be strong; it was not all for naught. But he could not help but feel keenly at the sudden loss of Ensign James Hecox.

"Let's go," he said hoarsely. He pulled on Shadow's reins and kicked him into a trot. Hell's Gate was now lost to them. Tallmadge could only hope that they would not be cut off by the British who were now sure to advance north.

INTERLUDE II

September 22nd, 1776

There were moments when Nathan wished he had more time to contemplate the peacefulness of death, the acceptance of it, and what God's designs were for him. But even for want of time, Nathan had come to the realization that perhaps some things were not for Man to contemplate. Still, he did not deny the beauty of the day God had created for him to witness before taking him into his arms.

It was a mild, beautiful early-fall day, the light breeze and shining sun seemingly a gift from the angels. With each step he took from the tent of Captain John Montresor, one of General Howe's aide-de-camps, it was as if he could feel the sins of his life grow lighter. His steps feel less burdened. He had written two letters a couple of hours earlier, one addressed to Enoch to ask for his forgiveness and to pray for his soul, and one to Lieutenant Colonel Knowlton. It was his final report and an apology to his commander for failing him as a spy. He had also conducted his apology to General Washington on his failed mission, and asked that his Commander-in-Chief pray for him once he reached Heaven.

During the night, he had time to reflect on his life, his mission, and his duty to his country. He knew that once news, if there was any, of his death reached his friends, they would mourn, but he hoped that they would not desert the cause. He hoped that they would take up arms for the cause and serve with the fervor and idealism that he had so believed. But if they did not, he would not hold them to it. After all, he had willingly become a spy and he would not expect his friends to do the same. Each man's patriotic feeling was unique. Each of them served the cause as they believed, in their own way.

He had reflected on his life with his friends, on the life he had with his family and was content with what he had accomplished in the years he was on God's green and blue paradise. He imagined William Hull's chiding remarks the night before he left and almost silently acknowledged that William had been correct. He had been too trusting, too open, and had fallen into Robert Rogers' trap. It was his own fault and his own arrogance for believing that he could easily identify Patriots or Tories in the taverns. He understood his mistake. Though he wished for another chance to correct it, by the time the morning sun rose, he had accepted that he had only received that one chance and had squandered it.

His thoughts had turned to another one of his friends, Benjamin Tallmadge. In contrast to William, Ben had acquiesced to his request not to tell him of the dangers and respected his wishes and choices. His friend had been the one to write the letter pushing him to join the Continentals after some months of indecision. In return, he had tried to give Ben advice on leading his men, on the conduct of an officer and of the strength that the enlisted needed to draw from him. They had constantly pushed each other to the limits while they had been studying at Yale and Nathan could only hope that if and when Ben received news of his death, it would push him, not crush him as news of friends and family dying did to so many others. He had a seen a glimmer of hope that Ben would move past death when he found out about his older brother William's fate on Long Island. Nathan hoped it was enough.

So many good men were going to perish in this war and the only regret he had was that he had just the one life to give for his country. He did not regret the undertaking of the mission – but hoped it would serve as a valuable lesson to those who came after him – those who would continue the mission; those, who were Patriots and fought wholeheartedly for the cause of freedom and independence.

"Any last requests?" William Cunningham, General Howe's provost marshal, walked beside him. He looked down from the beautiful blue skies and warm atmosphere to see that they had approached an apple tree with a hangman's noose on a branch, and a wagon next to it.

The site of his execution.

Nathan sighed softly and reached into the inner pocket of his jacket and pulled out his unsealed letters. "Would you please see these delivered. One is to my brother Enoch in New London, the other to my commanding officer, Lieutenant Colonel Knowlton. I have conveyed my apologies for my failed mission to him in these missives."

Cunningham took the letters and stuffed them into his own jacket pocket. "We shall see," the red-haired, red-nosed man sniffed. He had been a boorish host since Nathan's capture yesterday.

Nathan gave him a faint smile. He did not know if his request was to be honored, but then again, he would not be there to see it honored. It was his hope that Cunningham would respect his final wishes, but it was only that – hope. He squared his shoulders and cleared his throat as he approached the apple tree. It would be just a short amount of pain before darkness claimed him. The jerk of the rope and the snap of his neck. Then he would feel nothing and be embraced into the arms of his loving God.

Nathan stopped and climbed up to the back of the wagon where he allowed himself to be bound, the ropes feeling rough on his wrists. He supposed that in the last moments of his life on earth he would be sensitive to how unique the hemp and rough pull of ropes would feel. He could feel the stiff starchiness of the clothing he wore, smell the stale odor of the tavern he had visited the night before. It was as if he suddenly could feel everything as the heavy noose was pulled over his head, wrapping around his neck. The brush of his queue was pulled out and Nathan was acutely aware of the smell of salt water. This rope had been used on the Sound, or around water. Perhaps it had been one of the *Halifax's* ropes?

Smiling softly to himself, he looked out to where Cunningham stood before him, Montresor next to him. To his sadness, he saw that there was a glimmer of water in the young aide-de-camp's eyes and he shook his head a little. *Do not weep for me, weep for what may become of our country*, he wanted to say, but the words did not come out. He could not say them. Montresor had been a good confidante in the last few hours of his life but Nathan could not persuade him to betray his cause more than Montresor could save him from the hangman's noose. No, Montresor would have to decide on his own; as every Patriot did when they took up arms. Was it worth it? How long was a man to endure hardship for little to no reward, only to meet death? How much was to be paid for Patriotism and for the independence of this new nation?

"Captain Nathaniel Hale of Coventry of the Colony of Connecticut. You are hereby found guilty of the highest treason to the lawful ruler of these lands of the Crown, King George III. You will be hung until the death for the role of espionage, your body left to rot in an unmarked grave as a warning to those who rise up in rebellion against the law and order of these Colonies. Do you have any last dying speech and confessions to make?"

"I regret," Nathan looked out at the beauty of the cityscape before him, marred only by the still smoking clouds of a great fire that had consumed part of York City the day before. It was still a beautiful sight amidst such ugliness. "I regret, that I had not been able to serve my country better."

"Swing the rebel off!" the words were barely out of Cunningham's mouth before Nathan felt the movement of the wagon.

He felt the sudden burst of fear. It would only be a quick pain and it would be done. A quick pain, a quick pain-

3

October 4ᵗʰ, 1776

He felt like a musket ball had been shot into his stomach at point-blank range as he listened to the news. He could feel Colonel Chester's sharp-eyed gaze on him as General Wadsworth finished talking, but kept his eyes steady on the general. It was like listening from an extremely hollow point from one side of a house to another. It certainly explained why Captain Wells had insisted on accompanying him when he had been requested to report to Wadsworth at general headquarters. Wells must have heard it first before being sent to retrieve him.

Nathan was dead. Hanged for spying.

Tallmadge heard and even saw the words coming out of Wadsworth's mouth, but somehow he could not comprehend them. But he did see the moment when the general had stopped talking, and nodded mechanically. "Thank you, sir, for the honor of personally informing me," he said and saw something in Wadsworth's face soften. Tallmadge saluted stiffly, holding himself still even though the pain made him want to curl up and lie on his side for a while.

Wadsworth returned the salute before he spun crisply on his heel and left. He could feel both Colonel Chester and General Wadsworth's eyes on him as the door closed behind him. He knew what they were thinking – there had been no honor in

Nathan's death. A decorated officer who had bowed to the ungentlemanly function of such a low form of life – a spy. He knew they were evaluating him as they gave him the news, but did not know what kind of evaluation he had undergone. Was it a test of character? A test of his connections to a man that everyone now thought of as nothing more than a spy? Were they waiting to see if he had any additional information?

Tallmadge welcomed the thoughts, drowning out the roar of pain that he was feeling over Nathan's death. He barely recalled how Wadsworth had said the news was delivered. Something about a meeting for a prisoner exchange conducted by Captain Hamilton and a few others regarding future prisoner exchanges. A British officer by the name of John Montresor had supposedly given a letter that mentioned Nathan's death by hanging, a captured spy.

"Tallmadge?" Wells' hand on his shoulder pulled him out of his thoughts and he glanced over to see his captain staring at him with some concern. "Bad news regarding you family?"

With those words, Tallmadge realized that Wells had not been informed of Nathan's death. He had apparently been ordered to escort him, but had not been given the details or reasoning. He opened his mouth to tell him, but closed it as he wondered why there had seemingly been secrecy surrounding Nathan's death. He knew from experience that it was highly unusual for general, even a friend like Wadsworth, to be informing him, a mere lieutenant, of a death of sorts. It had been Colonel Chester that passed news to him regarding William's death and even then, it was only in a roster report that Chester managed to find when he had been at Wadsworth's meetings. But Wadsworth had personally told him about Nathan's death. Tallmadge did not recall mentioning that he and Nathan had been friends to Wadsworth or even Chester, even back before he had joined the militia. There had been no indication that his commanding officers knew of his friendship with Nathan, unless it had been by Nathan's own words – at least that was what he supposed.

It *was* a test.

And slightly horrified, he realized that it was a test not only for himself, but for the rest of the army. He remembered Nathan as boisterous, kind, helpful, and prone to speak not even a single falsehood. In his brief contact with Nathan while they were both stationed on Long Island, he remembered his friend caring for his troops, and the men he commanded, but most of all, caring for the state of the cause and of the army. Tallmadge had heard rumors regarding Nathan's popularity with the rest of the army – the occasional lapses in discipline that he had early during the Siege of Boston, but it seemed his friend was well-liked. The fact that Nathan had made references to William Hull trying to dissuade him from his assignment to spy behind the lines of the enemy told Tallmadge that his fellow officers in Lieutenant Colonel Knowlton's regiment must have also tried to persuade his friend to abandon his mission.

And with that knowledge, Tallmadge knew what the test was about. If Nathan's manner of death was revealed; if the army knew that one of their rising officers, a beloved captain, had been hung as a spy... He shuddered to think of the consequences. Morale would plummet; hope would be dashed. Someone of Nathan's caliber had sunk so low as to become a dredge of society to try to win against the British and had failed. They had already evacuated twice, from Long Island, from Kip's Bay and now were waiting at Harlem Heights – waiting with tension and nervousness, wondering when Howe would strike again. The brief victory that had been claimed at Harlem Heights by Knowlton's Rangers and the troops supporting them had been tempered by the knowledge of Knowlton's death.

Any knowledge of Nathan's death would spread fear once more in the camp.

Tallmadge swallowed, the pain that had initially felt like a punch in his stomach slowly ebbing away as he digested his own analysis. "Some bad news, but I will write my father later regarding it, sir," he lied, keeping his voice even and light. He could not tell anyone of Nathan's fate. The cause depended on the fragile boost they had gotten in the brief victory two weeks ago.

"Hard luck," Wells squeezed his shoulder once before releasing it. "I will leave you to your thoughts then, Lieutenant. I also expect your inventory report to me before tomorrow's general post. Do you have any duties to attend to General

Wadsworth that may prevent this?"

"No sir, but I believe the general is expecting me to report on the status of the battalions so he may make a formal report to General Washington himself," he said and Wells nodded.

Tallmadge had been formally appointed brigade-major to General Wadsworth's command staff two days ago, replacing the temporary Brigade-Major Fenn Wadsworth. During the evacuation of Kip's Bay and subsequent battle at Harlem Heights, the regiment's previous brigade-major, John Wyllys, had been captured and taken prisoner in the chaotic September days. Tallmadge still served as adjutant to Colonel Chester as well as a lieutenant in Captain Wells' 3rd Troop, but for the last two days his duties consisted of running messages back and forth between the six battalions camped at Harlem Heights. He also had to run roster checks and duties for his own troop and anything Colonel Chester wished him to convey to the rest of his troops of the 6th. It had been exhausting work and Tallmadge did the best he could.

He supposed it was luck that the whole of the regiment was camped at Harlem Heights at the moment. The only regiment that was not accounted for was Bradley's 7th Battalion. Colonel Bradley and his battalion had been initially deployed to Paulus Hook, New Jersey in case Howe decided to invade from Staten Island or further south. After they had evacuated to Harlem Heights, Bradley's battalion had been ordered to support the fortifications at Fort Lee under General Nathanael Greene's command as a special detachment and thus not officially in the chain of command for General Wadsworth and the rest of the Connecticut militia brigade.

"All right then," Wells nodded and left him, heading towards his own tent.

Tallmadge was left alone and found his own tent pitched next to Bulkley's. It had been a welcomed relief to sleep on a proper bedroll and straw-covered bed instead of the uneven crates and cobblestone ground they had slept on in the streets of York City.

"Bulkley!" he called out, and saw his friend stick his head out of the tent, spectacles perched on the edges of his nose. Tallmadge thought him too young to be wearing such accouterments, but Bulkley said that he needed them after so many nights spent on his family's ships reading manifest orders from a very young age.

"I have the list." His friend ducked back into his tent before stepping out and handing him a sheet that detailed what each man had in terms of ammunition and rations. Tallmadge had created the roster list himself and had given it to Bulkley to ask each one what they had and what they had salvaged since arriving at camp.

As he glanced at the paper, he noted that some of them had salvaged more things than others. "Was there a salvaging party sent out?"

"No. I remember seeing both Parsons and Dole's bags being held in lottery by the men the other day so they might have won the contents," Bulkley shrugged. He nodded – most of the time what was in a man's trunk after he died on the battlefield was given to the widows or families of said deceased person, but ammunition and rations were distributed among the rest of the men in a lottery of sorts to at least give the family some monetary compensation for their loss.

The contents of Ensign James Hecox's haversack and knapsack were distributed among the two of them, but they had already sent all of Hecox's personal effects back up to his family in Wethersfield. Captain Wells had written a letter of condolence to send along with the remains and Tallmadge could only hope that Hecox's family would find some comfort in the passing of their son.

"I'll check with General Wadsworth to see when the next salvage party is being sent out. Let Captain Wells know and to make sure to lobby for some of our men to be in that party," he said and Bulkley nodded. Technically he was still a junior officer to Bulkley's enlistment, but due to his promotion to brigade-major, he had more authority to authorize certain things under Wadsworth's orders. It was a feeling that Tallmadge was not quite used to, and he dared not abuse such power in certain aspects. In others, especially when it came time to keep the men supplied, he had already learned how to exert his station and influence to get 3rd Troop better equipped or favored in distribution of labor.

Salvage parties were occasionally sent out to either forage for fresh food, fish, or produce that would help feed the rest of the army. They were also occasionally sent to raid ammunition stores, working in tandem with a scouting party. 3rd Troop had been sent on one such occasion to ascertain the strength of the British occupying lower York Island, but they had not encountered any patrols and returned when the foraging party said that they had wagons full of goods for the army. He had heard rumors that General Washington had not been too happy with that particular patrol, hoping to find out what Howe's movements were, but could not confirm it. Tallmadge wanted 3rd Troop as part of the salvage party only because they would technically get first pick of things they found – even though it was for the whole of the army. It was a little underhanded, but he had seen many others return with smiles on their faces at their bounties and wanted at least some of his men to experience that to improve their morale.

"Davenport was a great help," Bulkley commented in an absent manner and Tallmadge gave him a look.

Ever since they lost Hecox, they were short one officer in the troop and with himself on detached duties as brigade-major, the reality was that they were short two officers. He knew he could easily blame Bulkley for shirking his duties, but he understood that his friend needed help in drilling the troops, or commanding them on the field in Wells' absence. It seemed with Hecox's death, Bulkley had become more vocal and insistent and Tallmadge had found himself becoming a little more resistant and stubborn to his friend's entreaties.

It was not that he did not consider Sergeant-Major Davenport a ill-fit to be promoted to ensign, but somehow he still felt *angry*, incredibly angry at himself for putting Hecox in such a position. He had not even had time to react before the young man had been literally blown apart. Bulkley could have easily suggested to Captain Wells the idea of promoting Davenport to ensign, but his friend knew it would be more effective if it came from Tallmadge. He would couch it in the fact that his responsibilities were numerous and while he could execute them to effect, the regiment would benefit from Davenport's promotion to an officer.

"I'll consider it," he replied, but knew that ultimately, Bulkley was right. It was only his third day as brigade-major and he was already feeling the tugs of exhaustion – now compounded by the knowledge that Nathan was dead.

He folded the paper and headed down to Wells' tent. He arrived shortly and cleared his throat, "Sir, it's Tallmadge."

"Enter," Wells voice called out and he pushed the flap aside and entered.

"Here is the list, sir," he said handing Wells the paper.

"So fast?" Wells seemed surprised.

"Bulkley and I drew up a list yesterday and started asking the men earlier this morning during inspections. Sergeant-Major Davenport was of great assistance when I was summoned to General Wadsworth's command post," he said and saw Wells nod, perusing the list.

His captain looked up at him. "Davenport has been assisting the troop lately since Ensign Hecox's death hasn't he?"

"Yes sir," Tallmadge replied. "I would highly recommend him for promotion ensign. He has the respect of the men and I believe can perform to great effect."

Wells made a noise of agreement. "We do need another officer in case James or John requires your services." There was something in Wells' tone that sounded different, almost as if he was expecting this, but Tallmadge could not quite tell. "I will put it in my report for Colonel Chester later tonight."

"Sir," Tallmadge replied, "if you do not mind, I would like to execute my duties for General Wadsworth at this time. I will return when we have late afternoon drills in a few hours, sir."

"Yes, that is fine." Wells dismissed him with an absent wave of his hand and Tallmadge left his tent.

He squared his shoulders and checked that he was dressed properly before heading down to where 1st Battalion was stationed, at the farthest end of the encampment that made up the Connecticut regiments. He normally would have started with the 6th itself or even the 5th considering that the 5th was stationed right next to them, but he knew from habits that Colonel Chester liked writing missives late into the night and would not receive a report from him until the early morning right before he was to report to General Wadsworth.

He did not want to start with the 5th since Colonel William

Douglas was a very cross man to deal with since his regiment received the worst public denouncement anyone had ever seen. It was delivered by General Washington himself, furious at how Douglas' men had abandoned the works at Kip's Bay without firing a single shot. Since then, Douglas had been shunned at every meeting and was in disgrace. There were already rumors about him resigning his post, but so far the man instead taken his anger and embarrassment out on his officers and the last brigade-major. It prompted Fenn Wadsworth's resignation. Tallmadge had not had the fortune of encountering Douglas, but with this first batch of battalion status reports to deliver, he would see for himself who Colonel Douglas was; but that would be later, after he went to the rest of the battalion commanders for their reports. He hoped that meeting the others first would give him some fortitude to finally retrieve Colonel Douglas' report.

Colonel Gold Selleck Silliman, 1st Battalion commander, was General Wadsworth's second-in-command as well as the commanding officer of Connecticut's regiment of Light Horse. Tallmadge was already familiar with the man. Silliman had a reputation of being soft-spoken, but with an intense fearlessness in the face of British troops. That fearlessness had been enhanced while his battalion had been stationed with General Knox's artillery company at the southern tip of York Island. When Knox and Putnam had led the evacuation of their forces, the 1st Battalion had held back the British that had tried to cut off their escape. There were losses, but it was said that there would have been more had it not been for 1st Battalion's actions.

Silliman also had a reputation of being utterly serious; but Tallmadge had heard rumors from more than one of his junior officers that it was a way for Silliman to test the resolve of new recruits or new officers who had purchased commissions or were promoted into positions that perhaps they were not ready for. He had interacted with the colonel only once and that was just to deliver a message from Chester to Silliman before being summarily dismissed without even a second glance. With his promotion to brigade-major, this would be his first time he would meet Silliman on official duties for General Wadsworth. Tallmadge would be lying to himself if he denied that he was a little nervous.

He stopped by Silliman tent, easily the largest in the area where 1st Battalion was stationed and saw the flap was wide open. The colonel was sitting hunched over his desk, writing. Tallmadge stopped by the edges of the tent, making sure that he was not blocking the officer's sunlight, but also close enough that he knew Silliman could see him out of the corner of his eyes. He saluted and cleared his throat, "Colonel Silliman, sir."

"Yes?" The man did not look up as he continued to write.

"General Wadsworth requests status reports on the Battalion's strengths," he said and saw the quill pause. He kept his posture stiff and at full attention.

Something akin to annoyance seemed to pass through Silliman's expression before he sighed and rubbed his eyes. "Couldn't James have asked this during the meeting yesterday?" he thought he heard Silliman mutter, but the other man pulled out a fresh piece of parchment and ripped it in half before scribbling down a few things. "Find Chandler, my second, and tell him to see the surgeon with this request. The report should be ready by late this afternoon."

"Sir," Tallmadge took the parchment and folded it. He had promised Captain Wells that he would be at the afternoon drills, but from what Silliman was saying, the report would be ready around then. He would have to find some way of getting the report from Silliman and also participate in afternoon drills. He saluted and left, headed down a few tents where he had seen a jacket with the epaulettes of lieutenant colonel hanging on the corner of a mirror.

"Lieutenant Colonel Chandler?" He paused in front of the open tent and saw the man seemingly asleep on his cot. The man's eyes opened with a snap and peered at him.

"Who are you?" Chandler rubbed his eyes, trying to clear the sleep away.

"Lieutenant Tallmadge, sir," he introduced himself and handed over the folded piece of paper. "Orders from Colonel Silliman, sir."

Chandler sighed and took the paper, unfolding it before looking back up at him. Chandler had kind eyes and the temperament seemed to extended to his personality. He folded the paper back up and nodded. "I will have those reports to

Silliman later this afternoon. Tallmadge, eh? Wadsworth's new brigade-major?"

"Yes sir," he replied.

Chandler made a small noise and Tallmadge could not decide whether it was approving or not. "Word of advice, Tallmadge, be true. Wyllys was good at his job because he became Wadsworth's arm. Good man, pity that he was captured. Fenn, well, Fenn thought he could use his relative's name to help him."

"Sir," Tallmadge nodded as he saluted, accepting the advice and left.

As he walked away from 1st Battalion's tents, a plan began to form in his mind as to how he was going to get Colonel Silliman's report. It would take some creativity and some shading of the truth, but it could not be helped. His only hope was that the rest of the Battalion would have their reports in before 3rd Troop started their drills. Otherwise, he would have his hands full trying to get everyone's reports. But, Tallmadge never shied away from a challenge. As he headed towards 5th Battalion's tents, he thought he could hear Nathan's phantom laughter, an echo of what once was, but could never be again after the death of his friend. He would deal with the hurt later, the pain of grief. Right now, he would execute his duties as best as he could.

"Silliman, you have a wicked mind," Colonel John Chester commented quietly, just out of the hearing range of General Wadsworth who sat on top of his horse overlooking the small bluff that had been turned into a mock battlefield for the late afternoon's exercises.

"Gives the boy some character," Silliman replied with a small shrug of indifference. "Besides, are you worried for him?"

"Not in particular," Chester replied, unable to keep the pride out of his voice as he watched the proceedings below them. This had been a joint drill between his Battalion, Silliman's 1st, and Silliman's 2nd detachment of the only Light Horse regiment to come out of Connecticut. Both were practicing their lines and formations and the Light Horse regiments were to practice charging the lines. Though there had not been much cavalry presence when the British had landed at Kip's Bay, a majority of the troops being infantry, General Washington had ordered most of the army to practice against cavalry incursions.

Chester and Silliman sat on the same small ridge as Wadsworth, both deciding to let their seconds command the afternoon's exercises. However it was not their seconds that they were focused on, but rather, one young lieutenant who sat proudly on horseback, directing his men under Captain Wells' commands.

"The boy needs some practice at seeing the broader orders at hand, but I think he'll pick it up quickly," Silliman observed. It was a bit of trickery that Chester had not thought of, but it made sense. Tallmadge needed to quickly learn how the posting of brigade-major worked and that not only was a favored appointment for him, but that he was able to do his duties.

He had heard from Captain Wells that Tallmadge had requested that an additional officer be promoted in his troop to ensign to handle some of his duties, so he could execute his other assignments. It was a step in the right direction even if Wells was not exactly happy to lose a lieutenant of Tallmadge's caliber – especially in light of the loss of one of their junior officers, an ensign by the name of James Hecox. But it was a lesson Chester thought Captain Wells needed to also learn – that he would lose officers, whether through transfers, desertions, or death on the battlefield. Wells needed to learn how to adjust. He had been a cautious appointment even though Chester liked the man. The captain was occasionally too afraid of change, but when he did accept such changes, he did so with a gusto and passion that was unrivaled.

"Still, a wicked plan." Chester watched as Tallmadge wheeled his horse around, a steady hand at controlling the beast. He had been surprised at how natural of a horseman Tallmadge was; he thought the younger man would have been a more deft hand at controlling small boats and fishing vessels.

A quiet snort made him glance over at Silliman, who had a slight smile on his face. He silently shook his head at his friend's antics, then turned his head back to watch the light horse practice their formations. The Connecticut regiment originally had twenty-four troops of light horse, one for each infantry regiment that were then organized into separate regiments and placed under detached command of Colonel Silliman.

"Ah, here he comes." Silliman's quiet voice was nearly drowned out by the thunder of hooves across the ground in front of them as the light horse were led on a brief charge before halting.

Chester looked to where his own Battalion were still turning in formation and saw that Tallmadge had indeed broken away from his troop and was heading on a curved path up towards them. Within a minute, Tallmadge made his way up to them and saluted. His arrival made Wadsworth turn a little, a mild look on his face at the young lieutenant's appearance.

"Sir," Chester noted that Tallmadge addressed Silliman specifically, "your report for General Wadsworth?"

Chester managed to keep his expression as neutral as possible as he noted one of Wadsworth's eyebrows rise up at Tallmadge's request. He wondered how Silliman did it, how he kept his expression flat and mild while reaching into his jacket's pocket and pulling out a sealed piece of parchment.

"Certainly, thank you Lieutenant," Silliman replied as Tallmadge accepted the report before taking a few steps over to General Wadsworth.

"Sir," Tallmadge placed the report into a small burlap saddlebag before lifting the bag up, "the status reports as you had requested. Shall I place this on your desk?"

"No, I will take them." Wadsworth seemed pleased and took the bag. "Thank you Lieutenant Tallmadge."

"Orders sir?" Tallmadge continued and Chester could feel a swell of pride rise in him. Not only had Tallmadge managed himself in wake of the news regarding Nathan Hale this morning, but it also seemed that he had dedicated himself to the duties that were now required of him.

"None, for the moment," Wadsworth nodded curtly.

"Sir," Tallmadge saluted, and Chester thought he was going to leave, but then the young man turned to him. "Sir, orders?"

This time Chester could not keep the smile of pride off of his face. Tallmadge still remembered that he was his adjutant which most in his position would have easily forgotten once they were given a higher position of power. "My compliments to Lieutenant Colonel Wills on a job well done," Chester replied.

"Sir," Tallmadge saluted before wheeling his horse around and galloping back to where the rest of the Battalion were finishing up their formations.

"John, a moment of your time," Wadsworth suddenly said and Chester shifted his horse a little as he saw Silliman move to the side to give them some privacy.

"Sir?" he looked at Wadsworth. The general looked even more tired than when they had last talked in private. He supposed that General Washington had not been very pleased with one of Wadsworth's commanders. The fact that William Douglas' troops ran from Kip's Bay without firing a single shot had sent the rumor mill in the army into overdrive. The man had been derided and muttered about behind closed doors. Even Chester himself had avoided him, unwilling to be associated with someone who could not clearly command the respect and steadiness of militiamen. He was not exactly sympathetic to Douglas' plight – Douglas was a hard man to like, abrasive and foul-mouthed during their meetings.

Still, it seemed Wadsworth had borne the brunt of Washington's ire for Douglas' failings and it made the general seemed more drawn and old. Truth be told, Wadsworth looked exhausted, the last month of skirmishes and of retreats eating away at him. He dared not wonder what Wadsworth was really thinking – but he knew from talking with Silliman that there were faint rumors that Wadsworth was frustrated by the lack of time he had to training his militia and possible threats of officers resigning from the army due to the series of defeats in recent months. Gone was the glorious days of when they drove the British out of Boston Harbor.

"Send one of your regiments out on a foraging patrol. They will be accompanied by Major Sheldon's command. We need to ascertain the enemy's movements," Wadsworth said and Chester frowned.

"You wish me to send out 6th Battalion's troops, sir," he stated and saw Wadsworth nod.

"Give the boy some more experience." It seemed he had read his commanding officer's mind as Wadsworth smiled a little before his expression turned serious. "There are only two, perhaps three months left in the men's enlistments and rumblings from Congress say they may authorize the raising of officers and an army instead of relying on militia forces."

"You think Tallmadge has the makings of a Continental officer," Chester stated and Wadsworth nodded once.

"Good head on his shoulders and was one of the few whom you said asked you about drilling troops while we were stationed in Long Island. He is true to the cause and passionate about it. We will need officers of his caliber in order to defeat the British," he stated and Chester nodded.

"Sir." He could sense that the conversation was coming to an end. "I will write the orders up first thing regarding the foraging patrol." Wadsworth nodded again and Chester could see that he was very proud of what Tallmadge had accomplished so far. He could see that the young man was starting to become aware of his own growing reputation and perhaps the favoritism that had been bestowed upon him, but at the same time he was still as humble as ever to respect the chain of command and to follow orders. Only time would tell if Tallmadge would continue to show the more daring side of himself – case in point, his antics with rescuing his horse – but Chester had a feeling that even the news of his friend's death had not broken him, but rather hardened his resolve.

October 21ˢᵗ, 1776

They had evacuated again, pulling back from Harlem Heights all the way to White Plains in an effort to fortify their positions and prevent the British from encircling them. Tallmadge had pitched his tent against Bulklcy's in an effort to keep their things from rolling down the hill where the 6th Battalion was stationed. It was called Chatterton Hill. The 6th was on official detachment from the main body of the Connecticut brigade, now under the command of General Joseph Spencer who had taken over after General Lord Stirling's capture. General Wadsworth still required his services as brigade-major from time to time, but since he and the rest of the battalions that had not been absorbed by other regiments were stationed with the main army further back, there was not as much need for him. He took the opportunity to help train the newly promoted Ensign Henry Davenport – formerly sergeant-major. Andrew Adamson had been promoted to Davenport's old position and William Pullings promoted to corporal to lead Adamson's group of soldiers.

Tallmadge was proud of his friends for receiving such promotions, a testament of how respected they were among the rest of the men for their bravery and efforts. For the last few weeks, he and Bulkley had been teaching Davenport the differences between an officer's commission and an enlisted man's commission. For a bit of levity, they had also engaged in a little fun at Davenport's expense. Davenport had taken it with good humor which reaffirmed his decision to put in for his friend's name for a promotion. The man understood that he was a junior officer, but also understood his responsibilities at the same time.

He supposed that the whole of the 6th, while somewhat diminished by the loss of Captain Bacon's troop to Knowlton's Rangers, along with a majority of Captain Marcy's troop during the retreat from Turtle Bay, was in good shape. But there was no denying the fact that the Connecticut brigade had suffered. 2nd Battalion had lost a majority of their command staff through the premature death of Colonel Fisher Gay, or through capture during the retreat from New York. The 2nd had been absorbed into the main army, dissolved by Washington himself, along with 4th Battalion since the capture and subsequent death of Colonel Samuel Selden. It seemed that General Wadsworth was officially in command of the 3rd and 5th Battalions, but even he was with the main army stationed on a flat plain of land above and a mile away from Chatterton Hill. Like the 6th, 1st Battalion under Colonel Silliman had been ordered on special detachment once again under General Israel Putnam's command.

Tallmadge did not understand the politics behind it until one early October day. He had been ordered to wait outside while Wadsworth talked with General Washington. Wadsworth was in an agitated state of mind after receiving a letter from one of Washington's aides the day before. Colonel Silliman had warned Tallmadge away from disturbing or asking anything of the general. It seemed Silliman had taken a liking to him since he delivered the man's regiment report to Wadsworth during the exercise. Tallmadge had only realized a few days after the exercise that it was a test of sorts by Silliman to prove his competency and apparently he had passed.

Although Silliman had warned him of Wadsworth's agitated state, he had only realized the cause as he waited outside General Washington's office. He did not mean to overhear, but one could not deny the quiet fury and intensity of Wadsworth's voice for his defense. It seemed that General Washington had made his final decision after Colonel Douglas' 5th Battalion's disgraceful retreat from Kip's Bay, and laid blame solely on the Connecticut brigades. Washington had all but called them unfit for duty and nearly discharged them save for those he determined had served with valor and honor.

Wadsworth asked if the Connecticut brigades were to be replaced by General Lee's army, which was rumored to be coming up from the south to reinforce them, along with others like General Smallwood's or Colonel Daniel Morgan's southern men. It was the first time Tallmadge had heard Washington be utterly blunt, with a mere 'yes.' He had never heard the general speak with such candor, and had always thought of him as one who directed with a gentle but firm hand. Thus, listening, eavesdropping on the conversation between Wadsworth and Washington – he wished he could agree with his friend and commanding officer that the Connecticut troops were able to serve with duty and honor, but if Washington had made such an assessment – he could not disagree with the Commander-in-Chief.

Thus in the next few days, when they had marched from Harlem Heights to White Plains, the 6th found itself serving under detached duty to General Spencer's regiment while the 1st and its Light Horse served under General Putnam. The rest of the Connecticut brigade was absorbed into the main army itself. Spencer also commanded a hodgepodge of military regiments from different states, but he seemed to be a fair man and treated the regiments he had taken over with courtesy and respect.

There were seven other regiments with them, totaling about 1,500 men and he immediately surmised that they had been placed on a key position. The Bronx River extended beyond them down the hill, deep in most places, but fordable in the area where they were stationed at. If the British were to pursue them, they could cross with little to no problems. The hill itself was also a flanking position and so if they fell, the whole of the army behind them would be overrun. Washington's headquarters had been set up in a small house belonging to one Mr. Elijah Miller. The main body of the army spread out to his left on a larger hill and those at Chatterton Hill were the vanguard of the Continental Army's right.

Summer's muggy grip had finally broken with several brief rainstorms and now the pleasant autumnal mildness whipped its cool winds around them. The leaves were an ever changing beauty of red, browns, yellows, and oranges, a cascade of colors that made Tallmadge long for spiced cider and apple orchards. He could smell the familiar whiff of firewood being tended day and night in the houses situated nearby, a far cleaner smell than the stink of York Island. York Island had too many animals, too many rotting elements to make any fire smell clean and crisp. Here, it smelled nice and fresh and reminded Tallmadge a little of his home in Wethersfield. The army had already received orders to settle and while a few had set up group fires for the rest of the troop to use, he would not partake of those at the moment. They had received orders to dig entrenchments along the ridges and farther down the hill near the swampland to their right. The swampland would make it hard for any soldier to pass, but it also provided some cover for them in case of advancement.

"Dig this way, not like that. You do it this way, you exhaust yourself even before night comes, lad." Davenport's loud voice made Tallmadge turn and he saw friend showing one of the younger soldiers how to properly hold a shovel. He smiled a little, nodding as both glanced at him before turning to inspect how the others were doing. The sounds of digging resumed and he heard Davenport's pleased hum of approval. Henry Davenport was a local farmer from Farmington which was near Wethersfield, wealthy enough from the onions and other crops he grew, but still humble enough to occasionally go out into the vast fields and pastures he owned and help his hired hands turn the soil each year.

The thunder of hooves made them look up. A young man on a rather nice-looking bay horse rode down towards them, then pulled his beast to a stop with a swift halt. "Lieutenant Tallmadge?" the young man called out, and he raised his hand.

"Here," he called out, but did not salute the young man noting that he had an epaulette denoting the same rank as he – a 2nd lieutenant. Instead, he nodded a greeting as the young man walked his horse up next to him.

"Sir, Lieutenant Charles Webb Jr. of the 19th Connecticut at your service. Colonel Webb requests your presence if possible. He would not give me the reason, sir. I've been sent to fetch you," the young man said and Tallmadge realized that the young Webb, more than likely Colonel Webb's son judging by his name, had been made an adjutant of Webb's regiment.

"Let me check with Colonel Chester. Where is your regiment located?" he asked, and Webb pointed north-east

"Eastern flank along the ridge, sir."

"I will meet you there, Lieutenant, thank you," he said as he glanced over to Davenport who nodded and walked a few steps over to him to take over general watching duties.

He trudged up the hill, using his hands to grip the slippery grass that was still wet from the recent rainstorm, before pulling himself to the top. A farmhouse bordered by stone walls and picket fences was where General Spencer had made his command post, shared it with the rest of his staff as well as other commanders of the regiments he led. The hill was also home to neat rows off-white tents, including his and Bulkley's.

A stabling area for horses had been set up to the left of the farmhouse, using the runoff of the Bronx River to water and care for the beasts without having to carry buckets up and down the hill. Tallmadge trudged up the slightly muddy road to the house and opened the door, stepping in. He walked to the front parlor where Colonel Chester, Lieutenant Colonel Wills, and Major Ripley had their desks on one side. The other side was occupied by one of Spencer's own divisions.

"Sir." Ripley looked up at him as he walked in and Ripley made a small movement with his hand before Chester looked up and smiled at him.

"Tallmadge, how goes efforts with the entrenchments?"

"Well, sir," he replied. He could see a bit of soft curved hand writing on Chester's desk and realized he had disturbed his commanding officer's reading of personal letter. "My apologies sir, but I wanted to let you know that Colonel Webb of the 19th has requested to talk to me. I do not know for what, nor was the reason given. I was told to report to him at my convenience, though it seemed a little urgent."

Something Tallmadge could not identify passed through Chester's face before he nodded solemnly. "I know what this is about." The colonel sighed deeply before waving at him. "You may go. I will let Captain Wells know where you have gone."

"Sir," he saluted and left. He wanted to ask Chester what it was about, but something on the colonel's face told him it was an intensely private matter, and he wondered what sort of private matter could have to do with him. He put that thought aside as he knew he would receive his answer in a scant few minutes.

He found Shadow absently grazing in the field with the rest of the battalion's horses. His horse nickered upon recognizing him and seemed to toss his head at the others as he trotted towards him, stopping shy of the makeshift picket fence that kept the horses penned in.

Tallmadge absently scratched Shadow's cheek before grabbing him by the bridle and leading him to one of the fife players who doubled as a stable hand. The boy was fresh-faced and gap-toothed, but executed his duties well. He found his saddle and Tallmadge placed it on Shadow securing it with practiced ease, before mounting his horse and starting him off at a fast trot towards Webb's encampment. The Continental lines extended roughly three miles from end to end – with his battalion stationed at the farthest edge and Webb's on the opposite side. It only took a few minutes to ride into Webb's encampment where he saw two horses, one belonging to Lieutenant Webb outside of a large tent, the other laden with what looked like a heavy travel pack and accouters that did not seem military, but more civilian.

He dismounted and tied Shadow to the post before pausing at the front of the tent. "Lieutenant Tallmadge reporting as requested," he announced.

"Enter." The voice was deep, fatherly sounding. He pushed the tent flap open.

He stepped in and paused as he saw who Colonel Webb's

guest was. "Enoch," he said quietly, recognizing Nathan's older brother.

Enoch Hale sat on one of two chairs in the large tent, sorrow etched across his features. He looked overdressed for the mildness of the season, as if he had been sleeping on the road instead of in an inn or tavern. Enoch had sharper features than Nathan, features that did not make him as handsome or as popular as his younger brother with the women during their years at Yale, but there was no denying the family resemblance.

"You are familiar with Mr. Hale, then, Lieutenant?" Webb looked at him and he nodded, remembering at the last second to briefly salute.

"Sir," he said. If Enoch was here...

"Only a select few had been told about Captain Hale's fate, but Mr. Hale here took it upon himself to check on his brother after his letters had stopped in early September. Mr. Hale was kind enough to mention that he heard rumors about his brother's fate on his way here and wished to confirm them." Colonel Charles Webb had a fatherly countenance about him, and there was a definite family resemblance between him and Lieutenant Webb who stood next to him in complete silence.

"Sir-"

"Colonel Chester and General Wadsworth are well aware that you have not spoken a single word about Captain Hale since you were informed. I believe that it was more than likely to be Captain Hull who spread such rumors when he inquired as to his friend's fate," Webb rubbed his chin, looking for a moment like a tired old man.

"Yes, sir." Tallmadge could not say anything else.

"Since Captain Hull is on patrol, I thought it best for you to perhaps give some closure to Mr. Hale here." Webb stood up, his chair scraping across a patch of grass with a wet squeaking noise. "I will leave you to it, gentlemen." With that, Webb made to leave, but Tallmadge turned, a sudden thought occurring to him.

"Sir, how..."

"...Did I know the last two people to whom Captain Hale spoke before he left?" Webb asked, looking at him with a raised eyebrow.

"Y-Yes sir." He realized he had spoken out of turn.

"Alas, that is something even I am not allowed to reveal." Webb gave him a brief sad smile before moving past him. The colonel left his tent with his son following him. Tallmadge knew the comment was supposed to be reassuring, but felt a sense of unease with it.

He supposed that the fact that he was not being punished for his indiscretion or anything he had said was a saving grace, but he could not shake the nagging feeling that maybe someone had sharp eyes on him – was watching him or somehow knew? Perhaps one of Hale's regiment had followed him and reported it back? It was supposed to be a secret spy mission, but Nathan had sought him out so he had not thought much of it back then. But, perhaps he had jeopardized Nathan's mission by being too careless with his information and questions.

"Benjamin, it's good to see you again." Enoch rose from his chair and walked over, hand extended.

Tallmadge pulled himself out of his thoughts and clasped the older Hale's hand. Even though he and Enoch were about three years apart, it seemed that life in the ministry had added some wisdom to Enoch's gaze that looked reminiscent of his own father's whenever he preached from the pulpit.

"I began to hear rumors a few weeks ago after Nathan's letters stopped arriving," Enoch started, before smiling a little sadly. "Those rumors were just confirmed by Colonel Webb, though he stated that Nathan had not been a part of his regiment since late August?"

"Yes," Tallmadge confirmed. "Nathan said that he was a part of Lieutenant Colonel Knowlton's Rangers on special detachment."

"Ah," Enoch nodded as he clasped his hands in front of him.

An awkward silence filled the tent as Tallmadge wrestled with what he knew versus what Nathan had told him before he left for his mission.

"Enoch-"

"Ben-"

Tallmadge paused, before Enoch gestured for him to continue. "Nathan was on a mission with orders apparently from General Washington, Enoch. He died a hero-"

"My brother was *hung*, like a spy, Benjamin." Enoch's voice became rough with emotion. "A *spy*. There is no honor, no heroics in that. Surely you know that as well as I do."

Tallmadge pressed his lips together as he shook his head. "He was on a mission for General Washington."

"And what honor, good sir, is that for someone to ask of another person? An officer of Nathan's abilities and caliber?"

"One not taken lightly, Enoch," he said quietly, "one which one understands the sacrifice made, the loss of honor and branding of a gentleman to degrade one's self to the lowest form to spy on the enemy."

He could clearly see that the knowledge of Nathan's activities, even if they were from Washington himself, was eating away at Enoch. The older brother could not believe that his young sibling had so willfully discarded the status of gentleman to debase himself by spying on the enemy. To get caught and be humiliated even in death with a hanging. But, Tallmadge had to find a way to defend his dear friend's honor, even if he had a dishonorable death. He had to defend his memory in the only way he knew how – to justify Nathan's actions for him because he was not here to defend himself from Enoch who was clearly in the throes of grief. He had promised Nathan not to lecture him on his choice when it seemed that William Hull had already done so; he understood that Nathan was holding firmly to his choice – that his friend had no regrets and thought he would succeed. Failure was never on his mind and from what he remembered General Wadsworth telling him, the man that befriended Nathan in his final hours, Montresor, had spoken of the calm dignity his friend had, the acceptance of his fate, his only regret that he had not been able to serve his country better with the single life he had been given.

And with that knowledge, Tallmadge half expected the gut-shooting pain he had felt when he had first heard the news to fill him again, but what surprised him was another sensation – wholly unlike the fiery anger he felt when he found out about William's mistreatment and death at the hands of the British. He expected fiery anger now, but instead it was icy and cold. Bitterly cold anger.

That cold anger engulfed him, fueling the knowledge that the

British would pay for what they had done to Nathan, to William, and to so many others.

"Nathan died proclaiming that he was a captain of General Washington's Continental Army, Enoch," he said, his voice surprisingly calm and measured. "He died knowing what he had done was right and just even though others may not see it. He wanted those who executed him to know that he died a soldier, not a spy, but a soldier."

Enoch's eyes widened as the older man rocked back a little, shocked by his words. "B-Ben..."

"He was hung, but he was no spy," Tallmadge continued. "He was a soldier doing his duty." It suddenly felt too hot, too stifling in Colonel Webb's large tent and Tallmadge nodded curtly to Enoch. "My apologies, Enoch. I need to get back to my post."

He could not say anything else to Enoch, could not stand to see the grief on the other man's face, but most of all, could still clearly see the disbelief in his posture – that Enoch still wanted to deny that Nathan had been a spy, had died like a spy. Tallmadge had spoken his piece, had dealt with his grief at his dear friend's death by turning it into an anger that armored him. It was now up to Enoch to deal with the knowledge and grief in his own way. While it seemed callous, he knew he could not help the older Hale brother.

He left the tent in an abrupt fashion and nodded once as he saw Colonel and Lieutenant Webb both look up from where they had been standing nearby. They nodded back as he reached and mounted his horse. He spurred Shadow's flanks and trotted away, unwilling to look back at the tent that held Enoch Hale. No matter what others thought of Nathan's fate, Tallmadge knew better – his friend had not died in vain nor in disgrace.

SANDRA CHEN

4

They had been given orders to advance to the entrenchments dug in along the banks of Chatterton Hill after word of British forces advancing on their position was brought by a hasty scout. Tallmadge heard the distant march of feet and boots behind them, General Alexander McDougall's regiment forming a secondary perimeter on the hill. General Washington himself had been inspecting the lines during the morning when the scout had arrived, prompting the flurry of orders. Though he had only seen the general from a distance, accompanied by his staff and a few of the other officers, he did see his own former commander Wadsworth break briefly from the group to greet them and offer his congratulations on a job well done with the entrenchments. Colonel Chester had been proud of that, a sentiment that apparently Washington had echoed a little later when he inspected their section with the briefest of nods.

Tallmadge steadied Shadow's gait as he moved down the hill and across the fordable part of the Bronx River with the rest of 3ʳᵈ Troop. Shadow pawed impatiently at the water, unsettled, but Tallmadge calmed his horse down with sharp tug of the reins. He could feel Shadow shifting a little at the rebuke. It seemed being stabled with the others did not suit his mount too well, since apparently he had become less prone to obeying his orders. He supposed it couldn't be helped since Shadow had only known Bulkley's and Wells' mounts for the most part.

Their orders were explicit. They were to slow down, if not stop the British advance. Long poles tipped with iron spikes offset the lack of bayonets and rifles on some troops that had lost supplies during the chaotic retreat into Harlem Heights. They had not had a chance to replenish supplies, and rifles taken from imprisoned British soldiers had been given to other regiments or scouting parties that had a higher need. Still, it was a way to attack and Tallmadge had his own small group line up in staggered rows, those with rifles forming lines while those with poles would stay behind until the British got close enough for them to use their weapons.

The morning dew had not yet disappeared when Tallmadge heard the distant sounds of drums and fifes. The enemy was coming. "Steady," he called out as he moved Shadow back and forth behind his men. He could see Bulkley and Captain Wells doing the same while some of the other officers of the force re-positioned their men.

He could see them now, the white lined tips of black tricorns coming towards them. No. Tallmadge frowned. What he had thought were white tips were actually plumed and as the drums and fifes got louder, he could see *gold* tips, a concave-like hat.

Hessians.

Hessian mercenaries were advancing directly towards them, their dark blue and yellow-gold uniforms a sight to behold. "Steady," he called out again, swallowing his own sudden bubble of fear at the fact that they were about to face ruthless mercenaries hired with British coin. They had heard rumors that the Hessians had looted and pillaged many communities on Long Island after the British had taken it over. The rumors caused some discontent and anger in the camp. These were men who were paid only to fight and had no stake in this country, this war for independence. Their reputation might have frightened some, but he could see more than one of his men gripping their rifle or pole tighter, wanting nothing more than to kill the interlopers.

"Steady," he called out as he saw the distant form of their commander riding on top of a white steed – Colonel Johann Rahl directing his men. "Make ready," he called and his first line placed their rifles on top of the entrenchments, kneeling into the soft-swampy ground. The second line held their rifles steadily behind the first line, ready for their commands.

His command was echoed by the others up and down the line as they watched the Hessians march, seemingly oblivious to the danger. "Aim," he called and estimated the distance to maximum effect of his men's fire. He heard the staccato command of 'fire' a few yards from him as a line of Hessians got into range, but kept his focus on the line that was advancing straight towards them. Out of the corner of his eye, he saw the line stagger under the fire of his fellow soldiers before he turned and swept his arm down. "Fire!" he shouted and his command was answered by a thunderous volley.

"Second line advance, first reload!" he called out, his ears ringing from the sound of musketry. He smiled grimly at the sight of the Hessians who paused and staggered against the volley his men had given them. He heard Bulkley's booming voice followed by Captain Wells' commands to fire almost at the same time as Davenport's hoarse yell.

"Fire!" he called as he saw the second line of rifles discharge, throwing more Hessians to the ground, some screaming in pain while the line itself looked to be in confusion. He pulled out his pistol as the enemy lines faltered, and aimed the field officer that walked with the Hessians. Firing his pistol, he saw that his aim was true. The young officer fell to the ground, clutching his leg and screaming for a retreat.

The Hessian line broke, some fleeing back while others stared at the fallen officer in confusion before grabbing the man by his shoulders and dragging him away. He heard a ragged cheer erupt from his lines. "Reload!" he ordered, and they stopped their cheers to follow his orders. He could hear a few of them chuckling to themselves as they completed their task, the sounds of musket fire echoing to the right and left. He glanced over to see that the Hessians near Bulkely's flank were not so keen on retreating. He would have to help his friend drive that troop of Hessians back.

Tallmadge took the quick opportunity to reload his own pistol, hammering the ball down the gullet of his pistol before half-cocking it. He pulled on Shadow's reins, his horse responding to his command to face the left. "First line, dress left and make ready-"

"Sir!" Adamson's urgent shout made him turn to see his friend pointing back to where he thought they had scattered the Hessian line. They were reforming and marching again.

"First line, belay orders, about face," he called and saw his men scramble to obey turning to face their original positions once more. "Make ready!" He could hear the faint mutters of annoyance and anger at the fact that the Hessians had managed to regroup so fast and advance again.

"British regulars!" Bulkley's agitated shout snapped his gaze to the left again. The British had crept up unnoticed on a hill on their left flank. They let loose a withering volley of fire into Bulkley's men.

"Sir!"

"Fire!" he shouted, looking back to the Hessians, who were now prepared for them, kneeling to firing positions. The first burst of fire from the first line sent several falling to the ground, but the Hessians held fast this time and returned fire.

"Take cover! Reload, second line, advance!" he called out. Bulkley's and now even Wells' lines were starting to collapse. He cursed silently as he looked back to his own line and saw his two of his men fall to the ground, screaming in pain. "Take them to the surgeon!" he shouted to two of his men who stared back at him, fear evident in their eyes.

"Second line, fire!" he called and saw the ragged discharge of musket fire, the discipline he had drilled into his men slowly giving way to the fear of the mercenary force and the fact that the British were advancing once again.

"Lieutenant, fall back! Fall back!" he thought he heard Colonel Chester's voice call from near the river behind them and turned to see him gesture earnestly for him to pull his men back. He ducked at the sudden whistle of a ball and felt Shadow dance underneath him. "Reload and fall back!" he shouted to his men and he heard his command echoed by Wells, Davenport and Bulkley. However, Bulkley's command was cut short. Tallmadge turned to see his friend grab his shoulder, clutching it as he hunched over in his saddle.

"I got him, sir! I got him!" he heard Davenport call out, and he pulled on Bulkley's horse's reins.

Tallmadge nodded curtly as he gestured widely with his free hand, still holding his pistol, "Come on men! Fall back!" He could see the drills they had done paying off as they retreated in a semblance of order instead of the ragged one that had been employed at Turtle Bay and Brooklyn. A few of them fell to the sudden onslaught of British and Hessian fire, but the rest retreated, some dutifully reloading while others tried not to flinch at the musket fire coming their way. He could hear the regiment's drummer pounding the march for retreat as he held the rear for Bulkley and Davenport's men, while Wells led the men to safety up Chatterton Hill. Adamson was in the middle of the combined 3rd Troop once more, urging the men to walk in an orderly fashion.

They splashed into the river, Tallmadge pushing his horse a little deeper towards the edge where the river was fordable to where the currents were swift as he waved the men to continue to retreat.

"Sir! Watch out sir!" The voice came out of nowhere and Tallmadge suddenly found himself violently pushed to the side, just as Shadow shuddered and buckled underneath him.

The weight of another person who had leap at him was too much and he fell from his saddle, his horse whinnying and neighing in distress. He slammed into the water, coughing and spluttering as the current quickly rose above his head. He saw Shadow splashing somewhere near him, having also fallen sideways into the deeper water. Tallmadge clawed at anything and everything as his felt himself being pulled underneath, the currents much faster than what he had expected when he first forded the river.

He dropped his pistol, his senses taking in the chaos of the murky river, his horse's dark form and feeling of someone tugging at his uniform. He lashed out, his kick slow and unsteady in the water, before he managed to break the surface and inhaled loudly, his heart beating wildly as he felt a tug on the back of his jacket. The sopping wet face of the regiment's reverend, Dr. Trumbull, surfaced next to him.

"Reverend-" he gasped, coughing as he swallowed water. He realized that the current had pulled them quite far along in those short moments. He could see the British entering the fordable area of the river. There were glints of metal starting to crest the hill to the right of the main Hessian advancement – more than likely artillery, but he wasn't too sure as he spat out a mouthful of water.

"Thank God," the reverend coughed, "one of the Jagers was taking aim at you, son. You would have been dead-"

A huffing snort made him turn in the water to see his horse trying to swim his way out of the river, but there was a sluggishness to Shadow's movements. As his horse briefly rose out of the water, Tallmadge could see what was causing the sluggishness. Shadow had taken the ball meant for him – directly above the heart. "No..." he whispered as he tried to swim towards his dying horse, but the reverend suddenly pulled hard at his jacket, nearly making him choke and sink back into the currents of the river.

"You can't son! We need to get to the shore!" the reverend tugged harder and Tallmadge wanted nothing more than to rip himself free, but he saw that the Reverend was indeed correct. The British and Hessians were already advancing across the river. He pulled away from the reverend's grip and started to swim towards the shore, the coldness of the water making him shiver. He could hear the reverend follow behind him and they managed to reach the shore after a few minutes of hard swimming.

The once mild fall air felt utterly *frigid* as Tallmadge surfaced and pulled himself to shore. He shivered as he turned to see his horse struggle against the current, pulled farther and farther downriver. He swallowed back the unexpected lump that had formed in his throat – there was nothing he could do for his mount and hoped that Shadow would drown first instead of dying slowly from the bullet wound.

"Surrender." A guttural, heavily accented voice spoke up next to him and Tallmadge turned to see the end of a bayonet pointed at him, two Hessians towering above him. One was sitting on a bay horse with dark hair, an officer judging by the single epaulet on the man's shoulder. The other was a rifleman, a sergeant by his stripes.

Tallmadge closed his eyes and nodded, raising his hands in

surrender as he stood up slowly. Opening his eyes, he could see Reverend Dr. Trumbull do the same, nervously looking at the musket pointed at him. Tallmadge could feel the point dig into his back as he turned and started to trudge up the hill. The distant sounds of Shadow's struggles down river were fading as it combined with the sounds of marching, occasional musket fire, and fife playing. He thought he would have felt fear at being a prisoner now, but it was oddly curious that he did not feel any sort of fear. Instead, everything seemed unusually clear – some how more focused than ever before.

As he started to march up the steepness of Chatterton Hill, taking a handful of grass to steady himself, he was acutely aware of the bayonet that was pointed more at him than at the good Reverend. It seemed that the Hessians knew that the man next to him was a chaplain while he was considered a greater threat due to uniform and epaulette. He could hear the heavy breath of the bay horse the officer rode beside him, see the beast's heaving flanks. He was aware of the glint of the officer's pistol hanging near the saddle horn, and the fact that the officer was looking to his left to see the advancement of his own Hessian troops.

As they made their way up the hill, Tallmadge started to bear right and heard the quiet exclamation from the officer who seemed puzzled, but did not order the soldier marching them to move them back to the main Hessian body.

"Lieutenant?" He heard Reverend Trumbull's hoarse whisper behind him, but ignored it as he continued to move right up the hill.

They were close now, he could sense it. He kept one eye on the advancing Hessian and British lines, the two forces combining their climb up Chatterton Hill. He made sure that he was parallel to the second line, but veering to the right. The hill itself had done its work and if he timed it right, he could take advantage of his situation. A few more steps and Tallmadge crested the hill with the Hessian officer and soldier in tow just as he heard the first exclamations of surprise and shock from the main infantry line of soldiers to his left.

That exclamation turned into shouts of surprise and screams of pain at the sudden concentrated volley of musket fire from behind the stone walls, trees, and fences of the small property at the top of Chatterton Hill. General McDougall's forces had combined with General Spencer's after retreating and were now making their stand on Chatterton Hill itself.

Tallmadge wasted no time after the first volley and spun, knocking aside the bayonet pointed at his back and startling the soldier. He shouted as Tallmadge punched him in the face and grabbed the man's jacket, pulling him close. At the same time he heard the shout of the officer on top of the horse.

"Stop, stop! You prisoner! You prisoner-" he thought he heard from the officer and turned with the soldier still trying to pry his arms off of his jacket just a pistol discharged near him with a loud bang.

The soldier slumped into his arms, dead from friendly fire. Tallmadge stripped the man of his rifle, fumbling a little before he jabbed it towards the officer on his horse. The man did not have a chance as he tried to pull back, but the smooth unsharpened blade of the bayonet slid into his gut. Blood poured forth from the man's mouth as he slumped, his face a mask of pain from his fatal wound. Tallmadge gritted his teeth and pushed harder, before firing the gun, ending the man's life as he pitched forward and fell off his saddle.

He released the rifle, letting it and the skewered officer fall to the ground in an unceremonious heap as he quickly mounted the bay horse. He reached down to the reverend who stood in shock at the quick carnage Tallmadge had wrought.

"Come on!" he shouted, startling the reverend as he saw the Hessian and British lines stagger under another volley, and start to stream back down hill.

The reverend grabbed his arm and pulled himself up, seating himself behind Tallmadge as he spurred the horse's flanks and galloped towards the Continental lines. He kept his head low as he heard the chaos of the Hessian line scattering behind him, a third loud volley of hundreds of Continental guns firing into them. Screams of agony followed by yells and braying of animals filled the air and he risked a quick glance behind him. The Hessians were staggering back down the hill, some tumbling end over end while others fell on top of their fallen comrades in a bid to escape the onslaught of concentrated fire from the American lines. There were bodies scattered across the hillside, blood marking the dew-covered grass with slick streaks, as if someone had hastily painted the ground.

Tallmadge turned back around just as another volley was let loose and jumped the bay horse over a fence into the general area of the small house. He felt the reverend grab at his waist in an effort to keep himself seated, but ignored it as he pulled the horse to a halt, the large animal snorting and pawing at the ground. Clearly it knew that it did not belong here, but Tallmadge kept a firm grip on the Hessian horse's reins. Its master was dead, but it seemed the animal did not know it.

"We're safe Reverend." He turned his head a little as the reverend tipped his hat and slid from the saddle.

"Thank God." Trumbull made the sign of the cross, sending a kiss up to the sky and he saw that a few of the soldiers around them cheer at their appearance. He supposed that they were cheering for the reverend's survival since he was considered a man of God. "Thank you Lieutenant, thank you."

"No, thank you Reverend for saving me from that shot." He shook his head. Trumbull seemed to protest his words, but abruptly stepped back just as he heard someone gallop towards them. He looked up to see that it was General Spencer himself.

"Tallmadge, where in the blazes did you come from?!" The general looked surprise. "We thought you lost!"

"Reverend Dr. Trumbull and I managed to escape in the chaos of General McDougall's reinforcements," he explained before gesturing to his new horse. "A kind soldier lent me his horse."

Spencer gave a wolfish smile, completely understanding his meaning. "Good, I need you to report to Washington on the situation here. We scattered them with the volleys, but I don't think we can hold onto the hill."

"Sir," Tallmadge replied, "I briefly remember seeing artillery possibly pointed towards our position."

"You sure?" Spencer looked concerned and Tallmadge shook his head.

"I'm not sure." He knew it was not the answer that Spencer wanted, but neither could he lie. "We were caught in the river currents before we made it to shore, but I do remember briefly seeing artillery in the woods before the Hessian and British columns advanced over my position."

"Include that with your report, Tallmadge." Spencer pursed his lips briefly as he nodded and Tallmadge saluted him before kicking the horse's flanks.

The beast leaped into action and for a second Tallmadge was startled by the horse's responsiveness as he galloped to the house that General Washington had made his headquarters. He could hear the scattered volleys of gunfire echoed by reports of return fire as he rode past rows and rows of tents, through several regiments who were on alert, waiting for the press of British forces. But as he got closer to Washington's headquarters, he saw many were on alert, but there seemed to be no sign of any British advancement on this side of the line.

His gallop into headquarters startled some of the soldiers. They dove to the side, clearing a path for him as he leaped off his horse, tossing the reins to one of the stable boys who caught them with a startled cry. He hurried in, brushing and squeezing past those who were gathered in the foyer of the house. He was a little surprised to see them step out of the way, but a quick glance at his own uniform told him the whole story. He was still soaking wet, blood staining the front part of his uniform from when he had killed the mounted officer, and he could feel the caking soot of rifling powder on his cheek from when he fired his pistol and the musket.

"General Washington, sir," he called out as he saw Washington standing by a war table with several other generals and his staff around him. He paused right outside the double set of doors that were swung wide open, with the general's lifeguards standing at attention outside. "News from Chatterton!" he called out.

Tallmadge had expected one of Washington's aides to call him over with a gesture of his hand. He did not expect Washington himself to look up from where he was studying his map and talking to General Putnam, and gesture directly for him to enter. It took Tallmadge a moment to collect himself and he stepped in and saluted as best as he could, now acutely aware of how disheveled he looked.

"Sir, General Spencer says we may not be able to hold Chatterton Hill. General McDougall's forces were able to cover our initial retreat up the hill, but the Hessians are advancing on our forward lines and the British are advancing on our left flank," he reported, using what he had glimpsed during the brief time he was made the Hessians' prisoner as well as what he had seen when his men had fallen back from the entrenchments. "Sir, I spotted artillery, but I do not know where they are pointed towards."

The concern was immediate in Washington's eyes. "Show me where, Lieutenant...?"

"Tallmadge, sir," he replied. Washington nodded and he approached, aware that some of the generals, including Putnam and Wadsworth who was standing nearby, had stepped away to give him room to look at the war map.

"Tallmadge, are you injured?" he heard Wadsworth whisper urgently, and he shook his head a negative.

"Sir, my men were located with General Spencer's advance forces here." He pointed to where two long blue tokens and two short ones sat on the valley next to the Bronx River. "We pulled back to here." He moved his finger to Chatterton Hill where McDougall's forces had provided them with volleys that had staggered the Hessian lines. "We are currently holding them off, but General Spencer says that we may not be able to for long. He indicates that Colonel Rahl and the Hessians are advancing from here." He swiped his fingers towards the red on a curve towards where the main bulk of the army was. "But the British are advancing on our left flank." He pointed to the other red tokens to the left of Chatterton Hill. As he spoke, one of Washington's aides leaned in and moved the tokens themselves.

"I saw artillery roughly...over here." He pointed back to where they had been massing to the right of the Hessians, on top of a hill that was not as tall as Chatterton. The same aide dropped a red token onto the indicated area and Tallmadge stepped back.

"Cavalry?"

"I do not know sir," he shook his head, "currently infantry forces."

"Sir, our scouts indicated that Robert Rogers and his band of rangers and light cavalry were not among the initial push of British forces. We think he may be headed due east," a general whom Tallmadge was not too familiar said.

"As noted, Mr. Scott," Washington murmured. "Mr. Wadsworth, what of Colonel Silliman's light horse?"

"Most are detached for reconnaissance duty, but I think Sheldon's regiment is still at camp. Right flank," General Wadsworth replied.

"Tallmadge, find Major Sheldon and have him coordinate a flanking attack from the left side of Chatterton Hill with Knox. After you've finished your task, notify General McDougall and Spencer that I want their forces to slowly pull back to the main body of our army. Have McDougall place Smallwood's Maryland men and the New York men to cover their flanks. Sheldon's light horse should cut off any immediate pursuit when this happens. Mr. Webb, send word to General Knox and Captain Hamilton that I want their artillery regiments to shell the enemy artillery indicated on this map."

"Sir," Tallmadge saluted with a curt nod and left the room, hurrying out the door to where the stable boy still held the reins of his horse. Not even as he finished mounting, he saw Lieutenant Colonel Samuel Webb, one of Washington's aide-de-camps, hurry out after him, whistling for his horse which was brought in a prompt manner. He wondered if this Webb was related to Colonel Webb of the 19th Connecticut militia that Nathan had previously served in. But there was no time to ponder such familial relations as he settled in his saddle.

"Good form there Tallmadge." Webb grinned at him and Tallmadge returned the smile. "Yours?" the man indicated towards his own chest and Tallmadge shook his head. He knew that Webb was referring to the copious amount of blood that soaked his clothing and had spread with the dampness of his recent trip into the river.

"The enemy's," he replied and the other man barked out a quick laugh of understanding before heeling his horse and galloping away.

Tallmadge wheeled the bay beast around and spurred his flanks, charging forward towards the other side of the army. He found what had to be Sheldon's light horse, the only small group of mounted men clustered together. Some were dressed in Continental uniform, others in the civilian clothing like the majority of the militia. They all looked at him as he pulled up short. "Major Sheldon?" he called out and saw a man walk his horse over from the group.

"I'm Major Elisha Sheldon." Sheldon looked to be several years older than he, with a fashionable queue that was pulled back, but not styled in the latest from Europe – powdered grey or white. Instead, he had a rugged look about him, his dark eyes sharp, but with a hardened quality that Tallmadge associated with those who had fought from the very beginning in the struggle for American Independence.

"Sir," Tallmadge gave him a brief salute, "Lieutenant Benjamin Tallmadge of the 6th Battalion, 3rd Troop. I've just come from General Washington's headquarters with orders sir. We require your help in coordinating a flanking maneuver when General Knox fires his artillery into the Hessian artillery line over at Chatterton Hill."

"Understood," Sheldon nodded, "Skinner, Seymour, hold here. The rest of you, boots and saddles, let's go!" His voice was unlike Bulkley's commanding boom, but it had the quality of command in it and Tallmadge marveled at how fast those who had not mounted their horses immediately stopped conversations and did as ordered. They were far more disciplined than Tallmadge ever thought possible. He felt a little envious.

"A fine horse." Tallmadge did not realized that Sheldon had addressed him until he caught the man's gaze staring at the horse he had taken, and coughed lightly.

"Hessian," he replied. "His rider did not need such a fine horse anymore."

"Suits you," the other man replied before gesturing with his chin to lead the way. Tallmadge felt the heat of blush rise up as he turned his horse and spurred it into a canter. He headed on the most direct route back to the front lines. Behind him, he heard the thunder of hooves as the rest of the cavalry followed him.

They arrived back on Chatterton Hill in short order, Tallmadge pulling to an abrupt halt. He saw that no one was firing and instead, all were waiting. "General Spencer!" he called out as the general himself stepped out of the house and hurried towards them. He was followed by General McDougall who looked utterly gruff, his dark hair shot through with streaks of white. Tallmadge dismounted and saluted. "Sirs, General

Washington wishes for us to pull back to the main lines in an orderly fashion."

"'Bout time we did that," McDougall rumbled. "My men got hit on the left flank pretty badly before Howe stopped his advancement for the moment."

"Sir, General Knox is to fire his artillery-"

"At the Hessians, figured that too." McDougall nodded curtly before gesturing with an arm down towards the small hill. "Looks like they want us off of this hill."

Tallmadge followed the general's gesture and saw that he had indeed seen artillery in the brief moment when he surfaced after losing his horse and accouterments. The Hessian line was now pointing their artillery directly towards them. He saw that General Knox was already moving his cannons to shoot over Chatterton Hill towards the Hessian lines. He thought he spotted the distant form of Lieutenant Colonel Webb near where Knox sat on his horse.

"Major Sheldon and his light horse are to coordinate with General Knox on cutting across the British and Hessian lines to halt their advance while we make our retreat," he finished and saw Spencer nod.

The general looked over Tallmadge's shoulder to address Sheldon who was still sitting on his horse. "Major, no unnecessary risks. The river is not fordable for most points except through Chatterton itself and near Knox's cannons."

"Sir," Sheldon tipped his plumed hat and left, the rest of his regiment following him as they rode down the other side of Chatterton towards Knox's artillery.

"Good work Tallmadge," Spencer turned back to address him. "Colonel Chester is over there." He pointed towards the middle of the hill. "You are in charge of 3rd Troop, Lieutenant. Your captain and 1st lieutenant both took injury during the retreat. Damn Hessian Jagers were trying to take down all officers during the initial charge."

"Sir," Tallmadge said, reminded of his own close brush. He nodded and led his horse to where he could see what remained of 3rd Troop hunched over a long stone wall. Some of them idly picked the grass while others rested against the wall with their backs facing the enemy, eyes closed in sleep or even in prayer he saw some mouths moving with soundless words. Some opened their eyes as he walked by with his horse, drawing a few smiles and surprised looks.

He ignored their attempts to flag him down, a little more than disappointed in the lack of discipline he had just witnessed in his own regiment, compared to Sheldon's men. He knew it was harsh of him to compare the two, but after his initial thoughts of how well his men had performed, it now seemed they had retreated after firing two volleys. The fear of death and fear of the British and Hessian forces still ate at his men and he vowed that once they were free of this engagement, he would train them better – make them as fearless as possible. Their morale had suffered and he knew why some had fear in their eyes as he walked by. Some must have witnessed Wells and Bulkley receive their injuries, and even now he did not know the status of his immediate commanding officer and his thick-headed friend.

"Sir!" Adamson hurried from where he had been conferring with Colonel Chester, Lieutenant Colonel Wills, and Major Ripley. "Sir, Captain Wells-"

"I heard," Tallmadge held up a hand, halting Adamson's explanation. "Thank you for taking care of 3rd Troop in my brief absence."

"Yes sir," Adamson looked relieved that he was back and saluted smartly. "Orders?"

Tallmadge nodded as he let one of the men take his horse's reins, and made his way down to where the three officers were. He saw some of the more junior officers of Spencer's regiment and McDougall's force, including young Lieutenant Webb, streaming towards the various troops. He realized that the 19th Connecticut was a part of McDougall's forces and felt warmed by Nathan's former regiment's presence. It had been over a month since his friend had passed, but he thought he could see the unyielding fighting spirit of his friend in Webb's regiment.

"Sirs," he nodded at them. "Knox's artillery is set to attack the Hessian line. We are to retreat to the main lines when that happens and Sheldon's light horse will halt any advance."

"Understood." Chester's eyes gleamed with pride before he nodded to Lieutenant Colonel Wills and Major Ripley. "Gentlemen, take your positions. Tallmadge, you are in charge of the 3ʳᵈ due to Wells and Bulkley's injuries."

"Sir," He took his leave, Adamson following behind him as he headed to where 3ʳᵈ Troop waited. This time, he did acknowledge his men with a short nod of his head and brief wave of his hand as they cheered for him.

"Most of the men saw how you took the Hessian officer's horse," Adamson commented quietly behind him and Tallmadge shrugged.

"I took the opportunity that was given and did my duty," he replied. He had a feeling that by the end of the day, the story of his and Reverend Dr. Trumbull's escape from the two Hessians would be told to others over the fires. It would more than likely be paired with the story of his rescue of his horse from Brooklyn Heights. There might have been a time he would have basked in the glory of the tales told about him and his exploits, but the recent two months of fighting did not seem so glorious. But he allowed it, knowing it would raise troop morale – that his actions might provide incentive to a soldier who was fearful to take that extra step and do what needed to be done.

"Form lines. We will be executing fighting withdrawal from this position. The enemy will not have gained this position for we will not surrender it to them. We will shed their blood before they try to lay their claim," he ordered, inwardly marveling at how calm and steady his own voice was; he was even more surprised at the cold anger he was feeling, but drew on it, fighting away the shivers he was still feeling from his wet clothing.

His men murmured their surprise, but they seemed pleased to be joining the main army instead of being the vanguard. As so, they formed their lines, muskets held at the ready and those who still had long poles with iron spikes for tips stood behind. The calls of others to form lines echoed across the hilltop just as the first gigantic boom of a cannon sounded behind them. Tallmadge swiftly turned as did several others to see General Knox's cannons roar to life, booms shattering the air as a concentrated volley burst forth.

He craned his head to watch the cannon balls soar and smash into the hill side across the river, some sending packed dirt and grass into the air, others throwing already dead bodies this way and that. From his vantage point, he could see the Hessians standing stone-faced in wake of the bombardment, not a single man flinching. Beyond them, the red-white uniformed British troops were also standing at attention, though he thought he could see a ripple of nervousness in their forces.

Distant shouts followed the roar of silence in the wake of the first bombardment and Tallmadge gestured for the soldier who had taken the reins of his horse to bring it to him. He mounted the large bay again, walking to the back of his troops. He drew his sabre, feeling it stick a little from the water in the scabbard, but it pulled free and held it aloft.

"Steady men," he called out as he saw the tiny forms of the Hessian artillery crew touch their cannons. Not even a second later, white smoke emerged from the barrels of the cannons the quiet of the field once again shattered by booms of artillery. Sharp whistles filled the air and Tallmadge forced himself not to flinch at their closeness – the returning fire reminded him greatly of the two ships firing on them at Turtle Bay.

Thankfully, they sailed over Chatterton itself and hit the valley between Chatterton and the hill where Knox's artillery were placed. A few minutes later silence reigned once. Someone blew on a bugle of sorts and the Hessians and the British started to march.

"Ready men, ready," he called out, tasting nervous anticipation in the air as they saw both armies marching towards them.

"Charge! For independence!" Sheldon's shout was accompanied by the thunder of hooves as they watched the light horse pour down the hill, sabers and muskets pointed at the incoming British line that was trying to flank them.

Tallmadge cheered with the others at the sight of the cavalry breaking up several British lines, muskets and sabres swinging and firing before they executed a sharp turn and pulled towards the back of Knox's artillery hill, their job done as the British halted their advance.

"Fire!" Multiple commands brought Tallmadge's attention back to his front. He saw several of the troops that were stationed farther down the hill fire their muskets, keeping with their formation against the incoming Hessians. He noted the sharp discipline that the front lines displayed and realized that they were the Maryland and New York Regiments that General Washington had been talking about – and far more disciplined than the Connecticut lines were.

The first line finished firing, stood up and reloaded while backing up the hill at a steady pace. The second line immediately knelt down and let loose another volley before doing the same as a third line covered the first two. By the time the third line finished their volley – the Hessians this time advancing without consideration to the loss of more men as they crossed the river and started to climb up Chatterton – the first line had finished reloading and held their muskets at the ready as they backed up the hill.

"First line, make ready!" Tallmadge called out just as the Maryland and New York militiamen passed by them, still holding to a strict discipline of a marching withdrawal. His call was echoed by the rest of the 6th and other regiments that were stationed after the Maryland and New York regiments.

He heard the guttural call of the Hessians making their own musketry ready. A second call, probably the Germanic word for aim, was followed by clicks of muskets aimed up the hill at them. "Steady men, steady," Tallmadge called out for reassurance. He could still see the first line of regimental defense slowly climbing past them and knew he could not fire. His men did not yet have a clear shot. But he knew that the Hessians had not compunction to wait, having taken at least three volleys of fire without firing a single shot. Tallmadge braced himself for the inevitable screams that would come at their command. At the same time, he watched the Hessian lines closely for any sign of Jager regiments that meant to shoot at him again now that he was remounted on a horse.

The gruff Hessian shout for 'Fire!' was answered by at staccato of musket fire and white powder filling the air. Then screams and sounds of balls piercing bone and flesh as the front line staggered. Several of those who had been retreating fell along with some of his own men. He winced, but kept his resolve as he pointed his sabre at the still-advancing lines.

"Aim!" he called out and could feel the palpable relief that rippled through 3rd Troop as the first line took aim. Some men who held the long poles dropped them and helped those who had been wounded, dragging them farther upland as the last of the first line of defense crested the hill.

"Fire!" His voice was drowned out by the roar of musket fire and the commands of others as they let loose their volley.

The Hessian line staggered once more, but their screams and groans were swallowed by the sudden thunder of cannonades filling the air again.

"First line, reload and withdraw!" he shouted, waving his sabre in the air, hoping that his command was overheard by the bombardment that had started up again. "Second line make ready!" he called out. He thought he heard his command echoed by Adamson near him, helping him manage the 3rd.

"Aim, fire!" He said just as he heard the same call from the Hessians. For a second Tallmadge heard nothing but the loudness of musket fire as white smoke filled the air. He waved his sabre in an effort to clear the smoke, coughing a little from the gunpowder. As the air slowly cleared and he saw that the Hessians had stopped once more, but a lot of his men of the second line were down, some clutching missing and bleeding legs, while others held up their shaking blood-slicked hands, fingers blown off. Others had fallen and lay still, dead.

"Second line, reload and withdraw," he called out and the men that heard him moaned in gratefulness as they stood on shaky legs and started to back away. They forced themselves to march in order, though he knew they wanted nothing more than to flee to safety. He turned his horse and followed them, making sure he was positioned behind them to reassure them of his presence. The third defensive line, the one stationed by the house that used to be General Spencer's command post, was filled with the remaining troops of both Spencer and McDougall and he thought he saw Colonel Webb's 19th positioned behind a stone wall as he and his troops marched past them.

He heard guttural Germanic commands again and braced himself, knowing that if he was to be hit by a musket ball, it would be now. "Steady men," he called out as he walked his horse behind them, "steady." He heard the distant shout of Sheldon's cavalry once more, the ground shaking a little from artillery fire exchanged with far more gusto and frequency than before. General Knox had apparently made adjustments since the first volley, and had found the area to aim for to cover them. The volley of artillery almost made him miss the Germanic command for 'fire', just before he heard the sound of muskets behind him.

It was quickly followed by a sharp blooming pain searing across his upper arm. He involuntarily pitched forward from the momentum of the ball that clipped him, and immediately grabbed his arm with his other hand, loosening the reins on his horse. He hissed as his hand and hilt of his sabre made contact with the wound and pulled it away, noting that it was slick with blood. He could feel the drip of blood running down the inside of his shirt jacket, mingling with the dampness of his clothing and jacket, but there was no hole, nothing to indicate that he had a ball lodged in his arm. Only a sharp shooting pain that seemed to spike with each bounce of the saddle or when he tried to move his hand.

Tallmadge gritted his teeth and hissed again as he forced himself to straighten and grab the reins once more. It was not a serious wound, he repeated to himself silently, as he rode past the third line, following his men who now marched with far less fear than they had displayed only a few moments. They knew they were safe now, with someone else holding the line while they retreated.

He continued to silently urge his men onward as he heard the third and final line make ready before firing their volleys. As he rode down the opposite side of Chatterton Hill, a small ragged cheer went up as his men saw the main body of the army come into view. He wanted to tell them to be quiet, to hold to discipline, but he too, felt a sense of relief at seeing the army ready to defend any charge. Out of the corner of his eye, he saw Colonel Chester gesturing for him to tell his men to fall in with the rest of the 6th, and nodded.

"Shoulder muskets and fall in to Colonel Chester!" he called out to his men who responded with palpable relief at being out of danger and happily situated themselves into a respectable column of marching.

He pulled his horse to join Colonel Chester, hurrying the beast a little as he saw that Lieutenant Colonel Wills was been seriously injured. Wills was hunched over in his saddle, hands pressed into his side as Major Ripley looked worriedly at him.

"Sir-"

"I'm fine." Wills' face was pale, seemingly drained of blood. He kept his eyes forward. "I do not need a surgeon-"

"Solomon-"

"I'm damn well *fine* John," Wills bit out harshly, glaring at Ripley. "I don't need-"

Tallmadge was riding just behind the lieutenant colonel and managed to catch him as he suddenly slumped backwards, nearly falling from his horse. Tallmadge grunted in pain as his own arm wound was jarred by the lunging move he made to keep Wills on his horse and by the weight of the man's body hitting his shoulder.

"Holy mother- Solomon!" Ripley grabbed Wills' shoulder and shook it as the officer's eyes rolled a little and closed, before he slowly blinked them open again. The man seemed to realize what had happened and forced himself to lean forward. "Wills, goddammit! Tallmadge-"

"I know, I'll get him to the surgeon." Tallmadge took the reins from Lieutenant Colonel Wills' limp hands and gently pulled his horse to keep moving. He saw the other man's head loll, but he seemed aware that he was now being led and so kept one hand gripped tightly on the saddle horn, his other still pressed into his side. Out of the corner of his eyes, he could see Major Ripley staring at them, his expression worriedly mournful. He knew the man wanted nothing more than to accompany Lieutenant Colonel Wills to the surgeon, but his duties and rank prevented it.

Tallmadge led them to the back of the main encampment where several surgeon's tents had been set up to receive the wounded and infirm. "Almost there sir," he called out quietly as he saw Wills' eyes roll again, seemingly unfocused and glass-like. "I need a doctor! Lieutenant Colonel Solomon Wills of the 6th Battalion is injured!" he called out to the nurses and servants who were running around.

"Here!" a surgeon gestured for him to stop. He clearly had just been operating on someone judging by how slick and coated in blood his hands were. The surgeon waved back to two nurses who placed their things down before coming over.

"Sir, sir, they're here to help," Tallmadge called out, placing a hand on the senior officer's arm as he slumped forward again.

"Catch him, catch him there-"

"Let me help." Tallmadge dismounted, ignoring the stabbing pain that traveled up his arm as he reached over and helped the surgeon and nurses steady Wills, the man limp and heavy as his feet flopped to the ground. Tallmadge reached down and lifted his feet as the nurses each grabbed a shoulder and together they carried him into one of the tents.

The smell that assaulted him immediately made his stomach roil. He clamped his teeth and lips together in an effort not to vomit at the reeking scent of death in the tent. It smelled of rancid onions and rotting fish, a heavy stinking blanket that threatened to smother him as they placed Wills on a wooden table. He blinked, staring at the dark blood weeping from the apparent stomach wound the lieutenant colonel had received. Wills himself was unresponsive and Tallmadge did not know if the man was still alive, but he hoped so. He backed away a little to let the nurses and surgeon do their work.

"Well, hey, if it isn't the Tall-boy." The voice was unmistakable, but it sounded slurred and almost drunk.

He pulled his gaze away from Wills' unmoving form to see Bulkley lying on a cot nearby, Davenport sitting on a stool next to him. Next to them was Captain Wells, with his eyes closed seemingly sleeping. One of Wells' legs was heavily bandaged, but it did not prevent the bright blooming spot of red from showing through.

"Tall-boy," Bulkley called out, a lopsided smile on his face, his eyes glassy and heavy with the effects of laudanum. He had been stripped to the waist and swathes of bandages covered a shoulder wound.

"Bulkley." He forced himself to move towards them and nodded a greeting. "Davenport."

"Tallmadge." Davenport looked exhausted as he rubbed his face. "Surgeon wanted me to give the lieutenant here laudanum before I left. I was just about to head back to the lines when I saw you carrying Lieutenant Colonel Wills in here."

"Gut shot." Tallmadge turned a little and saw the surgeon trying to extract the ball from the lieutenant colonel's wound.

There was a squelching that sounded abnormally loud in the nearly silent tent, and he suppressed the urge to shiver. It was so unlike the screams of the dying and wounded on the battlefield – here, it was so quiet and still. Almost as if Death itself hovered nearby, silencing those who were healing and those who were already on their way to its embrace.

"Wuzzat?" Bulkley slurred and gestured feebly with a shaking finger towards him and Tallmadge glanced down at himself, wondering what he was talking about before he remembered he was still stained with the blood of the Hessian officer he had killed.

"Not mine," he reassured his friend.

"No, zat," Bulkley gestured again and Tallmadge frowned.

"What-"

"I think he means to ask if you're wounded, sir." Davenport gestured with his eyes and chin towards Tallmadge's arm and he glanced at his wound, touching it absently. He winced a little, but it seemed like the pain had dulled. Then again, he was still a little cold from his damp clothes, so it might have numbed his arm somewhat.

"Mine, but it's not bad," he shook his head. "I'll see to it when we are settled. How's Captain Wells?"

"Sleeping like a babe after the laudanum." Davenport smiled a little. "Though I suppose I should not say that."

Tallmadge had to laugh quietly, too tired to summon up a reprimand for Davenport's words against their commanding officer. Even Bulkley chuckled weakly before he slumped a little, his eyes sliding closed, succumbing to the effects of the drug. A second later, a slight snore issued from his mouth and Tallmadge had to smile.

"Took him long enough," Davenport said before clearing his throat. "Apologies, sir. We thought the laudanum had the opposite effect on the lieutenant here, making him far more alert and awake after the ball was pulled from his shoulder."

"We knew he had a thick head," Tallmadge commented lightly and Davenport smiled a little. However, his smile faded as the sound of pounding hooves stopped abruptly outside. The tent flap opened and more people rushed through, some carrying soldiers on makeshift stretchers while others carried their wounded comrades in by their limbs, yelling for the surgeon or nurse.

Tallmadge straightened as he saw Major Ripley follow behind the small stream of wounded. He saw Davenport also stand up at attention as Ripley spotted them and headed over. The major barely acknowledged them as he rushed to the surgeon's table and grasped one of Lieutenant Colonel Wills' limp hands.

"Come on you stupid jerk," Tallmadge could hear the major mutter, "you can't leave me like this. Goddammit what the hell am I supposed to tell your father or your sister Maria?"

Tallmadge bit his lip. He started to feel the same stabbing pain in his stomach as when he was initially told of Nathan's death. He gestured to Davenport to follow him to allow Major Ripley his privacy, and they stepped out of the surgeon's tent. The immediate breath of fresh air was almost a shock to him, and he found himself breathing deeply to get rid of the scent of death that hung inside the tent. He inhaled deeply again, the pain in his gut fading with each draw of untainted air.

"Sir?"

"Come on, let's find where 3rd Troop was placed." He was sure that they were safely behind lines, even though the distant booms of cannonades still rang in the air. Knox and his artillerymen were keeping up a steady and heavy-sounding barrage it seemed. And the fact that he could not hear the quiet pops of musket fire told him that the army itself was not engaged in a major conflict which meant they had successfully integrated themselves into the lines and were now awaiting further orders. He knew Major Ripley would not have abandoned his post unless Colonel Chester had given him the order to take his leave. It also told him that Chester was hoping he returned soon to take command of 3rd again or at least have another officer among the 6th, as Lt. Colonel Wills and Major Ripley were indisposed.

"Take the lieutenant colonel's horse." He gestured to the two animals which surprisingly had not moved or bolted even no one there to handle them.

"Sir," Davenport mounted Wills' horse and Tallmadge mounted his bay. "Uh, sir..."

"Shadow was lost in the initial retreat," he explained before heeling his bay to start back towards the main lines.

"I'm sorry sir. He was a fine beast," Davenport replied and Tallmadge nodded.

"He was," he agreed and left it at that.

Colonel Chester informed the ranking officers and enlisted men of the 6th of Lieutenant Colonel Wills' death later in the evening. Heavy rain had stopped the bombardment by both side's artillery, and the battle drew to a close. Wills died during surgery and the announcement was followed by a moment of silence for the death of one of their officers. They had also been informed that General Washington would be pulling the army back to nearby North Castle for a more defensive stance against the next wave of attacks by General Howe.

Just a few days later, Tallmadge found himself standing outside of Major Ripley's tent. He was not that curious as to why the major summoned him, as he still served as Colonel Chester's adjutant, but a small part of him did wonder about the summons. He had been brevetted to captain rank just the day before by Colonel Chester due to Captain Wells' and Lieutenant Bulkley's injuries and officially placed in command of 3rd Troop. He himself had his injured arm in a sling, but he was considered fit for duty and it was something he had been ready to fight the surgeon on if he had not been considered viable and discharged from the tents.

"Sir, Captain Tallmadge reporting as ordered," he called out.

"Enter." Ripley's voice was hoarse. Tallmadge pushed the flap open and stepped in, ducking his head a little before he straightened.

He resisted the urge to wrinkle his nose against the pungent odor of alcohol that wafted in the air. He also noticed that the major's tent was in a disarray with scattered parchment, a half-spilled inkwell, and several empty bottles that once definitely held Madeira or rum. It looked like a complete mess. The major himself fared no better, his normally neat and tidy queue lopsided, loose strands of hair not even combed or slicked back with oil. His clothes were rumpled, as if he had slept in them, and he had perhaps two days' growth of stubble.

"Sir." Tallmadge said nothing about the state of the tent or of the major's appearance. Instead, he saluted.

The salute was returned in a careless manner. "Tallmadge, sit, sit, though...I suppose there is no chair here, sorry." The major's eyes were bloodshot as he held the neck of a bottle. "Drink?"

"No thank you." Tallmadge held up a hand to forestall the pouring of whatever the major was having. He stood by the edge of the tent, clasping his hands behind him. "You asked for me sir?"

"Tell me, Tallmadge, how did you do it. Huh?" Ripley took his declination of a drink as an excuse to drink straight from the bottle itself. "How did you do it?"

"Uh, do what sir?" he asked.

"Hale of course! Your friend, comrade, brother in arms. How did you do it?" Ripley looked at him like he was stupid.

"...Sir?" Now Tallmadge was really confused.

"He was hung for spying, neck stretched, spat on, marked, cut up, and you didn't even flinch. You stood stone-faced and you didn't even move. You acted like he wasn't even worth considering, but I know," the man nodded, a smarmy smile plastered on his face. "I know you Tallmadge. You felt it, didn't you. That pain...that hurt. It feels like someone cut you up and left you in the corner to rot and die, doesn't it? It feels like someone stabbed you with a bayonet that's rusted beyond belief and twisted it several times."

"Sir, I think-" Tallmadge began, but stopped at Ripley's sudden lunge towards him.

"Answer the goddamn question, Tallmadge!" the man shouted, his face a mask of fury, spittle flying everywhere. However, he did not get up from his scat and only glared at him. Silence filled the air between them before Ripley snorted and sat back. "Not even a bloody reaction-"

"Sir-"

"Answer, the goddamn question, *Captain*," Ripley snarled, this time his voice thick and quiet.

Tallmadge stared at his obviously drunk major for a long moment as he realized what the major was talking about. Not only did Ripley find out about the manner of Nathan's death, but apparently had heard the details and rumors that had spread around camp since Enoch's visit. It seemed Captain Hull – the suspected source of the rumors – had gotten more details on Nathan's death and had told others. He did not know why William would do that to Nathan's name and whatever was left of his friend's honor, but he guessed that William did not want others to forget Nathan or to think of him as only a spy. Somehow, Major Ripley had found out that Tallmadge and Nathan had been good friends before they both joined.

He now realized that Ripley wanted to know how he coped with the news of Nathan's death to help himself cope with the loss of Lieutenant Colonel Wills. Perhaps he thought of them as having a kinship of sorts – what Nathan was to Tallmadge, Wills was to Ripley. And in that realization, Tallmadge felt a little sympathetic towards the major's drunken state.

"I got angry, sir." He kept his tone quiet and respectful as the major stared at him. He gestured towards his own stomach. "It did hurt, but one day I found that it didn't hurt as much. Instead, it felt cold, sir. I was going to rip the heads off each one of those Hessians and lobsterbacks that I came across. They were, no, they *are* going to pay for what they did to Nathan, to my brother William."

He bit his lip and shook his head. "I am sorry for your loss, sir. All I can tell you is that it will hurt less with time. I cannot tell you when you will feel that anger, but it has helped me."

He watched as Ripley lowered his head, cradling it in his arms as he talked. Silence filled the tent again before the major muttered something incomprehensible.

"Pardon, sir?" Tallmadge asked.

"I said get out." The major's bloodshot eyes glared at him again and Tallmadge nodded.

"Sir," he sketched a quick salute and left the tent, walking quickly away without looking back. He did not know what impact his words had had on the major, but he hoped they at least would bring some kind of closure to the man for his loss.

INTERLUDE III

November 23rd, 1776

New York was closed to them now. The fall of Forts Washington and Lee all but ensured that the city was solidly in British hands. He sighed as he discreetly looked around the mostly silent house he occupied in Newark. They would be marching again tomorrow; no time to dally with Howe's forces so close by. The men would be exhausted, ragged, but he kept pushing them – he had to. If Howe truly knew the strength of the army – if he knew how many he had left to defend Peekskill under the command of General Charles Lee, then Howe would be able to defeat them before winter had settled over these lands.

Per custom, silence answered him and his glance around produced nothing of value, except for loosening the tightness that had gathered around his neck. General George Washington sighed again and set the quill down from what he was writing on his desk. Lee had arrived some time after he had pulled his forces back to North Castle and helped to consolidate their defenses. The arrival of his army had also provided a much-needed boost to morale, which had flagged after their defensive retreat from White Plains. The plan had been to split part of their forces to move down into New Jersey while the other was left to guard the Hudson Highlands that included Fort Westpoint, Stony Point, and other important areas along the Hudson. But Howe had decided to go after Fort Washington and then Fort Lee. Fort Lee had fallen three days ago and Washington did not know where Howe would go next. If Howe went north to attack the Highlands, he could turn his army around to provide an effective attack. But if Howe chased after him into New Jersey, then the force he left at the Highlands would be of little use.

He needed to know where Howe would strike and then send a missive commanding Lee to join him. General Putnam would be able to oversee the Hudson Highlands in Lee's absence, though he supposed the man's acerbic nature would rile the Lee after a short while. Perhaps it would hasten Lee's departure from North Castle and bid him to join sooner rather than delay. But even with the movements of the army, the one thing that had vexed him since being forced to evacuate Brooklyn Heights was the lack of actionable intelligence. He had received scouting reports and the like, which helped him determine where to place his army or draw them back, but they were not ideal for any long-term intelligence gathering.

He considered writing his friend John Jay who had been officially appointed by New York officials to lead their state-sanctioned organization the Committee and First Commission for Detecting Conspiracies. Jay's network of spies operated in a limited capacity, unable to give him much actionable intelligence as they were too busy ferreting out the last of the conspiracies against his life, which began when he first arrived at the city back in April. Now, with General Howe occupying the city, it would be too risky for Washington to send in another of his soldiers disguised as a civilian. He had learned that painful lesson with the triple loss of Knowlton, Knowlton's brave man, Captain Hale, and finally the report that the Rangers had all been captured with the surrender of Fort Washington.

Hence his need for eyes and ears in New York or within Howe's camp itself.

A knock came from the door and Washington glanced up to see his manservant, William Lee, or Billy as he was called, peer in. "Sir, Major Tilghman is here to see you," Billy's voice was quiet and polite, his eyes always downcast, but respectful. He had been one of Martha's slaves, part of her dowry, after Washington married her. Billy had proven to be a boon, helping him manage his estate as well as his needs during the months before he accepted the Continental Congress' decree that he was to be lieutenant general of the Continental Army – the de facto leader.

"Send him in, Billy," he said and the door opened wider before Tilghman stepped in, hesitancy on his face. Tench Tilghman had volunteered to be a part of his staff and thus received no official Congressional designation of rank or pay. But Washington had bestowed upon him the unofficial rank of major as his own thanks for the man's services and dedication to the cause. He was grateful for Tilghman's support, knowing that he had the man's confidence in serious matters.

"Your Excellency-"

Washington frowned and Tilghman cleared his throat.

"I apologize, sir." The young red-haired man looked nervous. Tilghman did not normally forget the fact that Washington disliked being called 'Your Excellency', even though it was a title Congress used in each of their letters to him. The fact that he forgot meant the news was serious. "Sir, we've received reports that Cornwallis is on the move at night sir, the Hessians at the front columns." He tried to keep his voice steady, but Washington detected a hint of misery underneath it, as if he was ashamed to be speaking like this.

"And?" he could hear the pause in Tilghman's words.

"Sir, we've lost at least fifty men since last count. They were a part of General Gates' reinforcements and said that their terms had expired. The army has dwindled to nearly four-thousand two-hundred men, sir."

Washington gritted his teeth and silently curled a fist, wanting nothing more than to pound the table. But he could not show lax discipline in the face of such words. "Inform the commanders that we are to move tonight. The men will have to rest when they can. We must make for the Raritan River in three days' time and cross into Brunswick. The men can rest then, after all of the boats have been cast away so Cornwallis and Howe's army cannot cross."

There was a hint of a smile on Tilghman's face as he nodded. "Very good, sir. I will do as you ask."

Tilghman left and Washington held himself still, counting

silently to ten after the door had closed before he finally let loose his anger and slammed a fist into the desk. The ink well, parchment and quill jumped into the air before settling. Damn everything, he thought. Damn Gates and his idiocy for not re-enlisting the men or informing him of their expiring terms. Damn the army and the lack of discipline from the soldiers that had been called up. He thought he had dealt with the worst of the lax discipline by dissolving most of the Connecticut militia line and re-assigning some of the better ones to shore up the loss of men in both Spencer's and Putnam's regiments. He had also absorbed the Connecticut men into the main army where he hoped their morale and fighting ability would be improved, but it did not seem to be the case.

He had angrily laid blame on General James Wadsworth for raising such men of loose morals and compunctions, and the general took it with good grace. But he could not blame him for the failings of men who had experienced defeat after defeat after defeat since late August. Now they were running from Cornwallis who had been sent with a part of Howe's army to chase after them. And the only thing he could find to try to bolster the troops' morale was to tell Tilghman that they were to cross the Raritan and cast all boats off to discourage pursuit. It was laughable, such a farce that Washington felt his anger growing again.

He shook his head and picked up his quill, angrily crumpling up the missive he had been writing. Scratching out a new header and date, he started to write to Congress once again, informing them of their progress. Except this time, instead of informing them of the state of the troops and their actions, he knew what he had to do. They needed an *army*, not militiamen. He had seen some of the junior officers in the militias that had been raised willing and ready to fight for independence. They were the ones he wanted serving in the army, ones who had such a passion for the cause and could inspire others. Militiamen could only go so far, but with proper training, the ones with passion and zeal for the cause could become the decisive lynch-pins for his army. There would still be militia and enlistment terms, but they needed those who were willing to fight not only for their farms and homes, but for others too. He had seen it from time to time on the battlefield. Men like Colonel Silliman who dutifully led his 1st Battalion, men like Smallwood, even Colonel Daniel Morgan and his Virginia riflemen. He mourned Morgan's loss, his capture at Fort Washington a blow to him.

He needed more men like Morgan and knew whom he wanted for the army. There were several he had his eyes on, hoping that if and when Congress proceeded under his recommendation, that they would join the army proper. One was the young Captain Alexander Hamilton who had served with distinction under General Knox's artillery. The others were mere lieutenants at the moment, but their actions in their respective regiments had garnered much admiration and lifted morale for the troops they served with. The army would benefit under their guidance – McLane, Clark, and Tallmadge by his reckoning.

Congress needed to authorize the raising of a proper army. Otherwise, their cause would be as short and swift as the nooses they would be hung from if Cornwallis, Howe, or any of the Hessian mercenaries captured them.

"Billy!" Washington called out and the door immediately opened. He finished signing his name and poured powder all over the parchment to let the ink set before blowing it off. "Find Mr. Webb."

"Sir," Billy closed the door. He folded the parchment and sealed it quickly. As he finished with the wax, the door opened again and Washington scratched out the address for Congress.

"Mr. Webb," he greeted without looking up at his other aide-de-camp, Samuel Webb. Webb was from Connecticut, and though he had no formal higher education, he had been carefully taught by his step-father Silas Deane. Washington greatly respected the man they had sent to France to help the war effort here. Deane's careful teachings to the eldest of the prominent Webb family of Connecticut made him an ideal aide-de-camp. His knowledge with words and prose helped Washington greatly when he needed to deal with Congress in a less direct fashion than he was comfortable with.

"Sir," Webb stood at attention. Webb had been one of the few who had requested to be commissioned when he accepted the position of aide-de-camp, and had been appointed by Congress as a lieutenant colonel. It was a mostly ceremonial position in terms of non-combatants, but it provided Webb with enough respect in the eyes of the other generals to know that he spoke with Washington's voice.

"Ride to Philadelphia and see that Congress gets this and addresses it immediately. There can be no delays by post," he ordered and the young man nodded, taking the letter eagerly. "Sir?"

Washington gave him a grim smile. "If we shall continue to fight this war, we will need a proper army come spring."

5

"I'm going to say something." Henry Davenport's eyes were dark with anger, but Andrew Adamson shook his head as he reached out and placed a cautious hand on his friend's arm.

"Don't," he warned quietly as they watched their mutual friend, Benjamin Tallmadge, walk by, his pace a little slower than before, but still just as determined.

"He's clearly exhausted. Look at him!" Davenport gestured with a hiss towards Tallmadge's retreating form. "The major's running him ragged and Wells has not said a thing!"

"Wells can't say a thing. He's been stuck on bed rest since his wound got infected, Henry." Adamson resisted the urge to roll his eyes at his friend's protests.

"Someone ought to tell the captain then-"

"And what's Captain Wells' going to do after? Tell Colonel Chester?" Adamson asked, looking at Davenport as his brows furrowed further together.

"He's running Tallmadge ragged," Davenport stressed. "You and I know that he's been running all over the place and the major's abusing Tallmadge's posting as brigade-major. It's like he's got some burr up his arse and won't do shite about it. Just what did Tallmadge do to anger the major?! Last I saw, the two were cordial with each other, even when Tallmadge was just a lieutenant!"

"He's still a lieutenant, Davenport," Adamson sighed, "just a brevetted captain since Wells is still on bed rest."

"Same difference now that he's leading our drills." The stubborn Hartford man would not give in and crossed his arms, glaring mulishly at Tallmadge's form which had dwindled to a speck across camp. "Bulkley-"

"Bulkley is an even worse choice if you're going to tell someone, Davenport." He arched an eyebrow at his friend. "And not the choice to go with."

"Well, someone ought to know!" Davenport looked frustrated, almost about to tear his hair out.

Adamson sighed, resting his head against the palm of his hand. "Henry, you want to help Ben, aye?"

"Aye," his friend turned from staring to look at him.

"Then be better than your rank, *Ensign*." He gave him a sideways look. Thankfully it was only the two of them and no one overheard a sergeant-major reprimanding an officer, even one just recently promoted to ensign rank.

"But I don't like the 'yes sir' 'no sir' you can't mingle with the enlisted men, sir," Davenport complained, "I don't want to be an ensign anymore."

"Don't look at me," he frowned, "I'm not giving up sergeant-major and getting demoted just because you don't like the rules of conduct between an officer and an enlisted man."

"You'd be better as an officer, Andrew. I'm not cut out for this and I'm blaming Bulkley for even thinking of suggesting it to Captain Wells," Davenport groused. While Adamson would have taken the compliment any day, he knew that agreeing or even thanking his friend for the compliment would lead to further complaining about the unfairness of the situation over the past month.

"I think it was Tallmadge who did that," he interjected and saw his friend's expression grow a little surlier.

"Someone ought to be told." Davenport crossed his arms across his chest. "It's not fair."

"Tallmadge doesn't seem to mind," he pointed out, and his friend gave him a look.

"This whole officer-non-commissioned officer shite is

idiocy," Davenport continued to grumble as he turned back to glare at the fire they sat around.

Adamson sighed quietly and ran a hand through his shaggy dark hair. It had grown since the summer, and though he kept it within regulations, trimming it so it could still be tied into a queue, he sometimes wished he had the freedom to just shave his whole head and buy a wig. Except wigs were a luxury he could not afford, not with his small bounty or meager pay.

He knew Davenport had a point. Tallmadge was looking a lot more ragged and exhausted since they were stationed with whatever was left of the Connecticut militia that had not been discharged. General Washington had split his army into two following the fall of Forts Washington and Lee. They had been initially bolstered by the presence of the famed General Charles Lee whom a lot of officers and enlisted men admired, but then came the news that a majority of the army was to cross the Hudson and head into New Jersey to prevent Howe from making overt moves on Philadelphia. The rest of them would be stationed at Peekskill in case Howe did decide to capture the Hudson Highlands.

The 6th, or what remained of the 6th, was stationed under the command of General Putnam while members of the other Connecticut battalions went with Washington. Colonel Chester had been left in command of the 6th, but had taken over most of General Wadsworth's duties when the man had left for Hartford to talk to the Connecticut officials. Rumor across camp was that Wadsworth was to take a leave of absence following what had happened with the Connecticut regiments at Kip's Bay. Adamson did not know much about it, nor did he ask Tallmadge when he saw his friend, but it had left a lot of the officers that had served under Wadsworth feeling uneasy.

He supposed that maybe Major Ripley was one of them, and perhaps that was why he had been driving Tallmadge so hard in the past month. Ripley had changed into a different man since the death of Lieutenant Colonel Wills. He was harder, more acerbic, more prone to yelling when things did not go his way or drills were not executed to his liking. Tallmadge bore the brunt of the major's rants, but he did so without even a single complaint – at least none that Adamson was aware of.

Adamson found himself keeping a close eye on Tallmadge since that first time he had seen Ripley verbally reprimand him in front of the whole troop. He also kept a close eye on the troop's morale and what the men were saying or hearing. It was something he picked up quickly when he had first enlisted and even before he received his sergeant's commission. The men loved to gossip, almost as much as his four sisters when they had social calls or invites to local Wethersfield fetes. He had told Davenport to not say anything, to only just watch and see, but now he could tell that his friend was nearing a breaking point. If something was not done, he would take matters into his own hands.

"Henry," he started quietly, taking a long stick and absently tending the fire. The wood crackled and popped as embers hissed into the cold late-fall air. He moved a little closer to the fire as he felt a gentle breeze pick up. "What would you do? If you confront the major, you *will* find yourself hung from a branch. If you tell Ben himself, he might just deny it or say that everything was his fault. Yes, we knew Colonel Chester back in Wethersfield, but I am sure that if Ben was aware of what Major Ripley might be doing to him, he would tell the colonel. He and Ben are good friends. You remember that day in Cambridge? The tavern?"

"Aye," Davenport nodded, his expression still surly, but his voice softened a bit with affection. "Tall-boy gave a rousing speech about joining the cause based on what he saw and what he knew. Good speech too...got us to join."

"Tallmadge will ask for help when he needs it, Henry. Have some faith." He reached out and clasped his friend's shoulder, shaking it. "In the mean time, we can help him in our own way."

"Huzzah, Ensign Henry Davenport." The sarcasm dripped a little thick, and this time Adamson did roll his eyes as Davenport grinned at him.

"You're a total arse," he shook his head.

"Language, Sergeant-Major," Davenport mock chided and Adamson sighed.

"Now you pull rank on me, Ensign?" He pretended to be wounded and his friend laughed loudly before slapping him on the back.

"Come on, let's see if Tallmadge needs help." Davenport pushed himself up from the fire, stretching.

Adamson followed suit, glad that he was at least able to dissuade his friend from doing anything rash this time around. However, as he and Davenport headed in the direction they had seen Tallmadge walk, he could not help but wonder how much longer he could hold his friend back. Davenport's point was valid and even Adamson was starting to chafe at the fact that neither of them could do anything for Tallmadge. Not when morale was so low and every whispered word hinted of desertion was met with swift reprimand or menial punishment. He could only hope that once their six-month bounties were up, things would be different.

Tallmadge supposed the saving grace was that the army was making preparations to stand down for winter, and that meant furloughs would be issued to the men. It also signaled the end of the six-month bounties, and while there were rumors swirling that Congress would authorize the raising of new troops for longer bounties, no official word had come from Philadelphia or been printed in the gazettes. He had already decided that if such news came through, he would sign up for a longer service, his mind hardened to the fact that he would honor both William's and Nathan's memories and do right by their actions and names. The only issue was that he considered joining up with a New York regiment instead or perhaps place himself under a different commander.

It was not that he disliked serving under Colonel Chester or Captain Wells; it was the current problem he faced with Chester's second-in-command, Major Ripley. Since the death of Lieutenant Colonel Wills, Ripley was tasked to fulfill all the responsibilities Wills had in maintaining and leading the men in Chester's absence due to meetings or other duties. The major had proven that he could occasionally take command, and had proven himself a somewhat traditional leader, but Tallmadge and some of the other officers were of the opinion that Ripley had changed since the death of Wills.

He would not go as far as to call the man touched in the head, but the major's behavior was perhaps reaching the apex in the past month. The major pushed them hard during the drills, critical of every single mistake that was made. He had yelled at some of the newly promoted captains, yelled at even the veteran lieutenants and ensigns of the battalion. He assigned menial punishment for tasks that could have easily been done without comment. All of it was done in a manner that kept Colonel Chester in the dark, but Tallmadge had heard his fellow officers complain to each other when they had time to themselves.

Tallmadge could not entirely fault the major for his actions. Since they had settled at Peekskill for winter camp, morale had plummeted and there were desertions reported almost every week. The men were disheartened and he could see part of the reason why the major pushed them hard during their daily drills. He wanted to keep the men focused, fresh, and thinking of next spring's campaign instead of the possibility that they would to lose the war for independence and the British would kill them all if given the chance.

But Major Ripley was aware that they were all going into the last month of their six month bounties. Their terms would expire just after Christmas. Some men had already taken it as a sign to desert, going home to their families. Others stayed, as General Lee had announced that the British were still moving and that they should be ready at a moment's notice to move to Washington's winter camp in New Jersey. But many had given up on the cause, seeing Washington's plan to split the army into two as a sign of hopelessness.

Tallmadge refused to see it in such a way and tried to encourage that thought in the men. But in the past month, it had been hard to justify his words when even he himself resented what Ripley was doing. He could not be sure, but he suspected his interference towards the major had turned his ire to him. Ripley had wisely not harassed any of the injured men, but those that seemed to be healing or had returned to their duties, he considered fit for duty and thus enacted the same menial punishment or drills on them as the others. Bulkley had been caught up in that, having returned to duty two weeks after receiving his shoulder wound at White Plains.

Tallmadge had seen the major belittle Bulkley for every

mistake he made during inspections and drills. He himself had been made brevet captain since Wells was still on bed rest. Wells' leg wound had taken an infection that prevented him from even walking or executing his duties. A little over a week before, Tallmadge finally had enough of the major's treatment of Bulkley and had used his new position and authority to stop the man from harassing his subordinate. It had only been stern words couched in a suggestion, but it worked.

However, Tallmadge had a feeling he had turned Ripley's ire to himself. For the past week he had found himself being summoned per his capacity as Colonel Chester's adjutant for all sorts of tasks. These duties he would have executed without complaint, but it seemed Ripley thought to spell them out to him as if he was a mere school boy. Some of the tasks were useless or redundant, but he could not dismiss them since he was a junior officer.

All in all, Tallmadge was exhausted after a week of almost non-stop movement along with the drills and duties he needed to execute as 3rd Troop's commanding officer. But he refused to let the strain show. It was not only a matter of pride, but also one of discipline. If the rumors he heard were true, he would have to present a strong case to be considered for another regiment that was not infantry nor under Major Ripley. He did not know Ripley well, but based on the man's actions he would not put it past the major to request him to serve under him if the bounties were renewed.

That was something he did not want.

"Tallmadge, hey Ben." He did not realize he had walked right past Bulkley's tent for the third time that night. He turned to see his friend peer out, shivering a little against the cold.

"Edward?" he walked over, wondering what Bulkley was doing up so late at night. The moon was already at its apex and he was pretty sure that it was past midnight. The 6th shared a small house with 1st Battalion's Colonel Silliman and his staff, using the bedrooms upstairs as their own quarters. The family that the house belonged to had been given a generous stipend and moved farther up river near Fort Westpoint.

"What's Major Ripper got you doing at this hour?" Bulkley asked and Tallmadge frowned.

"Bulkley," he warned, keeping his voice low. The enlisted men did not need to hear the nickname given to Ripley by the others who had faced his wrath.

"What's he got you doing now?" Bulkley ignored his warning and Tallmadge sighed.

"He wanted an additional stores and ammunition report on the battalion as a whole. Something about putting in a report to General Lee from Colonel Chester." He knew that when Ripley assigned it to him, the information requested was already in his carefully collated and sourced roster report, but Ripley demanded separate numbers. He had not even deigned to give him back the roster reports so he could copy the figures to a separate piece of paper. So after eating something quickly, he had to go back and forth to check the numbers again with the troop commanders. It was clearly make work and designed to keep him awake. But Tallmadge knew that if that report was not on Ripley's desk when the man awoke the next morning there would be serious consequences.

He had experienced those consequences firsthand a week and half before when he failed to deliver Ripley's request by morning light. It had resulted in him drawing the overnight watch the day before a parade in front of General Lee himself. Only with Bulkley discreetly jabbing him several times in his nearly healed arm wound had he managed to stay awake the whole time. The wound itself still ached, but the pain was fading day by day and Tallmadge knew it was on its way to healing once more.

"Shite Tallmadge, the man is-"

"Bulkley." This time he glared at his friend who stopped talking and pressed his lips into a frown. "You're not helping matters."

"Well, neither are you-"

"I'd rather think I am," he shot back, arching an eyebrow at his friend.

"How?"

"Every single assignment he gives me, I execute to the best of my abilities and in a timely manner. Every time it happens, he gets angrier or realizes that I've bested him." He shook his head. "His grief is overriding his rationale."

"That's not grief, Tallmadge, that is pettiness-"

"He is angry." He rubbed his arms absently as a brief wind picked up. He had felt warm while walking, but now, pausing to talk to Bulkley had made him a little cold. "And, I believe it is my error that made him this way."

"Come again?" his friend stared at him.

Tallmadge sighed. "It is nothing-"

"Ben-"

"It is *nothing*," he stressed, hoping that Bulkley would stop asking. It seemed to work; his friend mulishly frowned, but did not say anything else. A small part of him wondered if the words he had said to Major Ripley when he had been drunkenly mourning the loss of Lieutenant Colonel Wills had not been the right ones. He had been honest and told the man the truth – he was furious at the British for killing his older brother William and his best friend Nathan. That had resolved itself into a cold anger that he used as his armor, and a desire to see the cause of independence through and to honor the memories of those he cared about. It was how he conveyed it to Enoch when the man had clearly sought some measure of comfort in his words – words he could not say to Nathan's grieving brother. Words he could not say to a grieving Major Ripley.

Silence reigned between the two of them for a moment before Bulkley sighed.

"Davenport wrote up tomorrow's roster report and Adamson will come by an hour before drills start with hot food-"

"Bulkley-"

"We've noticed you've not been eating properly, only the hard tack that is in your haversack, not the food cooked around the fires-"

"I don't have time-"

"Precisely," his friend arched an eyebrow at him. "Adamson is coming by with something fresh and hot. You will eat it or else we will go straight to Colonel Chester rank and consequences be damned, and get us all hung from a rope because you are too stubborn to *not* eat."

Tallmadge sighed. "Fine. Anything else?" He rubbed his arms, feeling colder still.

"Good night Tallmadge," his friend said before he disappeared back into his tent and Tallmadge ducked into his own which stood beside it.

He could hear his friend move in his tent a bit before the sounds of movement stopped. His own tent was cold and he struck a small candle, setting it on the crates he had salvaged at camp to use as a makeshift desk and chair. At least they all had wooden cots and straw mats instead of having to sleep on the cold hard ground. He took his jacket off, hanging it on the edge of a crate, and shivered as his skin puckered from the cold. It might have been more prudent to sleep with his jacket on, but Tallmadge knew that any sign of a wrinkle on his jacket could cause Ripley to assign him another menial task.

He pulled the bed covers up around himself and blew out the candle, hoping that sleep would come soon as he tried to stem the shivers that engulfed him. A part of him wanted to keep moving around, to keep warm himself but another part yearned for sleep, having been awake for far too long. In the end, Tallmadge slept, but it was fitful and restless.

December 1st, 1776

"John, I say this to you with consideration to the years of friendship we've had, but also as a fellow officer in this army we both love and serve in." As soon as those words came out of Colonel Silliman's mouth, Chester knew the rumors he had heard were far more serious than he initially believed.

He placed his fork down and gave Gold his full attention.

"The rumors are true, John."

He sighed and reluctantly nodded as he picked his fork back up and continued to eat his breakfast. Chester considered himself a fair man and one who knew the intricacies of the army politics. But even he was stymied with the current problem he was having with his own command staff. He had heard about what Ripley had been doing to the remnants of the 6th Battalion. It had taken a while for him to confirm such rumors due to his daily meetings with General Lee and the others. Lee and what remained of his force brought up from Charleston, South Carolina, combined with Putnam's troops numbered roughly two-thousand. The meetings were of great import, discussions on defenses, patrols, orders for potentially following Washington or fortifying defenses. There was also talk of merging with General Gates' army further northward, but nothing had come of it so far.

He had left Ripley in charge of the 6th in his absence, but had been hearing grumblings about how the Battalion was being handled. It did not help that when he tried to corroborate such rumors, they were denied by Ripley himself and even some of the junior officers. He saw fear in their eyes, but without proof, he could not act. He had even discreetly asked Tallmadge about it, but the younger man had been surprisingly tight-lipped.

As a result, Chester was left with the only other option – he had requested as a personal favor for Silliman and his own staff to corroborate the stories for him whenever they could. General Spencer, who oversaw the 6th and Silliman's 1st, would have normally dealt with such matters, but Spencer had been sent with a small force to Rhode Island to effect a blockade of the ports to prevent the British from receiving winter shipments. It was why Chester had been left in charge of the 6th and why he and Silliman had been in meetings with Lee. The only problem was that Lee tended to end his meetings with parties each night. It made Lee very popular with the officers and men. Chester loved a good celebration as much as the others, but night after night of such mingling left him wanting to excuse himself. But in deference to company, he could not.

"Ripley refused to take the furlough I've offered since Solomon's death," Chester murmured quietly.

"Do not make it an offer?" Silliman made it sound like a suggestion, but Chester could tell it was anything but that.

"My fear is that he would take it and do something rash," he admitted, taking a bite out of a sausage. It tasted like ash. "He can still fight, I've seen it in him. He wants to fight-"

"He is running all of your officers ragged, John." Out of the corner of his eye, he saw Silliman politely sipping on his coffee.

Silliman had requested a private breakfast with him. It was not too unusual, considering that the two of them sometimes used the house they were boarded in to discuss strategy or anything of concern that came across gazettes or letters. But this morning in particular, the house was deathly still, the servants not making a single sound. Then again, the servants had been summarily dismissed after serving them breakfast.

"You mean to say you've noticed him wearing Tallmadge down." Chester pointed out and could see a small frown appear on Silliman's face.

"I heard Tallmadge wandering the house at one in the morning last night; ostensibly to place another report on Ripley's desk. He's been doing that every other day, John. *Every* other day. Even before morning drills," Silliman pointed out.

Chester knew his friend had taken a shine to young Tallmadge, finding him charismatic. He did not deny that Tallmadge had a natural charm that inspired others; his bold actions in recent months proved that. But Silliman was someone whom Chester had thought might view Tallmadge as a challenge and rival, not as someone to mentor. He was glad to be proven wrong, to see that another officer besides Wadsworth and himself recognized Tallmadge's latent abilities and hoped to nurture them.

Chester had decided long ago, especially after Solomon's death, that he would retire from the field and go home to tend to his family and to his business once his bounty was up. There had been too many deaths, and if he were honest with himself, something about Solomon's death and Ripley's current behavior reinforced his decision. He was getting too old to fight – too tired of seeing good friends die around him. There was a small part of him that refused to voice it, but he did not want to be anywhere near the battlefield if and when Tallmadge were to take a fatal British ball to the side. Tallmadge was reckless and Chester had sought to instill at least some caution in the young man he had raised to lieutenant. He had hoped the young man's adventures in retrieving his horse from Brooklyn Heights had tempered the recklessness. Instead, it seemed to have magnified Tallmadge's behavior. It was something that made Chester hesitant in guiding anymore of the young officers of his battalion since the retreat from Kip's Bay.

"John-"

Chester finally decided to come clean. "Sel, I am returning home after my bounty is up," He heard the annoyance in his friend's voice – a silent unspoken question as to why he had done nothing when he clearly knew what was happening.

"You are giving up the fight?" His friend did not sound very surprised.

Chester placed his fork down and looked up at Silliman. "For now, yes." He absently rubbed his eyes with his fingers. "It has been too long seeing nothing but death and burnt fields. I miss the green of crops, the gently rolling hills sloping down the Connecticut River. Too long has musketry been my lullaby, death my companion."

Silliman stared at him for a long moment before nodding. "The fight will have lost one of the better soldiers, John."

"The fight has long passed me, Sel," he shook his head. "While I appreciate your words, they are wasted on me. I have lead my men as best as I could, but you have already seen those in my battalion who are the future leaders. It is only fair that I give them a chance to prove themselves in battle and out of it."

"Aye," his friend agreed as Chester resumed his breakfast. "So what of Major Ripley?"

"I will talk to Ripley-"

He paused as a firm knock came from the front door before it opened and a messenger stepped in. "Excuse me sirs, important news from Philadelphia. General Lee has called for a parade in two hours."

Chester watched as Silliman took the pamphlet from the messenger's hand, nodding absently to the young man's salute before he left. He could see Silliman's eyes scan the pamphlet, his expression turning to one of astonishment. "Washington actually did it...he actually convinced Congress. Congress is authorizing the raising of eighty-eight regiments in all of the states. The terms of enlistment will be longer and the men considered an army instead of militia forces."

Silliman stopped speaking and met his eyes, shining with pride and joy. "John, do you understand what this means?"

"You've got a war to fight, Sel," he said and his friend nodded, but his smile tempered as he realized that even with the authorization and raising of an actual army, Chester would still not return and instead was committed to retire.

"We've got a war to fight," his friend insisted and there Chester had to agree. Even though he was to retire at the end of his service, he knew that there would be new orders, new assignments to be given. They had two hours before the troops were to be on parade. And two hours to see where John Ripley was to be posted. Two hours to salvage what was left of own legacy in the 6th before everything changed.

It was a very unusual sensation, the effects of at least three cups of coffee mingling with the exhaustion he had been feeling for the past week. It felt like a haze of sorts, but the saving grace was that it was cold and sunny and the cold kept him awake. The announcement from the army parade that General Lee had conducted earlier in the morning still sent a rush of hope through him. Congress had come through and declared the proper raising of an army instead of relying on militia enlistments. There were to be officers commissioned in the states' regiments, enlistments to be raised; anything and everything to continue the fight. It had emboldened the spirits of the men and Tallmadge had seen some of them cheer with hope and shout with joy. Those were the men he knew would more than likely sign up again. But he had also seen some men look away in shame, their zeal for the cause faded after the nearly six months of retreat after retreat.

Still, a summons in the afternoon to the house that Colonel Chester and Major Ripley shared with the officers of the 1st Battalion was nothing new. It was more than likely about another task Ripley wanted him to do in his capacity was adjutant. He hoped that perhaps he could seek an audience with Colonel Chester to ask about possibly applying for another officer's commission in a different regiment now that they knew the war would continue, but he also knew he would have to do it without Ripley's knowledge. In his current spate of pettiness, it would be just like the man to try to sabotage or prevent his transfer.

He entered, straightening his jacket as he did a discreet check of himself in the foyer mirror before walking to the closed door Colonel Chester's office and knocking.

"Enter." Colonel Chester's voice was muffled against the wooden door, but Tallmadge smiled inwardly. He knew Major Ripley would not do anything overt or petty – not with Chester there to reprimand him.

He opened the door and was surprised to see not only Colonel

Chester and Major Ripley, but also Colonel Silliman and General Wadsworth. He stepped in, closing the door behind him and saluting to General Wadsworth. "Sir, welcome back."

Wadsworth had a pleased smile on his face and Tallmadge was relieved that the rumors he had heard about why Wadsworth had departed camp to go to Hartford, Connecticut were not true. The rumor had been that Wadsworth was to ask for a resignation of his commission, but since he still wore the epaulette of brigadier general, he supposed that case was not true.

"Tallmadge, did you see Bulkley-"

The hasty knock on the door stopped whatever Colonel Chester was about to say. A rueful look appeared on his face. "Enter."

Tallmadge saw Bulkley step in, looking like he had rushed from the tents. His arm hung in its sling again; he had not worn it during their parade in front of General Lee. It seemed Bulkley had rushed to his tent to place his arm back in his sling before running here. Tallmadge knew that the doctors had told Bulkley he would regain full use of his arm in about a week's time.

"Pardon my tardiness, sirs," Bulkley saluted, a little red in the face as he realized who else was in the room.

Ripley looked like he had eaten something sour, but Wadsworth nodded his acceptance of Bulkley's apology with an easygoing smile. With Wadsworth's and Silliman's present, Ripley dared not speak out of turn.

"It's all right, Lieutenant." Wadsworth cleared his throat as he clasped his hands in front of him. "Now that we are all here, there are a few things to add onto the news General Lee delivered this morning. General Washington had requested that General Lee bring his portion of troops that had remained to join him in Trenton. It seems Howe is sending his Hessian mercenaries to potentially capture Philadelphia. General Sullivan will be second-in-command of the forces and has called for the battalions not assigned under Putnam's command here at Peekskill to get ready to move camp."

Wadsworth looked at all of them. "There have also been requests from General Gates to supplant the forces he sent down to General Washington from Albany to continue his campaign against General Burgoyne up north come the spring. Lastly,

General Spencer has requested additional forces to be sent to Rhode Island to help oust the British forces there."

As Wadsworth spoke, Tallmadge hoped that he would perhaps be part of the forces sent to help General Washington. While he did not think he would mind serving under General Gates, there was a man that served as brigadier general under Gates that he found boorish and rude. He had crossed paths with Brigadier General Benedict Arnold back when was been a student in New Haven and the encounter had not given him a good opinion on the man. Though he had heard of his exploits and credited him with a good head on his shoulders, it was his mannerisms that made Tallmadge disinclined to serve under him as a subordinate.

"But before we discuss assignments and the like, I have called you all here because I have the pleasure of giving all of you promotions by both Congress and General Washington's orders." Wadsworth smiled a little and Tallmadge blinked in surprise.

"Lieutenant Bulkley?" Wadsworth looked at Bulkley who had turned red again, but stepped forward.

Tallmadge could not help the smile that appeared on his face, his fatigue rapidly fading, as he watched his friend smile nervously.

"S-Sir," Bulkley looked like he wanted to be anywhere else but in this room, even if it was clear he was being promoted instead of reprimanded. Bulkley stood ramrod straight, his arms held stiffly to his side.

"Congratulations, Captain Bulkley." Wadsworth gestured for Chester to step forward and produced a single captain's epaulette. Tallmadge watched, his smile growing wider as Chester removed the lieutenant's braid on Bulkley's right shoulder and replaced it with the epaulette. He knew from the officer's regulation that if Bulkley was a captain for three years or more, he would be allowed to place another plain epaulette on his other shoulder. Majors received a more intricate three-clover style epaulette while those who were of lieutenant colonel rank or higher received fringes on their epaulettes.

"You've been requested to serve under Colonel Samuel Blatchley Webb who had been ordered to raise the 3rd Regiment of the Connecticut Continental Line. Currently you will continue to serve in Colonel Chester's battalion until the end of your current bounty then report to Colonel Webb come the New Year. Will you accept this commission?" Wadsworth asked.

"Yes, sir." Bulkley looked pleased as Chester shook hands with him. He saluted and stepped back and Tallmadge patted him on the back, grinning as his friend smiled back at his good fortune.

"Lieutenant Tallmadge," Wadsworth said and Tallmadge stepped forward, the sudden flutter of nervousness filling him. He kept his gaze forward and stood firmly at attention.

"Your rank of brevet captain has been made permanent," Wadsworth started, as Chester stepped forward once more, taking the braids of his rank off and replacing it with a lone epaulette. "Congratulations, Captain Tallmadge."

"Sir," Tallmadge saluted, as Chester finished his work and stepped back once more.

He received salutes from all four senior officers present and lowered his hand. He made to step back, but Wadsworth held up a hand for him to stay where he was. "What General Lee did not mention was that in the raising of eighty-eight regiments of infantry, there was also to be the raising of four regiments of the horse, dragoons. Major Elisha Sheldon has been promoted to colonel and placed in charge of one of these dragoons, the 2nd Continental Light Dragoons. He has specifically requested that you join him in the raising of such a regiment and in light of your recent actions against the enemy, you are to command a full mounted troop."

Tallmadge stared. He was to command a troop of horse. And it had been Sheldon whom he had interacted with only briefly during the Battle of White Plains, who had specifically requested him? He pulled himself out of his thoughts as he heard at slight clearing of throat from Silliman and felt himself warm a little in embarrassment.

"I might have said something to Elisha about your escapades with your horses," Silliman murmured, and Tallmadge colored further as he saw Chester try to hold in a laugh, while Wadsworth had a rueful smile on his face. He dared not look at Ripley, but could imagine a dark look directed at him.

"T-Thank you, sir," he managed to stammer out before nodding to Wadsworth. "And thank you also, General, for the opportunity."

"Don't thank me yet, Tallmadge," Wadsworth shook his head. "You will be traveling to Philadelphia with me to see to the procurement and raising of the regiment of horse from Congress itself. Since it has not been done in the brief history of our military, nor in our previous time as colonies, Colonel Sheldon has requested that you bring back any information you can regarding the raising of such a regiment to him in Wethersfield. He is currently there recruiting men for the task."

"Yes, sir," Tallmadge nodded, and stepped back as he realized to his delight and disappointment that while he would not be seeing anymore action for perhaps the rest of the year, he would most certainly not be beholden to Major Ripley's pettiness any further.

Bulkley slapped him on the back and he turned to smile at him. As he did, he could see Ripley beyond him, with an odd expression on his face. He could not quite tell what it meant, but the fact that his apparent promotion and reassignment had disturbed the man pleased him. The only thing Tallmadge regretted was that Bulkley had already received his orders to continue to serve in the 6th which meant he would be with Ripley for the remainder of the year.

"Major Ripley," Wadsworth said and Tallmadge watched as Ripley stood stiffly at attention. "Your service record is commendable and Colonel Chester has specifically requested that you receive your own command. It has been determined that your skills will benefit General Spencer's forces in Rhode Island come the spring and four troops will be commanded by you. Do you accept this command?"

Ripley was silent for a moment. Tallmadge saw something grief-stricken and terrible cross the older man's features as he lifted his head bit and spoke up. "Sir, I request a brief leave of absence to consider your request. Since we have settled into winter quarters I have been giving a lot of thought as to where I may serve the cause best and have made a few errors in judgment along the way."

The initial elation Tallmadge felt when he found out about his promotion rapidly drained as he realized what Ripley was truly saying. And the more he listened, the more anger began to build in him. It was not the solemn look Major Ripley had on his face; it was that Ripley had refused to even meet his gaze as he spoke what was as close to an apology as he would ever make. The officer was too proud to apologize for his actions towards him and the junior officers of the battalion, even in front of Wadsworth.

But it seemed Wadsworth had not been privy to what had happened in the past month as he nodded with a kind smile on his face. "Lieutenant Colonel Wills' death has affected us all and I know it hit you the hardest, Major. You have my condolences on his loss and I will grant you leave to see to his affairs and yours. Will you serve out the remainder of your bounty before taking leave?"

"Yes sir. I owe it to Colonel Chester here before I take my leave." Ripley nodded and Wadsworth seemed pleased with his answer.

"Then it is settled. I will write General Spencer of your request. I believe he will be expecting you by February. Will that be enough time?"

"Yes sir," Ripley nodded again and saluted, "thank you sir."

Wadsworth returned the salute as Ripley stepped back, avoiding his and Bulkley's quick looks. They both returned their attention to Wadsworth as he turned to face Silliman.

"Well, Sel, it seems that you've got a knack for this," Wadsworth chuckled, "Congratulations son, you've been made brigadier general."

Tallmadge had to clap at that news and was joined quickly by the others in the room. Since he had met the man, Silliman had given him sound advice, especially during the brief time he had served as General Wadsworth's brigade-major and when he had taken over the captaincy of 3rd Troop. Silliman seemed like a good man who commanded the loyalty and adoration of the men that served under him, and it was good to see that Congress rewarded those who were needed to lead others in the fight for independence. He watched as Wadsworth took the epaulettes off Silliman's shoulders and replaced them with the gold-fringed single-star epaulette of a brigadier general.

"Thank you sir." Silliman shook hands with Wadsworth after he was finished with his task and accepted a casual salute from Colonel Chester. On impulse, Tallmadge saluted him and the other man smiled and acknowledged his show of respect with a salute of his own.

"You're going to like the rank Sel, but probably not the assignment," Wadsworth continued, "You're commanding the 4th Brigade of the Connecticut Continental Line which will muster during the winter, but General Gates has requested you in Albany come spring."

"I see," Silliman nodded as Wadsworth gave him a slightly rueful smile and patted him on the back.

"Cheer up Sel, it's not that bad serving under Gates-"

"Not him, it's Arnold. He gets the job done and is effective with command, but he's pretty abrasive." Silliman shook his head and Tallmadge was a bit surprised that Silliman had the same low opinion of Brigadier General Benedict Arnold as himself.

"Well, I know you will make do with the best you've got." Wadsworth clasped his hands together and looked at all of them as Silliman took a step back. "Gentlemen, if you will, General Gates has also seen to it that the officers, both newly promoted and those who are in camp, are to attend to festivities tonight celebrating this good news and fortune. All officers are invited as an early Christmas party to celebrate the continued revolution for independence.. He gestured towards the door. "Now if you'll excuse me, there is a glass of wine with my name on it and a fire to warm myself."

Everyone laughed, including Ripley, who seemed in better spirits without the dour bitterness he had displayed since Colonel Wills' death. Silliman followed as did Ripley, but Tallmadge hung back and shook his head at Bulkley's questioning glance. He saw his friend shrug and follow the others as he waited for Colonel Chester. He did not miss the significance of the fact that Chester was the only one who had not been given a promotion after Wadsworth's announcements.

"Sir, a moment if you will?" he asked, as Chester rounded his desk and headed towards the door.

"That is fine, but do you mind if we talk on the way?"

Chester gestured for him to continue and Tallmadge nodded, matching pace with the older man.

"Sir, I do not mean any disrespect, but-"

"You wish to know why there was no promotion for me while all others were given such honors?" Chester finished for him with a wan smile and Tallmadge nodded.

"You do not seem surprised," he stated.

"Aye," the other man replied, "and it is because I've come to the decision to bow out of the cause after this bounty has run its course."

"But sir-"

"Tallmadge," Chester started, holding up a hand to stop his protests. "Benjamin. I am old, though I do not look it. Inside, I feel old. The things I have seen since responding to the alarm in Lexington, they have made me feel my age, feel beyond my age. I've sent good boys and men to die in the last two years and I believe that I cannot effectively command anymore if asked to do so."

"But sir, you were there with us at Turtle Bay, at White Plains-"

"And who, Tallmadge, who was the one to lead the men. Who led 3rd Troop?"

"Captain Wells, sir-"

"No," Chester interrupted, "that is not what I've been hearing from the rest of your troop and others who've witnessed your bravery and skill, Tallmadge. Captain Wells may have led the 3rd Troop, but it was the men who obeyed your orders. Yours and Bulkley's. Dear Solomon was like you until he took the shot at White Plains. He was the one who led the men while I was only there to give orders."

Tallmadge was quiet as he stared at Colonel Chester. "Sir..."

"Death leaves a unique perspective, Tallmadge." Chester sighed, and for a moment Tallmadge thought his former commanding officer had aged a hundred years. "For some, death becomes a motivation. For others, it breaks something in them."

"But sir, you have not died." He was confused by Chester's words.

"No, I have not," Chester agreed with a sage nod. "But like I told Sel, er, Brigadier General Silliman, too long has musketry been my lullaby, death my companion. I would like to have a moment's peace before death takes me."

"Sir..."

Chester sighed, long and loud, and turned to smile at him. It was not an insincere expression, but it made Tallmadge feel wistfully melancholic all of the sudden. "I will not abandon the cause just yet, Tallmadge. But you will need help with the Connecticut Assembly in raising troops. I can help in that regard, but please, do not ask me to send good men to their deaths on the field again."

"Sir..." he did not know what else to say after his friend's plea. He nodded. "Yes sir..."

"And, before you ask. I had written a letter to General Washington himself, marking you as fit for promotion to any post. You understand the men and the cause in a far better manner than I ever have, Tallmadge. You understand the difficulties that will lay ahead, but you also understand the consequences if we fail," Chester said, and Tallmadge understood that he was referring to both his late brother William and his best friend Nathan. He had not thought about Nathan much since his death, having put all thoughts of his friend out of his mind and instead had used his cold anger to fuel his desire to see the cause to the very end.

Chester looked out towards the camp, which had come alive since the news this morning. Tallmadge followed suit. Soldiers and fellow officers were celebrating in their own way, some already drinking by fires, while others wrestled with each other in celebration. The melancholic mood that had fallen over camp for the past month had lifted a little, as all realized that the cause was not lost. Some men were already preparing to move camp, likely having heard orders that they were to join General Washington at Trenton for the remainder of the winter until their bounties were up at the end of the month.

"These men will need new leaders for the rest of the war, Benjamin." Chester pressed his lips together for a second. "Lead them well, Captain. I give you permission to recruit from the 6th if you wish, but know that Bulkley will also be given permission. However, the men must first finish their bounties before they will join your new commands."

"Thank you, sir." Tallmadge had wanted to ask, but it had been impolite of him to do so. There was a long-standing order extra bonus pay was to be had if an incoming officer managed to pull some men from their original divisions into the new ones they were commanding.

Colonel Chester absently nodded as they approached the main encampment where the festivities were already in full swing. Tallmadge realized that he would not get another chance to talk to his friend if General Wadsworth was to leave for Philadelphia in the next few days.

"Sir," he called out and saw Chester stop and turn. "Thank you, sir, for giving me the opportunity." He saluted him and saw a sad smile flit across his friend's face before the salute was returned with a solemn look.

"The pleasure was all mine, Captain," Colonel John Chester replied.

About a week later, Tallmadge officially left camp and the 6th Battalion to travel with General Wadsworth to Philadelphia. Two days after, General Lee started to march his troops down to Trenton where General Washington awaited their arrival. Wadsworth had confided in him that Washington had been writing with some impatience for Lee to join him, but had been rebuffed with an air that bordered on insubordination. The confidence and general air of congeniality between him and Wadsworth was unexpected, but Tallmadge supposed that since it was just the two of them traveling to Philadelphia, they each needed a companion to talk to – otherwise, it would have just been silence.

Wadsworth was in better spirits since they departed camp. Tallmadge had learned that his friend was to be promoted to major general by Congress itself; the allocation of two such ranks given to him and to David Wooster. He had congratulated his friend and realized that Wadsworth had specifically returned to Connecticut to petition the Assembly for the rank. Though Wadsworth would technically be subservient as the second major general to Wooster's first major general of the whole Connecticut militia, it was a well-deserved rank in Tallmadge's opinion. Even though his friend had dealt with General Washington's ire over recent retreats, especially the one in Kip's Bay, the Commander-in-Chief himself perhaps saw the wisdom of granting Wadsworth such a rank given his ability to recruit men to the cause. At least Tallmadge hoped that to be the case.

Riding on Wadworth's good news and prideful smile, Tallmadge had added that he had already received verbal agreements from some of the men of 3rd Troop who wanted to serve in the 2nd Continental Light Dragoons come the new year. All of his friends, Adamson, Pullings, and Davenport, along with a couple of others, had agreed to join him in Wethersfield once their bounties were up. Wadsworth was immensely pleased with Tallmadge's recruiting efforts and congratulated him on retaining men who would be useful in training the newer men under his command.

Their journey to Philadelphia was slow and cautious. They took the back roads and avoided the main paths that they suspected General Washington was to march his troops over. Such avoidance was necessary due to a heavy Hessian presence in New Jersey. Tallmadge felt the pull of joining back up with Colonel Chester's regiment, now fully dissolved into the general army per Congressional orders, but he could not contain his relief at the reprieve from fighting or the rigors of camp. They arrived at Philadelphia eight days after setting off from camp and the city was already abuzz with news.

Tallmadge planned to find lodgings for him and General Wadsworth while the general met with the Connecticut members of the Continental Congress, but Wadsworth invited him along. He was surprised, but Wadsworth mentioned something about making important friends. He was honored at such an opportunity and followed.

They reached the house that had been rented out to the Connecticut delegation and Wadsworth knocked. Tallmadge noted a lot of activity about the streets and was about to ask one of the Continental soldiers stationed outside what was happening when the door opened.

"Brigadier General James Wadsworth and Captain Benjamin Tallmadge here to see Mr. Sherman, Wolcott, and Huntington. We are expected," Wadsworth said to the butler as they stepped in.

Tallmadge took his tricorn off and absently brushed his jacket as he stared at the sheer opulence of the house they had entered. Rich oak lined the walls and a simple yet beautiful staircase led to the upper floors of the house. The butler gestured for them to move into the parlor as he went in search of the gentlemen in question. The three names were known to Tallmadge, representatives from Connecticut to the Continental Congress.

"Silas Deane used to be the primary representative to Congress from Connecticut and had picked this house to live in," Wadsworth started quietly as they waited in the warm parlor. The crackling fireplace felt good and Tallmadge found himself drawn to it. He stretched his arms out to take in its warmth.

"Used to be?" Tallmadge asked and Wadsworth smiled a little.

"Mr. Deane has been sent to Paris to determine if the French are amenable to supporting our cause," a new voice spoke up behind them, Tallmadge turned to see a wiry rope-thin man with a sharp nose and bright eyes that complimented a seemingly youthful stature. He was dressed in a fashionable outfit that looked more like he would be fitted to the southern delegates' clothing than the simple, homespun designs of those from Rhode Island or Massachusetts. "Ah, James, good to see you again."

"And you as well, John." Wadsworth took a step forward and clasped his hands over the other man's. He then gestured to Tallmadge. "This is Captain Benjamin Tallmadge, one of the officers formerly under my command. He's been recently promoted to lead one of the dragoon troops under Colonel Elisha Sheldon." Wadsworth turned to him and gestured back to the well-dressed man. "Tallmadge, this is John Jay, a trusted friend and member of the Secret Committee of Correspondence for New York."

"Sir." Tallmadge shook hands with the reed-thin man. He wanted to ask why Jay was a member of a secret committee, but refrained from it, hoping that he would receive answers in due time.

Jay released his hand, seemingly pleased with his conduct or perhaps his lack of inquiry. He turned back to Wadsworth. "Do you have it?"

"The latest from Barnabas from our mutual friend overseas." Wadsworth reached into the pocket of his jacket and pulled out a small bound book. He handed it to Jay who took it, his smile brightening.

"Excellent." Jay tucked the book neatly into his own jacket before nodding to them. "Gentlemen. Please excuse my rudeness for not staying to converse any longer, but my compatriot is expecting me elsewhere at this hour and we have much to do before Congress meets again in Baltimore."

"Baltimore sir?" Tallmadge asked and the bright smile on Jay's face disappeared.

"You have not heard?"

"Heard what?" Even Wadsworth looked concerned.

"Lee was taken prisoner two days ago on the way to Washington's camp," Jay frowned. "Congress called for an immediate recess that day and it is the reason why they are holding the next session in Baltimore. They do not know if Philadelphia has been compromised."

"And the men?" Wadsworth asked.

"Sullivan finished the march. It seems Lee was caught unawares as he frequented White's Tavern near Basking Ridge in New Jersey and was taken prisoner by happenstance." Jay shook his head. "It is also why I was called here from headquarters to ascertain and help my colleague here."

"We shall leave you to your business then John. Best of luck and godspeed to your health and safety," Wadsworth nodded and Jay returned the nod before leaving.

Tallmadge stared at the door, confusion swirling in him. He did not exactly understand what had been said aside from the obvious about General Lee and his capture; the conversation seemed couched in shadowed words and things he was not privy to. However, he dared not voice any of his confusion. Part of him sensed that it was unwise to do so at this juncture. Instead, he turned back to the fire and continued to warm his hands.

Silence filled the parlor, save for the crackling of the fire. Tallmadge glanced towards the ceiling as he heard the sounds of footsteps walking above them.

"Remind me to introduce you to Barnabas. Good man, easily likable, and one I think you will find of great help should you have need of his resources," Wadsworth suddenly said, just as the footsteps descended the stairs. They both turned to greet the person walking into the parlor.

"Wadsworth! Always good to see you!" The man had thinning hair with spectacles perched on his nose, and seemed a jolly enough fellow. He was dressed rather conservatively, but with an opulence that showed in his choice of fine cloth and muted colors.

"Huntington!" Tallmadge watched as Wadsworth clapped the other man on both of his shoulders, a wide smile on his face. "You've lost weight!"

The other man coughed a laugh before shaking his head. "Kind enough for you to point out. I would have thought I'd gained weight by sitting around listening to the rest of Congress all day."

"I find it far more polite to say the opposite, Samuel." Wadsworth pursed his lips together before both men laughed. As their laughter faded, Tallmadge straightened as Wadsworth gestured towards him. "Samuel Huntington, this is Captain Benjamin Tallmadge of the newly formed 2nd Continental Light Dragoons."

"Your servant, Mr. Huntington," Tallmadge shook hands with the older man.

"Captain. Thank you for dedication to the cause," Huntington nodded and Tallmadge nodded, tried to hide his surprise at the man's words. No one had ever thanked him for his service before. It felt both odd and gratifying.

"I hope to continue my service until independence is achieved, sir," he replied.

"Oh?" Huntington looked at him, "such prose and command of words...Yale?"

"Yes sir, class of seventy-three," he replied.

"Good school, though I will admit I had not the chance to be educated in such a manner." Huntington placed an apologetic hand on his chest. "My education was self-taught. Still, it is good to see another one of Yale's finest with such devotion to the cause."

Tallmadge acknowledge the compliment with a brief nod as Huntington turned to Wadsworth. "I know you are here for that promotion, James. But Congress had recessed two days previous to your arrival. I'm sure you have heard of what has transpired to General Lee?"

"Yes, John was just here before leaving," Wadsworth nodded.

"Ah, yes, he was ensuring a particular matter was being dealt with, but back to the matter at hand. Lee's capture has forced us to recess until we can all meet again in Baltimore, which should be in about a week's time. Are you willing to wait until then for the ceremony?"

"I can." Wadsworth seemed relieved and Tallmadge realized he had been afraid that since Congress had recessed, they would not be issuing promotions that were mandated or promised. "However, I do believe Captain Tallmadge requires his immediately. He also requires your help in acquiring any resources that the 2nd Continental Light Dragoons require or any contacts you, Sherman, and Wolcott may know of."

"Ah, that I can do," Huntington nodded and turned back to him. "Captain, your papers?"

Tallmadge started a little and found himself fumbling for the papers he had been given to denote his promotion from lieutenant to captain. They had been initially signed by General Washington, but still needed Congress' formal approval. Bulkley's and even Silliman's promotions were already approved by Congress, but since his was for a brand new type of regiment, one that had never been attempted before, Congress was required to sign in person.

"Sir," he handed them over, fighting the rising heat of a blush on his face.

Huntington took the papers and turned. "Samuel!" A few seconds later, a young boy no older than twelve peered in and he handed the papers to him. "Find John Hancock and I don't care for what hour he thinks this is. Have him sign it and return it as soon as possible. No delays."

"Sir," the young man nodded and scampered away.

"My nephew," Huntington explained. "Bright young lad, very quick on his feet. If you will gentlemen, Mr. Sherman and Wolcott are both out, but do not let that deter you from accepting my offer to host your dinner tonight. Have you found lodgings?"

"Not yet," Wadsworth shrugged, and Huntington smiled.

"Then may I offer a suggestion of taking lodgings just down the road until we are to depart for Baltimore?"

"I will go and see to our rooms, sir," Tallmadge offered, understanding his place.

"Thank you," Wadsworth started, but his next words were overridden by Huntington himself.

"But please, do return Captain. I would like to hear of news from the front, not written in reports by the generals themselves. I am sure you have stories of our fight in the last few months, eh?" Huntington asked and Tallmadge nodded.

"As you wish." He sketched a short polite bow to the two of them and headed out of the door. It felt odd, but he supposed his rank now afforded him greater access and courtesy than that of a mere lieutenant. In the last three months he would have never have imagined receiving an invitation to dine with both a general and a member of the Continental Congress. Rank did have its privileges and he was beginning to understand why Wadsworth and even Colonel Chester had introduced him to certain persons. The last few months of fighting had taught him the scarcity of resources and the need to preserve of good men who would continue to inspire others to the cause. Otherwise, the fight for independence would be lost.

INTERLUDE IV

December 22ⁿᵈ, 1776

Washington wanted nothing more than to take the crumpled missive and throw it into the fireplace. Damn Charles Lee and his misadventures. He would have thought the man to have more sense and awareness, but the letter he had just read spoke the opposite. It also did not help his darkening mood which sat like an cloud of ill will for the past few days. He had only recently found out the highest and most personal of betrayals from within his own staff. Joseph Reed on whom he had thought he could rely, had been in secret correspondence with Lee and had disparaged his character in agreement with the latter. He had long known that Lee coveted his position as Commander-in-Chief of the Continental Army. Lee thought that he could do better than Washington and he had ignored the man's veiled formalities and sloth of duties. It was why Lee had taken his time leaving camp at Peekskill, and Washington could not help but wonder if Lee had been captured because of it. The news made him want all the more to damn the man to hell.

A knock on the door, and he looked up to see Billy peer in. "Sir, Major Tilghman wishes to speak to you."

"Send him in." He slid the crumpled parchment beneath several pieces of paper. It would do Tench Tilghman no good to see the missive. Tilghman was present when he had loose his wrath against Lee's misadventures, bearing the brunt of an ire that he was not supposed to bear. Washington had gruffly apologized afterwards and told Tilghman he should not infer that any blame was upon him. But Washington knew that the sight of the crumpled parchment would inflame the younger man's nerves once more and that was something he did not need at the moment.

The door opened wider and Tilghman stepped in, his nose red from the cold. "Sir, the person in question has been detained."

Washington felt his mood lift. That was welcomed news. He stood up and rounded the desk as Billy scrambled to retrieve his cloak and hat. He accepted them without comment as he swept out of his office and the house he occupied. They had retreated from Trenton, New Jersey to Newtown, Pennsylvania across the Delaware River. Newtown was near Philadelphia, a preventative measure in case the rumors of General Howe's troops marching to take the capital city were true.

Billy closed the door behind him, but did not follow; Tilghman stepped neatly into the void that Billy would have occupied. He knew Billy would find the paper that he had crumpled and dispose of it in the proper manner. His manservant was well versed in his moods and this was something Washington found invaluable.

"House three, sir," Tilghman murmured behind him and Washington headed across camp to the proper detainment house. There were five 'houses' total, tents in actuality, but known as detainment houses for soldiers who crossed lines and for civilians who happened by camp and were not recognized. The houses were isolated from the main body of the camp, but not so isolated that those who were treated as prisoners could escape or be rescued by their compatriots.

Washington dismissed the two soldiers on duty who were stationed outside house three with a wave of his hand. Tilghman would see to their discretion. He stepped into the tent, letting the flap close behind him. He could hear his lifeguards taking their posts outside.

"Are you in need of a doctor or surgeon, Mr. Honeyman?" Washington ran a critical eye over the state of his agent. John Honeyman was a familiar face to him, having served in the

Seven Years War, though in a different regiment. He had also run into him while he was in Philadelphia during the time he represented Virginia in the 2nd Continental Congress. Honeyman had craggy features with some of his teeth missing, but a head full of hair and full beard that made him look more a butcher than a weaver, his secondary trade. But that was not what drew Washington to him – it was the keenness of Honeyman's eyes. Clear-eyed and immensely observant, Washington had bumped into him by mere happenstance as they retreated from the Hudson Highlands to Trenton.

"Nah," Honeyman spat out a wad of something dark to the side, "but if you got drinks..."

Washington smiled thinly, a game he knew very well, and lifted the flap a little. Tilghman was already there with two glasses and a small bottle of wine. Washington took the proffered gifts and let the flap close once more. He set them down on a small table and poured a half-measure for himself, while giving Honeyman a full glass.

The man accepted his offer of the glass with his hands and feet still bound, but drank deeply and exhaled loudly after he was finished. "Nothing like a good wine to whet the palate, eh, sir?"

"Agreed." He waited patiently, knowing that Honeyman would speak when he needed to.

"I'll be feeling the bruises your men inflicted, but it is nice to know that some of them still can fight." Honeyman looked a little roughed up and even winced in pain as he moved, but he seemed no worse for wear. "Thank you for your letter to my wife and family. It will save them from reprisals."

"It was the least I could do. How goes business?" he replied, refusing to let his impatience bleed through his words. But it seemed something must have shown on his face as Honeyman set the glass down on a nearby barrel and sat forward, grimacing as his movement aggravated some injury.

"Cattle sold well." Honeyman's sharp eyes gleamed. Washington leaned forward to take in the information his spy gave him. "Sold a nice fat one to the Hessian Colonel Rahl and his fellow officers. They said that they were going to celebrate Christmas by slaughtering it and even asked for two more for the men under their commands. Their bellies are going to be full and sleepy by the time they are finished with my cows."

"How did Rahl seem to you?"

"Could not stop talking about what happened at White Plains. Said that it was not surprise that made him initially pull back, but the fact that he wished to give your men a chance to surrender the field of battle before he charged the hill. He knows you're here, sir, but he saw the littering and burning of supplies all along the way to Trenton and thinks the boys will just starve themselves and flee by January. He crowed about it to the other officers when he was looking at my cattle. Says that I should only sell to him and not to the poor skinny bastard, some kind of Germanic swear I think, sir, that seems to demean you, sir."

"Does he now." Washington had no love for Hessians, but he had always held their officers to the same standards of respect he had for the British. This new information regarding Rahl and his utter contempt for his forces and the Continentals soured his opinion on the man.

"Didn't really get a good count, but I say you're looking at the same amount of forces that attacked you at White Plains," Honeyman continued, before picking up his empty glass again. Washington obliged the unspoken request and poured him some more, though this time he made sure to pour only three-quarters instead of a full glass. "Thank you, sir," Honeyman raised his glass in a salute and downed it in two gulps. He set the glass back down again. "As to the matter of my release..."

"There will be an accident with a haystack near this area. Mr. Tilghman will see to your bonds after I leave. Do not make your intentions known."

"Your boys are going to shoot," Honeyman pointed out, and Washington gave him a bland look.

"If they do not I will be sorely disappointed in them," he replied, and saw the other man smile a little.

"Better their shots than the Hessians, sir. Though I do hope I do not get hit." Honeyman seemed a little worried, but Washington knew the man was wily enough to avoid being hit. "You wish for me to pass word to our esteemed Hessian colonel?"

"You have seen the state of my men." He trusted Honeyman's discretion.

"Aye." The other man seemed to want to say more, but refrained as he picked up the glass again and held it out to Washington who took it, hiding both glasses and claret of wine underneath his cloak as he stood up. He nodded his farewell to Honeyman who, for a moment, looked at him with solemn pride before the same cocky expression overtook his features as he schooled himself to becoming a Tory sympathizer once more.

Washington stepped out and nodded once to Tilghman who immediately stepped in to discreetly loosen Honeyman's bonds so he would have an easier escape tomorrow morning. Billy would be sent to "accidentally" set a nearby haystack on fire, providing the necessary distraction for Honeyman to escape from camp. As he headed back to the house, he could not help the small smile of hope that appeared on his face.

All he needed to do was to cross the Delaware back into Trenton.

6

January 3rd, 1777

Tallmadge was surprised when he found that the current residents of his old house in Wethersfield had readily allowed him to re-board there for the winter. Though he did not occupy the master bedroom, he had been given the converted parlor as his private quarters and office to use whenever he wished to retire for the day. He had arrived back at Wethersfield the day after news had been published about the rousing success of Washington's forces against the Hessians at Trenton. The town's spirits had been buoyed and celebrated the victory all the way into the New Year. Tallmadge found himself thrown immediately into processing the slew of new recruits who eagerly signed up, their fervor and patriotism renewed by the Christmastime victory.

Tallmadge had cheered at the news of Washington's victory, celebrating it with a small officers' gathering that Colonel Sheldon arranged with some haste. Though Tallmadge knew the 2nd Light did not yet have its full quota of officers – with more applying, petitioning, and paying for commissions day by day – he had relished the chance to meet the others he would be serving alongside.

Samuel Blackden was Sheldon's second, given the commission of a major, while Josiah Stoddard the rank of captain. Tallmadge had met the two and learned that both had served with Sheldon during the Ticonderoga campaign back in 1775 under General David Wooster, before Sheldon was given command of the Light Horse attached to then-Colonel Silliman. Both seemed fair-minded and Tallmadge learned that Captain Stoddard had been a lieutenant under Bradley's 7th Connecticut battalion which had been assigned to Fort Washington. Along with a handful of other officers and enlisted men, he had escaped capture by the skin of his teeth whereas the rest of the battalion had not been so lucky. Both were Connecticut men from Salisbury and were acquaintances. Stoddard was junior to Tallmadge by at least fifteen days, having been commissioned on December 31st. However, he was not the most junior of the captains, that distinction belonged to a New Jersey man along with one from Massachusetts.

There were technically three open positions of captain, one of which would be serving with Colonel Sheldon himself, but one of these had already been filled by a Frenchman who had petitioned Congress for posting. While Tallmadge welcomed any French aid, knowing that it would help them greatly against the British, he was puzzled by the posting of the man in the 2nd Light. His name was Jean Louis de Vernejout and he had already proven himself to be dismissive and borderline contemptuous of his fellow officers. Tallmadge had immediately disliked him, and he was not surprised to see his own feelings reflected in some of the other officers. It seemed that Captain de Vernejout had only adhered to the barest of respect for Colonel Sheldon and Major Blackden. Tallmadge had already caught Stoddard and another talking about the Frenchman behind his back.

He supposed that he should be thankful there was only one Frenchman who had decided to join the 2nd Light as an officer, as they were still short two lieutenants and a handful of ensigns. Ezekiel Belden and John Shethar had both applied; Shethar was from Litchfield and was a friend of Blackden's, while Belden had been known to Stoddard and had served with the other man under Bradley's battalion at Fort Washington. He too, was one of the few who had escaped when the British captured the fort late last year. There were to be six troops of horse and acquiring said mounts was to be determined by each troop's commander.

Tallmadge felt he was up to the task, but since he had no lieutenant of his own to delegate to, he had spent the last few days inquiring about purchasing proper mounts for his men. He had also spent time recruiting men from around the area, since he knew many of the families by virtue of being their former schoolmaster. It was hard work and Tallmadge found himself dropping into his bed without even properly greeting his hosts the last few nights. He would have to remedy that soon, though they were gracious enough not to comment on his apparent lack of manners.

"You keep hunching over like that and you're bound to get a permanent curve to your back, Tallmadge." The familiar booming voice of Bulkley pulled Tallmadge from his work of copying over the latest recruits to the rosters. He turned from his desk at regimental headquarters – ironically the house next to his former schoolhouse – to see his friend wander in with three others who had given him their promise to join after their initial militia bounties were up.

"Bulkley!" He set his quill back into the inkwell and stood up, greeting his friend with a back slapping hug before pulling back to look at him. Bulkley was a little soot and dirt covered, but his arm was out of his sling and looked none the worse for wear. "Davenport, Adamson, Pullings," Tallmadge greeted the other three.

"Captain," Adamson murmured as the three knuckled their foreheads out of respect.

"You all are looking well." He was glad to see that none of them looked injured, though their uniforms were covered in telltale dried blood and dirt.

"Trenton was a grand affair, Tallmadge," Bulkley grinned, slapping him on his arm. "You missed it. No injuries, we even got Colonel Rahl that Hessian bastard. Pullings nearly took a dunk in the river, but we managed to pull him back on board without having him swim with the ice."

"It wasn't that cold," William Pullings shrugged. He had slightly beady eyes, but was great shot with a Pennsylvania rifle. He was one of the few soldiers who declined taking a standard issue musket and instead, preferred his trusty rifle and a sheathed bayonet to do the job. Captain Wells had not made much of it, but Tallmadge knew that with a regiment like this, Pullings would have to conform to regulations.

"When we left, Washington was making for Princeton. Wells and some of the other men stayed to serve a quick six-week term, but we got back here to see if we could recruit more boys to the cause," Bulkley grinned. "Colonel Webb's got his men stationed up here for recruitment, plus there's a guest of yours we were asked to escort from Fairfield."

"A guest of mine?" Tallmadge stared, puzzled. He had not been expecting anyone to call on him nor to visit.

"He's waiting out in the foyer, thought it too impolite to come into regimental headquarters when he is but a civilian." Bulkley had a mysterious twinkle in his eye and Tallmadge smiled hesitantly, wondering what his friend was on about as he stepped out of the shared office.

He did see a man standing by the foyer, examining a beautiful painting of the seascape with his hands clasped behind his back. The man turned at his entrance and Tallmadge found his smile growing wide at the sight.

"Father," he greeted as he walked towards him and heartily shook his hand. His father surprised him by pulling him into a firm embrace.

"Let me look at you." Reverend Benjamin Tallmadge Sr. stood back, determined to examine his third oldest. Tallmadge stood tall, pride shining on his face. He had only received his new uniform and colors a few days ago, just before the New Year. Blues and buff in the style of the Continental colors adorned him, while his breeches were also of buff-yellow gold. A red sash was tied around his middle denoting the status of officer-rank. While most Continentals wore a long jacket with tails, cavalry officers required shorter tails to best accommodate their time in the saddle. The only thing that had not arrived was his helm – supposedly a gold-burnished coloration with a white-horsehair plume.

"Sir, we will report ourselves to Major Blackden for enlistment into your troop, sir," he barely heard Adamson say quietly behind him, but acknowledged his friend's words with a wave of his hand.

"I am so proud of you, Benjamin." He passed his father's

examination as the man reached out and grasped his arms. "So proud."

"Thank you father." Tallmadge suddenly found it hard for him to speak, an unexpected lump forming in his throat. He was reminded of the fact that William had died mere months ago, and that he'd only had time to write his father twice in the interim. "I...I have to ask-"

"Your brothers John and Issac are safe, as is Zipporah," his father started. "Do you remember Selah Strong? Nancy's husband?"

"Yes." Tallmadge remembered that Selah Strong had served in New York's provincial congress before war had broken out. He was an outspoken Patriot and his wife, Anna, who was more known by her nickname Nancy, was a constant fixture by his side. Tallmadge had grown up knowing Nancy, but had known the Strong family a little more due to their familial connection. His father's second wife, Zipporah, was part of the Strong extended clan.

"Selah helped Zipporah settle with the rest of his extended family in New Haven along with the boys after we arrived in Fairfield. We made plans to flee after Long Island was taken by British forces." The elder Tallmadge looked grim. "I was inquiring about yours and Samuel's regiments when some of your men happened by. The meeting was most opportune. A sign from God that he is watching out for all of us."

"Aye." Tallmadge did not feel so compelled by religion as his father, but neither could he disagree with the words said. He still carried memories of a boyhood growing up in a stern, religious household. "How is Samuel?"

"Last I heard, he was still serving in the 4th," his father replied, and Tallmadge nodded.

"I am sorry about William, father," he said quietly and his father sigh deeply. For a moment, he could see the age and weariness in the older man's eyes, the same eyes that had refused time and again to talk about his service in the Seven Years War. The same eyes when he had presented himself to his father last year in August, after receiving his commission. He knew his father had been rather reluctant for him, William, and Samuel to join the Continental cause, but they were no longer part of his household; they were men who had grown into their own and had free and independent thoughts.

"I am sorry about him too," his father replied, "but it is not an apology for you to make, Benjamin. William knew of the consequences, and I have come to terms with the fact that you and Samuel have both readily accepted them as well. Otherwise, you would not have joined."

"Aye," he agreed, just as the clock in the foyer chimed. He glanced at it with some trepidation, knowing he had to get back to his duties.

His father seemed to sense it also. He bowed a little and placed the hat he had taken off back onto his head. "It was good to see you, Benjamin."

"Please stay at least for the night. I am currently lodged with the Wakefield family. I am sure that they would not mind you as a guest for tonight's dinner and lodgings."

His father looked hesitant, but nodded. "All right. I shall make my introductions to them and see you at supper."

Tallmadge smiled and nodded as his father tipped his hat at him and left the house, the door closing behind him. He stared for a moment longer, savoring a brief respite before turning back to his office and sitting down at his desk to continue working the roster rolls for the 2nd Light. It was good to see his father again, even if only for a brief moment.

January 11th, 1777

His name was John Webb, known to his family and friends as Jack. He had no service record prior to his enlistment. Webb had a spark in him that Tallmadge found kinship with as he watched the younger man drill the men of 1st Troop. He had requested the lieutenant's commission for Webb himself and had presented it to him just yesterday. The younger man had proudly accepted it and he had watched with some amusement as Adamson, Pullings, and Davenport gently poked fun at Webb's new rank during morning drills. He was glad his friends had accepted him as a fellow officer, to be respected and treated as such, considering that Adamson was the only one the same age as

Webb merely seventeen years old.

Webb was from Wethersfield, though he said he had been considering studying at Yale before the war broke out. The young officer said he was encouraged and inspired by family members to join. Webb's older brother Samuel was known to Tallmadge; he had met the elder Webb briefly at White Plains as Washington's aide-de-camp. Jack Webb's sense of dedication had touched something in Tallmadge and he had immediately set the young man to work before giving him his lieutenant's commission.

The last of the commissions for lieutenant had been given to John Shethar of Litchfield, owing to the fact that he had paid handsomely for it. The funds had been necessary and helped in the purchasing of supplies for the regiment. The 2nd Light had been allocated one-hundred dollars per head of horse and Washington gave specific instructions that the horses be serviceable trotters of sufficient size. This meant no stallions or mares, but geldings, fillies, and colts were allowed provided that they were not white or grey colored.

And that was Tallmadge's latest problem. He had created a *manage* to corral and break in the animals they had acquired, but they were still woefully short of the number of appropriately colored horses. For a dragoon regiment, white or grey horses were too easily seen by the enemy when patrolling, and both colors were also used for high-ranking officers of the army itself. He searched through several reports he had from local farmers in the area. "Webb, how many does Sheffield's farm have?"

"Three sir," was the quick reply. Webb dropped a piece of parchment on his desk before moving to his own desk, rifling through his own papers.

Tallmadge plucked the paper given to him and placed it with three others. They were from local farms willing to part with their horses. He had been surprised how reluctant some of the so-called Patriots in nearby towns and cities were to part with their beasts, even though they were compensated quite handsomely with a hundred Continental dollars a head. It was more pay than most of them made in a year.

"The inoculation reports?" he asked.

"Going well, sir." Adamson was in the office with them, but

he sat on one of the couches in the general area, paper spread around him as he too sorted reports. Tallmadge had placed Adamson in charge of inoculating 1st Troop which Sheldon had given him command of following the acquisition of the nominal number of captains. "I've shared my findings with the other sergeant-majors of the troops."

"Good," he replied, a little absently as he searched for the report he had written regarding horse numbers and which farm had been willing to part with some. Another shadow crossed the corner of his eye and he saw Adamson's hand withdraw, leaving the report with the inoculation numbers. Tallmadge took a quick glance at it and saw two 'x' marks. "Adamson, what-"

"Sergeant Nathan Smith and Jonathan Dallaby both are gravely ill after inoculation, sir. Surgeon is keeping them isolated so the men are not frightened by such measures," Adamson replied. Tallmadge pressed his lips thinly together.

"Did the surgeon say whether or not they will survive?"

"No, but he did make the sign of the cross, sir," Adamson replied, and Tallmadge wanted to sigh, but he instead rubbed his eyes tiredly. Along with the order for specific horses, Washington had requested that all of the 2nd Light receive smallpox inoculation. They had all been subjected to it the previous week and Tallmadge had only received a light head-cold that soon went away with warm food and good company. His men had been inoculated in the last two days, and to hear that two of his men had come down with the pox itself worried him.

"Let the surgeon know I will be visiting them tomorrow." He stopped rubbing his eyes and scratched a small reminder to himself to do so before morning drills commenced.

"Yes sir," Adamson replied.

"Damn it, where is that report?" he muttered as he set aside his current sheaf of papers and picked up another stack. A few more minutes of fruitless searching finally yielded the report he was looking for and he placed it in front of him. He grabbed the three pieces of paper he had set aside and started to copy down numbers. Once he was done, he sat back and stared at what he had written.

The numbers were poor.

"Webb," he called out as he stared at the damning figures, "are we sure of the amount that can be provided from Sheffields, Westwood's, and even Davenport's own farms?"

"Yes sir." He heard the scrape of a chair across the wooden floor and the tapping of feet as Lieutenant Webb approached him. Tallmadge glanced up at his lieutenant, noting the frown on his youthful features. Jack Webb had intelligent brown eyes and dark brown hair that was tied back in a queue. He raised the paper up to Webb who took the silent offering and stepped back, his frown growing even more pronounced as he read the numbers.

"Sir-"

"Colonel Sheldon and Major Blackden's staffs will have the horses they require if they so wish, but unless it is divided up by all officers of the regiment having each of these horses, the men themselves will not have such mounts." He shook his head. "There is no other way around it."

"Yes, sir." Webb looked disappointed as he handed the paper back. Tallmadge took it, all but tossing it onto the table in frustration.

"I'd never thought I see the day that Benjamin Tallmadge is frustrated by a piece of paper." Bulkley's booming voice echoed from the doorway and Tallmadge turned to see his friend leaning against the frame, a smile on his face.

"Bulkley," he greeted shortly, not exactly in the mood for his friend's teasing especially in the presence of two junior officers.

"I'm here to make sure that Lieutenant Webb here is at the dinner tonight at the Deane house," Bulkley smiled. Tallmadge started, a frown on his face. He had almost forgotten about the dinner at the Deane house. He had been invited as General Wadsworth's guest, but did not realize that Webb had also been invited.

There was a very put-upon sigh from Webb and Tallmadge turned in his chair, puzzled as to why his young lieutenant had made such a noise.

"My brother Samuel expects me to arrive on time to the fete instead of stopping by, say, a tavern before I arrive." Webb shook his head, scoffing a little. "He forgets that I am an officer like himself and still tends to treat me like a child."

"He is only concerned for your well-being, Lieutenant," Bulkley chided gently, and Tallmadge felt a bit of sympathy for his lieutenant. He remembered his two older brothers William and Samuel both treating him like a child when he first enrolled and went to Yale. Granted, his first two years there were not exactly full of hard study; he had relished the sheer freedom he had encountered, without his father or older brothers to curb his more adventurous impulses. He and Nathan had much fun during those years so he understood where Webb was coming from and why he seemed a little dour at the moment.

"He's smothering me," Webb groused.

"He may be, but I am under specific orders from your *brother*, my commanding officer, to bring you there. And since I do not plan on receiving a reprimand so early in my captaincy career, I will order you to march there," Bulkley replied with a tight smile.

"Hard luck, sir." Adamson slapped Webb gently on the back from where he was sitting and Tallmadge could see that his friend was trying very hard not to laugh at Webb's expression which shifted from dour to resigned.

It was hard to keep the smile from his expression as Tallmadge stood up. "Tell you what, Lieutenant. I will accompany you and let your brother know of your most recent efforts, and perhaps it will help change his perception."

"Sir..." Webb sounded even more reluctant, but seemed to accept his fate as he realized the two of them would not let him escape his duties. "Yes, sir..." Webb stood up, brushing himself down before turning to face him. "Sir, with your permission, I'd like to conclude my duties for tonight due to an engagement of a personal nature."

Tallmadge noticed Bulkley smiling in good humor at Webb's somewhat stiff and formal request but ignored his friend's look. "Of course," Tallmadge replied, giving the young officer credit where it was due. "Thank you for your efforts for today. We will reconvene tomorrow at the same time in the morning after drills."

"Sir," Webb saluted and Tallmadge returned it as the young man left the room followed by Bulkley.

"Adamson," he turned to his friend who sat up in attention.

"Check on Smith and Dallaby tonight and let the surgeon know of my visit tomorrow. Probably around noon if you will. If you can also clean up here-"

"Will do," his friend waved an absent hand at him, knowing that neither Bulkley nor Webb would be able to see. "Go enjoy yourself, Ben."

Tallmadge smiled and shook his head. He would not have normally allowed Adamson to act in such a manner unfitting his rank, but it had been a long frustrating day of trying to acquire horses and figuring out other logistical elements in outfitting the rest of the 2nd Light. "You and Davenport better not get too drunk at Pullings' family tavern tonight. Drills at morning light tomorrow."

Adamson only returned the smile as Tallmadge stood up and headed out of his office. The requisition for dragoon helms had not come through yet, so he had to content himself with no helm to wear to the formal gathering. He would have normally worn his tricorn, but it denoted infantry and Tallmadge was prideful enough of his station that he wanted his helm to be the only type of headgear he wore.

He met Bulkley and Webb in the foyer as they headed out of the regimental headquarters and down to where the Deane house was. They arrived in short order and Tallmadge did not miss that several carriages were waiting outside, some dropping off ladies in all their finery while others had soldiers waiting beside them.

"Ah, Jack!" a voice called out and Tallmadge looked towards the source to see the familiar sight of Colonel Webb. A young woman was attached to the man's arm and was smiling behind her hand.

"Sir," Bulkley saluted the colonel as they stopped before them.

"My compliments Captain Bulkley." Colonel Webb nodded to Bulkley who beamed with pride.

"Sir," Tallmadge also saluted, "it is a pleasure to meet you again."

"Ah, Tallmadge was it? I knew you looked familiar. James Wadsworth kept on talking about you." Webb smiled a little. "I also remember what you did at White Plains and my cousin Charles seems also to hold you in high regard for your integrity."

"Sir." Tallmadge was a little embarrassed at the praise and the knowledge that General Wadsworth had mentioned him in passing – several times if Colonel Webb was not mistaken – as well as being mentioned by Nathan's former commanding officer even though they had met only briefly before. He did not know that Washington's former aide-de-camp was so sharp-eyed.

"Sir, if you'll excuse me," Bulkley quietly interrupted, and Webb nodded, dismissing Bulkley with a casual salute. Tallmadge saw his friend stare at him with amused incredulity in his expression before leaving them.

"So, what brings you-"

"Samuel! Jack! And Benjamin!" Wadsworth's voice was far more boisterous than normal and he turned to see the major general walking out of the front door, a glass of wine in his hand. From the faint light of lamps, he could see that Wadsworth was already rosy in the cheeks.

"James," Colonel Webb greeted as did Lieutenant Webb, though he was a little more hesitant and faint.

"Sir," Tallmadge saluted his friend who returned it before circling an arm around him and pulling him forward.

"Tallmadge's here as my guest, Samuel," Wadsworth said. "Jack, your sisters are looking for you."

"Sir," the young lieutenant belatedly saluted Wadsworth as he headed inside, followed by a polite excuse from Colonel Webb's guest on his arm who hurried accompanied the younger Webb. It left the three of them still standing outside, though General Wadsworth gestured for them to enter.

"I see I need not make introductions?" Wadsworth asked as they entered the house.

Tallmadge was immediately struck at how opulent the wood panelings were, a dark mahogany with an atypical staircase winding up the right side of the house instead of the traditional Georgian-style he was used to seeing in Wethersfield. The left hand side had a table already set, a few people mingling around it while music filtered down from upstairs.

"Captain Tallmadge and I were briefly acquainted at White Plains," the elder Webb replied, plucking two glasses of wine from a passing servant and handing one to Tallmadge.

"Thank you, sir," he replied, and Webb only smiled.

"Come now, you can call me Samuel when we are at such fetes as this," Webb waved away the formalities. "It is a chance for a celebration!"

"Then please, call me Benjamin," Tallmadge said taking a sip of the wine. The sweetness of the vintage felt good after a long day's work and he felt himself start to relax.

"This way, my boys, this way." Wadsworth guided them up the stairs, past the awning that held a string quartet and into what looked like to be a ballroom. No one was dancing at the moment, but then again it was only the start of the party and he suspected that there would be more merriment as the night wore on. "So White Plains, eh?"

"Sir," Tallmadge remembered Wadsworth asking about the blood-soaked uniform he had on when he rode into Washington's headquarters to deliver his report from Chatterton Hill. But there was no forthcoming comment as Wadsworth looked around, a puzzled frown on his face. It seemed he had been expecting to find someone up here with the other mingling guests.

"Dear me, I do not know where Barnabas went." Wadsworth pursed his lips before turning to them. "My apologies gentlemen, I had wanted to introduce you, Benjamin, to Barnabas Deane, but he seems to have gone off somewhere. If you'll excuse me." With that, Wadsworth left them.

"Check with Haggar, James, he may be next door helping Joseph," Webb called after him, and the other man nodded. The elder Webb turned back to Tallmadge with a rueful smile on his face. "Barnabas is my step-uncle. This is actually my step-father Silas Deane's house, but since the war started and my older brother Joseph is taking care of the family's affairs, there is no one to take care of Silas' affairs except for his brother."

"Your step-father is currently overseas...?" he trailed off, remembering the off-handed mention of Silas Deane and his mission overseas when he and Wadsworth had been in Philadelphia. Webb nodded.

"In Paris," the other man replied, "seeing if the French are amenable to the cause. It was Silas who initially brought me to Philadelphia and petitioned Congress to give me my commission and posting."

"Ah yes, I remember Mr. John Jay mentioning it when I

briefly met him in Philadelphia." Tallmadge nodded and saw something spark in Webb's eyes, a clear interest in what he had said.

"You are acquainted with John?"

"Of a sort," Tallmadge shook his head, "Mr. Jay seemed to be in the midst of helping an acquaintance while Congress had relocated to Baltimore last month. I dared not inquire into his affairs as he seemed tight-lipped about it."

Webb chuckled, sipping his wine, "John Jay is a man who does not trust easily. He is a good man for the cause, zealous and understands what needs to be done, very much like the general himself."

"I am very glad that Congress was able to see the wisdom of raising Continental soldiers instead of relying on militia," Tallmadge said. "Though I do not deny the militia's fervor for the cause, I believe with soldiers, it will be easier to maintain discipline and an army instead of relying on six-month bounties and that sort."

"Aye," Webb agreed. "It seems you have also seen what many others have seen. Though I do have to confess that there are those who have declared our independence a lost cause."

Tallmadge paused mid-sip and hastily swallowed the wine in his mouth as he wrinkled his brow. "You jest-"

"No," Webb shook his head, before he looked around for a brief moment and leaned closer. "Before the general crossed the Delaware to make his assault on Trenton, he dismissed General Gates from camp after he arrived with his men from the Hudson Highlands. Words were exchanged and Gates left camp without any of his aide-de-camps or lieutenants."

Tallmadge was surprised. He had heard rumors, but realized that what Webb had been saying was true and was not prefaced with any words because Webb had been present at the dismissal. "But Gates-"

"It is during the lowest and harshest of points when you find out who is truly dedicated to the cause." Webb looked solemn and Tallmadge nodded slowly.

"Aye," he agreed, the words reminding him of what he had told Enoch Hale back in October about Nathan's supposed last words or feelings. Truth be told, he did not want to listen to the rumors that William Hull had spread as it still hurt from time to time.

As if Webb could easily pick up on his thoughts, the other man suddenly spoke up, "I also wished to express my sorrow for your loss, Benjamin."

"Pardon?" Tallmadge looked up, confused.

"I had wished to seek you out for some time now, but circumstances prevented me from doing so until today." The colonel turned the glass of wine in his fingers. "When the general found out about Captain Hale's demise, I expressed that we should at least tell his family the circumstances surrounding his death so that they would not be ashamed. Circumstances and hearsay eventually prevented such a thing, but my cousin Charles told me of what you said to Captain Hale's brother Enoch when he visited."

"Nathan-er, Captain Hale died with honor," Tallmadge reiterated. "I would like to have think he died a soldier doing his duty, even if it was spying, because he was doing it for General Washington and for the cause."

"Aye, and it is an unfortunate truth that most do not understand, the need for such secrecy," Webb stated, and Tallmadge nodded cautiously.

He was surprised that the colonel had such views. He knew that while the cause for Independence was strong, many considered themselves gentlemen and thus did not sully their hands with such shadowy methods. Considering what Webb had said about Washington before, the colonel and general were of the same mindset. Tallmadge pursed his lips for a second as he thought on it. He supposed from the general's point of view, intelligence was needed and though military scouting was common, the ability to ascertain the movement of troops and potential foray was limited. It was why vedettes and patrols were set up. They were a form of honorable scouting of intelligence against enemy movements.

A thought occurred to him. "The French cannot openly war against the British, can they? It was why your step-father was sent to ascertain their intentions?" If such words were the truth, it certainly explained why Congress had decided to give high-ranking commissions to the Frenchmen who joined the cause –

and certainly explained Jean de Vernejout's posting as a captain even though he had no discernible background in military affairs.

His question caught Webb off guard and Tallmadge saw the other man stare at him for a moment before a faint smile appeared on his face. Tallmadge sipped his wine and nodded. He had been thinking of why Wadsworth had introduced him to John Jay and mentioned Jay as head of the Secret Committee of Correspondence, before mentioning Barnabas Deane in relation to it all. It made a little more sense now given Webb's lack of words.

Like Nathan, he suspected that Webb's step-father was overseas serving in some capacity of espionage on a diplomatic mission for Congress. He had sent a book of sorts back to Barnabas Deane, who was in charge of his affairs and Barnabas had given it to Wadsworth who had given it to John Jay. It meant that Jay's Secret Committee of Correspondence was gathering intelligence and more than likely providing it to Congress and possibly to General Washington if such threads were tied tightly together.

The fact that Webb had become reluctantly tight-lipped about it reminded him of Nathan's reluctance to talk about his mission for the general. In Tallmadge's mind, it confirmed that Webb was involved to some extent in espionage and intelligence gathering or at least was privy to parts of it through his connection as Washington's former aide-de-camp. It also made him appreciate the other man's condolences regarding Nathan even more.

"Samuel?" a feminine voice spoke up near them and they both turned to see the woman that had been on Webb's arm standing near them.

"Elizabeth, my apologies." Webb graciously held out his arm for the woman to take before gesturing towards her. "Benjamin, this is Elizabeth Bancker."

"Captain Benjamin Tallmadge of the 2nd Continental Light Dragoons, Miss, and your humble servant." He bowed to her and she nodded.

"Pleased to meet you," she said before she turned to Webb. "I'm sorry Samuel, but Jack-"

"Not again," Webb interrupted with a quiet sigh and Tallmadge wrinkled his brow, staring at the colonel. Webb turned and looked at him. "Benjamin, I hope you do not hold this over my younger brother as your lieutenant. He tends to celebrate in excess from time to time."

Tallmadge shook his head. "I will not. I believe that I thought I drunk Wethersfield dry when I received my lieutenant's commission."

"Good man," Webb patted him on the arm before bowing slightly to him. "Excuse me, Benjamin." With that, he left, headed back down stairs just as Tallmadge saw Wadsworth come up two other men trailing him.

"Sir," he nodded once to his friend.

"I suppose it is good timing too." Wadsworth glanced back as Webb and his guest disappeared from view down the stairs. He turned back and gestured to the two men. "Benjamin, let me introduce you to Barnabas Deane and my cousin Colonel Jeremiah Wadsworth of the Commissary Department, both of whom I believe you'll find to be excellent conversationalists as well as of help for your regiment's needs."

Tallmadge squared his shoulders, pushing all thoughts of espionage, Nathan, and the enlightening conversation he had just had with Webb out of his mind as he shook hands with the men. There would be time later to think on the words spoken.

INTERLUDE V

February 3ʳᵈ, 1777

"Would you like something to drink after your long trip Nathaniel?" Washington offered as he poured himself a thumb of whiskey.

"No thank you, I am fine," said the other man, who sat by the roaring fire in the Georgian-style house Washington had taken as his quarters for the winter in Morristown, New Jersey. He was a little heavyset, with fingers that looked like miniature sausages. Washington knew those fingers held a surprisingly delicate stroke of penmanship and articulation not thought possible. Spectacles were habitually perched on the man's nose, his curly hair untamed by the queue tied back. He wore plain clothing, and for all intents and purposes, looked like a traveling schoolteacher.

If the British only knew, but that would defeat the purpose of his visit and painstaking measures put into place for a man like Nathaniel Sackett to even succeed as a member of John Jay's Committee and First Commission for Detecting Conspiracies. Washington set the decanter down on the small tray and took a seat at a wide table with maps that had been cleared to the side for a meeting with some of his generals. Dinner had followed before Sackett had arrived at camp.

Washington had managed to talk to John Jay during the month that the army was stationed at White Plains, since it was the headquarters for the Committee, but nothing much had come of it. Jay had expressed his support in gathering intelligence from York Island, but he could tell that his friend had far more pressing matters on his mind – especially in regards to Philadelphia and the lands between that city and New York. Jay did not trust easily, constantly vetting and evaluating even his own agents for any signs of Tory sympathies. But with Nathaniel Sackett here, it gave Washington some hope that Jay had taken his words seriously.

While he was not so familiar with Sackett as a person, he was familiar with his body of work. Sackett had unusual methods for spycraft including some that Washington recognized as his own from his days in the Seven Years War. But it seemed that his previous methodologies had been expanded upon by Sackett. Sackett had worked with Jay in running agents in and out of hostile areas, including New York. He had seen limited success in the reports that came across his desk, but he hoped that with Sackett here, more could be done.

"Then I shall get right down to business Mr. Sackett." Washington set his own glass down after taking a small sip of whiskey. "I need eyes in New York to discern General Howe's intentions. Some of the men I have sent have not produced the results that I wish for."

"They were executed or imprisoned as spies," Sackett stated bluntly. Washington was taken aback at the man's words, not used to such bluntness. "I can try to procure spies and agents, but it will take some time."

"That is a luxury I must confess we may not be able to afford come the spring," he replied. He was already receiving disturbing reports on the procurement of supplies for the British, but could not verify them save for the occasional scrap of intelligence he got from Jay's limited network or from local merchants who were free with their information. "I have someone who has generously volunteered-"

"A soldier," Sackett scoffed and Washington frowned. He did not like to be interrupted and Sackett was already testing his patience with his bluntness. "Soldiers are too visible, too easily seen-" The man trailed off mid thought as a curious expression crossed his bespectacled features. "Unless there is a good cover story to go along with it. It may work, but I do not know if it will provide the necessary intelligence you require, General."

"Please describe your plan." Washington's ire died a little as he realized this was how the man thought: in bursts of words, chains of ideas, possible approaches.

"Your officer, what rank-"

"Major." Washington lifted a hand and saw Billy move from where he was near the door. "Billy, please fetch Major Clark from the drawing room."

"Yes sir." Billy hurried out of the room and returned a few minutes later with a polite knock on the door, before letting Major Clark in. Billy followed and closed the door behind him, resuming his post.

Sackett made a humming noise as he turned in his chair to study Clark. Major John Clark was a Pennsylvania man who commanded the 2nd Battalion of the Pennsylvania Flying Camp. He had been drawn onto General Greene's staff on detached duty and used as an advance scout from time to time. Greene had recognized his intuitive abilities to ferret out information or come to accurate conclusions and had personally recommended him after dinner inquiry a few nights ago. Clark was tall, with fair skin and light brown hair and light eyes.

"Sir," Clark saluted and Sackett made a harrumphing noise before turning back to face Washington.

He waved the Major to ease. "Your assessment?"

"It will be hard, but he will need a plausible cover." Sackett frowned as he tented his thick fingers together. "He acts too rigid, too precise, so we will have to discard all manner of civilian covers for him."

"It is the time for re-supplying," Washington murmured mostly to himself as he thought on the idea of covers for Major Clark. He was used to fielding double agents, but providing cover for Major Clark that was not simply pretending that he was a Tory loyalist instead of a Patriot soldier was new to him.

Sackett clapped his hands together. "We will use that. But he cannot slip directly into New York itself. We will have to go either from New Jersey's coast or perhaps through Connecticut or Rhode Island in order not to attract suspicion."

"Sir, if I may?" Clark spoke up. Washington inclined his head for him to continue. "I believe that Connecticut would be the ideal place to insert into Long Island. Admiral Howe's fleet is still lying in wait between New Jersey and Long Island. We may be able to use one of the privateers or whaleboats to deliver myself to Sag Harbor or somewhere near there, and I will slowly make my way into the city itself to acquire intelligence. I can pose as a quartermaster or a part of the Commissary department looking to trade for goods on the London Trade or with Patriot farms."

"It is a good plan, but we need proof." Sackett pursed his lips and adjusted his spectacles. "Many an agent are caught with false proof or no proof at all."

Washington was reminded of Nathan Hale's failure. The man had been enthusiastic and Washington had been taken in by his charm and willingness to do whatever it took for the cause. But Hale's death had been a harsh lesson on providing adequate cover for his agents, that would not be easily discerned by Tories or British soldiers. Sackett was right, they needed something to prove Clark was procuring supplies for the Continentals. Something that would have him scouring the whole of Long Island and even inquiring into York Island itself-

Horses.

The idea struck him so fast that he froze for a second and saw the others in the room react to his stillness. "Horses," he stated, and saw confusion ripple through both Sackett and Clark's features. He stood up and rounded to his desk where he rifled through several papers and reports. He found the two sheets that were addressed to him. One was from his friend Jeremiah Wadsworth who was in charge of Connecticut's Commissary, while the other was written by a young newly promoted Captain Benjamin Tallmadge.

Tallmadge had impressed him with his boldness in retrieving his horse on Long Island after they evacuated, his fearlessness in leading his men to cover the retrieval of a lone and sorely needed cannon when they retreated to Harlem Heights, and his accurate and composed report on the status of Chatterton Hill while he was covered in blood, soot, and powder, fresh from battle. He possessed a calm clarity that reminded Washington greatly of the eye of a fierce hurricane – coldly still, yet deadly when provoked. He had also received a favorable report from his former aide-de-camp Colonel Samuel B. Webb of Tallmadge's amenability towards future intelligence sources.

"I have here a letter from Colonel Jeremiah Wadsworth of Connecticut's Commissary and one from Captain Benjamin Tallmadge of the 2nd Continental Light Dragoons. Both have expressed a concern for lack of horses needed for our dragoon regiments and request that liberties be taken with the requirements. I will be writing a letter back to Captain Tallmadge allowing the procurement of horses not to the color that I had initially requested, but I require you Mr. Sackett, and you Major Clark, to go to Tallmadge personally and recruit him for your mission. He will provide you with the cover required. Is this to your satisfaction Mr. Sackett?" He looked at the other man who nodded solemnly.

"Of course," Sackett tented his fingers again, "there is also the other matter..."

Washington nodded as he saw Major Clark salute, sensing that he was neither wanted nor needed for this part of the discussion.

"If it will please you, sir, I wish to take my leave to prepare to leave camp tomorrow," Clark asked, and Washington dismissed him with a nod. Clark left the room, the door closing quietly behind him by Billy's hand.

"I am willing to part with a stipend of fifty dollars a month," he started, "for your care and trouble in this business. You will have an operational fund of four-hundred-"

"Six-hundred, sir," Sackett shook his head.

"Five-hundred," he frowned a little, and saw Sackett tilt his head in agreement.

"Five-hundred dollars."

Congress would not be pleased, but Washington knew he could cover some of the funds from his own coffers. They had already given him nearly unlimited authority for the next six months in order to build an army ready to fight the British. This would be part of the expense.

"Then we are in accord. Thank you, General." Sackett

extended a hand and Washington shook it. Clark would be the first of many agents he hoped Sackett would procure to feed back intelligence before spring came and the campaign resumed.

7

"Sir," Davenport's voice preceded the knock on the door to his office at regimental headquarters. "There is a civilian here requesting to meet with you."

Tallmadge pulled himself away from the letter he had received from General Washington stating that he was allowed to allocate horses of the grey variety, but which still forbade white. It was a compromise, but one that was sorely welcomed. He had dispatched Adamson and one of his newer sergeants to forage for grey horses on farms they had initially scoured. With Adamson out on his current duties, he had drafted Davenport to serve as his runner today. He had been surprised when Davenport asked to be demoted to sergeant instead of taking the lateral posting of cornet from ensign, and his friend had declined to tell him the reason. Lieutenant Webb had been placed in charge of the day's drills, helping the men that had been placed in 1st Troop learn how to shoot and fire from horseback with the horses they currently had.

It had been relatively quiet that morning and Tallmadge had been enjoying some personal time with letters he had received from his father as well as other correspondents more feminine in nature. He must have made an impression on Colonel Wadsworth as he had been duly invited to a few parties and dinners. During some of the dinners, he had struck up light conversation with the women there and had corresponded with them. He had not made any overtures, keeping his tone conversational and light. But the letters were a balm to soothe the headaches he was starting to realize were a part of command.

He sighed, folding up the letter from Washington. "What is his name and purpose here?"

"He says he is a Mr. Nathaniel Sackett and he is here on business from Army Headquarters. He says that he has a letter of introduction from General Washington himself." Davenport sounded puzzled, confusion crinkling up his large features. Tallmadge raised an eyebrow.

"Send him in." If the man was truly from General Washington, he must be important. But the reason as to why Washington would send a civilian specifically to *him* was something Tallmadge could not guess. As far as he knew, he had only met Washington once – at the Battle of White Plains – and had written to him only once just weeks ago regarding the state of acquiring horses to his specifications. There had been a quiet sense of respect he had gotten from Washington's letter, but as far as he knew, he had not done anything of merit to be noticed in the general's eyes.

"Wait, Davenport," he called out before his friend peered in again. "Does Sheldon know of this meeting?"

Davenport looked away for a quick second before turning back to him. "Mr. Sackett says no."

"Oh." Now Tallmadge's curiosity was truly piqued. "Send him in, Davenport."

"Sir," Davenport knuckled his forehead as he opened the door wider and a slight heavy-set man stepped in. Tallmadge stood up and walked over as Davenport closed the door behind him. Sackett stood a head shorter than he was, but Tallmadge was immediately struck by the sharp eyes that gleamed behind the man's spectacles. Sackett took his tricorn off as Tallmadge extended a hand and shook his hand.

"Mr. Sackett, Captain Benjamin Tallmadge of the 2nd Continental Light Dragoons," he introduced himself.

"Nathaniel Sackett, formerly of the New York Secret Committee of Correspondences, now currently under the employ of General Washington," the other man replied. He pulled out a small letter that was still sealed and handed it to him.

Tallmadge managed to keep his surprise from showing as he took the letter and flipped it over to look at the seal. It was Washington's. And the fact that Sackett had mentioned he was a part of John Jay's organization, but now was under Washington's employ was telling. He broke the seal over the letter. It confirmed what Sackett had said, that he was under Washington's employ and was here specifically to see him without the knowledge of his commanding officers. It did not take long for Tallmadge to realize that Mr. Nathaniel Sackett was a spy of sorts.

A spy here specifically to see him.

He wondered if Sackett was perhaps part of the Diplomatic Corps or even an emissary, but a quick study of the man slowly pacing about his small office told him that he was used to wearing the simple, elegantly cut clothing he had on, not the luxurious cuts of other types of clothing. He had seen his fellow Frenchman Captain de Vernejout look decidedly uncomfortable in the dragoon uniforms and helms they had been issued. Even though the Frenchman had joined and served as a brevetted captain in the Continental Army after their evacuation from Harlem Heights, he had apparently had no such command and worn a French military uniform.

Tallmadge folded up the letter and handed it back to Sackett, then cleared his throat and stood with his hands clasped behind his back. "So, you are here on General Washington's orders?"

"For a mission that you will find of good use and of benefit for myself," Sackett replied, a pleased smile on his face. Tallmadge had the feeling he had passed a silent assessment, but did not know for what.

"You should have received a letter from the general indicating that the restrictions have been lifted regarding horses of a grey color. Since you still need mounts to outfit the rest of the 2nd Light, I believe you will find farmers along the Connecticut coast as well as the shores of Long Island who would welcome some form of coin to part with their animals," Sackett explained.

"And nothing else?" he asked, staring at the other man with

some suspicion.

Sackett spread his hands out and stared at him, wide-eyed. "Nothing else. That is it, Captain."

"Why Long Island?" he asked. "Surely there are farms across Massachusetts and in Connecticut that would suit our needs. My orders for obtaining horses were also restricted to New England mounts. Long Island, last I heard, was not part of the so-called New England states."

A brief grimace flitted across Sackett's features as his fingers delicately plucked an invisible mote of dust from his tricorn in a fit of nervousness. Tallmadge knew he had either anticipated something the other man had not, or had discerned an intention that Sackett did not wanted to reveal at this juncture. Whatever it was, Tallmadge was a little pleased.

"We require you to work with Major John Clark who is awaiting our arrival in Fairfield." Sackett finally stopped pacing and stood, hands clasped in front of him. "Major Clark has volunteered his services to seek out enemy intelligence and obtain it by any measure. Unfortunately, since he is of military posture and bearing, I cannot do my good work in changing him to a civilian identity. He will need a plausible cover-"

"And you mean to use my orders as that," Tallmadge interrupted.

"Yes," the other man replied. "It is the best we can do under these circumstances for now. Should you wish to accompany Major Clark across the Sound, you would have the legitimate excuse to purchase horses and accouterments to outfit the 2nd Light-"

"While Major Clark ascertains the necessary intelligence of the British forces," Tallmadge finished for him.

"Aye," Sackett replied.

"How will Major Clark depart?" he asked, keeping his voice neutral. He had heard rumors of the cover Nathan was given for his ill-fated mission. Clark's sounded far better. But Tallmadge still needed to know how Clark would avoid detection while in enemy territory. "Will I be required to accompany him the whole time?"

"No, no," Sackett shook his head. "He will maintain himself as perhaps a part of your regiment on special detachment-"

"Allowing us to part ways if necessary," Tallmadge murmured. Sackett nodded his assessment. He pursed his lips and looked away, contemplating what had been said. It was a solid plan, with little risk to himself since he did have legitimacy in his orders for furnishing horses and saddlery to his regiment, even if he was captured or discovered by British or Tory forces on Long Island. The risk was far greater for Major Clark. If Colonel Sheldon was not to be notified of this mission per Washington's letter, then Clark would have no ground to stand upon if his deception was discovered. Tallmadge could only do so much as a captain, especially given his junior rank to Clark.

He knew that questioning orders was ill-advised, but Sackett was clearly civilian and thus not his superior. However, as he glanced at the man he could sense that asking such a question would be a mistake. It was very much like words veiled in shadow and secrecy that Webb had alluded to along with words uttered between John Jay and General Wadsworth back in Philadelphia. If Colonel Sheldon was not to be notified, the reasons for that were known only to General Washington and Tallmadge would keep that confidence. If Major Clark was caught, he would do his best, but he was certain that the major was probably aware of his precarious position and would act accordingly.

"When is the major expecting us?" he asked and saw something flit across Sackett's eyes before he reached into the folds of his jacket and pulled out another small letter, this also with Washington's seal.

"In three days' time if possible," Sackett said. "This is a letter you may give to Colonel Sheldon informing him of a special assignment you have been detached to perform."

"Does it say anything else?"

"I thought it best to leave it up to your discretion," Sackett smiled faintly.

As Tallmadge took the letter and put it into his jacket pocket, he started to work on the reason why he would be performing this special assignment. A thought occurred to him, "Mr. Sackett, in order to best serve Major Clark's needs, I will have to ask one of my men to accompany me if possible."

The faint smile immediately disappeared from Sackett's face

as he paused for a moment. "Do you have one of your officers in mind that can be discreet?"

"Yes." Tallmadge knew exactly who he wanted. "He has already been performing such duties and is due back later tonight. I will tell him what he needs to know and nothing more."

"Good," Sackett nodded solemnly, and placed his tricorn back on his head. He extended his hand again and Tallmadge shook it. "It was a pleasure meeting you Captain Tallmadge. I look forward to seeing you in Fairfield in three days' time at Whitehall's Tavern."

"Three days' time then," Tallmadge replied.

Lieutenant Webb was not too happy to be left in charge of 1st Troop for the next three weeks as Tallmadge prepared to depart camp. Tallmadge had given Sheldon the letter from Washington authorizing him to be detached on special assignment and his commanding officer had surprisingly accepted it with some amount of grace. Sheldon had also accepted his explanation of finding more horses for the 2nd Light without any comment.

That had left him to inform Lieutenant Webb to continue his current efforts in getting the men trained and proficient with their weaponry and caring of horses. He made Davenport and Lieutenant Belden, who served under Major Blackden's Troop, as Webb's support since Belden was familiar with training soldiers due to his experience in Bradley's battalion last year. Webb and Belden were familiar with each other, both from Wethersfield, and apparently an officer's commission had brought them into the same social circles. The two had also become friends with Captain de Vernejout's Lieutenant Thomas Y. Seymour and the three had been seen around the regiment, executing their duties together.

Still he could understand Webb's reluctance to be left in command, when he had little to no experience. He had tried to reassured the younger man and Webb had blushed and grumbled something that Tallmadge could not discern before accepting the fact that he was to be left in charge.

"I cannot decide which one smells worse, Fairfield or New

Haven," Adamson commented over the sounds of the horses' feet on the muddy road. He wrinkled his nose at the stale stench of brackish water and decaying fish that hung in the air.

"Are you going to include Stratford in that assessment?" Tallmadge asked. He could not deny that the smell of seawater mixed with fresh water was noticeable even in the dead of winter. It did not help that it also smelled with the foulness of feces and rotting things left in the piles of snow on the side of the roads.

He had specifically chosen Andrew Adamson due to his former student's unassuming quiet mannerisms. Adamson was not prone to loud outbursts or heated arguments unlike Davenport. He was also able to follow orders without question, something that Pullings had been reprimanded for a few times while they had all served in the 6th Battalion 3rd Troop. That said, Tallmadge sometimes wondered if Adamson's lack of boldness was what made him pass beneath the notice of their superiors, thus reducing his chance for promotion. Tallmadge would have liked to have seen some kind of boldness in the young man, but settled for the fact that at this juncture, Adamson would surely keep their mission a secret.

"Aye, if it pleases you," Adamson smiled, "may I amend my previous statement to include all of Connecticut's coastline from New Haven all the way down to Stamford?"

"In the legitimacy of the fact that they have an unusual sense of odor about them," Tallmadge replied, and saw his friend nod before he laughed a little. "Something to drink to then." He pulled his horse to a halt and dismounted. It was a dapple-grey mount purchased from one of the farms that Colonel Wadsworth had some investitures. He had traded the bay horse he had stolen from the Hessians for this dapple-grey, the owner finding the bay of far more interesting color and stock. It had been a fair trade, and while he was sad to see his bay horse leave his service, the animal had been hard to control.

His new mount had a far calmer manner that reminded him greatly of Shadow. He had named the horse Castor after the Greek myth of Castor and Pollux – Castor being the horsemaster, Pollux the boxer. Tallmadge thought it appropriate considering if Nathan had lived and joined the 2nd Light, his friend would have more than likely named his horse Pollux. Nathan was always more athletic than him while they were at Yale. He had Castor outfitted with black straps and black bear-skin holster-covers. The small number of horses his Troop had acquired were also covered in such accouterments and the men were appreciative of such splendor. Tallmadge could see that they were drawing appreciative gazes from civilians as well as from fellow Continentals and militiamen stationed in the town.

Fairfield was home to a mix of Loyalist and Patriot forces, but it was also known as a hub along the Long Island coastline where privateers of both British and American boats patrolled. Currently the town was home to the Patriot whaleboats, and he could see some of them docked or being outfitted in the distant marshlands. Whether Fairfield would become a Tory hub in six months was unknown. It was a fate that had befallen both Stamford and Norwalk, which were closer to New York and the contested lands of the Westchester area.

He knew that the Patriot forces held points from Dobb's Ferry northward along the Hudson, while the British had taken the lower Hudson strongholds of Forts Lee and Washington back in October. That left the area outside of York Island, the start of White Plains and Westchester in and around the Bronx River as heavily contested lands. There were already general orders calling for patrols, in response to the increase in both Tory "cowboys" and Patriot "skinners" roaming the area. But the towns at the southern tip of Connecticut belonged to Tory privateers and raiders while Patriot forces currently held Fairfield as the edge of their stronghold. It extended eastward, up the coast past New London, but avoided part of the British fleet stationed in Newport, Rhode Island.

"I don't know if I wish to drink to the smells of brackish water, sir." He turned to see Adamson a little green in the face at such a prospect and laughed lightly. "Might be drinking brackish water itself."

"There is truth in those words." Tallmadge tied his horse to the post as Adamson did the same. He secured the single pistol and carbine on either side of his horse, along with a spare sabre. Washington's orders had been specific regarding the armed state of the dragoons, totaling three sorts of firearms and two sabres for officers, while enlisted men received three firearms; but unlike two officer's pistols, they had three carbines. Carbines were shorted-styled muskets, easier to wear on horseback than the full length musket. The other two carbines were holstered on either side of the horse's saddle. Adamson bore such armaments, but with the nearly identical outfitting, one could not easily tell which horse was an officer's and which was an enlisted man's without seeing the riders' uniforms.

After checking to make sure his own weaponry was secure, including the hidden dagger he kept inside his boot, he secured his helm against the saddle horn of his horse and headed into the tavern. The familiar roar of cheerfulness and general rowdiness in the tavern made an unbidden smile appear on his face as he moved among patrons who were exiting, entering, or going from table to table.

"Well, if I live and die, look at the Tall-boy!" He turned at the sound of a boisterous voice he had not heard in a very long time, and saw the last person he had ever expected to see in Fairfield.

He had a full woolly beard that was clearly dashed with the white of salt. A slick longcoat of dark oilskin covered him from head to toe, and he wore a longboat man's hat with a wide brim that looked like it had been waterproofed, judging by the beads dotting the brim. Tallmadge's smile grew wide as he reached out to embrace his childhood friend, the pungent odor of whale oil and salty-sea not withstanding.

"Caleb Brewster, you old sea-faring salt!" Though Brewster was seven years older than he, Tallmadge had fond memories growing up with his rambunctious friend who sometimes got the two of them into trouble.

"Benji Tall-boy Tallmadge!" Brewster pounded him hard on the back and Tallmadge nearly choked at how powerful the man's blows were. He pulled back and shook his head.

"Whaling seems to have treated you right," he commented, and Brewster laughed.

"Felt that one didn't ya?" Brewster had a cheeky smile on his face as if he had done what he had done with deliberate intent. "And look at you, all done up in blue and gold here?"

"Continental Army, 2nd Continental Light Dragoons," Tallmadge said proudly and Brewster smiled, his yellowing crooked teeth splitting his bushy beard.

"Captain too," Brewster flicked a casual salute to him. "Sir."

"What about you?"

"1st lieutenant, Continental Artillery under Colonel John Lamb, though I'm on detached duty right now." Brewster shrugged as if it was nothing of consequence. "Got myself a privateering license from the New York Assembly to you know, help our boys out here in the Sound."

"The artillery explains your arms," Tallmadge commented and saw Brewster grin.

"You think? The ladies sure love it," Brewster laughed, patting him on the back. "Come on, let me introduce you to some of my friends-"

"I'm actually here looking for someone-"

"Come on Tall-boy, just meet them. You'll like 'em." He felt himself prodded along by Brewster and sighed. He followed the man past a couple of tables before he saw a table where the familiar face of Mr. Sackett sat along with another dressed in the blue-white of Continental infantry. Tallmadge noted the three-clover epaulette of major on the man's shoulders and realized that the man sitting next to Sackett was probably Major Clark. He glanced at Brewster, mildly surprised that the whaler knew of Sackett and Clark. But Brewster did not respond to his look and instead guided him to the empty chairs.

"Mr. Sackett, Major Clark, sir," he nodded his head at Clark who took the aborted salute for what it was in such a casual setting before sitting down with Adamson taking the seat next to him. Brewster smiled ruefully as he took fifth seat and propped his feet up onto the empty sixth chair at the table. "This is Sergeant-Major Andrew Adamson, his discretion can be counted on."

"Sir," Adamson aped his nod at Sackett and Major Clark.

"You're just a kid, aren'tcha?" Brewster stared shrewdly at Adamson and Tallmadge could see his friend bristle a little.

"I was born with a musket pointed at the British," Adamson shot back, and Brewster laughed, long and loud as he slapped his thighs.

"I like him, Tall-boy. Can I keep him?" Brewster asked. Tallmadge rolled his eyes.

"No." He could see Adamson was a little offended at Brewster's comment, but had let it slide. Whether it was out of respect for his status as an officer, or perhaps because Major Clark was sitting directly in front of him across the table, he did not know. But he was inwardly proud of Adamson for keeping to himself and proving to the other two at the table that he was able to be discreet.

Sackett cleared his throat. "Now even though you have just arrived, I myself, must leave as I have other matters to attend to elsewhere. I will leave the details of your operation to yourselves, but please do inform me on matters of great import." He slid a small piece of paper towards the middle of the table. "This is where I will be staying for the next couple of months."

"Mr. Sackett?" Tallmadge was a little confused as Sackett stood up. As the man drained the rest of his ale, Tallmadge held up a finger to the tavern owner to order two for him and Adamson.

"My dear boy, you do not think that your operation here is the only one I am overseeing?" Sackett had a look on his face that greatly reminded Tallmadge of one of his teachers at Yale – when he had done something utterly stupid or asked the wrong question.

"Sir, I have three weeks for this..." He dared not speak the word "mission" as the noise suddenly dropped with several of the rowdier patrons leaving the tavern.

"Then I believe, Major, that is your time frame." Sackett glanced at Clark who nodded silently. Sackett glanced at all of them once before leaving as two more ales were delivered to the table.

Tallmadge drank a mouthful of his ale, the last few days of travel washed away by the bitter, good taste of alcohol. He could see Brewster playing with the lip of his cup and Clark absently swirling the small amount he had left. He quickly studied the man, noting the tall, broad-shouldered frame and the grizzled look about him. Clark was several years older, with puckering fair skin along his neck and the telltale sign of flash powder from musket fire on his light eyebrows and hair.

"So, what's the plan?" Brewster asked. Tallmadge set his glass down.

"You said Archer's and Green's farm a few miles away have horses for sale?" The question was clearly directed at Brewster, but spoken in general to the table. Clark 's calm, unassuming voice belied his broad frame.

"I'll need to ascertain the quality of the horses," Tallmadge said, "and perhaps inquire as to counterparts on the Sound which may provide such necessary mounts."

It seemed his forward thinking pleased Clark as a faint smile appeared on the man's lips. Even Brewster looked impressed, but Tallmadge wasn't trying to prove his worth to Brewster – he was looking to prove himself to Major Clark. This was the man General Washington had specifically chosen to ascertain intelligence and who would more than likely be reporting his conduct, as well as that of those subordinate to him, to Washington if his mission was a success.

"Well, my men can row you across when you want," Brewster chimed in. "There are a few manifests that we're keeping an eye on though."

"Any with necessary goods?" Tallmadge was starting to realize that besides helping Major Clark with his intelligence, he could also acquire goods and needed accouterments for the 2nd Light.

"Depends on what you're looking for, Tall-boy," Brewster shrugged.

"Saddlery, bridle, the like," he said and Brewster frowned a little.

"Hard to do specifics, but I can inquire on the Trade if you want-"

"Please do," Tallmadge nodded.

"My boys and I'll swing by the drop area every three days or so, that okay Major?" Brewster asked, and Clark nodded.

"Why not light a signal fire?" Adamson asked, confused.

"Kind of hard to see with the Sound kicking up this much in the winter and if a squall rolls through, like it always does, you ain't seeing shite, kid," Brewster shook his head. "Makes for great whaling and shanties though."

"Who's the garrison or militia commander down here?" Tallmadge asked Clark.

"Brigadier General Gold Selleck Silliman," the other man

replied and Tallmadge smiled a little.

"You know Silliman?" Brewster had caught his smile.

"We served together under General Wadsworth's Brigade," he said, and saw Brewster shake his head.

"You leave little sleepy Setauket and here I find you moving up on the world, Tall-boy," Brewster joked. He drained the rest of his ale and stood up, stretching widely. "Well gents, it's been nice. I'll see you in two days' time!" With that, Brewster patted him on the shoulder and walked out, flipping a few coins to the tavern owner for his drink.

"Sir, if I may," Tallmadge asked, as the noise of the tavern engulfed them again. "You know of Brewster?"

"We received a favorable report regarding Brewster's abilities. Seems that in November, he crossed the Sound with a party of Long Island refugees and Connecticut rebels to some town called Setauket. They ambushed a party of British soldiers, killing a few and taking some prisoner. Offered a trade for those on British prison ships, but managed to raid and get more prisoners while avoiding the British patrols." Clark shrugged, and Tallmadge was starting to recognize that the other man was not prone to grand gestures or statements that spoke of his approval or otherwise. His shrugs were akin to praise. For such a tall and broad-shouldered man, it was utterly baffling yet impressive to Tallmadge how unassuming he was even wearing his Continental uniform.

"That sounds like Caleb." Tallmadge shook his head in wonderment.

"And yourself?"

"Oh," Tallmadge took a sip of his ale, "Brewster and I grew up together."

Clark had a faint smile on his face as he finished his ale and stood up. Tallmadge did too, even though he was not finished as did Adamson who had stayed quiet as a mouse since Brewster left. He tipped his forehead as Clark nodded in response to his casual salute and left them. Tallmadge watched as the taller man weaved his way through the crowded tavern with the ease of someone practiced at moving through thicker crowds, perhaps even the battlefield. As soon as Clark was gone, he sat back down and took another sip, the soothing sour taste melting in his mouth.

"What now, sir?" Adamson asked.

"Introduce ourselves to General Silliman and head to the farms tomorrow," Tallmadge replied, as he played with the lip of his glass. He could feel the excitement building in him at what he was about to undertake.

February 25th, 1777

The trip to Archer's and Green's farms held far more success than Tallmadge had initially expected. He thought he would receive perhaps one or two horses, but he received a total of seven horses from both farms that would be delivered to the regiment up at Wethersfield by way of New Haven and barge. He had also learned what Major Clark's cover was as the major silently observed him interacting with the owner of Archer's farms with Adamson beside him. When they had approached Green's farms, the major requested that he try his hand and Tallmadge allowed it, Adamson providing the necessary help and articulation of requests for the 2nd Light. Clark had proven himself a quick study and by the end of the day Tallmadge suggested that Adamson accompany Clark across the Sound. They had also learned of several farms in the vicinity on Long Island where horses may be sold.

At night, in the tavern, Clark had quietly proposed that while he would make the initial introductions at the farms and initial inspections, it should be Adamson who would be doing a majority of the negotiations so the risk to Clark would be minimal. Adamson would then contact Brewster on the three-day check up with any intelligence that needed to be delivered across the Sound and Tallmadge would be there to give it to Sackett.

Tallmadge had agreed with the initial plan, but pointed out that the farther inland Clark went, the longer it would take to give intelligence back to Adamson. He proposed that he himself would make regular trips after the initial intelligence drop to ensure that whatever cover Clark had come up with would be bolstered by his presence. Clark had readily agreed with another faint smile before they finished their evening meals and retired for the night.

The next day as much as Tallmadge wanted to see the three off, he knew that discretion was the better part of valor and instead he busied himself with riding to the Stratfield area of Stratford. He had heard from Archer's farm that the family farms of Daniels and James both had horses they would consider parting with.

Three days later, Adamson passed on a small scrap of intelligence to Brewster who then gave it to him. Tallmadge left it sealed within a letter to the inn where Sackett was staying. Another three days after, there was no intelligence, but Brewster reported that Adamson reported that the local population was worried about British troop movements from Sag Harbor, a port town where the tip of Long Island jutted to meet the Atlantic.

Another three days had passed. It was the middle of the second week when Tallmadge found himself crossing the Sound in Brewster's whaleboat, ostensibly to provide the extra cover that both Adamson and Clark likely needed. He pulled his cloak closer to his body, shying away from the harsh winds that blew across the boat itself.

"Where did you drop them?" Tallmadge asked after the wind had died down a little. The familiar coastline of his childhood drew closer with each stroke from the rest of Brewster's crew. The whaler manned the till.

"Just west of Setauket. Even though the boats in Sag Harbor are at the south fin, can't be too careful," Brewster replied. "You've been home yet?"

"Before we evacuated Long Island last year," he replied, looking towards the left of the approaching coastline. The wind was good and strong today, pushing their fast clip. Though the waters were a bit choppy after a brief squall had blown through two days prior, Brewster had declared it safe to sail even with the ice floes in the Sound.

"How is old man Reverend Tallmadge? Settled in New Haven?" Brewster asked, making a small adjustment on the rudder of the whaleboat. Tallmadge glanced at his friend, who smiled and shrugged. "I helped him evacuate along with some of my own family members after New York you know."

"He's fine." Tallmadge nodded his thanks, and Brewster only

grinned in reply. "Settled I think. You heard about William?"

"Aye," the whaleman shook his head. "Damn shame Ben. Sorry about your loss."

"Thank you. How is your family?"

"They're safe. Got family elsewhere. Can't show my face back at home, suppose you can't show yours either, so I guess we're both stuck on the other side of the Sound until the war's over."

"Or we're both shot."

Brewster pursed his lips, a rueful smile appearing on his lips. "Or hung." His smile was a touch wicked and Tallmadge laughed lightly, finding bleak humor in his words.

"We're in uniform-"

"You're in uniform-"

"Privateering uniform," he pointed out, and Brewster acknowledged the distinction with an agreeable nod.

"Privateering uniform," he said.

"We're accorded the duties of our stations."

"I suppose you're right, Tall-boy." Brewster stood up, his hands gripping the rudder as they approached the marshy coastline. He began to steer hard towards the landing spot on a rocky outcropping that looked like it had been eroded by the recent storms. "I think Nancy's moved back into the manor she sold to the Smiths. Saw the clothesline look a mite different in recent weeks. More petticoats than men's clothing," Brewster commented absently. "Didn't realize that with her husband and all..."

"My father said that Selah's family helped him when they landed in New Haven." Tallmadge supposed that a woman would not be overlooked for her husband's Whiggish ideals. Still, it was nice to know that not all the Patriot-leaning families had been driven out of Setauket.

The boat ran aground a few minutes later and Tallmadge hopped out, helping the small crew of whalers pull it securely ashore. Brewster and his crew would stay the night to rest before heading out before dawn's light.

"Kidlet should be behind the two pine trees over that ridge," his friend pointed out. He stared at the whaler, wondering what Brewster meant by calling Adamson by that nickname.

"Kid-let?"

"He's a kid," Brewster protested, but not with heat. Tallmadge shook his head. "Good kid too. Was going to call him young pup, but I think he probably would have plotted my demise on our first crossing. The major laughed his head off when I suggested it to him."

"Major Clark?" Somehow Tallmadge could not imagine the cool and confident major laughing as Brewster had just described.

"Not exactly what you might think of laughing loudly, Ben. More like...this..." Brewster adopted his best impression of Clark laughing, which consisted of him giving a small smile and shaking his head.

He shook his own head. "Caleb, I think you've been burning whale oil for far too long."

"I saw mermaids," Brewster countered and Tallmadge had to laugh. "No it's true, mermaids! They were so pretty and their bosoms so full that one could use them as pillows-"

"I'll see you in three days Brewster." He waved his goodbye over Brewster's lively and somewhat vulgar description of 'mermaids'. Brewster continued his digression, this time to the rest of his crew. As he walked toward the meeting spot Adamson had designed, he could hear the soft sounds of singing from the rest of the whaling crew as they started up a sea shanty.

The noise faded as he crested the sloping ridge and found the two pine trees that Brewster had talked about. He approached them, watching the area cautiously.

"Sir," Adamson's quiet voice spoke from behind one of the trees and he stepped out, a smile on his face. The young non-commissioned officer huddled in his cloak, shivering a little.

"Adamson," Tallmadge greeted.

"I did find a couple of farmers who were willing to sell horses, but a few miles to the west of here, towards York Island, is Fort Slongo." Adamson grimaced as he handed over a half a piece of parchment. "Major Clark scouted it a few days ago, but said he was going to bypass it since he had already taken the numbers there and move farther west."

"What's the strength of the Fort?" He did not remember receiving any numbers or indications about Slongo in the last missive sent by Adamson.

"That's the thing, Major Clark didn't give me the numbers the last we met, about five days ago." Adamson looked a little confused. "He just told me to tell Brewster about Sag Harbor movements."

Tallmadge frowned a little, wondering why the numbers would not be reported. He supposed that Clark either wanted to get confirmation of the numbers, or perhaps he suspected Slongo was unoccupied. He put the thought away as he focused again on Adamson. "Where are you staying in the mean time?"

"A tavern-inn just a few miles away. Some of the local farmers have been giving me rides to the nearby farms." Adamson gestured for him to follow.

They walked a short distance to where a farmer was waiting with his horse-drawn cart and a bale of newly brought hay. Tallmadge saw Adamson wave to the farmer who waved back, but as he got closer, Tallmadge was brought up short as to who was waving at them. He could see recognition bloom across the other man's face as his eyes grew wide with surprise.

"Ben? Benjamin Tallmadge?!" The man had a slight rasp in his voice, but there was no denying the familiar sounds of another childhood friend who sat holding the reins to the horse-drawn cart.

"Abraham Woodhull." Tallmadge started walking again and met Woodhull's outstretched hand with his own. "Good to see you."

"And you as well, though...I don't think you should be here, Tallmadge." Woodhull was several years older and while they had been cordial and friendly with each other, Tallmadge had found Woodhull to be pessimistic. Woodhull was a quiet sort who loved living the bachelor life. Still, between him and Brewster, he had received a healthy education outside his father's teachings of the word of God.

"Still as sour as ever." Tallmadge released Woodhull's hand and rounded the back of the cart, climbing aboard. Adamson settled himself on one side of the bale of hay while Tallmadge did the same.

"No, I don't think you should be here Tallmadge. Town's becoming a lot more Tory since your father left." Woodhull clicked his tongue and slapped the reins and they started off.

"So why help Adamson here?" Tallmadge asked.

"He paid in coin and there's nothing to be said about helping someone out with supplying soldiers." Woodhull sounded indifferent.

"My sergeant-major here sent back numbers and I want to make sure we're getting a fair price." Tallmadge could not sense if Woodhull suspected anything, but it seemed like Adamson had kept to his cover, along with Major Clark. The fact that Woodhull did not mention Major Clark was telling – which meant that Clark was elsewhere, more than likely pushing farther west and allowing Adamson to continue his work here in finding horses for the regiment.

"The Johnson farm has a few I think, maybe even the Hunters," Woodhull supplied.

Adamson pulled out two folded parchments from his jacket and glanced through them. "Two from Johnson, both bays. They're in fair condition though perhaps it was me that spooked one of them. I am not too sure. Hunters I was going to check, but the squall that rolled through prevented me from doing a proper inspection."

"Hunters farm if I remember correctly is about a mile that way?" He pointed vaguely in the southerly direction.

"You want me to drop you off there?"

"How much extra?" Adamson asked and Woodhull glanced back, a mirthless smile on his narrow face.

"Since Tallmadge is an unexpected ride here, it'll be free this time. If you want me to wait for the return trip though-"

"We'll manage." Adamson looked dour at the prospect and Tallmadge glanced between his two friends.

"Where were we going originally?" he asked.

"Roe's tavern-inn," Woodhull replied.

"I could use a warm meal," Tallmadge countered and saw Woodhull sigh and nod. "It's cold, Woodhull."

"You want to head to Hunters later, don't find me." His former neighbor seemed a bit annoyed and he wondered if he had done something to warrant the chilly reception he was getting.

"Adamson?" He sat back and glanced at his sergeant-major

who had a flat look on his face.

"Woodhull's right, sir," Adamson whispered, his voice barely carrying above the sound of horse and cart running along muddied roads. "Tory presence has increased significantly since Clark and I were here. Might account for ship movements at Sag Harbor and maybe troops being billeted from York Island to here."

"Is there any perceived immediate danger?"

"Not that I can see, but I try not to get in the townsfolk's way when I stay at Roe's. There were one or two that looked like Continentals passed through last week, but no others except for me since then," Adamson replied.

"Their names?"

"Didn't catch them sir," Adamson shook his head. "Though they didn't seem too friendly either. Kept to themselves. I don't know what regiment, but they looked like they were infantry. One of them was missing his powder horn though."

Tallmadge absently nodded and filed the information away in the back of his mind as they rode the rest of the journey to Roe's tavern and inn in silence. They soon arrived and Woodhull promptly dropped them off before leaving without even a goodbye. He watched the narrow-faced man disappear around a bend of the road. The reception he had gotten from his former neighbor was odd, almost hostile. Surely Woodhull wasn't a Tory, was he? He had always assumed Abraham was a staunch Patriot, though he had refused to join the local militia or even serve under his cousin General Nathaniel Woodhull's regiment.

Putting that thought aside, he headed into the tavern-inn and nodded a greeting to the owner, Austin Roe, who seemed surprised to see him. He and Adamson took their cloaks off and draped them across two empty chairs at a table. Apparently Adamson had made a favorable impression on Roe during his stay as the man promptly brought two glasses of ale.

"What will it be for tonight, gentlemen?" Roe had a fashionable queue, and unlike Brewster whose unruly hair seemed out of place amidst the clean-shaven fashion of the day, he kept his beard neatly trimmed. It made him look like a cross between Brewster and himself if Tallmadge was inclined to compare. "Mr. Adamson, your usual?"

"If it pleases the missus," Adamson smiled and Roe laughed.

"It'll please her. If you aren't careful she'll adopt you as her own. I might find myself in need of a new wife after being cuckolded." The tavern-inn keeper chuckled and Tallmadge was reminded that Roe and Brewster were neighbors growing up. Both had the same ribald sense of humor.

"I would not dream of it, sir," Adamson blushed, and Tallmadge smiled a little at his friend's expense.

"Stew and two pieces of bread if you will," he asked, and Roe nodded.

"Right, Tallmadge. Though I fancy seeing you here." The older man looked at him curiously. "Your father did leave in a hurry after everything last year, you know."

"I know." Tallmadge had the sense that even Roe was not exactly happy that he was here. "Wintering supplies."

"Ah," was all the man said as he left their table.

Tallmadge turned back and cleared his throat, then he took a sip of the house ale. It tasted just like he remembered from his childhood. "So what did you find?"

"Here, sir," Adamson hastily pulled out the pieces of paper with crooked lines of numbers written on them. Tallmadge realized that Adamson must have used an ember from a fireplace to write down what he knew while wandering around the farms. There were more numbers, elegantly scrawled at the bottom, which were clearly written with ink. Tallmadge pulled the papers to look at them. He could see that there were a total of ten horses that Adamson had found, two of them bays from Johnson with a plus sign next to them, which meant the transaction was confirmed.

"They agreed to the payment of one hundred Continental dollars?" he asked.

"Yes. However sir, I was not able to give them the Continentals up front." Adamson looked sheepish and Tallmadge glanced up at him.

"Oh?"

"I think the farmers here might have taken advantage of my lack of bargaining knowledge." The younger man looked ashamed and Tallmadge raised an eyebrow.

"But you were with Sergeant Mills-"

"Mills handled a lot of the negotiations and I am ashamed to admit that a lot of them were based on Commissary promises and the like." Adamson frowned and Tallmadge resisted the urge to sigh in exasperation. It made perfect sense now, how he was suddenly able to get a lot of horses. Mills, having transferred from Wadsworth's Commissary, must have had inside knowledge and business transactions at the ready.

"You ran out of money," he stated, and saw his sergeant-major shrink a little in embarrassment.

"...Yes, sir..." He thought he heard his friend mumble just as the heavy thumps of Roe's footsteps made him look up.

The tavern-in keeper placed their food on the table, leaning in a little too close-

"Tallmadge, I really think you shouldn't be here. Neither should you, Andrew," Roe warned with a quiet hiss, before leaving as if nothing had happened.

"Sir?" Adamson asked as Tallmadge tentatively dug into the stew that had been provided. That was the second person to warn him that he should not be here and he looked around the tavern, but could not discern what prompted the warning.

"Sir, should we leave-"

"No," Tallmadge shook his head as he continued to eat. "If we leave now, it would draw further suspicion if anyone is aware of our presence."

"But sir-"

"Eat your stew, Adamson. We'll leave after we finish, but not before." He could feel eyes on them, but could not tell if they belonged to friend or foe. It was rumored that this was how Nathan had been captured, but Nathan had been talking with supposedly Patriot-leaning townsfolk, not sitting in a tavern with full Continental uniforms to bear. Still, Tallmadge could not shake the ghostly feeling of his friend's presence – as if Nathan was watching him this very moment; protecting him or warning him, he could not tell.

He glanced at the numbers again and sighed. They would have to leave immediately if Roe's warning was any indication which meant he could not purchase the horses that were on this list, even though they numbered at least ten. Ten possibly good mounts for the dragoons to use...and if they left with Brewster the next morning, there was not any way of getting in contact with Major Clark to warn him that they all were compromised.

The door to the tavern opening and the sounds of booted feet pulled Tallmadge from the notes. He caught a glimpse of Adamson's eyes widening in fright as he turned to see three British officers, one of them at least a colonel, walk in, pulling their gloves and hats off as they dusted the weather from their cloaks. A pit of worry and apprehension formed in Tallmadge's stomach at the sight. If the soldiers were just outside- He dared not think of possibly being captured like General Lee outside of Basking Ridge at White's Tavern.

"Good evening gentlemen, what can I do for you?" Roe was immediate and prompt.

"Good evening, I am Colonel Richard Hewlett of General Oliver Delancey's Tory Brigade and these are my staff-" the senior officer started to make introductions, gesturing and looking around before he spotted them.

Tallmadge put his spoon down and slowly stood up, the scrape of his chair on the wooden floor abnormally loud in the deathly silence that had befallen the tavern. A second scrape told him Adamson had done the same.

"I did not know your tavern accepted patronage from rebel-"

"I believe Mr. Roe was compelled, Colonel Hewlett," Tallmadge interrupted loudly, staring straight at the colonel who had a sallow face and beady eyes. He wore a typical fashionable white-wig under his tricorn hat and his lips were thin, making him look a little like a bullfrog.

"Compelled," Hewlett stated as he walked forward and Tallmadge unconsciously drew himself up, staring the senior British officer straight in the eye. He could see the two staff officers behind Hewlett place their hands near the holster of their pistols, but made no such overt movements of his own.

"Yes, sir." Tallmadge dared not look to see what Roe's expression was. He did not want to give any indication to the British officers that Roe may have Patriot ties. "Captain Benjamin Tallmadge at your service, sir."

"Captain Tallmadge, eh?" Hewlett glanced at his epaulette, disdain evident on his face as he looked him up and down.

"Of the 2nd Continental Light Dragoons, sir," Tallmadge

added with an edge to his tone. The reaction from Hewlett was subtle, but noticeable as the man took a small step back at his regiment's designation. Dragoons, especially British ones, were well-armed and had a deserved reputation for their formidable skills on horseback and when dismounted. It seemed that Hewlett had taken the British reputation and applied it to American ones.

But whatever small advantage he had gained by intimidating Hewlett was lost as the colonel mastered his brief moment of fear and stared at him. "And, pray tell, captain, what you and your sergeant-major are doing here?"

"Winter supplying," he offered, and picked up the pieces of paper with numbers and farms written all over them. "Mr. Roe was...kind enough, after some manner of persuasion, to provide us with food and shelter."

His words had the desired effect. Hewlett frowned heavily and glared at him. "You are no gentlemen to be conducting yourself in such a manner." The British officer seemed offended as he snatched the papers out of Tallmadge's hands and looked them over. "Hmph, it seems you speak true, *Captain.*" Tallmadge did not miss the sneer at his rank.

"If you will excuse me, we must be on our way-"

"No," Hewlett shook his head and the two officers behind him grabbed their pistols, but did not draw them. Tallmadge's eyes narrowed as he read the perceived threat. He wondered if there was a troop of soldiers waiting just outside, ready to burst in and arrest them.

"I do not think you will be foraging for winter supplies anymore on this part of the Long Island coast." Hewlett folded up the papers and pocketed them. "You are free to go, but you will forage for supplies on *your* side of the Sound. Long Island has returned to the King's fold and I will treat no rebel party here for provisions and raids against the Loyalists of this colony."

"Sir-"

Hewlett held up a hand, stopping one of his staff officers from speaking up. "Am I clear, Captain?"

"Perfectly," Tallmadge replied, his voice cold. He gestured with his chin towards the door. "May we be excused now?"

"Of course," Hewlett said with the politeness of a viper lying in wait. He stepped to the side and gestured mockingly for them to leave. Tallmadge grabbed his cloak and put it on, clasping it as Adamson scrambled behind him, the two of them heading out of the tavern without a backward glance.

As soon as they were outside, Tallmadge headed towards where he knew Brewster's ship was pulled ashore, his feet sinking a little in the muddied ground. The cold wind whipped at them again and dark inky night gave way to the shine of moonlight on the ground – giving them at least the semblance of light to find their way down the road.

"Sir-"

"We need to leave, now." He had no doubt that Hewlett did intend them to leave, but sensed he would only give them this once chance. Word would more than likely be sent to Fort Slongo to search for any other Patriots in the area, and if they lingered, they could be caught and held prisoner.

"Sir, what about the horses-"

"Damn those horses!" he cursed and Adamson fell silent. "And damn you for writing the farms down!"

"Sir-"

"Be quiet, Adamson," He did not want to voice his suspicion that those on the list would be targets of retaliation by Hewlett. But neither could he fault Adamson for only doing his duties. He only blamed himself for allowing such a thing to happen, especially behind enemy lines.

"Sir, are you sure it was wise to let them leave?"

"Alert Fort Slongo's garrison. I want the men and the garrison to sweep Setauket and surrounding areas for any other rebel soldiers that might be in the area. Also find the location of these farms. They have horses that may be useful for General Tryon or Delancey." Hewlett waved a hand of dismissal to his major who rushed away. He turned to the tavern-inn keeper and bowed his head.

"I am terribly sorry that you had to suffer the presence of such filth, good sir," he began, and saw him look a little relieved.

"I warned him to leave, but he would not," the tavern-inn keeper shook his head. "I am only grateful that you were able to make him leave without any sort of violence."

"You are perfectly welcomed, now, if I may-"

"Yes, please, tonight's meal is on the house, Colonel." The tavern-inn keeper gestured for him to take whatever seat he wished. "Thank you again."

"Sir, are we sure about these numbers?" His other staff member, a sharp-chinned man by the name of Captain John Graves Simcoe looked at him with suspicious eyes.

"It seems he did not discern anything about Tryon's affairs. He was truly just looking for horses. Take your troop tomorrow, burn the farms that have already promised him horses for credit, and take the horses to Slongo," Hewlett replied and the sharp-chinned man nodded.

"Yes, sir."

The odd hooting whistle clearly did not belong to any owl that Tallmadge had ever heard of. He looked beyond the two pine trees and saw several dark forms peering from it. "Ho, there!" he called out hoarsely.

"Tallmadge that you?!" Clark's voice was also hoarsely quiet.

"Major Clark!" He scrambled up the long sloping hill and stopped by the twin trees, catching his breath as Adamson wheezed behind him. It had been a long walk from Roe's tavern to where Brewster had landed and Tallmadge was sure that they had not been followed since the bright winter's moonlight had provided ample light for them to walk without getting lost.

"We thought you lost-"

"Almost, sir," Tallmadge shook hands with Clark, the man's cold palms sending a jolt of surprise through him. "Colonel Hewlett of Delancey's Brigade let us go without issue."

"Thank God." Clark seemed relieved and Tallmadge was surprised at how the tall man's body seemed to bow in relief, "I ran into heavy resistance at Fort Slongo and overheard that Hewlett was being sent to Setauket. I was looking for Adamson when they marched in. I thought Adamson to be here waiting to drop off the usual message, but just found Brewster here-"

"Hey Tall-boy, you didn't get yourself caught!" Brewster spoke up from where he was leaning against one of the trees.

"Caleb," Tallmadge greeted before turning back to Clark.

"We will not be able to continue the mission," Clark shook his head, and Tallmadge found himself frowning in disappointment.

"But sir-"

"It's too risky. I will have to convey my failure at the lack of intelligence gathered to the general himself, but there is one piece of news we can report back to him that is not a total failure."

"Sir?"

"Long Island has become a Tory stronghold." Clark looked grim.

INTERLUDE VI

March 4ᵗʰ, 1777

"Come in, Major." Washington gestured for Major Clark to enter the room at his headquarters in Morristown, New Jersey. He had not been expecting Clark to return so soon, and when Tilghman announced his presence, it put a halt to his day's reports. He gave some time for the major to gather himself and rest after his arrival at camp, and the officer did not disappoint.

"Thank you, sir," Clark said as Billy pulled the door closed, leaving them in the near silence of the house. There were occasional commands shouted outside that were muffled against the walls and windows of the room, but they were few and infrequent. Winter still had its cold grip on them and there was not much one could do without dampening the powder or properly march in the heavy wet snow that had fallen a few days prior. Spring was arriving though, small birds making their presence known since the last winter's storm had blown through. Soon the rivers would be swollen with snow melt and the roads turned to mud by the constant rain. But it would be warm enough for the men to properly start their drills and on dry days, the firing of muskets and artillery would signal the resounding horn to war.

But at this very moment, Washington was not concerned about such matters. Intelligence had no season, unlike warfare, but if he had to give it a season, it would be winter – cold, merciless, and seemingly unending. One slip, one wrong word, and a man could find himself in death's icy grip. "Drink?" he offered, gesturing to the decanters sitting to the side. With some pleasure, he saw the major shake his head, declining his offer. Clark was a good man, a loyal and staunch officer who declined any form of drink, unlike Honeyman or the other local agents in his direct employ. He knew that in any other circumstance, Clark would have accepted such a drink as was custom to his rank as a battlefield commander, but in this case, Clark knew exactly who and what he was at this very moment – not a military officer, but an intelligence agent. And one who clearly refused any vices that could affect the clarity to his words.

"I am the bearer of bad news, sir," Clark said, his voice grave. "Long Island is lost to us."

"Oh?" Washington watched as his major stood at ease, hands clasped behind him as he made his report. Washington rounded the war table in the corner of the room and shifted one of the papers that covered his main map of lower New England and the Atlantic states. Long Island seemingly stuck out like a sore thumb.

"The Tory presence had grown stronger since I arrived there and I was only able to move to Fort Slongo before being cut off by a force sent out by General Oliver Delancey." Clark sounded frustrated and he glanced up to see the major look to the side, disappointed by his perceived failure in obtaining any useful intelligence.

"Delancey's Tory Brigade is supposedly situated in Westchester, is he not?" Washington asked, half rhetorical as he studied the contested region. Putnam had his garrisons near there, but Putnam had not reported anything amiss. Oliver Delancey's Tory Brigade had quartered themselves in the lower portion of Westchester for the winter.

"Yes sir. I believe that this new regiment is drawn from the Loyalist citizenry of New York and those on Long Island," Clark replied. "According to Captain Tallmadge's observations, they are led by Colonel Richard Hewlett."

"Hewlett is known to me." Washington pressed his lips thinly together as he took one of the red tokens lying on the side of the map and dropped it in the middle of Long Island. He was already receiving reports regarding Sag Harbor and the small British fleet stationed there, used for raids along Long Island Sound and to assist the British fleet stationed at Newport and along the Jersey coastline. It was a fortified position to be in. "Were you able to discern any movements of sorts?"

"None, sir." Clark shook his head. "I believe that this force was put together to weed out any Patriot families who have not fled and to suppress any sort of uprising that might happen."

"Bad luck then," Washington concluded with a soft sigh. He curled a hand into a fist and touched it to the map. It was what it was, just bad luck and bad timing for Clark. Perhaps if he had sent him earlier- Washington pushed that thought out of his head. Trenton and Princeton had been his primary concerns and he knew back then he had to keep the army together and give them victory or else with the expiration of the enlistment papers, there would have been no army come spring. The fight for American independence would have died without a sustainable army.

"Sir," Clark said neutrally.

Silence reigned in the room as he contemplated his next move. Sackett would have already been informed of Clark's departure to camp and the failure in this particular mission. One consolation, he supposed, was that they now knew the status of Long Island. The other consoling fact was that Clark and, it seemed, Captain Tallmadge, had both escaped the Tory net cast over Long Island with their lives. He was determined not to repeat the mistake he had made with Captain Hale. Which led his thoughts to one man in particular.

"Your thoughts on Captain Tallmadge?" he asked, glancing up at his major.

"Eager, competent," Clark straightened a little as he made his formal report. "He had bright ideas and is able to think on is feet, sir. His discretion was greatly appreciated as was his caution."

"Caution?"

"Caution when needed, but he had bold plans, sir." There was a small smile on Clark's face and Washington knew it spoke volumes. Clark was not prone to smiling or even giving overt praise, himself reserved and almost detached from events.

"He was able to point out the officer in charge of the Tory militia that stormed across Long Island and occupied Setauket. The questioning of the non-commissioned officer that had helped us – who was also able to keep his discretion on such matters – told me that by all rights, Tallmadge should have been arrested, but managed to effect his escape with nary a shot fired."

Washington raised an eyebrow, surprised at the news. Bold indeed, much like the reports he had read from the young officer's previous commanders. He could only surmise that Tallmadge had received his letter, received the letter Sackett had carried upon him, utilized his orders, and expanded and interpreted in a way to help Major Clark as much as possible. But he also had the foresight to escape the enemy without any undue harm befalling himself. It was clever work indeed and it pleased Washington that one of his officers was so fearless and fast-thinking.

"Anything else to add, Major?"

"No, sir," Clark replied the smile still on his face.

"Good, then I have another assignment for you, if you will," he began as his eyes moved back down the map to Philadelphia.

"I am at your service, sir," Clark nodded sharply.

"General Howe has stopped his movements towards Philadelphia, but there is no denying the fact that he intends to take the city at some time. I would like you to establish a network of agents to discern both the populace's intentions as well as if and when Howe intends to capture it," he said, and saw Clark frown.

"Sir, Howe would be a madman to try to take Philadelphia-"

"He has already captured New York, Major," he chided his officer who had the sense to look ashamed at his words. "He will intend to capture Philadelphia whether it be this year or the next, or even the one after that. We can hope to stop him, but we need to be prepared in case he or perhaps even Burgoyne if Schuyler or Gates is not successful in containing him upstate, decides to march their forces down to our capital."

"Sir," Clark nodded tightly.

Washington looked towards the door. "Billy, summon Mr. Hamilton, please."

"Sir," Billy's muffled reply echoed through the door before

his footsteps faded away. They returned soon after, and Billy opened the door to let Washington's newest aide-de-camp in.

"Major," Washington gestured to the young Alexander Hamilton who stood at rigid attention. His fingers were dark with ink after writing reports and correspondences to Congress that Washington had assigned him this morning. "This is Lieutenant Colonel Alexander Hamilton, late of Major General Henry Knox's Artillery Corps. He is my newest aide-de-camp."

"Sir," Clark saluted Hamilton, who returned it with a nod.

"Mr. Hamilton, this is Major John Clark," he said and saw his young aide-de-camp stare curiously at Clark since he had introduced him without a regiment attached to his rank and name. Hamilton had proven himself a fine gentlemen who had surprisingly declined staff positions on Greene and Knox's command, preferring the battlefield and artillery. He and his Hearts of Oak division had served with distinction in New York, Trenton, and Princeton. Washington had also learned that Hamilton had a way with words that was unusually deft, and so had asked the young man to join his staff. For the last three days Hamilton had been observing him with a sharp eye. The young officer had proven his intense loyalty. He also knew exactly what Congress needed to hear in regards to both troop status and the lack of actionable intelligence and funds.

Now, he would not only be bringing Hamilton deeper into his staff, but entrusting him with intelligence that would be given to him without further elaboration. It was the same way Washington had brought Tilghman into his confidence, as well as Colonel Webb. In a way, it was a test not only for Hamilton, but test for Major Clark.

Washington would teach Hamilton the knowledge and skills he would use with Major Clark in establishing this line of intelligence from Philadelphia, but it would ultimately be between him and Clark to discuss the finer details. He needed actionable intelligence, that was the result and did not need to bother with the finer details. It would be a good way for him to assess Hamilton's capabilities.

"I wish for you to help Major Clark oversee the establishment of a network of intelligence agents in Philadelphia. You will not be required to leave camp at the moment, but you will assume the duties that I expect you to on my behalf from time to time," he explained and saw Hamilton's eyes widen slightly as he realized the magnitude of what was being asked of him.

"Sir," Hamilton nodded sharply.

"Major, please let me know of an operating budget that will be suitable after you and Mr. Hamilton have finished discussing the details." He looked at the two of them and both saluted before leaving his office. Billy closed the door behind them, leaving Washington alone once more. He glanced back down at his war map and shook his head a little in frustration. Long Island was closed now. He could only hope that Sackett had established new lines of intelligence on York Island or even Brooklyn that had started to bear fruit.

8

March 24ᵗʰ, 1777

"These cannot be the correct numbers, Captain." The sheer amount of disappointment and disapproval in Colonel Sheldon's voice made Tallmadge cringe inwardly. He wanted nothing more than to leave the room. But protocol demanded he stay and face the consequences of what he presented to Sheldon at his weekly meetings on the status of the dragoons. Only officers with the rank of captain or higher were in attendance and it was a chance for the junior officers to handle the men for the day's drills and general orders. "Only forty serviceable horses?"

"Yes, sir." Tallmadge steeled himself. "The rest were lamed by hard use during the winter when we began to train the men in proper dressage and maneuvers."

"Hmph," Captain de Vernejout, the French officer who had been appointed by Congress sniffed. "Back in France, we would not have allowed such a thing to happen. The horses are treated with respect and cared for as they are the cavalry's lifeblood."

"Yes, sir." Tallmadge could not give voice to whatever ill-willed thoughts he had on de Vernejout's uncalled-for comments.

"Drain the horses of the blood and eat them did you?" Captain Stoddard muttered mostly under his breath, but it seemed that his comment did not reach Colonel Sheldon. Instead, he got a reprimanding glare from Major Blackden who was sitting on Sheldon's left. Sheldon sighed and placed the report back onto the table. "Options, gentlemen?" Sheldon asked, and Tallmadge could see the rest shifting in their chairs.

This was not normally how meetings were conducted, in such a democratic way. But Tallmadge knew that times were desperate. Sheldon needed ideas on how to raise more horses for the regiment. They were already flush with some needed supplies, but there was only so much that could be done given the slowness of Connecticut manufacturers. They were servicing not only the 2nd Light, but also fielding requests from other regiments that had decided to muster men in Connecticut and were wintering there.

The good news was they had nearly the full complement of men needed for the regiment and so had taken to training them in infantry tactics due to the lack of horses at the moment. But they could only do so much before the men would need to train *on* horses. The fact that the horses they had received and used for the initial months of training were worn down and unfit for service spoke of the desperate need for animals. Tallmadge wished his mission to Long Island had not ended so poorly. Those ten animals that Adamson said were promising could have been a godsend.

He knew Sheldon had penned another letter to Washington regarding the dismal lack of equipment and horses. But Washington's reply denied the request to search for horses outside the New England area and was a little biting in tone about the fact that taking horses from other areas meant there would be a lack of mounts for the other three dragoon regiments being raised. He himself had penned a letter to Brewster a couple of weeks ago, which had produced minimal results. His friend had apologized for the lack of military equipment on the ships that they had raided and plundered. Brewster did mention there were a few luxury goods if he wanted them, but Tallmadge only thanked him and passed on the offer.

"Sir, what of the Commissary?" Captain Epaphras Bull asked, breaking the uncomfortable silence that had fallen across the room.

"I've written to Commissary-General Trumbull, but without effect." Sheldon sounded defeated and Tallmadge grimaced. It was uncomfortable to see his commanding officer act in such a manner.

"Sir, I can see if there is anything Major General Wooster can do for us-"

"The reply will probably be no, Bull," Stoddard interrupted with a shake of his head, "Wooster's more than likely managing his own troops."

"But, sir, when I was with the Commissary of Prisoners, we were able to ration and scrounge up supplies to good effect-"

"And those supplies were used for *prisoners*? Did not realize the lobsterbacks merit such gratitude from us." Stoddard had a sour expression on his face and Bull fell silent, his attempt at a solution falling on deaf ears.

"Sir," one of the other captains spoke up, "I can write the Massachusetts Assembly in Boston if you wish. Some of my men in the troop hail from the area and may be able to persuade their fellow men to part with needed horses and accouterments that we are currently lacking."

Sheldon held up a hand to prevent Stoddard from making another sarcastic comment. "Please do. Let me know if there is anything I can do to help expedite or persuade the Assembly to at least properly mount and outfit the men of Massachusetts."

"I'll do the same for my fellow New Jerseymen," another Captain said and Sheldon nodded at the suggestion.

"I guess that just leaves us, Connecticut folk." It was only by virtue of sitting next to Stoddard that Tallmadge heard the other man's grumbling whisper. He had to turn his head to prevent himself from glaring at the senior captain for his remarks. Stoddard was not helping matters and Tallmadge was tired of the man's defeatist attitude. Never had he imagined the man to be so ill-willed. His initial meeting with Stoddard had been well-received and he had thought the man flush with relief from his escape from Fort Washington, but he was beginning to wonder if it was not relief, but something else had been stirred in the captain.

"No other suggestions?" Sheldon asked into the silence that had fallen across the room. "Then please, gentlemen, continue your efforts. Dismissed."

Chairs scraped loudly across the floor as they stood up,

throwing salutes of various quality to Colonel Sheldon and Major Blackden before they left. Tallmadge could see the two captains from different states huddled together, more than likely drafting similar letters to their states' assemblies. De Vernejout was already on the main road headed to what looked like Pullings' family tavern and Tallmadge was more than inclined to leave the caustic Frenchman alone. He was glad he did not have to interact with the man on a day-to-day basis; he had more than once seen the man's lieutenant, Seymour, wander to his part of the encampment with a frustrated look on his face. He was beginning to wonder how de Vernejout treated his junior officer to have the young man wander so frequently into his part of camp. At least de Vernejout was headed to the tavern, it would give Lieutenant Seymour some time to himself.

Tallmadge headed towards his own section of camp, his mood lifting a little at the ragged sounds of carbines firing. Webb was leading the men of 1st Troop on another drill and it seemed the men were improving day by day. Before Webb had become his lieutenant and led the drills, it had been a part of Adamson and Davenport's duties as non-commissioned officers. However, they were still in charge of drilling the men in the proper care of their weaponry and also how to properly shoot. A lot of the enlisted men initially protested such heavy-handed treatment, but his two friends had pulled a technique that had set the men straight. Adamson had stood near the targeted area while Davenport took one of the loaded pistols and fired it into the air directly next to one of the men's ears. He continued every twenty seconds or so, loading the pistol and firing a round off as the man tried to load his own carbine with the same speed. After about two minutes, the man finally finished loading his carbine, but was too scared to properly aim it and the ball went high into the air, completely missing the target, and by chance, Adamson, who had spent the time loading another pistol and also firing it into the air.

Adamson had then walked over and stated to the gathered men that they would be expected to load at the speed he and Davenport had loaded, while also under fire. The men were humbled after that day and told the story to new recruits as they joined. Tallmadge could not have been prouder of his friends for setting a good example.

As he rounded the bend to where his troop usually held their exercise, he could see they were divided into two groups. One group was farther away, turning in odd circles before shouldering their carbines and firing or stabbing downward with their bayonets. Tallmadge surmised they were pretending that they were on horseback, shooting and stabbing moving targets below them. The other group had half the men on horseback, half on foot. Surveying them, he and saw that the men on the ground were attempting to pull off the ones on horseback who were trying valiantly to stay on their horses.

Walking closer, he saw that Pullings was leading the horseback riders while Adamson led the ones on foot. As for the ones doing odd-looking maneuvers, he saw the distant form of Davenport yelling at them, his booming voice cutting clear across the hilly field, though his words could not to be discerned. He spotted Lieutenant Webb near the edges of a wood, galloping his horse across a small area and pulling abruptly to turn his horse around. He could see that rotten pumpkins and winter melons of various sizes had been set up on small wooden posts; Webb was trying to cut pieces from them, without good effect.

There was a frown across the younger man's face and he pulled at his horse's reins in frustration. His horse was apparently not disturbed by the lack of manners from Webb and responded to his abrupt commands, but Tallmadge knew the horse would probably lose its patience soon enough at such rough treatment.

"Webb!" he called out, making the young man stop and look up.

"Sir," Webb saluted him with sabre still in hand and Tallmadge frowned at the motion. It seemed his expression got point across. Webb hastily transferred his sabre to his other hand and saluted him properly.

"*Better*," he stressed the word with a slight edge to his voice. Since taking the young man as his lieutenant, he had noticed a few idiosyncrasies about Webb. While bright and eager, Webb had an indefinite laziness about him that appeared when he was not put to work or given tasks that occupied his time. He was timid to try new things, but once he tried them, he was eager to master such tasks. Tallmadge could still see the potential in

Webb, but he was also starting to see that the young man expected praise every time he did things correctly or mastered something. While it reminded him greatly of himself back in his early days at Yale, it made him wonder if Webb's expectations were a little too high and he was setting himself up for failure down the road.

Tallmadge saluted back and Webb lowered his hand, transferring his sword back to his right hand as he gripped the reins. "Sir?" the young man inquired.

"Show me how you are attempting to cut," he ordered, and Webb nodded before wheeling his horse around and setting off at a fast canter. Tallmadge watched as bits of melon and pumpkin flew into the air, but there were more than a few misses along the short path. Webb turned around and trotted back, his lips pressed thinly as he knew he had missed a lot of the targets.

Tallmadge walked over and lifted Webb's sword arm, examining it. The blade was sharp, but Webb's grip on his sabre was weak. "Hold your wrist firm, but do not snap it completely straight. You'll break your wrist and arm in that fashion when you do hit something. Rotate gently at the angle needed and keep firm." He let the young man's arm go and watched as he gingerly flexed it before nodding at him. Tallmadge stepped back and gestured for Webb to try again with the adjustments he had made.

Webb spurred his horse to another canter and this time scored more hits than before, though he still missed some. Still as Webb stopped and turned his horse around, Tallmadge saw a pleased expression on his lieutenant's face. "Your wrist will feel sore for a few days after today's practice. Just think of it as writing lines over and over again," he called out, and saw the smile drop a little from Webb's face.

He shook his head in amusement and left his lieutenant to his practice. He decided to mount up and headed to the nearby stables to find his horse, Castor. Castor whickered a greeting, nibbling at his hand for any sorts of treats. Tallmadge reached into his pocket to pull out half a carrot, which the horse eagerly ate as he saddled Castor up with full weaponry and mounted him. He trotted out of the stables, checking to make sure he had his ammunition pouch, and headed to where Adamson and

Pullings were.

"Sir," they both called out and stopped the men from their exercise as he approached. He nodded to them.

"How many of the men have horses?" he asked.

Adamson glanced towards the men. "Twelve sir. I was about to allow some of them to get their horses-"

"Those who have horses, boots and saddles, on me. Those who do not, bayonet drills."

"Sir," Adamson saluted and turned to and bellow the order to the men who immediately sprung into action. The seven men already on their horses, immediately went about checking to make sure they were completely outfitted while three others headed towards the stables to prepare their horses, along with Adamson and Pullings. Both had gotten their mounts from their families in a fit of generosity, and Davenport's mount from his farms had been traded for a dapple-grey from New London a few days before.

"Sergeant Mills, lead the men on bayonet drills," he called to the former Commissary officer, and the man saluted before organizing the remaining men without mounts to continue their training.

Tallmadge waited as the men returned from the stables, completely dressed and looking superb, in Tallmadge's opinion. He wheeled his horse and started to where Davenport was training the men in the firing line. A flutter of excitement spread through him. He hoped they would receive the proper amount of horses soon and his whole troop could be accoutered and displayed in such fashion. As he led them past where Webb was practicing, he could see his lieutenant look up at them, brow wrinkling in a silent question. Tallmadge waved the younger man back to his original exercise and Webb nodded reluctantly as he wheeled his horse around to continue practicing against the melons and pumpkins. Webb would join in the exercise soon enough. For this one he needed the men to utilize what they had been learning for the last two months and apply it on horseback.

"Sir," Davenport called out as the last ragged fire of carbines echoed in the area. He saw the seventeen other men stop what they were doing to stand at attention.

"Sergeant, have your men set up the targets for a staggered

line of fire. After you've finished that task, you may have them join Sergeant Mills in bayonet drills," he ordered, and saw the slight crestfallen expression on Davenport's face, but he nodded and gestured for the men to do as he asked. He knew Davenport wanted to join them on horseback, but he needed at least another non-commissioned officer to oversee the men on bayonet drills. Like Webb, Davenport would have his chance soon enough.

The task was completed in good time and Tallmadge turned his horse and faced the mounted men. "You will ride single file, going no slower than a trot at the targets and fire all of your firearms at a number of them. Once you've finished, you will reload at least one of your carbines while maintaining movement in your horse before you reach this point again."

"Yes, sir!" was the enthusiastic response, but Tallmadge could see some of them puzzling over the task. None of them, save for perhaps Pullings and Adamson, had practiced reloading their firearms on horseback. It would be a challenge, but he hoped their practice with reloading would become second nature and they would adjust to the motion of the horse.

"Go!" he ordered and watched as Adamson led the charge, firing his first carbine as he started at a fast canter, then slowing to a trot to fire his other two and holstering them. Tallmadge noted to his pleasure that Adamson slung his first carbine behind his back, then took his last carbine to reload as he trotted his way back. The men murmured their appreciation. Pullings was next. But Pullings worked differently; Tallmadge saw his beady-eyed friend go at a trot instead of a fast canter and carefully aim each carbine with perfect headshots on the straw scarecrows they were using as target practice. The men cheered with his last shot, but unlike Adamson, Pullings took the carbine that was slung across his shoulder and reloaded that one. His horse was now at a gaited fast walk on the way back instead of trotting like Adamson's.

Tallmadge watched the next man go, James Dole if he remembered correctly, and saw him fumble a little, his horse slowing from a trot to a walk before he managed to spur him faster for the rest of his firing. However, Dole struggled with reloading and by the time he returned, he was finished reloading his carbine. It was the same for the next few men. When the last one finished Tallmadge watched them with expectant eyes.

"Reload all of your weaponry and repeat this exercise," he ordered calmly. He did not expect them to get it on the first try or even in the next few, but he also understood he could not show any emotion regarding their perceived successes or failures at his orders.

"Sir," they all replied as they went about to reload the rest of their weapons. He could see some of the horses shifting underneath the men as they moved around in their saddles. Some struggled to control the animals, unused to dividing their attention between such matters.

"There are other options," he called out as the men continued their task. "Some that require firing into the enemy at close quarters or from afar, some that use bayonets as a fourth weapon." He accepted a carbine from Adamson to use as an example. "As you well know, your fire will not be as accurate with the bayonet situated at the end of your weapon. But if you are to engage the enemy in close proximity, you may find yourself firing at one enemy and running through the next."

Some of the men looked up at what he said. He saw them nod, renewed in their understanding of what dragoons truly did on horseback. He handed the carbine back to Adamson and moved Castor back a few paces.

"Again," he ordered and the exercise began once more.

April 7th, 1777

The promotion was unexpected, but not unwelcome. Tallmadge stood at rigid attention in front of his fellow officers. Colonel Sheldon was in the midst of pinning the second of his silver three-clover epaulette that denoted him as a major. The only explanation he had been given for the promotion was that his service the last four months since the raising of the regiment had been impeccable and that General Washington had authorized the promotion of one officer for each rank. Blackden had received his commission of lieutenant colonel and he received the promotion to major.

Sheldon had also said that while he would remain in nominal

command of 1st Troop, former Lieutenant Belden, now promoted captain, was to command 1st Troop in his absence if he was called away for staff officer duties. It was something that left an unusual feeling in Tallmadge. While he relished the chance to accept a field officer posting, he also continued to feel the pull toward directly in command of a troop. His desire for the chance to exact some measure of punishment on the British for what they did to Nathan and to William was still running hot.

"Congratulations, Major." Sheldon finished with his work and stood back. Tallmadge saluted crisply and it was returned with equal enthusiasm. His fellow officers all clapped, though he could easily tell that some were jealous of his new rank. The Frenchman, de Vernejout had an especially sour expression on his face, but Tallmadge ignored him. De Vernejout had railed not only against Sheldon, but against Congress for not giving him a higher rank – though it was all completely out of earshot of Sheldon himself. He and the other captains who were subjected to the man's rants all but ignored him. The only one willing to engage the Frenchman was Stoddard, but not in defense of Sheldon to Tallmadge's surprise. Instead, the man antagonized the Frenchman, trying to find twists and turns in his rants to turn against him. Tallmadge would have expected since Stoddard knew Sheldon, and had even been friendly with him, he would have defended their commander, but it seemed the long winter months had changed the man. One the other captains, Barnett, was also party to the whole exchange, but Tallmadge had long learned to stay out of Barnett's way – the man sometimes reminded him too much of Major Ripley.

Still, now that he was of higher rank than his former fellow captains, he supposed he could curb their attitudes a little and perhaps conduct them towards defeating the British instead of fighting among themselves. At least that was his hope. Though they still needed supplies and a full complement of horses, there were rumors swirling that the French had sent aid. Tallmadge did not know if it was true, but he hoped it was. Perhaps at tonight's celebration dinner hosted by Colonel Wadsworth and his family, he would inquire about those rumors.

April 28th, 1777

The warning bell woke Tallmadge with a start. He quickly threw on his jacket and boots, grabbed his sabre, pistol, and knife and rushed outside to see some of the men of other troops rushing about. Colonel Sheldon rushed by, hand gripping his sabre tightly, and Tallmadge hurried towards him, half-buttoning his coat. "Sir!" he shouted, hailing Sheldon.

"Tallmadge, get whatever men you have in your troop on horses. We make for Ridgefield as soon as possible!" Sheldon paused for a moment. "Governor Tryon burnt the stores at Danbury and everyone has been called to alert. We're the only cavalry force nearby. Muster at the edge of Wethersfield."

"Sir," Tallmadge quickly saluted, his blood quickening in anticipation and anger at what he had just heard. He spun on his heel, finishing with the buttons on his jacket and cupped both hands to his mouth as he reached the tents where his troops were stationed. Some of them were already peering out sleepily, while others who had been on duty looked confused.

"1st Troop, 2nd Light, boots and saddles!" he bellowed, walking down the line of tents, "1st Troop, 2nd Light, boots and saddles!" He repeated his command twice more as his men drew awake, scrambling from their tents. He saw Captain Belden, and Lieutenant Webb emerge from their shared tent, followed quickly by his troop's newest cornet, Elijah Wadsworth. He had only just enlisted earlier in the month, and as a favor to both General and Colonel Wadsworth, Tallmadge had taken the young cousin of the Wadsworth clan as a cornet.

After the dismal meeting with Sheldon a month and a half earlier, he had been invited to another dinner with Colonel Wadsworth and his family and had accidentally let loose his frustration at the lack of supplies. To his amazement, Wadsworth had only given a mysterious smile before presenting to the 2nd Light accouterments that apparently were secretly sent by the French. While it was not enough to cover the whole of the regiment, it was still a godsend in terms. Wadsworth had also made inquiries for more horses and had delivered enough that all of 1st Troop were now mounted on dapple-greys, though Sheldon and the rest of the troop awaited their horses. Sheldon had decided to mount his own troop on bays and blacks while others opted for a multitude of other colors. The few horses had been delivered yesterday and Tallmadge was planning for his troop to assume formal training during the next month before they received the call to join the main body of the army encamped at Morristown, New Jersey.

That boon of accouterments was something Tallmadge could not even begin to thank his good friend for, but he supposed taking a member of the Wadsworth clan as his cornet was as good a start as any. Surprisingly, his friend had asked that since they knew each other well, to start calling him Jeremiah and write him when he got to the battlefield of any troubles he had in terms of procurement. Wadsworth had then confessed he had spoken to Barnabas, who had sent a missive to his brother in Paris who in turn responded with the armaments. Wadsworth had said they were all fighting for the cause and it greatly warmed Tallmadge that he had found two friends who were as ardent Patriots as he. He had privately thanked Barnabas later and the man had modestly waved his thanks away.

As Tallmadge made his way to the stables, his men crowded around him, some asking questions he did not answer, while others silently followed, breaking away to prepare and mount their own horses. He quickly saddled Castor and checked his armaments before mounting him and securing his helm on his head. "Muster at the west edge of town," he called out and watched as his men slowly mounted and trotted. Cornet Wadsworth, unsurprisingly, was the last man out, having received his horse just yesterday. He had not had time to practice much saddling and checking of weaponry before mounting.

As Wadsworth rode past, the young man muttered an apology that Tallmadge did not deign to answer. He turned Castor and followed Wadsworth, arriving at the edge of town in short order. He could barely discern the sight of his men; a few lamps held up reflected against some of their helms. The night was damp and smelled of recent rain. It was roughly sixty miles to Ridgefield, a night's ride if they kept pace. He hoped rain would not come again, as it was wont to do in April. If it did rain, they would be limited to their bayonets and sabres if they fought the invading British forces.

He heard the neigh and whinny of more horses turn to see more of the 2nd Light, looking to be Lieutenant Colonel Blackden's men and some of Captain de Vernejout's. There was no sign of Stoddard's or Bull's men which meant Sheldon more than likely told them to stay behind in case the British decided to move against Wethersfield. Colonel Sheldon approached and he tipped his golden-burnished helm at him.

"Sir," he greeted.

"Tallmadge, designate your men every five miles for messenger duties. We ride without stopping tonight, but we need a line of communication back to Wethersfield in case we need to muster more men or to let Stoddard and Bull know to head south to New Haven," Sheldon started without preamble, and Tallmadge nodded.

"Form columns!" Sheldon called out and the men started to group together into two lines. Tallmadge slotted himself on the outer edges of the line in order to direct his Troop to stay at designated points. That they were going to ride to Ridgefield without stopping suggested the haste and uncertainty of the situation. The British had struck early and Tallmadge wondered if there would be any reports of mustering to Morristown or perhaps Washington was already on the move, even with the swollen rivers this time of year.

As they started off at a quick trot, Tallmadge pulled along side Cornet Wadsworth, noting that the young man was holding both the 2nd Light's colors and 1st Troop's colors proudly in one of the holsters on his horse's saddle. As cornet, Wadsworth was solely responsible for the Troop's colors in and out of battle. Since he was a junior officer, he had a sabre instead of a bayonet like the rest of the enlisted men. He also lacked an extra pistol since the flags occupied one of the holsters on his saddle.

He saw Wadsworth glance at him before nodding grimly, understanding his duties. Tallmadge smiled in return before slowing his horse a little to where Sergeant Mills was. "Mills, you're first."

"Sir," he replied. True to form, when they reached roughly five miles, Mills pulled out of the two-column formation and waited in the pastoral field as they passed by him. Tallmadge glanced back to see Mills tipping his helm at them, as the rest acknowledged his action with brief muted cheers or with their own tips of respect. He turned back and continued to ride, tagging the next person to stop. This continued for the next ten miles until they reached relatively open, and unplowed fields and Sheldon started them at a brisk canter.

Tallmadge knew the mileage would now go faster and tapped two people at once as they rode down towards Ridgefield. He designated Pullings somewhere at the midpoint, trusting that he would be able to respond in a faster manner than the less experienced men if need be, and finally when they were about five miles out from Ridgefield, he pulled aside Adamson, who would know exactly what needed to be done if word needed to get out quickly. That left Belden, Webb, Wadsworth, and Davenport as his officers in case his men needed to form lines or effect a charge.

But it seemed they need not have rushed. As the late morning light spilled across the town the acrid smell of fire and smoke from some buildings to the south of the town center made them halt. They saw townsfolk and militiamen running back and forth. Some were putting out fires while others helped the wounded. They had clearly arrived too late. Sheldon hailed a private who had bandages and pieces of cloth in his hand.

"You, where is the command post? And who is in charge?!"

"General Silliman, sir! He's just returned after he and General Arnold's led at least five hundred men down to Compo Hill near the Saugatuck River to chase those fleeing red-coated bastards!"

"Language, soldier!" Sheldon admonished loudly and the man looked chastened.

"Sir, they are at the church yonder," the soldier pointed out, and Sheldon angrily waved him to continue his duties as he heeled his horse and led them to where the local Presbyterian church was.

"Blackden! Get the men situated. Tallmadge, with me," Sheldon called out. Tallmadge and Sheldon dismounted, tying their horses to a nearby post and headed in. Behind him he heard Blackden getting the men sorted. They would stay mounted in case they were needed to continue the action against the British forces.

As they entered the church, Tallmadge could smell the

metallic effect of blood in the air. However, he did not smell the distinctive odor of rotten onions and decaying fish he associated with death. At the far end of the church using one of the pews as a makeshift workstation, Brigadier General Silliman was talking with some of the men.

"Sir," Sheldon called out and Silliman pulled himself away from his conversation to see them. There was a hard expression on Silliman's face, and parts of his uniform were smeared in blood, with one streak reaching to his hairline and tricorn hat. This was a far different Silliman than Tallmadge remembered briefly greeting in February when he was stationed in Fairfield. That General Silliman was gregarious and optimistic, had struck up a tentative friendship with him while they were encamped at White Plains and Peekskill before being disbanded and transferred to different regiments.

This Silliman was one who had seen much fighting in recent days.

He and Sheldon stopped, saluting smartly.

"Colonel Sheldon, Major Tallmadge," Silliman greeted without preamble. Tallmadge had almost forgotten that Sheldon served directly under Silliman while he was in charge of both 1st Battalion and the Connecticut Light Horse regiment last year. It felt like a lifetime ago and he was briefly reminded of the man's recommendation of himself to Sheldon to serve in his regiment.

"We rode here as soon as word reached us-"

"Arnold has chased Tryon and his troops to the Southport section of Fairfield and I presume by now Tryon had affected his escape across the Sound," Silliman shook his head. "I am grateful for your arrival, but the damage has already been done. Danbury has lost all of its stores and Ridgefield, as you can see, has lost some of its stores and a field hospital. Tryon was effective in his strike."

"Sir..." Sheldon could not say anything after that disappointing report and neither could Tallmadge.

"General Wooster has taken a mortal wound and is not expected to live much longer." Silliman looked to the side and Tallmadge felt like someone had hit him in the gut. Wooster was dying? Though he did not know General David Wooster personally, he had heard about the man's fame and prowess on the field. He was famed for being part of the expedition to Quebec and Montreal and was one of the first generals in Connecticut besides Arnold to actively encourage men to sign up with the militia.

"Do we have news from Colonel Lamb, Huntington, and Ludington?" Silliman turned to an aide who shook his head before running out of the church for the possible news.

"Lamb's New York artillery was a godsend, as was Henry Ludington's militia forces," Silliman explained, "but the men were too inexperienced, Elisha, just too damned inexperienced."

It took a moment for Tallmadge to realize what Silliman had just confessed and he bit his lip, wanting to deny the sharpness of the statement. But even as he opened his mouth to protest the man's words, he realized he could not say anything. A majority of the men they had recruited and enlisted since January were inexperienced. This was more than likely their first taste of battle, and the speed and discipline of the British soldiers, even Loyalist militia, had caught them off guard.

The sudden burst of noise and whinnying of a horse made all of them turn towards the doors. They opened to, reveal a very disheveled-looking General Benedict Arnold. Tallmadge was familiar with the acerbic general, whose pasty complexion and long face were now marred by blood and flecks of hair stuck to his cheeks.

"So the cavalry has finally arrived," Arnold spat out as he limped towards them, his face a cloud of anger.

Silliman stood up and pushed past him and Sheldon. "Benedict, you're wounded-"

"Not much, only my pride and but a flesh wound," the general finally had enough of limping and sat down on one of the pews, gesturing with a hand towards his blood-soaked breeches. Tallmadge got a glimpse and saw that it was truly a flesh wound; a ball had merely scratched him. "Lost a second horse though," the man laughed, sounding bitter and at the same time exasperated. "Found another one at one of the local farms, Green's was it? Aye, Green's Farms."

"You'll have to let the quartermaster know-"

"Compensation, yes, yes," Arnold waved away Silliman's concern. "Those damned lobsterbacks escaped, Sel. Escaped and scurried away like the damned rats they were! And you, that your cavalry out there?!" Tallmadge held himself at rigid attention, as did Sheldon, at Arnold's foul mood. He glared at them.

"Yes, sir," Sheldon replied carefully. "Colonel Elisha Sheldon of the 2nd Continental Light Dragoons, sir."

"You're late," Arnold scoffed. "Where were you when the alarm sounded-"

"Benedict-"

"Oh leave me alone Silliman." Arnold looked annoyed at Silliman's warning tone before he sighed heavily. "Wooster?"

"Mortal," Silliman shook his head and Tallmadge was struck at the sudden change in mood as the anger rushed out of Arnold.

"Where is he being cared for?" the general asked.

"Nehemiah Dibble's house in Danbury. I'll have one of my men escort you up there after-"

Tallmadge did not get to hear whatever else Silliman was saying to a slightly protesting Arnold about his wound, as Sheldon leaned over to speak to him quietly. "Tallmadge, take the men except for Blackden's troop back to Wethersfield," he said, and Tallmadge nodded before saluting the two generals and Sheldon and moving away.

He exited the church and waved to Lieutenant Colonel Blackden who dismounted and came over. "Colonel Sheldon says for your troop to stay here while I bring the men back to Wethersfield."

"Then the fighting is over?" Blackden had an odd expression on his face, as if he could not decide whether to be grateful or disappointed.

"Yes, sir," Tallmadge replied.

"Then you have your orders. Leave one man every fifteen miles in case we need to pass messages, Tallmadge," Blackden said and he saluted.

They parted and Tallmadge untied his horse from its post and mounted it. "2nd Light, on me!" he called out, just as Blackden called for his men to stay. He nudged Castor into a light trot and led the rest of the men back to Wethersfield, a myriad of emotions swirling in him at what had happened.

It was roughly a month later through the gazettes and newsletters distributed throughout the states - also aided by a jaunty letter from Brewster - that Tallmadge learned of the counter-stroke to Governor Tryon's attack on Danbury and Ridgefield. Lieutenant Colonel Return Jonathan Meigs led a bold attack across the Sound, using thirteen of Brewster's whaling boats to ferry roughly one hundred seventy men to the northern 'fish tail' at the end of Long Island – the sleepy town of Southold. There they relaunched the boats to attack Sag Harbor. The valiant force achieved total surprise and captured a slew of provisions that were taken back and distributed among the regiments still mustering along the coastline. They also captured at least ninety British prisoners and to everyone's delight, not a single man was killed in the action.

The triumphant return of the conquering forces had swelled enlistment numbers and emboldened the Patriot-leaning towns to call up their own militias to fortify themselves from further attacks. All, in all, Tallmadge was glad that some measure of revenge was enacted for the death of General Wooster and the men who tried to save their stores at Danbury and Ridgefield.

June 22ⁿᵈ, 1777

The letter had come by fastest courier and General Washington's wording could not be clearer nor his anger more evident. They were to make haste to Morristown, New Jersey, to join the rest of the Continental Army. Tallmadge had about a day and a half to make sure his men were as accoutered as much as possible. It seemed that this was not Washington's first request for them to join. Sheldon handed him the order and told Tallmadge to tell Washington that the rest of the regiment would join in a few days – held up by the lack of proper accouterments.

The journey was one hundred forty miles from Wethersfield to Morristown and it took a total of three days of moderate to hard riding through rough terrain to arrive at the main encampment. He, Bull and two other troops had made the journey, though Bull and his troop had been ordered to remain on detached duty with General Putnam at Peekskill in the Hudson Highlands as they passed by it on their way.

They thundered in and Tallmadge directed the men to set camp up near a small pond that seemed suitable for their mounts to drink from. He delegated the task to Captain Belden of his own troop while he made his way to the encampment's headquarters. Their arrival drew stares from the encamped soldiers and Tallmadge walked with a certain amount of pride, the regalia that denoted the 2nd Light keeping his head high and steps sure. Sheldon had picked the helms himself, burnished gold with a white plume of horsetail crowning the top. They stood out from the rest of the infantry's tricorn hats and everyone knew they would draw the attention of British troops whenever they faced them in battle – which was the point. Tallmadge had imagined the regiment as the vanguard or the flank of a formation, sent in to cause confusion among the British lines before retreating just as fast to let the infantry regiments and artillery finish their work.

"Major Benjamin Tallmadge of the 2nd Continental Light Dragoons reporting as ordered," he introduced himself to the aide-de-camp who met him at the door of the house that Washington had made into his headquarters. He took his helm off and held it at his left hip.

"Major Tench Tilghman at your service, please wait here," the aide-de-camp said, his voice surprisingly youthful given the slightly aged look of his features. His red-hair was thinned along his crown, but tied up in a respectable queue.

"Sir," he nodded as Tilghman disappeared into one of the rooms near the back of the house. The major came out a few seconds later and gestured for him to approach.

He entered the room and saluted General Washington, who sat at his desk seemingly signing a handful of reports. The general looked wearier than when he last saw him back at White Plains, but Tallmadge could not help but feel a warm glow of pride at being able to present himself to Washington. Lowering his hand, he stood at attention as Washington finished signing the reports and handed them to Major Tilghman who took them and left the room, closing the door behind him. Tallmadge noted one other person in the room, a negro and more than likely

Washington's servant. The negro stood patiently still in his corner of the room, waiting on any command Washington was to give him.

"Major Tallmadge," the general finally looked up at him with a neutral expression on his face.

"Sir, I have brought at least three troops of the the six of the 2nd Light with me. Per your orders, one troop under Captain Bull has been left with General Putnam at Peekskill and Colonel Sheldon will be arriving in a few days time due to issues outfitting the rest of the troop." He dared not further excuse Sheldon's absence, having read the letter that had demanded that the 2nd Light report immediately to Morristown. Judging intensity of the Commander-in-Chief's stare, Tallmadge had a feeling that any excuse that seemed frivolous or long-winded would not be well-received.

"And how fare your men?" Washington asked.

"Equipped, sir," Tallmadge replied "Each man has at least two carbines to their persons. We have outfitted the enlisted men with bayonets to offset the lack of sabres, sir."

It seemed his answer was satisfactory as Washington made the barest inclination of his head at his words. "You will report to Middlebrook tomorrow for review and from there; be placed under the general command of Colonel Theodorick Bland of the 1st Continental Light Dragoons."

"Sir," Tallmadge saluted again, sensing the dismissal and left the room as Washington's servant opened the door for him. As he walked back outside, he placed his helm back on his head and secured it.

As he walked across the camp, he did his best to shake off the chilly reception he had received from Washington. He knew it was not directed at him, but rather at the regiment as a whole, and by extension Sheldon. But since Sheldon was not here he had to bear the brunt of Washington's ire for now. He could only hope that tomorrow's review would bring the 2nd Light back into some favor with their Commander-in-Chief.

"Sir," Belden was there to greet him as he walked into their section of camp. He saw the other two captains in the distance and waved them over. As soon as they were all gathered, Tallmadge began without preamble.

"We have orders to report to the forward camp and command post at Middlebrook tomorrow for review and further orders. We will be joining Colonel Bland's command until further notice."

"Sir, Bland commands the 1st Light-"

"I know," Tallmadge held up a hand to stop Belden's confused protest. "He is senior cavalry officer and will be accorded the due respect he is given until Colonel Sheldon is present."

"Sir, will the 2nd Light be on such attached duty to other regiments in the foreseeable future?" one of the other captains asked, looking sour.

"That I do not know, Captain." Tallmadge was unsure of the 2nd Light's status. If they could muster as a whole, he supposed that Washington would use them in feints and battles instead of attaching them to other regiments, but at this very moment, since they were at half their strength, they could not be fielded as a whole regiment without incurring significant losses. "For now, these are our orders. The men may pitch tents, but I wish them to be ready by morning light."

"Sir," the captains all saluted and left to spread the order to the rest of their troops. Troop reviews were usually conducted in the mid-morning hours, and Tallmadge had no intention of arriving late to Middlebrook.

He headed towards where he had last left his horse and found that Castor had been taken care of, brushed with care and left to graze the pond grass and drink along with the others of the regiment. Tallmadge patted his horse gently on its rump, and it looked up before resuming its meal. The rest of the horses were already fed and watered or were in the process of being brushed down by the junior enlisted men of the regiment. Leaving Castor in peace, he found his pack on the ground nearby.

His pack was minimal, containing a bedroll of blankets and a small haversack of quills, ink bottles, and spare paper along with his wax seal and several sticks of wax for candling and sealing his letters. He also carried a pouch of lead cubes he could melt down to make his own ammunition, along with the necessary tools to do so, packed tightly against one another with his whetstone and shaving knife lodged in between. He had bundled his spare clothing into his bedroll, and there was also a tin of food, but he carried no tenting equipment or trunks with spare uniforms and clothing. Since they were mounted regiments, each man was expected to carry light. Those who had trunks and spare equipment could send them ahead to camp or await their arrival at a different camp, but most packed their things like he had. They could be posted on one front for weeks on end and then suddenly be posted on three different fronts on three different days. For the last two weeks before they had been called to join the main army, the men had been learning how to both catch sleep on their horses during patrols and also to be ready at a moment's notice.

Swinging his pack onto his shoulders, he headed towards where he could see some of them pitching tents brought over from the wagon that had followed them from Wethersfield. When Sheldon arrived, he would bring with him the rest of the tenting supplies, but for now, Tallmadge knew that instead of three or four men, they would be packed tightly, perhaps six or seven per tent. He glanced up and saw the cloudless sky. If the weather held, he knew many of the men would more than likely sleep outside the crowded tents.

"Sir, your tent has been set up," Adamson hailed him with a broad wave of his arm.

"My thanks, Sergeant-Major."

Adamson smiled and left to pitch his own tent that he would share with Davenport, Pullings, Mills, and a couple of the other more senior corporals of the regiment. By virtue of rank alone, Tallmadge was the only one in the three troops to have his own tent. Just mere months ago, he knew he would have felt embarrassed and perhaps a little ashamed at what such a rank deserved, but now he understood why all the majors, even those of higher rank wished for the privacy of their own tent. For one thing, the tents were not only used for sleeping, but also for reports, signatures, and letter writing. Most of all, they were a place where one could collect his thoughts without distraction.

Being a major seemed to have doubled or even tripled the work. Now as a staff officer leading three troops in Colonel Sheldon's stead he greatly valued the privacy of his own tent to write and plan in peace.

He ducked into his tent and set down his pack, unrolling his bed roll and smiling a little at where Adamson had pitched his tent. It was next to the remnants of a fence post which gave some flatness to the ground nearby, and allowed him to lean against it if he wished to sit. Adamson had chosen well and Tallmadge silently thanked his friend for it. With his bedroll set for the night, he pulled out a piece of paper and his inkwell and quill, along with a small book he had carried with him since his days at Yale. It was a gift from his father, a small prayer book, but with blank pages near the end for him to write whatever he wished. Nathan had once found the book and in a fit of amusement, composed a silly verse about him that spoke of their friendship. Tallmadge had read it with some chagrin, shaking his head at the last few lines of rhyme, which pleaded for him to help finish the verse. He had refused and declared Nathan's attempts a failure. His friend had given him a wounded look, but even that had not stopped their laughter. Tallmadge had vowed never to show his father what had become of his gift that Nathan had all but doodled upon.

Now, though, Tallmadge flipped to the last pages and stared at a couple of lines before closing the book and placing it against his knees and covering it with the paper on which he had started to compose the journey's report to Colonel Sheldon. Those days of whimsy were long gone and though Tallmadge was glad that he had some way of remembering his friend, it hurt to be reminded of his death. He took a deep breath and let it out slowly, letting the brief cold anger that filled him die to a simmer. In his report he made compliments to the conduct of the troops and the steadiness of the horses on their hard journey down to Middletown. He also related Washington's orders for them to journey to Middlebrook, they hoped to engage the enemy. Tallmadge quickly finished his report with the proper valediction to Sheldon and put the letter to the side to dry.

He pulled out another piece of paper and ripped it in half before writing a quick note to Barnabas Deane wishing him well and good health. He thanked him again for his missive to his brother in Paris for procuring needed armaments and again wrote that they were going to Middlebrook, but made sure to omit any potential mention of action or review. Barnabas had proven himself a wonderful correspondent when the man was traveling between his sister-in-law's house in Wethersfield to his own business elsewhere. It seemed Barnabas was taking care of his brother's business ventures as well as his own and thus traveled all across the state. Though Tallmadge had seen much of Connecticut, he was rather fond of the way Barnabas described the state in his own words. He decided to add his own observations of the landscape of New Jersey, having never been to the state until now. He noted the rolling hills and vivid green grass dotting the landscape. Finished with his letter, he set that aside and took the other half of the paper to write to Jeremiah Wadsworth.

He asked after the health of the Wadsworth family and sent his love to Jeremiah's wife. He had visited enough times that Jeremiah's children had started to call him 'Uncle Tallmadge'. He was touched by the sentiment, having been easily and readily adopted into the family and so decided to dedicate the rest of the letter to describing for the children the horses and all sorts of animals he had seen on the way down from Wethersfield. The last he had seen of the children, they had been pretending they were on a hunt, that one was the prey and the others the predators. They were to catch the prey, but the prey could occasionally turn into a predator if they caught the other one. Finished, he set the letter to the side and began the process of folding and sealing the others.

Task done, he stepped out of his tent and sought out the area where the post riders stayed, near headquarters, and approached one that looked like he was about to ride off for the night post.

"Corporal, which direction are you headed?"

"North, sir," the enlisted man replied, giving him a salute as he noticed his ranks.

"Do you mind taking these with you? All for Connecticut," he said and the Corporal nodded as he took his three letters and bundled them into his own bag. He thanked the post rider and headed back to his section of camp. He could see that most of the men were already sitting around small fires, eating rations for dinner or re-organizing their supplies. Tallmadge approached the fire that seated the captains of the troop along with a couple of their lieutenants.

They greeted him with a cascade of 'sirs' before someone

offered him a small tin of what looked like dried pork made into a stew. Tallmadge took the offering and tentatively tasted it before eating it completely. It was not bad, but the pork was more than likely starting to go rancid after being salted for so long.

"Squirreled it away since the winter sir." Belden accepted the tin back. "Figured we'd celebrate arrival to camp with it."

"Good way to celebrate," Tallmadge agreed. Meats would be hard to come by now that they were part of the regular army. He would probably have a better chance of getting fresh meat since as senior officer he would be offered the invitation to dine with other officers, but the fact that they were mounted regiments did not bode well for fresh food.

"Sir." He took the offer of the same small tin, now filled with a bit of rum.

"To your health, Captain, and to all of our successes," he toasted, and the rest of the officers cheered. Tallmadge drank the rum and hoped that they would serve well and serve with distinction.

June 24th, 1777

Colonel Theodorick Bland was not what Tallmadge expected when he and his detachment of the 2nd Light were placed under his command. He did not know many Virginians, General Washington being one of the few exceptions, but they seemed to have an air of aristocratic disdain that bothered him. Bland seemed to consider the Connecticut horsemen to be beneath his Virginian brethren. Granted, Bland was in command of the 1st Light and it was a well-deserved command to raise a regiment of dragoons in service, but Tallmadge would have thought the other regiments of dragoons would be held in the same regard. That seemed not to be the case even after they were reviewed by Washington himself.

Tallmadge could not help but glow in pride at the Commander-in-Chief's commendation of his detachment. Washington had especially taken note of the regal and smart appearance of Tallmadge's own former troop, all outfitted with dapple-greys, black bear-skin holster covers and black straps. Tallmadge had seen Captain Belden and Lieutenant Webb fail to smother their own smiles of pride, but did not reprimand them after the parade was finished. He was too proud of his work and let the men bask in the praise.

After the parade had finished, he and the officers of the troops had been introduced to Colonel Bland and officially placed under his command for movement the next day to nearby New Brunswick. They were part of General William Alexander's forces – or rather General Lord Stirling, who had been exchanged back earlier in the year during the wintering period after being held as prisoners of war. Colonel Daniel Morgan had also been returned, much to Tallmadge's own relief. He had heard of the exploits of Morgan's sharpshooters and knew that with Morgan's riflemen to support them, they would not have faltering lines of any sort.

But for now, he and the rest of his detachment were part of an advance group led by Colonel Bland who were following the Raritan River towards the New Jersey coast. The British had been spotted crossing from nearby Staten Island to the village of Perth Amboy. They were to give a show of force to judge General Howe's true intentions. The Raritan River snaked from the southern edges of the hills that made up Middlebrook, the forward camp, all the way back to Middletown itself where headquarters was located. New Brunswick was at a south-easterly direction from Middlebrook in the valley area of the hills, between Middlebrook and Perth Amboy. General Stirling and his forces, about 2,500 men strong, would wait nine miles behind them as Colonel Bland and the advance party made their show of force.

They were stationed with a majority of the 1st and 2nd Light up front, with Colonel Moylan's 4th Dragoons corralling Daniel Morgan's riflemen in a protective column. Tallmadge had recently learned that a majority of Moylan's 4th Continental Light Dragoons hailed from Pennsylvania, and that they too were held in odd contempt by Bland for not being *Virginian* horsemen. Though it seemed Moylan's men were held higher than he or his Connecticut men; Pennsylvania and Virginian men had served as mixed regiments since the beginning of the war. Moylan had expressed a bit of sympathy, but Tallmadge could see the man was more occupied with other matters than Bland's favoritism. He had learned, to his silent amusement, that Moylan's 4th Light had taken a lot of their uniforms from captured British stores, that they had recently had been forced to dye the facings a different color to prevent the Continentals from accidentally shooting them. The dye used still had a pungent odor. Tallmadge was glad that he was marching up front instead of downwind.

They numbered a total of 260 dragoons, and 300 of Morgan's riflemen. Tallmadge rode along side both Moylan and Bland while the rest of his men were spread out behind in the columns.

"We should be seeing them by now." Bland shifted in his saddle, peering ahead before turning to Tallmadge. "Major, send one of your men forward, let's see if they can properly scout out the enemy."

"Sir," Tallmadge ignored the taunt. Bland had been throwing such challenges his way since they had met the day before. He trotted back to where 1st Troop was marching and nodded a greeting to Belden and Webb who headed 1st Troop's column. "Borrowing Adamson," he stated, and Belden nodded again before catching the eye of Adamson who broke away from his formation.

"Sir?" Adamson asked, as Tallmadge turned his horse again so that he rode along side 1st Troop with Adamson alongside Belden and Webb.

"Scout ahead and report back what you see," he ordered, and Adamson nodded sharply before heeling his horse and galloped ahead. He watched his friend's form become smaller and smaller before disappearing over a small crest in the road.

They did not have to wait long. Adamson rode back with some haste and pulled his horse short before them. Bland held up a hand to stop the rest of the column from advancing. Tallmadge frowned a little as he noticed that Adamson looked a bit frightened, but managed to keep a resolute expression on his face.

"Sir," Adamson addressed Bland, "I count several battalions that may number to nine or ten thousand, sir. There were also artillery positioned behind them, but they did not look like they were loaded with shot."

"Were they marching?" Bland demanded and Adamson shook his head.

"No, sir. They were waiting."

Bland waved a hand of dismissal and Tallmadge caught Adamson's eye and gave him a sharp nod of approval as he rode back to rejoin his troop.

"Theo, we should show ourselves then retreat back to Stirling's lines for reinforcements," Moylan spoke up, his voice cautious. "We're nine miles out-"

"Forward," Bland cut Moylan off and started his horse at a trot. They followed and soon came upon the small hill in which Adamson's horse's muddy tracks could still be seen. The ground had been soaked with rain, rushing into the thickets and wildflower fields that contained brush and small saplings. The valley had apparently flooded in recent days and the water had only recently receded. As they rode up the hill, Tallmadge's eyes widen at the sight of hundreds, if not thousands of red uniforms dotting the horizon and beyond that, the blues of the Raritan Bay that bounded one side of Perth Amboy.

"Sir, we should-" he started as he realized that Bland was not pulling his horse to stop.

"We have the element of surprise, we should attack-"

"Theo are you mad?! We're nine miles from Stirling-"

"We have the *element of surprise!*" the man shouted and Tallmadge looked back and forth between Moylan and Bland, shocked by the sudden change in tone.

"Sir-"

"Ready your men, Tallmadge, I want your men to flank left. Moylan, take the 4th and flank right. Morgan!"

"Sir?" Colonel Daniel Morgan was a square-jawed man with a sharp chin and nose. He had keen eyes and a no-nonsense demeanor about him. He was also one of few infantry officers that were horsed. Tallmadge had heard of the man's exploits and that of his regiment, who fought like Indians using tactics many considered dishonorable. He himself had no opinion on the man's tactics. They inspired victory and caused chaos within the British ranks – he'd rather the British be given no quarter due to the lack given to Nathan and to William while they were prisoners. Morgan's respect and care for his men was well-known, and he could see a slight wariness in the colonel's posture after the surprising exchange between Bland and Moylan.

"Take your men to the brush to ambush the soldiers once we draw them in," Bland ordered and Tallmadge glanced back to see Morgan, acknowledge his order with a sharp nod. Morgan pulled away and began to direct his men.

"Sir, we've carbines-"

"Tallmadge, you should be preparing the flanking attack," Bland gave him a sharp look. Tallmadge pressed his lips thinly together, knowing his protests about the range of their guns was falling on deaf ears. He pulled his horse out of formation as he turned back.

"2nd Light on me!" he called out before he spurred Castor to go into the brush and thickets as the rest of the 2nd Light following behind him. He could hear Moylan calling for his 4th to join him and Bland calling his 1st to form up behind him on the main road. He moved at a fast trot through the brush, ignoring the whipping branches of saplings that bent, but did not break under the weight and speed of his troop's horses.

"Sir, what are we doing?!" Belden looked aghast as did the other two captains.

"Bland wants us to flank the left while he charges up the center to draw the British towards us," Tallmadge said tightly. He was furious at the orders he had been given – Bland was a complete idiot. Roughly five hundred of them were going up against a force of ten-thousand! "Belden, hold fast here. Barnett, Crafts, take your troops and form a defensive wedge. Belden, single file, carbines fire once. Call out any hits you make."

"Sir-"

"They have musketry, yes, but we must do something." He shook his head against Belden's protest and his captain nodded reluctantly before he and the other two captains started to bark orders to their troops. Tallmadge fell in with Belden's troop, riding along-side both Davenport and Adamson as he turned to his right to watch Bland wave his hands in short bursts, giving his orders. The whole of his regiment leap forward to charge at the enemy.

"Sir...Ben, what is Bland *thinking*-"

"You will kindly keep your thoughts to yourself, Sergeant-

Major," Tallmadge hissed back at Adamson who immediately shut his mouth and straightened in his saddle. He did not need any sign of dissent, even Adamson had been the one to scout out the enemy.

"Forward!" he shouted as he drew his sabre and pointed towards the British lines which were now charging at them with bayonets held at the ready. He could see Moylan's 4th doing the same, the two of them troops converging on Bland's position as they drove straight into the lead British line. Moments later, Tallmadge and his forces crashed through the line's left flank, just as the ragged scattered fire of his men sounded in the air. He pulled on Castor's reins and slashed at a soldier who tried to unseat him, spraying blood into the air before turning and stabbing at another soldier. The man fell to the ground, holding his neck as blood poured out, but Tallmadge was already pulling away, heeling Castor to ride back to rejoin the rest of Belden's troop, which had made their initial pass. The other two troops also pulled back, each man firing one shot.

Tallmadge heard the distant call of 'make ready' followed by cries of 'load!' from the other British lines and braced himself at the sound of their firing muskets. He heard cries of men in the distance and saw that the British had hit the retreating dragoon lines, just as the branches and saplings near him snapped and popped, struck by musket balls.

"Pull back!" he called out to his men as he sheathed his sabre and swung his carbine around. He turned back in his saddle to fire, but the distance was too great for him to do any damage. He and the rest of the 2nd Light pulled to where Morgan had set up one line of men. He could see them covered in the brush, their muskets ready to cover them.

"Make ready!" Morgan's call was echoed by his lieutenants and the brush before them came alive with the rustling of soldiers as they pointed their muskets beyond them. Tallmadge spurred his horse and jumped across one line of thicket, landing heavily in the thorns, which caused Castor to whinny with displeasure. "Fire!" the command came not even a second later and he was deafened by the sound of muskets going off all around him.

He wheeled Castor around and watched one of the lines of

British halted from the return fire. Then he saw Colonel Bland and his 1ˢᵗ Light racing down the direction they had come from.

"Pull back! Pull back!" The command shouted by Bland and his lieutenants echoed oddly in Tallmadge's ears as he waved for his own captains to pull back with them. He shook his head to clear the brief ringing from them.

"Go! We'll cover you!" he called down to Morgan's men who were looking a little confused in the brush.

"Reload and pull back men, pull back!" Morgan's lusty shout echoed across the thicket.

Tallmadge wheeled Castor around again, pulling his carbine in case the British line did advance once more as Morgan's men pulled back. He could see all three of his captains holding their troops in order to cover the riflemen's retreat, carbines held aloft. But at this distance, Tallmadge knew that the British had the clear advantage with their muskets.

The crackle of enemy fire snapped more branches and leaves, but Tallmadge refused to flinch as he felt Castor dance beneath him. He glanced back, judging the distance to which Morgan's men had double-quick marched their retreat, and saw Moylan's 4ᵗʰ Light once again surround the men in a protective barrier of horses. "2ⁿᵈ Light, on me!" he called out as he shouldered his carbine set off at a fast canter to rejoin the retreating group.

Amid the thunder of hooves he barely discerned the horn calling for the British forces to halt from pursuing them. Tallmadge finally let loose a sigh of relief. He and the rest of his men caught up with Bland's retreating forces and made their way back towards New Brunswick. That had been a little too close for his comfort. He spent the rest of the mostly silent ride glaring at the back of Colonel Bland's head for what he had done. There did not seem to be any casualties, but it was perhaps the Grace of God that had they had escaped the foolish charge. Just what had the man been thinking?!

They decided to camp three miles from Stirling's front lines. The men were exhausted after marching the nine miles and engaging the enemy, then quickly retreating at a dead run for two miles before being allowed to resume a marching formation. Silence had fallen over the camp as the three dragoon forces split among themselves. But Tallmadge could see that many of Bland's men were avoided; Moylan's Pennsylvanian men were the only ones who were remotely friendly with the Virginian horsemen. Morgan and his riflemen ignored the three dragoon regiments and instead tended to their own wounded which the British had fired upon seeing them as a bigger threat than the dragoons and their carbines.

There had been one attempt by his own men to engage Tallmadge about what had happened earlier, and he shut that conversation down with a pointed look and silence. But he knew he could not do anything about the dark looks thrown towards Bland and his 1st Dragoons throughout the night – not without calling himself a hypocrite for doing the same. The only thing that made it somewhat tolerable, at least in the men's opinion – but not Tallmadge's – was that they had captured one Hessian and his horse who had wandered a little too close to Moylan's 4th during their right flanking maneuver. Said Hessian had paid them in whatever coins he had and was now tied to a tree to prevent him from leaving camp and alerting the British of their position.

Bland had made a sport of it, acting seemingly cordial to the Hessian officer, but in reality mocking him subtly for his broken English and criticizing his horse. After a couple of hours of this, Tallmadge found the situation to be intolerable and politely excused himself from the senior officers gathering to check on his men. It was not that he objected to make fun of the Hessian officer whose horse did look like it was covered in too many layers of fur in such warm weather. It was that he was still livid at Bland's incompetence for trying to attack an enemy who was far more numerous and armed with *muskets* while they had only carbines.

Now, he found himself staring up through the leafy green branches of a large maple tree, unable to sleep because of his anger. Sharing the space under the tree to his right was Castor who absently grazed on the bits of grass that grew between the roots. To his left was Adamson and his horse, both asleep. At least that was what he thought until Adamson opened his eyes and seemingly stared at nothing in particular. Other men of the detachment had also taken up postings around trees, finding use for the shade and trunk to rest on, while others had taken to sleeping out in the open, using only their bedrolls for cover.

"Ben?" Adamson's eyes still stared to the far distance. "Do you think we're ready?"

"We trained, we taught them what we knew, what we learned." Tallmadge settled his gaze again on the branches above him. He knew what Adamson was asking, but in good conscience he could not give him the answer he wanted to hear. Tallmadge could only reassure him, both as his friend and as his commanding officer.

"Some of the boys, Ben, they were scared," Adamson sighed. "Could see the fear in their eyes, fear running straight through their horses."

"They'll learn quickly." It was up to each man to master his fear on the battlefield, the fear of death, the fear of being wounded, the fear of being shot and the fear of watching friends die. Tallmadge remembered his first time witnessed death on the battlefield during the evacuation of Long Island. He could not begin to describe the sensation it produced in him, but it had been solemn in nature. He had felt reluctance to even attempt to take the life of another person. Then his training screamed at him to shoot or be shot, and he had fired. His ball pierced an advancing soldier clean through the hip, throwing him to the ground in a pantomime of a spinning faint. The soldier had not gotten up and Tallmadge remembered the drip of blood, the wafting odor of rotten onions and fish – the scent of death. He had felt nothing but relief after that...that he had survived while the soldier that would have killed him did not. He had come out the victor.

"They'll learn quickly, they must." He blinked once before shifting a little. "Get some rest Andrew."

"Yes, sir," the formality of rank had returned to Adamson's voice and Tallmadge heard his friend shift against the tree trunk. Soon the sounds of Adamson's even breathing echoed in the air.

"To arms! To arms!"

He was moving even before he knew he was awake, his eyes

blinking open and reacting to the perceived danger by throwing the blanket off himself and drawing his pistol. He blinked again, wakefulness hitting him as he saw several troops of British soldiers advancing on their position through the small hills and fields. "2nd Light boots and saddles! Boots and saddles men! Hurry!" he shouted, startling some of the others who had not wakened with the alarmed cry.

He rolled his bedroll into a hasty bundle and tied it onto Castor as his horse shifted nervously with the perceived danger around them. The rest of his detachment also hurried to pack up their bedrolls and saddle their horses.

"1st Troop, on me!" he called as he swung into his saddle, the others following suit. "Barnett, Crafts, take your troops and cover Morgan's men!"

"Yes, sir!" they called out as they spurred their horses towards where Daniel Morgan's riflemen were hurrying onto the road for a quick walking march back to Stirling's lines.

He pulled his horse to where Captain Belden and Lieutenant Webb had been camping for the night. "Belden, Webb, break the men into groups of twelves, three columns, ragged fire and effect a retreat as soon as the men finished firing."

"Sir," they nodded and started to organize the troops.

"Pullings!" he called out, bringing his friend over. He pulled Castor close to his horse and spoke in a low tone. "Pullings, find the officer of the lead troop and shoot him." His friend's eyebrows knitted in understanding as Tallmadge pulled away and took his place at the lead of the formation, with Pullings right behind him. It was highly ungentlemanly what he was asking Pullings to do, but they needed to buy Morgan's riflemen time to retreat, being that they were infantry. He and the rest of the 1st and 4th Light could move faster on horseback. The fastest way to buy time was to shoot the officer giving commands.

"Charge!" he called, drawing his pistol and pointing it at the advancing troop closest to their camp. He heard Bland's shout of surprise as they thundered past the still retreating 1st Light and 4th Light, but it was drowned out by the cheer of relief from Morgan's men as they discerned their intention.

Tallmadge cupped a hand around his mouth as he saw that what he thought was one troop advancing, was actually four.

"Belden! Left two!" he shouted to Captain Belden who relayed his orders as they peeled away to deal with the two troops to the left of the main formation. "Webb! Right!" he turned to Webb who nodded and set his men to their task. Tallmadge leveled his pistol straight at the center of the formation as he saw the main body of the troop halt, the soldiers loading their rifles and readying to shoot. They quickly came upon them and Tallmadge fired blindly as he heard the staccato of carbine fire from either side. Then he pulled sharply on Castor's reins and turned to charge back the way they had come. Even before he spurred his horse to continue, he glanced back to see the officer that was ordering the men to make ready fall to the ground, clutching his leg in pain from Pullings' shot. He smiled grimly as the rest of the men fired their carbines two, three at a time at the troop, which was thrown into chaos by the wounding of their officer.

He eased Castor's hard gallop to a slow canter as the rest of the troop formed up around him. A quick glance showed no one was injured. Most of the men were reloading their rifles, per their training. "Good job," he called out as he heard the muskets finally fire behind them, but no one flinched which meant that the returning British fire was well short of their position.

"Sir! They're halting," Davenport's voice echoed from the back of the staggered column. He turned in his saddle to see that the British had indeed halted after being stopped from their initial charge.

"Let's go," he called, spurring Castor to a faster canter and they soon caught up with Bland's retreating forces. As they came up, some of Morgan's men glanced behind them and waved their tricorns, but Tallmadge did not acknowledge their greeting. He waved for Belden to organize the men into proper rear-guard formation. He did tip his head in acknowledgment to the rest of his detachment, as he passed by on his way to the front.

"Four advancing columns, sir," he immediately reported to Colonel Bland as he pulled his horse to a slow ambling gait. Castor whickered, shaking his head, but Tallmadge steadied him from moving too fast. Clearly his horse had enjoyed the exertions and wanted to move again. "I did not see any sign of artillery."

"Oh, they're there," Morgan spoke up as he took the rear

position of the three-line column. He nodded greetings to Morgan's lieutenants who were riding alongside him. "Good form, Tallmadge," Morgan said.

"Sir," he acknowledged the compliment with a curt nod of his head. He was still angry at Bland's actions the day before and the fact that they had almost been ambushed and captured by the advancing columns while they were so far away from Stirling's main camp.

"What of the Hessian, Tallmadge?" Bland asked, turning his head a little so that he could hear his words. He did not seem to acknowledge his report or what he had done even with Morgan's thanks. Tallmadge suspected that Bland was trying to save face from what happened yesterday, but he could not really tell.

"I did not see him when we passed through the campsite."

"Must have escaped into the brush," Moylan commented with a small shrug. "Alas, no loss. We have his horse and his money."

Tallmadge thought he saw something akin to annoyance flash through Colonel Bland's expression, but it was masked quickly by a non-committal grunt from the other man. He glanced over to Moylan, but the colonel of the 4th Light's face looked like it could have been carved from stone. An uncomfortable but welcomed silence descended upon the small group of officers as they rode the three miles back to Stirling's main lines.

When they arrived, Bland immediately ordered them to the rear guard and to stay mounted as he reported to Stirling. Morgan was the only officer who went with him and Tallmadge hoped the man would give an accurate account of what had happened instead of letting Bland spin the whole tale.

"Morgan will do it," Moylan commented absently as he leaned against the saddle horn. The two of them stood side by side as they waited with the rest of their detachments under the heavy wooded shade on one of the small hills dotting the area.

"Will do what sir?" Tallmadge asked as he unbuckled his helm and lifted it from his head. He wiped the sweat from his brow before placing his helm back on and securing it. The heat was starting to feel stifling, even in the shade. Standing on the hillside, the summer felt more humid here in New Jersey than it had in Connecticut.

"Make sure you get your due credit, Tallmadge." Moylan

glanced at him as he absently shucked off his gloves and tried to fan his face with them. It was ineffective judging by the disgusted look Moylan threw at his gloves before leaning against the horn of his saddle again.

"I do not care for credit for the idiocy that happened." He was inclined to test what Moylan's thoughts really were on Bland's actions, but decided to forego subtlety.

He was rewarded with a quiet snort of agreement from the other man. Looking down the hill, they could see the sea of red blocks slowly advancing towards them. Judging by the sheer amount of red, which nearly blotted out the green fields, it was most definitely Howe's army that had been encamped in New York for the winter. The British were not quite in range yet, and they had arrived at camp in time to warn Lord Stirling of Howe's advancing troops. He heard the distant command of 'load!' followed by the clanking metallic sounds of artillery to his right and turned to see the small artillery regiment that had accompanied them getting ready to fire. There was a brief nervous twitter among the gathered dragoons, and he raised a hand for the officers to steady their horses. He saw Moylan do the same with his men.

Resounding thunderous booms of cannon fire rendered the air and Tallmadge shortened the reins on Castor as his horse danced in startled fright. He heard the shifting and braying of the other horses behind them, but all the men managed to get their beasts under control. "That's a good boy." He patted Castor gently on the neck as the next cannon fired, shaking the ground once more. His horse tossed its head as Tallmadge looked towards where the shots had landed, digging deep brown marks across the ground. They were well short of the advancing British troops and he knew the artillerymen were more than likely making adjustments to their cannons before firing again.

His attention turned from the starting battle to Colonel Bland, who rode up to them, halting abruptly. "Tallmadge." Bland had a neutral expression on his face that bore no hint of whether he had received a reprimand or praise for his quick actions.

"Sir," he acknowledged.

"Take your men and report to General Washington at Middlebrook for further orders. Moylan, 4th and 1st are rear guard to Stirling. He will be conducting a marching retreat."

Tallmadge tipped his helm to Moylan who waved a glove in return before he wheeled Castor about and headed towards his men. "2nd Light on me," he called out and his men spurred their horses in the direction of the quickest road to Middlebrook, five miles away from the main lines. He was a little disappointed that they were not to fight in the battle, and instead would retreat to the safety of the fortified hills, but his disappointment was abated by the fact that he was no longer under Colonel Bland's direct command.

They arrived at Middlebrook in about half an hour and Tallmadge directed his captains to wait at the edges of camp in case they were called to ride out to Lord Stirling's position again. He directed them to a pond near the edge of camp, so the horses could get some water while he rode to Washington's command tent. He tied Castor to a post, unstrapping his helmet and attaching it to his saddle horn. He turned and saluted the general's lifeguards as one of the aide-de-camps peered out from the tent at his arrival. To his surprise, it was Alexander Hamilton whom he had briefly met while at Hell's Gate; except the man had been promoted to a Lieutenant Colonel.

"Lieutenant Colonel Hamilton, sir, news from Lord Stirling's forces," he said, and Hamilton peered at him for a moment, before recognizing who he was.

"Major Tall...madge, was it?"

"Yes sir." He was glad that the former artillery officer had remembered him.

"Please wait." Hamilton closed the tent flap, but reappeared after a few seconds and gestured for him to come in. Inside, Tallmadge saluted Washington, who had his back towards him and was staring at several maps scattered on his war table.

"Sir, Lord Stirling has affected a marching retreat," he started. "It is confirmed that these are General Howe's British forces from New York numbering in the thousands."

Washington nodded before glancing at the two of them. "Mr. Hamilton, please inform Knox, Maxwell, and the others that I wish to pull them back to the previous defensive line we have already established."

"Sir," Hamilton saluted and left without another word.

"Tallmadge, what of your forces under Bland?"

"Bland released us from detached duty with the 1st and 4th, sir," he replied. "Where do you wish to deploy us?"

"Here for now, though I will send word if we need the 2nd Light to assist in the marching retreat. Where is Bland now?"

"Colonels Bland and Moylan are both deployed as rear-guard to Stirling to effect the retreat, sir." Washington nodded before waving a hand to dismiss him. He saluted once more before departing the tent.

As he mounted Castor, he could not help but feel a sense of disappointment at what had happened. They had arrived with such haste, some of the men with bare minimum equipment and accouterments – but enough to impress Washington during the review – only to find themselves sent into a foolhardy charge at the enemy far greater in numbers, then nearly ambushed. And now, they were relegated to waiting as the first major battle of the year became a minor occurrence – a retreat. Tallmadge was frustrated and wished they had been deployed under more auspicious circumstances.

But he could not deny that his men now had battlefield experience. He hoped they would learn the valuable lessons of a fighting retreat on this day. And he thanked God that not one man had been lost from the 2nd Light. And all had performed admirably, just as he had taught them during the winter.

9

August 8ᵗʰ, 1777

Morale was low among the 2ⁿᵈ Light and Tallmadge could sense the men were restless and divided. Colonel Sheldon had brought the other two troops from their wintering quarters in Wethersfield after the Battle of Short Hills was fought, but instead of being one cohesive regiment, Washington had directed they be parceled out to other regiments or serve as piquets and scouts. While he understood the need for such duties, it disappointed Tallmadge that they were not to serve as one regiment. Captain Bull and his troop were still at Peekskill on the Hudson with General Putnam and did not seem to be returning any time soon. Lieutenant Colonel Blackden was also stationed with them.

Around mid-July they had learned that Howe's ships had sailed from Sandy Hook and Washington was trying to counter any movements along the seaboard. Though some of the men had conducted themselves well in the harried movements of going back and forth between the areas, he could see they were restless, some wanting action while others were simply bored with their duties and piquets.

That boredom led to infighting among the men – and Tallmadge knew that the officers were not above it, even though they were supposed to be gentlemen and beyond reproach. He tried to stay out of the bickering for the most part – letting the captains sort it out among themselves, but he had noticed that Colonel Sheldon did not exert discipline among the bickering officers.

They were currently camped at Newtown, New Jersey, on the left wing of an extended line stretching from the edges of Philadelphia to the Jersey coast, to watch General Howe's movements. Colonel Sheldon had proceeded to nearby Roxboro to oversee a court martial and left Tallmadge in charge.

Tallmadge sat around one of the camp fires, melting a block of lead to make ammunition. He had spent the last couple of hours cleaning his pistols with a small vial of whale oil that Brewster had sent in his last letter to him about a month ago. His friend had cheekily said that he owed him for the amount whale oil sent – which Tallmadge knew could run more than ten pounds on the black market. The letter also provided him with news from his childhood home of Setauket. Brewster had heard from local farmers and smugglers who plied their wares on the London Trade that Colonel Hewlett had taken over his father's church and turned it into a barracks. They had also destroyed part of the burial grounds in their construction of a stockade. Tallmadge was ill with anger at the thought of his father's church being destroyed in such fashion, but Brewster's letter indicated that he had not shared the news with Reverend Tallmadge in New Haven.

He had immediately written back to Brewster thanking him for the information and also the consideration to his father. He then forwarded Brewster's letter to General Putnam at Peekskill to see if anything could be done, but knew that whatever orders Washington had given to Putnam would put his request as a low priority. Tallmadge did not expect anything to be done, but he kept some hope.

"Aye, but then why do you not serve in perhaps the 3rd or even the 4th Light?" Belden's voice suddenly rose from the quiet murmur of another campfire near the one Tallmadge worked at.

Technically there was a row of tents that bisected the space between the two campfires, concealing him from the one with the captains and their lieutenants, but he could see shifting movement of the uniformed bodies of his subordinate officers:

Belden and Webb of 1st Troop, the Frenchman de Vernejout and Lieutenant Seymour, Captain Crafts, Stoddard, and their respective lieutenants. A small group of cornets and sergeants sat by another fire a few feet away, half concealed, but visible to both him and the officers' by the angle they sat at. Tallmadge saw that Belden's loud comment had stopped the brief murmuring conversation at the junior officers' fire and that one of the cornets, another Frenchman by the name of John Simonet de Valcour, had taken a particular interest at Belden's comment – his whetstone and sabre lying forgotten on his lap.

"Your Congress thinks there is too much of French and others serving in the more prestige regiments and thus wishes for me to serve with these...gentlemen..." De Vernejout's disdain was clear and Tallmadge resisted the urge to sigh. It was the same argument he had heard since Wethersfield – though it seemed now that since de Vernejout had an audience not familiar with his grievance, he seemed to relish again in his contempt for his assignment and rank.

"You mean rabble, don't you, Frenchie?" and like clockwork, Tallmadge heard Stoddard's growl of provocation to de Vernejout's words. "Well, you had your fill of killing those Loyalist bastards yet? Killing lobsterbacks? Slicing through them and cutting them apart-"

"Josiah, language!" Belden admonished, but was answered by a snort of contempt from Stoddard.

"Listen Zeke." Tallmadge glanced over to see Stoddard leaning towards the fire, tapping a wicked-looking hunting knife in his hand as he ran his whetstone quickly down the blade. "Those bloody lobsterbacks, well, they deserve every inch of this blade that I have here. So does anyone else who aides them."

"Captain, what if they're innocents?" Seymour spoke up a frown on his face. Tallmadge saw Stoddard shake his head a little.

"There are no innocents in this war, pup," Stoddard shook his head. "You fight or you are against us. Neutrality doesn't mean shite. We're bloody laying down our lives for independence, for those people who would want to see us hang or shot than help us. They'd better give us quarter or they better help us."

"Then how does this make us better than the British or even

the Tories? You heard what they did to Patriot towns right?" Belden, apparently derailed from his questioning of de Vernejout's loyalties, turned his energies to this argument. Tallmadge thought he heard Webb echoing Belden's question with a firm aye, but could not quite discern it through the sudden crackle of his own fire.

He glanced down and realized his lead block was burning a little before quickly taking the melted metal and pouring it into the molds.

"We've got the greatest commander in the dragoons, boys!" Stoddard crowed, rather facetiously in Tallmadge's opinion. He glanced up to see the man throwing his hands up in the air.

"Cheering declaration Captain, considering that I've seen you and the colonel butt heads back in Wethersfield," one of the lieutenants spoke up, sarcasm dripping in his voice.

"Elisha and I go back. He just needs a little push in the right direction from time to time. Being that *some* captains don't appreciate his leadership-"

There was an angry burst of French from de Vernejout that Tallmadge did not understand. But out of the corner of his eye he caught the young French cornet at the other campfire sitting up straighter, eyes widening in fear and surprise. Judging by the young cornet's expression, whatever de Vernejout said were strong words.

"What the shite was that, Frenchie?!" Stoddard's tone was hostile and Tallmadge straightened in concern, his tools forgotten.

"Something only you provincials cannot understand since you all smell like the backsides of pigs," de Vernejout said, spitting to the side.

"And you bloody well think that you're better than us?! You haven't even seen anything. You've just got your fancy little rank from Congress and you don't even know how to properly control your damn horse or even shoot straight. Don't deny it, I've seen you shoot and it's a pretty poor shot there. Not fit for any type of mounted combat!"

"Neither have you-"

"I fought at Fort Washington you little shite. Don't tell me what it was like when all you're here for is just for glory and riches. You don't even care one whit about independence and you can rot like the rest of the bloody Tories or lobsterbacks."

"Your Fort Washington was nothing more than a glorified surrender. Your vaunted commander did not even think to fortify the post or to ensure that his men would be able to defend the place. He left you there to die and you should have done so-"

"Sir-"

"No, Hazard, shut up," Stoddard interrupted his lieutenant. "I want to hear what else Frenchie thinks of us provincials. Come on, you got something to say-"

"*Oui.* Just because you think you are *friends* with Colonel Sheldon you benefit from knowing someone. No, you are trash, nothing but the waste that leaks into the outhouses. Sheldon does not know what to do with his commanders, and promotes such provincials to be my betters. They do not-"

"Sir-"

"Uh, sir-"

Tallmadge had hardly realized he had automatically stood up from his own fire and walked over to the 2nd Light's captains and lieutenants, until wide-eyed silence fell among them. He stood, arms folded across his chest as he stared at both de Vernejout and Stoddard, both of whom slowly turned.

"Would either of you care to repeat what was said?" Tallmadge marveled inwardly at how calm his own voice was as he looked around those assembled around the fire.

"Sir, I-I was to defend-"

"Defend what?" Tallmadge asked, raising an eyebrow at Stoddard's stuttering.

The man pressed his lips together and looked away, unable to meet his gaze. Tallmadge knew he could have easily called out Stoddard's supposed defense of his 'honor' of the slander that de Vernejout had subtly voiced, but he knew Stoddard would not have done such a thing. Tallmadge had seen the flash of anger, the jealousy in Stoddard's gaze when he had been passed for promotion to major. Even Tallmadge had been surprised at the promotion. Since Stoddard knew Sheldon previously and had even been friends with him, Tallmadge thought he would have been promoted first. He understood nepotism, knowing it was sometimes a good thing, sometimes a bad thing. But he thought that Sheldon would want someone like Stoddard who had a zeal for killing the British, but also for achieving independence at any cost, to lead the men. It seemed Sheldon thought otherwise.

"Captain de Vernejout?" he focused his icy stare at the Frenchman, "would you like to explain since it seems Captain Stoddard lost his voice?"

He could see something ugly flit across the Frenchman's face, but whatever it was, de Vernejout refused to voice it and instead shook his head and looked away too. Tallmadge affected a noise of curiosity as glanced back and forth between the two feuding officers.

"It seems that neither of you are willing to talk," he started. "Ensure it stays that way regarding what was said or perhaps not said. Dissent will not be tolerated, and neither will this sort of talk." He flicked his gaze between the two, but made sure he addressed his other captains since he had also heard them join in the debate. "You are officers and you should know better. The men we command do not have the experience either one of you carry from service or from foreign countries. It is your job to teach them how to be soldiers and how to be gentlemen. This is not the way gentlemen behave."

He gave them one last look. "Do better."

This time, all the officers refused to meet his gaze, shamed by his words. Having said his piece, he turned around and headed around the tents back to his fire. He wanted to sigh and run a hand through his hair in frustration, but he could not show such lax discipline in front of the men, especially after what he had just said. Instead, he picked up his tools and glared disgustedly at the melted lead, which was over cooked. The metal had turned to an ichorous black sludge and he tapped it against a stone near the fire, dumping the contents into the pit.

He glanced at his captains and saw that some of them were getting up with silent, stony expressions on their faces, the reprimand still stinging in their ears. Belden patted a good night to Webb, who made his way to the campfire of the cornets and sergeants and sat down next to Cornet Wadsworth with a miserable look.

He looked away as he saw Wadsworth turn his gaze towards where he was sitting, and pulled out another small lead block to melt.

"Sir." The gentle prod at his shoulder caused Tallmadge to start awake, his hand halfway to pulling his dagger from underneath his straw pillow. "Sir." He managed to stop himself short as he recognized the voice, and squinted into the inky night.

"Adamson?" he croaked, before clearing his throat a little.

"Sir, Cornet de Valcour says you should come quickly." Adamson sounded grave and Tallmadge blinked his eyes, trying to clear the sleep from them as he sat up, and sheathed his dagger into its place in his boot. He had slept with his boots on tonight, after a late walking patrol around the edges of camp to ensure that there were no other fights or dissent among the men.

"What time-"

"About early light sir," Adamson replied as he backed away, pushing the tent flap open some more.

Tallmadge saw that indeed, it was nearly dawn, the dark blues of night giving way to the lighter blues of morning. He rubbed his eyes and stepped out, meeting Cornet de Valcour's salute with a slightly lopsided one of his own.

"What is it?" he asked and saw Adamson move to the cornet who fidgeted and looked nervous. His friend prodded the young officer, who jumped a little before composing himself.

"Sir," de Valcour's accent was not as harsh as de Vernejout's, but it was still noticeable, as was his slightly broken English. "I apologize for lack of manners my fellow countryman displays. He has conducted a...how do you call, it, uh..." The young officer fell silent as he muttered something in French before looking back up at him. "Pistole, to fire, du-duel, yes, duel-"

The word sliced right through Tallmadge's sleepiness. He straightened and stared hard at the young officer. "What," he stated flatly.

"Duel, sir, duel, pistole and-"

"Yes, yes," Tallmadge shook his head impatiently, "I know what a duel is, but where, Cornet? Where?! And with whom? Speak man, speak!"

"T-They move over there, I think, over the hill?" de Valcour looked frightened as he pointed in the general direction of the sloping hill that descended into the small valley they had been using as a watering spot for the horses.

Tallmadge cursed silently as he turned to Adamson, "Get six men you trust. They are to be armed. Wake Webb and Belden, they are coming with me."

"Sir!" Adamson quickly headed away as Tallmadge pointed a finger at de Valcour.

"Wait here," he ordered and the young officer nodded.

Tallmadge ducked back into his tent and slung his jacket on before grabbing his sabre and pistol. He buckled the belt around his waist before heading back out and gesturing roughly for the young cornet to follow him. The young man tripped on his heels as he hastily followed his long strides across camp. As he passed by another row of tents, Belden and Webb hastily ran towards him, half dressed and similarly armed. He thought he saw Adamson's shadow cut across a few tents as he woke the six men he trusted to follow after them.

"Sir-"

"Sir, what's happening?!" Belden asked as he adjusted his weaponry while Webb pulled at the sleeves of his jacket and tried to make himself presentable.

"Stopping a duel," he replied curtly, furious anger filling him. How stupid was de Vernejout and the other man – he had a feeling it might be Stoddard – to challenge each other to a duel? He never understood the supposed custom between two gentlemen, even officers, and thought it barbaric. While at Yale and even during his time teaching in Wethersfield he had seen or heard about duels between those who thought they had been slighted, and had shaken his head in disgust at the nonsense a duel produced. It was even more disgusting now that they were all officers in the army. Why needlessly kill each other when they needed to unite and fight the British! That was the enemy, not each other. There was no honor gained in shooting a fellow soldier; duels were just a waste of life and time. Especially between two of his captains!

"Oh shite..." He heard the whispered curse from Webb, but ignored it as he glanced at de Valcour who nodded that this was the direction he had seen his fellow Frenchman and his opponent go in.

"That explains why Seymour wasn't there all night," Belden muttered and Tallmadge glanced back to see Belden duck his head in shame. "Apologies, sir, but Lieutenant Seymour bunked with us and was not in the tent for the night. We thought he was perhaps performing a task for Captain de Vernejout but-"

Tallmadge growled out his disgust and Belden quieted as he marched up the hill, his grip tight on his sabre's hilt. He knew that Belden, Webb, and Seymour were all friends, but it seemed that Captain de Vernejout had tapped Seymour to possibly be his second in this duel and Tallmadge wished he had been more aware of the situation. He should have put the Frenchman under house arrest after his comments by the fire.

"Sir! Look!" Webb called out as they crested the hill. Five people stood by a small ridge near a brook. One was in the process of moving up to higher ground, turning himself away to have deniability. The other two who were clearly holding pistols were checking their weapons while their seconds stood near them.

"Hold fast!" he shouted as he descended the hill, starting to jog as he drew his pistol, but held it loosely by his side. All participants looked up at him, startled by his appearance. Tallmadge's anger grew as he saw de Vernejout's opponent – Stoddard. His second was Lieutenant Hazard and Lieutenant Seymour was de Vernejout's second. The fact that the two captains had involved their lieutenants in this mess greatly incensed him.

"What the *hell* are you doing?!" he shouted as he approached. Both lieutenants looked nervous at the sight of him while de Vernejout and Stoddard had stony expressions. The fifth man, apparently the doctor that was to administer to either wounded party looked a little like Stoddard, but he too seemed startled – and perhaps a bit relieved – by his appearance.

"Solving dispute, sir," de Vernejout's tone of voice seemed to indicate that he was trying to point out the obvious and Tallmadge had enough.

He holstered his pistol in case he could not contain his anger and was tempted to shoot both men for their foolish stupidity. He jabbed a finger at the Frenchman. "You, good sir, are treading a dangerous line of insubordination." He glared at the two. "You will both stop this foolish nonsense-"

"Sir, the duel has been accepted and honor lost-"

"Honor has not been lost and I will not allow this duel to proceed even if the challenges have been accepted, Stoddard!" he roared at the captain, who flinched a little at his tone. "You two are officers! Act like your commands! As long as you continue to serve under the 2nd Light, I will not allow *any* man, especially an officer, to challenge any other man in the regiment to a duel. You two are as idiotic as the British! Do you honestly think that by killing or wounding each other when we are so short of officers will do the 2nd Light well?!"

He could see both men fighting to say something, but the protocol of rank and respect overrode their impulse. "Do I make myself clear?" he asked, lowering his voice so that it was now even and cold. "You wish to duel each other? Then transfer yourselves out of this regiment and be gone from my sight. You wish to sully the name of the 2nd Light and the honor to be a dragoon – do it away from this regiment. We do not need men like you who would recklessly throw their lives away just because you think your honor has been lost."

He heard movement behind him and turned to see Adamson and the six men he had gathered coming down the ridge. All were armed with their carbines and they half slid, half walked down the hill. He heard de Vernejout mutter something in French under his breath.

A sharp intake of a breath followed by an indignant splutter from Cornet de Valcour made him turn. The young officer's frowned as he flicked a quick fearful look at him. "Is not true, sir!"

Captain de Vernejout smiled nastily and muttered something else in French and de Valcour turned a little red in the dawn light. Tallmadge stepped between the two, shielding de Valcour from any other reprisal or vocal abuse from Captain de Vernejout. He met the two feuding captain's gazes. "Captain Stoddard and de Vernejout. Both of you will be placed under house arrest until Colonel Sheldon returns. You may keep your weapons, but three of these men will escort you back to your tents where you will stay. You can be assured that I will be writing a formal report to the colonel and to General Washington regarding your actions and conduct today."

He nodded to Adamson, who directed three men to escort both captains up the hill. They surrounded the two in a silent formation and Tallmadge nodded once to Adamson, who left with the six he had brought.

"Lieutenant Hazard, Lieutenant Seymour." He turned to face the captains' seconds and saw the two shift nervously. "What do you have to say for yourselves?"

"Coercion, sir," Seymour blurted out. "I...I apologize for allowing this to go so far, sir, but-"

"Oh come off of it, Thomas," Hazard scoffed. "You were waiting for Stoddard to shoot de Vernejout just because you hated him too."

"Quiet," Tallmadge said his voice firm. "As seconds, both of you were supposed to at least negotiate to the point to prevent this from happening."

"...Sir..." Seymour shifted uncomfortably before hanging his head, "Lieutenant Hazard is correct...I...did not engage in any effective negotiation due to my own feelings as both Captain de Vernejout's second and the poor service I performed as his second."

He saw Webb put a palm to his forehead, but ignored the movement as he focused back on the two lieutenants. While he himself disliked de Vernejout for his sour disposition and inflated sense of self-importance, this confession from Seymour was truly revealing. It seemed the 2nd Light was truly discontented with de Vernejout's presence. Tallmadge would have to talk to Sheldon about remedying that before another duel happened or perhaps an 'accident' of sorts on the battlefield involving the Frenchman.

He sighed quietly and shook his head. "The two of you will report back to your men and assume temporary command of your troops until this whole thing is sorted out with your captains. Be advised, if there is any talk regarding what has happened here, I will hear of it and I will know where such rumors have come from." He knew that he could not wholly prevent such rumors from spreading across camp, but perhaps he could prevent some of the more scandalous details from spreading. If either lieutenant valued their careers in the 2nd Light, they would know not to say anything incriminating beyond the basic fact that yes, their captains challenged each other to a duel.

He waved a disgusted hand at them, "Get out of my sight."

The two lieutenants left with Belden and Webb escorting them and Tallmadge turned to face the fifth man who was privy to the duel. He was clearly dressed in civilian clothes and had spectacles perched on the edges of his nose, much like Mr. Sackett when Tallmadge met him in February. However, he carried a large leather purse that indicated he was a doctor.

"Doctor Darius Stoddard at your service, Major..."

"Benjamin Tallmadge." He reached out and shook hands with the doctor, noting the family resemblance between Doctor Stoddard and Captain Stoddard.

"Josiah is my brother, sir." The doctor released his hand and smiled hesitantly. "I happened to have been in the area on my way to Philadelphia to visit a few of my clients when my brother sent word of this duel he was having with Captain de Vernejout. I hope he has not brought shame to the regiment or to you, good sir."

"That is something for Colonel Sheldon to decide," Tallmadge was decidedly neutral in his reply and he saw something flicker behind Stoddard's expression. If the man was trying to protect his brother from reprimand or punishment by flattering him, it was falling well short. Tallmadge was in no mood to accept any form of flattery.

"Seeing that this terrible business has been dismissed, may I be excused or do you request my presence here?"

"If you would please stay for a few days before proceeding onto Philadelphia, I am sure that Colonel Sheldon would like to hear your version of events that transpired and led up to this," Tallmadge asked and saw the doctor nod once.

"Of course, if I may be furnished with some paper to write to my clients about my delay?"

"Yes, I will have one of my men provide you with needed pen and paper and will send it by express post," he replied before gesturing to Cornet de Valcour. "Cornet de Valcour will conduct you to the house that Colonel Sheldon has made into his temporary quarters. There is a guest bed in one of the rooms you may use during your stay."

"Certainly, sir," Stoddard smiled congenially and started to head away.

"Oh, Doctor Stoddard?" Tallmadge called out as the doctor turned back. "Due to Captain Stoddard's current situation, please refrain from calling upon him."

The smile the doctor gave him was definitely not as friendly as before. He nodded and started to walk up the hill towards the camp.

"Sir," Cornet de Valcour tipped his head at him, but seemed to hesitate for a moment before shifting a little. "Sir, I want to apologize for my countryman's words to you. He questioned your sense of honor and your valor on battlefield for not allowing gentlemen to duel in manner. I told him it was untrue. He called me a traitor..."

Tallmadge managed to keep his expression neutral in light of de Valcour's words. He did not need defending by the young cornet, but appreciated it nonetheless. De Vernejout certainly knew of his military experience and was more than likely trying to get a rise out of his fellow Frenchman for siding with him. Even if de Vernejout had questioned his valor and military prowess publicly, it was something Tallmadge would never respond to – the men knew and the officers knew; and it was something de Vernejout would have no ground in questioning so it would make him seem all the more foolish for doing so.

"Colonel Sheldon will mete out punishment as he sees fit when he returns, Cornet," he replied, and the young man nodded before leaving to escort Dr. Stoddard back to camp. That left Tallmadge alone in the dueling site. He glanced up at the dawning sky. He had prevented one crisis from happening, but he had a feeling that this was only the beginning of his headaches.

Tallmadge counted his blessings and silently thanked God for Colonel Sheldon's return later that afternoon from the court martial he had been overseeing. He met Sheldon with the report of what had transpired in the few days he had been away and could see that his commander was visibly annoyed but resigned to what had happened. Tallmadge knew that this was not the first time Sheldon had to deal with both captains, but he also knew that the quarrel between them had escalated this seriously since they had mustered at Wethersfield.

He was dismissed with compliments to return after Sheldon had dealt with the two, and so Tallmadge found himself back in his tent, debating whether or not to take a nap or finish compiling reports regarding the troops' status. Oddly, one of the troops had gone through powder and balls at a faster rate than the others. There was also the problem that some horses had proven themselves to be unsuitable mounts for long-term use as they were starting to lame. Tallmadge had directed the men to try to rehabilitate the horses in case they were called upon, but had also requested fresh horses for the men.

He stared at the half-finished reports on his portable traveling desk, an unexpected gift from his father. Apparently his father had it commissioned when he returned to New Haven after his brief visit in January. Tallmadge used it to great effect since the tentage and supply wagons had arrived along with the larger pieces of furniture that could not initially travel with the officers. At the moment, however, Tallmadge decided to leave the desk alone and catch up on his interrupted sleep from the morning.

It only felt like a few minutes, but the sun was lower in the sky when he awakened to the scuffling sound of boots near his tent. "Sir," Webb spoke up beyond the flap of his tent. "Colonel Sheldon requests your presence."

"Understood." Tallmadge pushed himself up from his cot and brushed himself down, making sure his clothes were presentable. Outside, he shifted his weapons belt and gripped the hilt of his sabre as he made his way to the small house Sheldon had taken for both his quarters and his office. The house itself was small, with a main living and sleeping quarters, along with one storage room and a secondary bedroom which the owner of the house was relegated to after they arrived. Dr. Stoddard was more than likely using the storage room as a makeshift guest room.

On his way to the house, he saw that Adamson and the men he had utilized to guard both Stoddard's and de Vernejout's tents were still in place. It seemed Sheldon was content to let both men think on their actions and the punishment received.

Knocking on the door, he heard Sheldon's muffled command to enter and did so, closing the door behind him. "Sir," he saluted and stood at attention.

Sheldon waved for him to relax his stance. "I appreciate your handling of the situation, Tallmadge," his commander began, "as the men do need to learn that their petty disagreements are not more important than defeating the enemy or being in a prepared state if we are to be called upon."

"Yes, sir," he replied.

"I would however, like to ask your opinion on Captain de Vernejout, if you will?" Tallmadge shifted a bit.

"My personal opinion of the man, sir?" he asked.

"Yes," his commander replied, looking at him. "Everything said will be in confidence, Tallmadge."

"Yes, sir." He was not exactly comfortable with speaking in such a frank manner about someone, preferring to vent his frustrations in a satirical letter to one of his friends or summarize succinctly in a report. He had done the former after Colonel Bland's disastrous attempt to charge the enemy before the Battle of Short Hills.

"Sir, I believe that Captain de Vernejout is lowering morale among the men." He stared at Sheldon. "And his actions and words have provoked some of the others to rash actions as well as resentment towards foreign aid."

"Oh? You believe we need foreign aid? That we would overthrow one dictator for another?"

Tallmadge nodded once. "Yes and no, sir. It is my belief after what we had seen last year that we do need foreign aid, if only to a certain point. The French provided us with arms and ammunition, and while it is my hope that our ambassadors in France ensure that we do not end up falling under the yolk of the French monarchy after we win independence, we do need their help."

"Then what of Captain de Vernejout?"

"Nothing more than an adventurer who seeks glory only for himself in a rank that he has not *earned* yet," Tallmadge stressed and saw Sheldon incline his head at his words. "I do not know why Congress saw fit to give him such a rank, nor do I know of his previous military history and exploits, but I do know that the men that serve under him are not confident in their abilities nor sure in their discipline to adhere to commands given."

"Could it be a result of the inaction they have seen since their arrival?" Sheldon asked.

"I do not know, sir," he replied. "I was focused on training 1st Troop during that time, but I do know for a fact that de Vernejout's lieutenant, Thomas Seymour has spent time with my subordinates and has asked me questions regarding the training of horses and of men while we wintered, sir."

Sheldon pursed his lips and tented his fingers as he looked up at him. "Tallmadge, speak true and tell me if you would be comfortable giving an order to Captain de Vernejout if we are to see action."

"What kind of order?" he asked, and a faint smile appeared on his commander's face.

"A wise question," Sheldon acknowledged, before he sat back and let his hands rest on his desk, "but perhaps it is with a bit of providence from God that I received a letter from General Washington requesting that I send a troop to serve with General Gates and the Northern Army in his campaign against Burgoyne. It was something I had considered before I was appointed to this court martial, but now, it seems fate has provided me with an opportunity and excuse to handle such a situation."

Sheldon sighed and shook his head as he looked to the side, "De Vernejout did come with military experience, that much is certain, but how much of it was inflated to Congress we will never know. I have decided to send Captain de Vernejout and his troop on detached duty to aid General Gates in his campaign against Burgoyne. Unfortunately I do not have the power or clout to cashier out such a man without drastically reducing our standings in the eyes of the French."

"Very good, sir." Tallmadge was relieved to hear that de Vernejout was not going to trouble the 2nd Light for a while. Perhaps it would stop the bickering and infighting among the men, or at least reduce it when one of the biggest antagonists was gone. "Sir, if I may ask, what of Captain Stoddard?"

"Captain Stoddard will be reprimanded and his brother will be talked to," Sheldon's tone told Tallmadge that he would speak no more of it and he nodded. He knew that Stoddard and Sheldon were acquainted, if not great friends, but at least it was being handled.

"Sir," he acknowledged the order. "Will we see action soon?" he asked.

"Unsure, but since Washington had seen the main body of Howe's fleet launch from Sandy Hook, we are currently to be on watch for any sign of landings. We may see action yet, but at this moment, I do not know," Sheldon replied and Tallmadge sensed the dismissal in his commanding officer's tone.

"Sir, if I may take my leave," he saluted and started to leave.

"Tallmadge," Sheldon suddenly spoke up and he turned to see his commanding officer look at him with curiosity in his eyes. "I heard an interesting comment from some of the men regarding your disposition towards dueling?"

Tallmadge paused, wondering how he should address said comments before he squared his shoulders and answered truthfully. "It is a detestable action that one man may inflict upon another, sir."

"Not even if their honor was questioned?" Sheldon asked.

"There is no honor in killing those whom we call friends and allies," he said, "when we all should be killing the enemy instead."

Sheldon snorted quietly before allowing him to leave with a wave of his hand. Tallmadge turned back around and left the small house. He was not sure what his commander personally thought of dueling, knowing that it was a way to affirm a gentleman's social status against slights of honor. And therein lay the problem, in his opinion. While the European aristocracy was known for its duels in their classes, many of the officers and men of artisans or other classes their European counterparts would consider low, not worthy of the status of gentlemen. Only those who were landed owners would be considered gentlemen – but even then still viewed as country bumpkins. De Vernejout's sneer towards them was indicative of this. Tallmadge knew the Frenchman thought of them as nothing more than peasants trying to become officers without having the pedigree or lineage to back up the prestige of rank. This was why Stoddard and so many of the others found de Vernejout to be highly disagreeable.

At least the matter involving Captain Stoddard and de Vernejout had been settled. Hopefully they would see some action soon to bolster the men's spirits and also to have them focus on the enemy instead of the petty infighting.

In the month that followed, the 2nd Light found themselves on support duty assigned to General Greene at the White Clay Creek area of Delaware. General Howe and his British forces finally landed at the Head of the Elk after what seemed to be a month at sea, owing to stormy weather that delayed his fleet. It had given the Continentals precious time to fortify their positions around the Head of the Elk. There was talk of possible action, but the 2nd Light did not find themselves in the heat of it. Instead, they were dispatched to guard supply trains, a vital and necessary duty, but not one that Tallmadge expected would boost morale among the men.

He also found out during this time that his initial intelligence gathered by himself, Adamson, and Major Clark back in February had been put to use. A force led by his friend Colonel Webb crossed Long Island Sound on August 22nd, and attacked the Tory garrison under the command of Colonel Hewlett at Setauket. Unfortunately the garrison was too fortified and the mission was considered a failure as Webb retreated without loss or gain. Tallmadge was disappointed to hear that his childhood hometown was still under Tory rule, but what he and Clark had done was not for naught.

Tallmadge knew it was only a matter of time until Howe launched his attack towards Philadelphia.

September 11th, 1777

"Can I at least maybe eat one of the cows?" Pullings' slight nasally whine grated on Tallmadge's ears, but he ignored it as he rode at the head of the small escort party.

They had been detailed to escort several wagons full of provisions, ammunition, and general supplies to camp under the detached command of General Greene. It seemed the other three dragoon regiments had been utilized in the same fashion. He wished the 2nd Light had drawn scouting duty, as it required a full troop or more, but it seemed Washington knew exactly where he wanted to stop Howe, Cornwallis, and the Hessian forces days ago. The scouting routes had been disbanded and utilized for the more mundane but important purpose of making sure the army's supplies were protected from any raiding parties.

The last he heard, Washington had placed the army near Chadd's Ford and surrounding area along the Brandywine Creek while he and rest of the 2nd Light had been sent to retrieve supplies that were needed during and after the battle. Most of it was ammunition for the cannons, but some was needed materials that the men lacked, like working muskets or lead blocks for ammunition. That was two days ago and Tallmadge and his small party were on their way back, escorting the wagon train that was sent with the supplies. The wagons numbered four, and his party had eighteen men including Pullings and Adamson. Davenport, along with Sergeant Mills, had been detailed with Captain Belden and Lieutenant Webb's party with another supply wagon two miles behind them. Essentially the whole of 1st Troop had been split in half, as were the troops of the 2nd Light.

"Are you offering to pull the wagon after eating the cow?" Adamson joked with a cheerful smile on his face as he rode beside Pullings.

"What?" Pullings looked confused.

"There is strength apparently in eating that much meat. It must translate somewhere into that skinny form you have there," Adamson continued, and Pullings' expression became an exaggeration of distress.

"Abuse! I pronounce abuse!" Pullings mocked being shot in the heart. "My dear Adamson, how you wound me with your words!"

"It's just a cow." Adamson's cheerfulness turned sarcastically flat before the two erupted into laughter at the pun. The laughter cascaded through the rest of the men who surrounded the wagons on both sides. Even the wagoners laughed and some clapped at Pullings' performance.

Tallmadge had to smile at the clever wording as he glanced at his men. He caught Pullings' eyes and nodded once. "You seem to be in better spirits Corporal Pullings."

"Yes, sir!" Pullings gave him a jaunty salute. "And it is all thanks to the cow I may yet eat at the end of this journey!"

"Then you're definitely pulling the wagon for the rest of the journey if you wish to earn your share of the cow," Tallmadge shot back, and saw his friend look mockingly wounded.

"My share, sir. Only a share? Can I not have the whole of the cow?"

"Not if you want to have a cow." Tallmadge could see Adamson laughing into his saddle horn at his continuation of the pun. The others applauded behind Tallmadge as Pullings mocked injury again before turning back. But Tallmadge saw his expression suddenly change from cheerful to wide-eyed fear.

The road they were traveling overlooked the fords and shallow valleys that made up the Brandywine Creek. The area was dominated by rolling fields, some filled with farmlands, and others with dense trees packed together in tight clusters. He held up an absent hand to stop the train from going farther as he saw what had become of General Washington's position down in Chadd's Ford, and what had triggered Pullings' fear.

Fire, ruin, and utter devastation littered the area. Across the blackened ground, which was gouged by cannon fire, he could see tiny blue dots; mixed with red dots, Continental and British soldiers. There was the occasional brown or black dot form of horses that had fallen in battle. In general there were far more blues than reds strewn on the pockmarked green ground. Tallmadge pulled out his spyglass and extended it to survey the battlefield.

He swallowed, his throat suddenly dry. He could see the tiny movements of red dots and multi-colored ones, British and Hessian forces that marched undaunted across a shallow ford. He glassed upwards and saw the distant forms of blues moving away in the easterly direction they had come from, but also moving south. The army was in full retreat.

Tallmadge lowered his glass, placed it back into his pouch and gestured to Pullings.

"Sir?" He ignored the slight fear in his friend's voice.

"Ride back to Belden's train and tell them to head back the way they came from. We'll circle around back to where the army is retreating. Have him send out two to scout out the location and report back," he ordered, and Pullings nodded before wheeling his horse and galloping off.

Tallmadge turned to stare at the other men and the wagoners who looked a little nervous. "We'll be turning around," he announced. "Do not fear, we will rejoin the army as soon as possible." A few of the men nodded bravely at his words, but he knew they all saw what he had seen. The fact that they were now well out of the protection of the army meant a higher chance of the supply train being attacked if the British got wind of their presence; Tallmadge would be damned if he let the supplies fall into the hands of the British. The defeat at Brandywine now put his supplies at a great import and he would do all he could to ensure their safe passage to the retreat point.

They arrived at Chester, Pennsylvania in the early afternoon, three days after the army's defeat at Chadd's Ford after taking a rather long route around the rolling hills of Brandywine Creek. Chester was a small village located east of Chadd's Ford along the Delaware River, just south of Philadelphia. There was some minor fanfare to their arrival. Many troops were still getting themselves organized and tending to the wounded and dead, but those that saw them cheered as they approached. Tallmadge ignored their cheering and directed the supply train to the proper area before he and Belden reported to Washington himself.

His arrival garnered the thanks of the Commander-in-Chief before he was dismissed to see to his horses and men. Due to the long route and little to no rest for the horses, a couple of the men of 1st Troop reported that their horses had been spent and were lamed. Tallmadge also learned that the other supply trains and scouting parties that were sent out were slowly being recalled, though the supply trains had priority to getting the army re-equipped.

Colonel Sheldon and two troops had been sent up to reinforce the Hudson Highlands with General Putnam's division after conflicting reports of defeat and victory up north by Gates and Burgoyne had prompted the necessary division of the 2nd Light. He learned they would also be sent out again to escort another wagon of supplies, this time north of Philadelphia to ensure that the men had adequate supplies, and so set forth four days later. He returned a few days after that to find Stoddard and his troop had seen some action after being detached to serve under Lieutenant Colonel Benjamin Temple of the 1st Light. The 1st Light had been assigned to serve under General Wayne and a piquet had been formed to guard the main body at nearby Paoli.

Stoddard and his troop had been challenged by General Grey's men who had a somewhat frightening reputation of not using their muskets but only bayonets as their method of attack. It was a route at Paoli, with Stoddard and his troop barely escaping with their lives, while fifty others died and a hundred more were wounded and captured. Stoddard's troop had lost a couple of men and their horses, thinning their effectiveness once more. The long routes and supply trains had worn down more horses of the 2nd Light and Tallmadge checked with the other dragoon regiments to find that they too were not faring well in terms of keeping their horses healthy.

Morale lagged further and Tallmadge found that he could not do much to keep the men's spirits up. When the news came on September 27$^{th.}$ of the capture of Philadelphia, even Tallmadge wondered what they were going to do now that the British had both New York and Philadelphia. His answer would come on October 2nd.

10

October 2ⁿᵈ, 1777

The General Order of the day was swift and decisive. Brigadier General Casmir Pulaski had been summarily placed in charge of all mounted regiments and requested that all commanding officers of the light dragoons and their seconds report to him. Only those who were on detached duty or duties deemed too important to abandon were allowed respite. Since Sheldon had been sent along with Lieutenant Colonel Blackden to the Hudson Highlands and Captain de Vernejout and his troops were still serving Gates and the Northern Army, that left Tallmadge once again, nominally in charge of whatever remained of the 2ⁿᵈ Light; which was about three troops. He picked Belden to go as his second. By virtue of when he had received his commission, Stoddard would have had that honor, but he had received a minor wound at Paoli and was currently recovering. Tallmadge also preferred Belden because he was reliable and had led 1ˢᵗ Troop with a steady hand.

The two of them reported to Pulaski's tent and found the rest of the dragoon regiment commanders there. A slight sense of awe filled him as he realized this was truly the first time that all four light dragoons had been assembled in one area. He wished that Sheldon and Blackden were there to witness such a spectacle. However, it did not undermine the gravity of the army's need for cavalry forces since the defeat at Brandywine. As he removed his helm and set it on a small table where the others' helms rested, he tipped his head at the assembled officers. Colonel Bland nodded back, before turning to the side and coughing. He looked a little ill, but not ill enough to miss a meeting of this magnitude. Moylan greeted Tallmadge with a curt nod.

"Lieutenant Colonel Benjamin Temple." The officer next to Bland stepped towards him and extended his hand and Tallmadge shook it.

"Major Benjamin Tallmadge," he introduced himself as he released Temple's hand and gestured to Belden. "This is Captain Ezekiel Belden of 1st Troop."

"A pleasure," Temple seemed reasonably personable enough in an informal way as he shook hands with Belden. "How is Captain Stoddard?"

"Recovering, sir," Tallmadge replied. "He sends his greetings."

"You've got a fierce captain there, Tallmadge," Temple smiled, "absolutely fierce and a good man against the British."

"Yes, sir," Tallmadge replied, mildly surprised at the compliment that Temple had paid Stoddard. Then again, he supposed that for all of his disagreeable words, Stoddard did hate the British with a passion that was unrivaled. The only issue was his seemingly hostile attitude towards Tory families or neutral parties. Tallmadge glanced over as another man, dressed in the red-green jacket of the 4th, approached them.

"Major William Washington at your service," the man introduced himself with a slight rolling accent that Tallmadge recognized as a rural Virginian. He had a round sallow face that seemed dour except for the friendly tilt of his eyes. His cheeks were rosy as if with too much drink, but Tallmadge did not see any glass in his hand.

"Sir," he shook hands with the fellow major. There was a resemblance to General Washington and supposed that Washington was perhaps a relative of the general himself.

"We would have met back in June had I not been detached on assignment, Tallmadge," Washington shrugged. "Moylan spoke highly of you and your 1st Troop. I am glad to see you and

Captain Belden here."

"Thank you sir." Tallmadge glanced back to see Belden color a little from the high praise. Washington stepped back as did Temple, as another Lieutenant Colonel approached them. He was dressed in an off-white jacket with blue panelings.

"Major Tallmadge?" the man asked, and Tallmadge nodded.

"Sir," he tipped a casual salute to the man before gesturing to Belden. "This is Captain Belden of my 1st Troop."

The lieutenant colonel nodded before turning back to face him. "Lieutenant Colonel George Baylor of the 3rd Light. It's a pleasure to finally meet you."

"And you as well, sir." Tallmadge again reached out and shook hands with the officer. He noticed that Baylor was the only one who did not have a second-in-command with him.

"Most of my men are on detached duty, so I expect any offensive we conduct in whatever Pulaski has cooked up will be with the 2nd Light since you are also short three troops."

"Yes, sir," Tallmadge quelled his disappointment at being put under another officer's command. He had become used to conducting his own reconnaissance and missions for the last few months. But he supposed that with Pulaski gathering all available cavalry forces, it was inevitable. He was the most junior commander there.

There was a shuffling sound as the tent flap opened again and a young captain who looked harried and out of breath stepped in. The captain looked like he had rode in hard and Tallmadge suppressed a rueful smile.

"Apologies, sirs." The captain seemed to realize he was not late as Brigadier General Count Casmir Pulaski himself was still missing. The young man turned and extended his hand to Tallmadge. "Captain Allen McLane, sir, Delaware Horse."

"Major Benjamin Tallmadge, 2nd Light," he replied, shaking hands with the enthusiastic young militia captain. He gestured towards Belden. "My 1st Troop commander, Captain Ezekiel Belden."

"A pleasure to meet you." McLane shook hands with Belden, seemingly relieved that he was not the most junior officer there. Tallmadge knew the feeling, having experienced it when he was with the Connecticut Brigade the previous year. To him, that seemed like a lifetime ago, but the feeling that never quite went away, especially in a company like this.

He stepped to the side as the other officers made their introductions to the junior officer. Belden gave him a covert amused look, perhaps coming to a similar thought as he had. The young captain was not even half way through introducing himself to the others when the flap opened again and Tallmadge involuntarily straightened at the presence of Brigadier General Pulaski. The others did the same as Pulaski looked sharply at all of them before sweeping deeper into the tent. Pulaski's uniform was unique in that it looked a little like the Hessians', but with more medals and weight to it. It certainly was grand to look at, but Tallmadge had long learned that gaudiness and looks did not necessarily translate well to effectiveness and efficiency of command – case in point, Captain de Vernejout.

Behind Pulaski was another officer that Tallmadge did not recognize. He wore the epaulette of a major, but was smartly dressed and bore the regal air of southern aristocracy about him. He had a round face and wide eyes that seemed soft and untested by the rigors of war. But Tallmadge noted the sharp way the man held himself and guessed that the major before him was anything but untested. It also seemed that he knew his place. He paused and saluted the senior officers before following Brigadier General Pulaski to the back of the tent. Tallmadge and the others followed as the unnamed major withdrew a large map from his jacket and quickly unfolded it, placing it on the general's war table. Pulaski himself rummaged through a small bag and dumped out a handful of tokens, both red and blue colored, along with a couple of others that were oddly shaped and made of metal.

"Good evening sirs, I am Major John Laurens, one of General Washington's aide-de-camps and will assisting General Pulaski in this briefing," the major looked up, clasping his hands behind his back as Pulaski reached over and started to arrange the tokens on the map.

Tallmadge saw that it was a detailed map of the area surrounding Philadelphia. As Pulaski began to scatter the red-colored tokens in and around the city, he noticed that there were two concentrated clusters, one in Philadelphia itself, more than likely Howe and Cornwallis, while he other was clustered in a village just six miles northward, outside of the city called Germantown. On the northwest corner of the map was one blue token denoting their camp at Pennebeck Mill. The other blue tokens were placed to the side of the map, as were the odd-looking metal ones.

"This," Pulaski began without preamble, his accent heavy and gruff as he grabbed one of the odd-shaped silver tokens, "1st Light." He placed it down in no where in particular on the map. The token denoting the 1st Continental Light Dragoons looked a little like a griffin, but he could not be sure. Out of the corner of his eye, he saw Lieutenant Colonel Temple smile a little, happy that his regiment was designated with a stylized mythical beast.

"This," Pulaski pulled the next token and placed it next to the griffin and Tallmadge saw it was a falconing bird of sorts with the hood on and its wings folded, "2nd Light." He met the cavalry commander's eyes with his own and nodded once without comment. He did not quite know what to make of the fact that his 2nd Light had been designated as a falconing bird, especially as he studied the other tokens on the table, which were rather impressive-looking creatures of myth.

"3rd Light," Pulaski placed a rearing snake-like thing that Tallmadge realized was a dragon, similar to ones he had seen on very fine china. He guessed it must have been from the orient.

Apparently he was not the only one who had a hard time figuring out what it was as Lieutenant Colonel Baylor peered a little closer and hesitantly reached out to touch it before a glare from Pulaski stopped him. "It's a dragon depicted in oriental fashion, sir," Laurens supplied, as Pulaski took the fourth token and set it next to the three. It was definitely a depiction of a hydra, though it seemed a little burnished from constant use.

"4th," Pulaski said without other commentary before placing a fifth one next to first four. This one was of a mermaid. "Delaware Horse."

"Sir." Tallmadge had almost forgotten about McLane, but the captain spoke up next to him and he moved to the side to give McLane a better view of the battle map.

"Mine," Pulaski put his last silver token down and Tallmadge smiled at the obviousness of what denoted Pulaski's command. A regal charger half-rearing into the air. It seemed his attempt to induce some humor in them had the right effect as the rest of the room chuckled lightly before the Polish commander cleared his throat again, signaling for silence.

"Two wings." Pulaski placed two blue tokens at Chestnut Hill just north of Germantown, before gesturing for Laurens to continue.

"Sir," Laurens nodded once before gesturing to the two blue tokens, "Germantown has four major roads that lead into it from our current position. Major Generals Greene and Sullivan will be leading the two attacks on the wings. Greene on the left, Sullivan on the right. General Washington will form at the center, but be a part of Sullivan's forces. Sullivan, taking the right flank, will be supported by General Wayne and Conway as the flanking corps. They are to enter town and move forward without stopping. General Lord Stirling with Maxwell and Nash under his command will follow the initial column as reserve forces. General Armstrong will be a part of the right wing, but he will be sent down the Manatawny road to guard it from any attempt by the British to outflank us."

As Laurens spoke, he moved one small blue rectangular token down Wissahickon Creek which was next to the bulk of the red tokens that made up the force at Germantown. At the same time, he placed three tokens at spaced intervals that ran down the main road leading into Germantown from Chestnut Hill. Tallmadge could see that the road's name was Skippach. One was clearly Sullivan's forces, while the other was more than likely a combination of Wayne and Conway's forces and the one in the rear was General Lord Stirling's reserve forces. Here, Pulaski reached over and placed the tokens denoting the 1st, 4th, and Delaware next to the middle of the three lines of tokens. Tallmadge could see that both Bland and Moylan had tight pleased smiles on their faces at being on the right wing, the center of the attack. Tallmadge glanced over at Captain McLane, who had a solemn expression on his face and was studying the map with some seriousness in his eyes.

Pulaski was not finished. He reached over and dropped the token that denoted the 2nd Light, the hooded falconer, right in the front of the attack – with Sullivan's men. Pulaski had a grim look on his face as he pointed to Tallmadge. "You, punch, punch..." He jabbed his finger several times at him speaking the rest of his sentence in Polish before catching Moylan, Bland, and McLane's gaze. "The rest-" Pulaski made a sweeping motion and Tallmadge nodded.

It was a vanguard position that the 2nd Light had drawn; they would to be the tip of the spear that would initially cause the most confusion to the British and Hessian forces in Germantown. Then, they would push forward before the 1st, 4th, and Delaware would sweep in to continue to fight. It was a daring position and Tallmadge was pleased that his regiment had been picked to do such a thing. His only worry was that the farther they went into Germantown, the more likely the 2nd Light would be to suffer losses. He hoped that the drills and combat experience they had garnered so far would be enough for most of them to survive.

"Good." Pulaski saw that all four commanders understood their part in the plan. He gestured to Laurens to continue.

Major Laurens scattered a few more tokens on the left side of the map. "The left wing, General Greene, will be attacking the British right wing with General Stephen and flanked by General McDougall's brigade. They will enter Germantown village at the Markethouse by the lime-kiln road." Like Sullivan's formation on the right, the blue tokens signifying Greene's regiments were split into three, with McDougall's as the attacking force, but also the rear guard of Greene's left wing. Laurens dropped two more tokens to the right side of the map. "Generals Smallwood and Forman will follow Old York road until a convenient opportunity should bring them along the right flank of the enemy." The move exactly mirrored that of Armstrong's extreme position on the opposite side of the village.

Tallmadge marveled at how effectively the plan would cut off all four roads that led to the small village. The Schuylkill River was an effective barrier to stop the British from advancing and flanking their position outside of Philadelphia, therefore funneling all forces through Germantown. Pulaski reached over and placed the token denoting the 3rd in the front of Greene's forces, and looked at Lieutenant Colonel Baylor's eyes. "You, vanguard."

"Sir." Baylor understood that he needed to provide support

exactly as the 2nd Light did for Sullivan's forces. They would parallel each other as they cut through Germantown. Pulaski placed his own token as part of the second line before moving the one denoting the 4th over to his side.

"You, move here during battle," Pulaski pointed to Colonel Moylan, who nodded.

"Sir," he said before Pulaski pushed all four tokens – the 1st, 4th, Delaware, and his own – forward.

"We sweep," he said, and Tallmadge nodded as he saw the fullness of the plan. It was chillingly effective. He and Baylor's dragoons, though hindered by the reduction of their troops, would be the spear points and the dragoon regiments with the most troops would be the ones in the thick of the fighting as they swept in behind the initial surprise attack.

"Sir, when are we to attack?" Colonel Bland covered his mouth to cough once after speaking up.

"Tomorrow," Pulaski replied before a grim smile split his bearded visage. He spoke something in his native language before chuckling in a rather dark manner. They all turned to Laurens for any semblance of a translation, but the young major only shook his head a little.

"General Pulaski had commented during the initial briefing with General Washington that he can smell a fog coming in, so if the weather holds, we will attack tomorrow evening," Laurens replied. "If there are any questions?"

At this clear sign that the briefing was at an end, the officers broke away from the table to talk. Some crowded around Laurens and Pulaski with specific details or questions they had while others studied the tokens. Tallmadge studied not only where Sullivan was going to advance, but also where his troops were headed. He hoped the map was as accurate as possible; he noticed small square blocks that denoted houses, but not hedges or fences that he was sure were there. There was one particular landmark he saw was called Chew Mansion, but it seemed not to be of any consequence as he looked at the map closely. He deftly ignored the silver tokens on the map and traced a finger in the air from the path of the roads along the path of the 2nd and 3rd Lights' assignments.

"Sir?" Belden spoke up to his left and Tallmadge glanced at

the young captain. He was also looking at the map, but his eyes were roaming instead of truly studying it.

"I need you to find Wadsworth and Sergeant Mills and acquire as many pistols with the quartermaster department as you can before tomorrow. Give at least one to each man. They will carry this along with the rest of their armaments." He looked back at the map. Judging by how close each of the blocks denoting houses were, and the fact that they would be the tip of the spear and thus be pushing fast and hard through town – the men needed pistols instead of carbines. They would still be able to reload, but in case they ran into unexpected resistance, they needed a weapon for close-quarter combat besides their bayonets.

"Sir," Belden nodded and headed out of the tent. Tallmadge cast his eyes around for a rod and found one at the edge of the table.

After picking it up he measured out the appropriate length of twine, placed it on the map and started to measure. The village of Germantown had four main roads converging in the center. As part of Sullivan's left wing, they were to make their way through one of two center roads, pushing up the middle. Tallmadge could see that their line of attack was dotted with several houses and barns – all of which would make good fortifications for entrenched soldiers or perfect places to ambush sleeping soldiers.

"Tallmadge?" he heard Baylor speak up and glanced over to see the senior officer peering at him.

"Measuring how many carbine balls my men will have to carry if we are to move swift and fast in the attack," he explained and Baylor nodded.

"Excellent call." The lieutenant colonel pulled out his own rod and twine and moved to the other side of the map where he too began measuring the distance and speed needed to reload his men's guns. Tallmadge thought he heard a pleased grunt from Pulaski near them, but was not too sure. It seemed that speed was essential in this plan and instead of carrying heavy packs of lead and unneeded ammunition along with their bedrolls and accouterments, they would leave those behind at camp.

Satisfied with his calculations, he placed the borrowed rod

and twine to the side and gave the map one last look before searching out General Pulaski. He spotted him nodding and talking with McLane and Moylan, but caught the cavalry officer's eyes and nodded once before saluting him. Pulaski returned his salute with a brief nod and Tallmadge left the tent, heading immediately back to the 2nd Light's encampment to debrief and prepare his men for tomorrow's action.

They moved at nightfall the next day, the damp chill in the air providing the fog that Pulaski had predicted. It was roughly nine o'clock when Sullivan's wing of the army arrived at Chestnut Hill. Tallmadge pulled on the reins of his horse as he halted by the general's order, a few paces to his right. To his left was General Washington and his staff. Tallmadge had known he and the 2nd Light were to be part of Sullivan's wing, but he had not exactly known his placement until they had formed up. It had been both a pleasant surprise and a boon to the men's morale that they were placed right between the major general and the Commander-in-Chief of the army. He could still feel the nervous excitement rolling off the men and horses that made up the three troops of the 2nd Light behind him.

Major General John Sullivan was a gruff man who did not like to mince words and expected every order to be obeyed. Unlike General Putnam, who was of a manner similar to Sullivan, Sullivan gave his orders in a calm fashion. Tallmadge remembered how Putnam gave his orders – with a lot of yelling that sometimes rallied the men, but more often than not, terrorized the lot of them. He saw Sullivan raise his saber, turning it so the shine of the blade reflected off the fog that enveloped the area. Tallmadge heard someone to the far right give the order to march, the drummers beating a steady rhythm, the fifes silent to not give way the element of surprise with their piercing sound. They would more than likely start up during the thick of the battle once the drums were not able to be heard.

General Conway and the infantry regiments under his command began to move forward and soon disappeared into the murky fog. A few minutes passed before Tallmadge heard the distinct report of muskets going off followed by windows being broken and the cries of those shot. He saw Sullivan wave his sabre in a sweep and nudged his horse forward at the unspoken command. The rest of his men followed as they trotted forward into the fog.

"Ready!" he called out, as he swung his carbine around and held it with one hand, his other guiding Castor's reins. He had had all his men load their rifles at half-cock before they rode into combat. It was a dangerous practice for the most part, especially with the bounce of the horse's gait, but he had drilled them during winter to do such a thing in the absence of sabres. The only thing he did not have them do was to load their second or third carbines. They would fire one shot and have spare ammunition if they had the chance to reload, but would use sabres and bayonets for the majority of their engagement. Belden had been unable to procure much in terms of pistol, so Tallmadge had resorted to this plan. Those who had pistols kept them in their holsters to use as the last resort.

He had made sure the men knew what to do when they rode into the village. In the chaos of battle, each man would have to rely on what they learned from the battle plan to watch what the others were doing. They could not rely on drums or fifes, as they were to move swiftly through each division of British forces. Sullivan and the infantry behind them would also be attacking, with Wayne and the horses of 1st, 4th, and Delaware sweeping. The sappers and engineers would remove the obstacles left behind, like fences and debris so General Knox's artillery could come through.

There was a brief moment of thick fog and Tallmadge almost could not see his fellow dragoon next to him before it thinned and they came upon the ongoing skirmish at a nearby house. Tallmadge immediately fired his carbine, felling a British soldier from a window, then shouldered it and drew his sabre. He pulled hard on Castor's reins as screams and gunfire filled the air. Tallmadge involuntarily ducked as he felt a couple of muskets and carbines fire near him, then swept downward with the blade, spraying blood into the air. He cut down another British soldier who was distracted by the fire just as a shot in the center of his forehead rendered the soldier dead. Tallmadge glanced to his left and Pullings grinned at him from the end of his carbine. Pullings then drew out his other carbine with a bayonet and stabbed towards one of two British soldiers who were charging him, before knocking his horse full into another one.

Tallmadge had a sudden hairsbreadth of warning and jerked out of the way of an incoming bayonet, meeting the frightful eyes of the young British soldier that had tried to stab him. He swung and cut him down without a second thought. "Forward! Forward!" he called out, pointing his sabre towards the next house as he heeled Castor and charged forward. He heard the neighs of horses and shouts of infantry behind him and knew that Wayne was bringing up the sweep and they needed to press forward.

He managed to get a bit farther before a volley of musket fire rang from the house in front of them. Tallmadge flinched, but the musket fire was not for him. A group of soldiers hiding behind a stone fence with hedgerows cried out from the attack. Limbs and blood flew and Tallmadge waved his sabre in the air.

"2nd Light, halt and reload!" he shouted, and heard Webb and the others repeat his order across the fog in a distorted echo that was almost drowned out by scattered musket fire and the cries of the wounded. Tallmadge breathed a quick sigh of relief. All around them, the volley of enemy fire was returned with equal enthusiasm. He glanced around him, trying to steady Castor as more fire filled the air. "Aim towards the Allen House!" he shouted, "Fire!"

The shots were uneven, but Tallmadge heard windows being broken along with screams of those inside before he swept his sabre forward. "Onward!" He heeled Castor again. "Bayonets at the ready men!"

They moved forward again, but Tallmadge could see the initial line he had formed with his men faltering a little due to the increase in enemy troops. Their initial attack had awakened the sleeping Hessian and British forces and they streamed down from the village center. He thought that General Greene and his left wing would be there to counter the increase in troops, but he saw and heard no sign of them or of the 3rd Light yet.

"Sir!" Adamson suddenly burst forth from a dense bit of fog. He was leaning forward in his saddle as he pointed towards one of the roads ahead and to the left of them. "Enemy reinforcements! I think it's the 40th Regiment!"

"Go! Let Sullivan know!" He waved Adamson to take his report to the general as he spun and slashed downward at another soldier. He felt Castor move and lurch, the scream and crunch of bones behind him telling him that a soldier had tried to attack his horse and had gotten kicked for his troubles. Tallmadge pulled on Castor's reins and slashed at another British soldier before the loud drum beat signaled for them to halt the advance.

"Halt, 2nd! Halt!" he shouted, and heard the distant echoing calls. One was suddenly cut short and Tallmadge knew the man was wounded or had been killed. The sudden rush of Continental infantry emerging from the fog behind them startled Tallmadge, but he managed to halt his sabre's downward descent as they rushed towards the house. He watched the enemy forces still inside turn to meet the incoming attack. There were brief flashes of musket fire, shouts, before a soldier peered out the window and waved. The Allen House was taken.

Tallmadge cheered, his voice hoarse from shouting his commands as the staccato of musket fire echoed in the night. The fog was getting worse, but he could at least make out shadows moving to his left and right.

"Men dress right! Move onto the fields!" The order for the infantry was shouted and more soldiers moved past them. Tallmadge caught a glimpse of their standard; they belonged to Conway's division. Had General Armstrong not arrived at the extreme right flank of the attack to support them? Had they encountered British forces that they did not account for on the right wing? And where was Greene and his left wing for that matter? There was still no sign of them in the murky fog.

"Tallmadge! Looking for Major Tallmadge!" He turned to see an aide-de-camp, Major Sherbourne of Sullivan's own staff, riding out.

"Here!" he called out, raising his sabre. The major trotted quickly to him and halted.

"Sullivan wants you to move to the right wing and shore up the defenses there. We have not heard from General Armstrong or his flanking wing," Sherbourne directed and Tallmadge nodded.

"I sent word about Colonel Musgrave's 40th Regiment-"

"They were last seen retreating to where you are to be sent," Sherbourne said just as he saw Adamson emerge from the same direction Sherbourne had come from. Tallmadge nodded again, understanding what he needed to do.

The 2nd Light was going to drive Musgrave's infantry back further in order to allow some slack for the next push towards a rather large house that had been clearly labeled Chew Mansion on the map, from what he remembered. Washington had predicted that a great number of forces would be inside and so it would take a concentrated effort on Sullivan's right wing in order to drive the men from there.

"We're on it!" He turned his horse again and raised his sabre high as Sherbourne rode back into the fog. "2nd Light on me!"

He heeled Castor into a slow trotting gait and rode behind the infantry line that was set up next to the taken house. The rest of his men followed. "Good work men!" he called back, and he saw the slight fear, but awe in the men's eyes. He caught a glimpse of Webb clutching his shoulder. Pain was evident on his face, but he continued to ride, undeterred by his injury. Several others were bleeding from cuts and wounds, but they looked determined to continue the push forward. He turned Castor to a slightly unused path next to the Wissahickon Creek and rode along the edges as he directed his men to form three columns. Tallmadge felt sweat pouring down his face, stinging the minor cuts he had received from flying pieces of rocks and debris. The sweat was cold down his back, the autumn air doing him no favors.

"First four, reload!" he ordered. "The rest, bayonets and sabres at the ready!"

He would try to drive Musgrave's infantry back into the center of the village, where they hopefully would be swept up by the incoming forces by Sullivan and Wayne. He thought he heard the distant booms of artillery, but was not sure as the sudden ragged discharge of musket fire to his left occupied his attention. They were nearing the Chew Mansion, which meant that any moment-

"Fire!"

The enemy command roared forth and Tallmadge was confronted with a sudden discharge of smoke and gunfire that burst through the wall of fog in front of him. Castor reared and snorted in distress as British musket fire peppered their charge. "Charge!" he shouted, just as a musket ball tore through his arm. The pain seared into his consciousness as he folded into himself, clutching his fresh wound. He heard the cries of pain and surprise from the men behind him and his own arm felt like it was on fire. He tried to steady Castor and kicked his flank to send him forward. They could not falter, not after that surprise attack.

He burst through the dense fog to see two lines of enemy infantry that had fired at them, furiously reloading. A cry of fury emerged from his mouth as he pointed his sabre at the British soldiers, and was echoed by the rest of the 2nd Light around him as three columns of horse and mounted soldiers crashed into them.

The men were instantly bowled over. He kept his grip tight on Castor's reins as his horse trampled and crushed their bodies. He could hear the heaves and braying of the animals as he rode past the fallen enemy soldiers, and the others shouted and screamed as they discharged their weapons or swept their bayonets and sabres at the rest of the enemy forces. Soon the shouts of retreat filled the air. Tallmadge turned his sabre to the right and directed the three columns to leap over the small creek to avoid moving too far ahead of the other advancing forces.

Tallmadge saw that Musgrave's men were running for the Chew Mansion and directed the 2nd Light to leap over the small creek's banks once more. They arrived in short order back behind the original infantry line that was set up next to the Allen House, startling some of the soldiers as they to emerged from the murk.

Tallmadge pulled Castor to a halt and waved his men past to take a moment of rest behind the lines. He could see that many of them were wounded. Some injuries looked serious, while others were seemingly minor, similar to the musket ball gash across his arm. It was a similar wound to that he had received before, except on his other arm. Pain flexed along his hand each time he tugged at Castor's reins, but Tallmadge pushed the pain aside. He could still fight.

"Wounded, get yourself back to the surgeon-"

"Begging your pardon, sir, but no," he heard Belden speak up and saw the man was bleeding from the forehead. One of his eyes was closed, but he stared defiantly at him, and Tallmadge snorted before nodding.

"Good man," he stated, and Belden grinned tightly as did some of the enlisted men near him who were also injured. "Bandage your wounds then, and reload for one shot," he ordered. "Adamson!" he barked out.

"Here sir!" his friend called out and Tallmadge turned to see that Adamson was also injured, his hand covered liberally in blood. "It's not bad, sir," the younger man shook his head, "ball just nicked me in the shoulder. See?" Adamson turned to show him a jagged wound that was clearly weeping blood, but also showing bits of flesh and a small shard of bone.

"Get your wound bandaged and report to Sullivan and Washington that Musgrave retreated to Chew Mansion after our advance-"

"Fall back! Fall back!" The cries of panicked soldiers in front of them in the fog were followed moments later by several regiments of Continental infantry rushing past them.

"Adamson, go!" He realized that whatever regiment had been sent to clear out Chew Mansion had encountered Musgrave's 40th Regiment. Musgrave must have sent a majority of his men in the house and fielded a token force to receive him beyond Chew Mansion as a feint.

"Sir." Adamson wheeled his horse around and galloped away to deliver the news.

"Major," he heard a voice to his left and saw that it was Sergeant James Dole of 1st Troop, who leaned over in his saddle and handed him a folded piece of cloth. "For your wound, sir."

Tallmadge stared at the cloth before looking at his wound. He shrugged, sending renewed waves of pain down his left arm. "Nothing but a scratch, Sergeant."

"Aye, but an annoying scratch, wouldn't you say?" the sergeant grinned at him and Tallmadge nodded, accepting the long strip of cloth. "You injured, Dole?"

"No, sir," the sergeant shook his head before tapping his golden-burnished helm. "They singed me, right here, I think-" He lifted the tip of his helm and through the darkness and murky fog, Tallmadge could see a rather large dark mark streaked across Dole's forehead.

"Very lucky of you," he commented. It was lucky indeed for if the shot had been a few inches to the man's right, it would have taken his head clean off.

"Aye, sir," Dole tipped his helm at him as Tallmadge set his sabre on his lap, bloodying his breeches with the still wet bits of blood, sinew, and bone that he had cut from soldiers, and tied the strip of cloth tightly around his upper arm. It hurt and he resisted the urge to hiss in pain though he could feel sweat popping underneath his helm.

The sound of a horse snorting made him turn to see Adamson emerge from the fog, still pale and with his wound still untreated. "Report." He glared at his friend for disobeying the order to get his wound treated. Dole helpfully reached behind him and pulled out several pieces of ripped cloth as Adamson pulled his horse along side the two of them.

"Sir, we are to hold position for now. General Knox and Maxwell are bringing up artillery to shell Chew Mansion. Once they begin, we will be heading on the right flank with Sullivan's men while Wayne will go up the left."

"Any sign of Greene or his wing?"

"No, sir-"

"Listen soldier, when the Major gives you an order, you damn well obey it." Dole's grizzled visage was lit up in a crooked smile as he grabbed Adamson's arm, ignoring the yelp and wince of pain as he slapped a large wad of cloth on his wound. "Hold this, will ya?"

"Are you *trying* to make me pass out old man?!" Adamson sounded faintly indignant, and Tallmadge could see his friend's lips trembling with barely contained pain as he held the cloth in place. Dole quickly ripped a large piece of cloth one into several strips and started to wrap the cloth into place. To Tallmadge's dismay, the cloth was already bleeding through, but it was at least something.

He patted his friend on his leg in sympathy and Adamson gave him a watery smile, trying very hard not to pass out on top of his horse. Turning away to give him a semblance of privacy and dignity as Dole continued his rough, but effective ministrations, he picked his sabre up again and moved Castor to inspect the rest of his troops.

"Sir," many of them greeted him as he walked Castor by and he nodded at them. He could see they were either reloading their carbines or making cursory inspections of both horse and man. They all paused as the loud boom of artillery split the air behind them and Tallmadge knew that General Knox was beginning his shelling of Chew Mansion.

"Stoddard," He greeted the volatile captain with a brief nod and got a respectful one in return. The man had recovered from being routed at Paoli in time to join the rest of 2nd Light in the attack. Tallmadge could see he was glad to be back in action.

"Sir." Stoddard held up a bandaged hand, blood soaking through the cloth in a line across his palm. Tallmadge smiled a little in acknowledgment. He surmised that the man must have caught an incoming sabre with his bare hand, but he did not seem discomforted by it.

He continued on and checked in on his other two captains, along with their respective lieutenants. Webb still seemed dazed, but there was a rather large patch of cloth on his shoulder stemming the blood from his wound. The young lieutenant gave him a half smile before nodding to show he was still able to fight. A few of the men in his troop sported bandages on their legs.

"They slashed at us, trying to unseat us." Belden saw where he was looking and provided the explanation. "Bastards also tried to take our horses." In the inky darkness, Tallmadge could barely discern slash marks on some of the horses' flanks, blood from the cuts blending with the dapple grey and dark of the horses' stockings and lower body.

"Any losses?" he asked.

"Not that I know of, so far." Belden smiled tightly, finishing the wrap around his own head wound. "God willing, none tonight at the next charge."

"Keep it up, men," Tallmadge called out as he made his way back to his original position. There was no cheer at his statement and he did not expect one from the men. He could feel the pull of exhaustion and hoped they were to move out soon before the bone-cold chill of the autumnal night settled into him.

He received his wish a few minutes later as he heard

Sullivan's distinct voice ring out, ordering them to advance. The men at the Allen House line moved forward and to the right. Tallmadge lifted his bloodied sabre once more and walked Castor forward.

"Tallmadge, take the left flank of the column." He glanced behind him to see Sullivan himself along with his staff *and* General Washington and his staff emerging from the fog.

"Sir." He pointed his sabre towards the left as he spurred Castor and the rest of the 2nd followed, some with their bayonets and sabres drawn, others holding their carbines in their free hands. Tallmadge thought he caught a glimpse of Pullings and Davenport near the rear, both holding two carbines in their hands, guiding their horses with the reins in their teeth.

Artillery whistled overhead as they passed Chew Mansion. Some of the men fired as they passed by, but Musgrave's 40th Regiment was occupied with pouring fire on the infantry forces behind the hedgerows and bushes in front of the mansion, who were trying to find some way of dislodging those inside.

They slowed to a walk as they passed General Conway's men, who held a somewhat fortified position behind some wooden fences. Tallmadge caught a glimpse of the main road where Wayne's division was making its way up and nodded as he caught the eye of both Colonel Bland and Moylan. The outer flanks of their regiments were firing indiscriminately into the small pockets of resistance, as Sullivan's infantry had done in the front. Tallmadge thought they had finally converged to the center of town when there was a sudden discharge of muskets *behind* them.

Everyone immediately halted to assess the new threat before the cries of men filled the air. Another volley of musket fire was returned, but this time, Tallmadge thought he saw Wayne's men firing back behind them. He could not tell for sure. Brief flashes lit up the fog in a myriad of bright colors. "We're being attacked from behind!" He heard the cry through the fog before it was taken up by the others.

Tallmadge made to turn his horse to meet the new attack before another cry from the front came. "Cornwallis has been spotted! Hessian grenadiers! And with him, General Grey!"

The mention of General "No Flint" Grey, given what he had

done to the piquet at Paoli mere days ago, sent a shockwave through the troops. At the same time Tallmadge heard murmurs of retreat start to build. But before he could do anything, he saw the fog literally bulge in front of him. Continental soldiers started to pour out from it, running back towards the safety of the original lines.

"No! Damn you, no!" he thought he heard General Washington shout somewhere behind, as more men came swept through, fear evident in their eyes. Musket fire resounded both behind and in front of them. The booming artillery at Chew Mansion now sounded as if it coming from above them, but Tallmadge could not tell what was happening.

"Major Tallmadge! Stop them!" The fog parted just enough for him to see Washington point directly at him, and he nodded once.

"2nd Light! On me!" he shouted as he charged left to the main street. "Stop the men from retreating!" He urged Castor across, to the middle of the street, as his men formed around him, waving their arms and armaments to try to rally the retreating troops. "Stop!" he shouted as he saw Wayne's troops running, fear gripping them. Tallmadge turned back to see if the 1st and 4th Light might help, but the fog had enveloped the other dragoons. He could hear the bray and whinny of frightened animals, but could not see no one.

"Stop!" His command was echoed by the others as they tried to stop the retreating men.

It did not help that the continuing sound of musket fire echoed oddly in the fog. The shots sounded like they came from the houses around them, making him flinch, but there was no passing shot, nothing to indicate they were being fired upon. He tried to turn Castor's flank against the running bodies, feeling him jolt and push against the men that were now desperately running into one another. It felt eerily like when the 5th Battalion ran into him during the evacuation of Kip's Bay, but he ignored the thought. They could not falter now, not when they were so close-

"Stop! We are not being fired upon-"

"Oh shite, sir! Look!" Private Elisha Johnson of 1st Troop's agitated shout next to him made him turn his head. He looked towards where Johnson was pointing. A regiment of Hessian grenadiers emerged from the thinning fog. Their hulking imposing forms were advanced at a steady pace, and behind them, a small host of familiar British red along with officer horses.

Tallmadge cursed under his breath as he looked around. Castor danced beneath him as he tried to hear any orders regarding the new enemy forces that had appeared-

There was gurgling cough next to him, and Johnson suddenly fell off his horse. The man was clearly dead, a gaping hole where the lower part of his face used to be. Tallmadge stared, momentarily stunned. He looked up but the fog thickened and he could not tell where the shot had come from.

"2nd Light! Fall back! Fall back!" the familiar voice of General Muhlenberg, one of General Greene's staff, shouted behind them. He saw Muhlenberg riding towards them, gesturing frantically for them to follow him. Tallmadge realized that despite all of his efforts, they were actually to retreat from the battlefield again. He knew that Washington would never call for a retreat unless it was needed, but he had hoped that the men's resolve had been strengthened prior to battle. It was not the case.

"2nd Light, fall back on me!" he shouted, but was cut short as pain scored his right leg. Tallmadge grunted as he automatically swung his sabre and hit something. The gurgle of someone dying told him he had struck true at the soldier who tried to gash him. He winced as he quickly examined the wound. Blood stained his breeches, but it did not look too serious. He heeled Castor and followed in the direction General Muhlenberg and saw the rest of his men following behind him.

The sounds of Continental artillery shattered the air once more as they fell back past the Chew House towards the Allen House. He saw the distant forms of Continental soldiers retreating in a far more organized fashion, having been whipped into a semblance of order by the generals who were farther back. As the fog thinned he saw that they were truly in full retreat. All the regiments were falling back, some walking backwards with their muskets at the ready to prevent anyone from attacking their flank, but most were limping away. It was also then that he spotted General Greene and his left wing. It seemed most of them were intact, but what had delayed them was a mystery.

Tallmadge slapped Castor's reins as he spotted both Sullivan and Washington's staff and heard his men follow. There were cheers behind them and he resisted the urge to turn and glare at the British as they celebrated their apparent victory. Both generals and some of their staff turned in their saddles at his approach and he tipped his helm at them in apology. The only acknowledgment he received was a nod of affirmation from Washington himself before they turned back to continue the march.

Tallmadge was disappointed at what had happened. The plan Pulaski had explained to them had every possibility of working, except...all he could think was that if they had not tarried, or perhaps if he had struck faster... His thoughts were a storm in his head so much that he almost missed seeing Lieutenant Colonel Hamilton approach on horseback.

"The general would like a word with you once we've returned to camp." Hamilton flicked a quick look down at him, "and after your injuries are tended to, sir."

"Yes, sir," Tallmadge replied as neutrally as he could. Hamilton nodded before heeling his horse to rejoin the rest of Washington's staff. He thought he saw him stop next to Major Laurens, who was hunched over in his saddle, injured. Tallmadge turned his gaze away from the two as he contemplated why Washington would summon him after all of this.

A sense of dread started to form in him at the thought of what Washington might say to him. Would he be reprimanded for his inability to stop the men from retreating? Should he have said certain words to rally them? Would he be stripped of his command of the 2nd Light? He was not sure. He had sent Washington constant updates on the 2nd Light's needs and requests as well as any useful information they had scouted since their arrival with the main army back in May. But all of that could not stop the bitter taste that filled his mouth at the near victory that had slipped through their grasp at Germantown. And to top it all off, he realized that he had just lost the first man under his command. Private Elisha Johnson had died, and they did not have a victory to make his death meaningful.

By Tallmadge's reckoning, it was perhaps early dawn when he made his way to General Washington's tent after they retreated back to camp at Shippack. The camp was still alive with the surgeons at work along with the carousing of men on watch as they discussed the night's action. Tallmadge was mildly surprised at the mood of the camp in wake of their retreat, the good spirits, and took it to heart as he checked on the rest of the 2nd Light before making his way to Washington's tent. His own wounds had been checked by the surgeon and bandaged properly. He walked slowly, so as not to jar the shallow gash on his leg. The surgeon had estimated perhaps a week for it to fully heal and scar while his shoulder wound would take an additional three weeks. He had wrapped it in a makeshift sling and Tallmadge wore the sleeve of his jacket outside of it to prevent it from moving and shield it from the cold.

At least twenty men from the 2nd had come off with small scrapes and cuts and were declared fit for duty. As for those who were injured, the surgeons had said they would not be ready until the month's end. One of them was Adamson, who had eventually passed out on the way back to camp and had to be kept in the saddle by Davenport. Webb had also unexpectedly passed out, and it was only by virtue of riding next to the young man that Tallmadge had caught him before he fell off his horse. Tallmadge supposed that the only good news to come out of the failed attack was that there had only been one death among the three troops. Private Johnson would be mourned by the others, but the fact that they had all survived the battle after such fierce defense by the Hessians and British was not lost on him. He had not receive. any reports about loss of horses, but he had seen a few fall, shot out from underneath the men or, lamed by constant riding.

Tallmadge had told his officers to get their men settled and to also rest before they were to report to him later in the morning. He would get the tally of horses then. Sleep would be fitful for men who were not given laudanum to numb the pain, but nonetheless be a chance to rest after hours of non-stop fighting and riding. Tallmadge wanted nothing more than to lie in his tent, but he also suspected Washington wanted to know the status of the 2nd Light.

As he approached the large tent, he could see two of the general's life guards at attention outside. There was light peeking from the flaps before they opened and Lieutenant Colonel Temple of the 1st Light stepped out. Major Tilghman accompanied him and bid him a goodnight. Washington was most definitely still awake at this hour. Tallmadge approached and Tilghman spotted him before gesturing for him to enter. He followed after the major and was immediately engulfed in the warmth of the tent.

"Sir." He saluted Washington who was sitting at his desk, scratching out numbers. The general looked up and acknowledged his salute with the barest smile on his lips before gesturing for him to take a seat in an empty chair near his war table.

"Are your injuries serious?" Washington asked as he set his quill back into his ink well and turned to face him, folding his hands together.

"S-Sir?" That was not the question that Tallmadge had expected, but he quickly recovered and shook his head. His wounded shoulder protested the movement, but he ignored it. "Uh, no sir. Just grazes," he replied, oddly touched by the fact that his Commander-in-Chief's first question was of his own health. "T-Thank you for your concern."

Washington merely nodded. "Please let me know if you require the services of an able surgeon. One of my newer aide-de-camps, the Marquis de Lafayette has an excellent physician who saw to his wound after Brandywine."

"S-Sir," Tallmadge felt a little embarrassed at the attention and wondered what he could say to deflect the apparent concern his Commander-in-Chief was showing for him. He had only officially met the general three times, the first time at White Plains. Knowing Washington held him in such regard, Tallmadge could not help but reciprocate the general's apparent good will. He knew Washington would not commit his forces unless there was no viable alternative, would not devise plans that would waste their lives and he hoped his men would be able to live up to the task at hand.

The tent flap opened and Tallmadge was saved from saying anything as a man with a youthful countenance burst in. He immediately identified him as a Frenchman, judging by the uniform, and saw he had the epaulette of a major general. He immediately stood up to salute him, jarring the wound in his leg by his sudden movement. "Sir." He refused to let the pain show on his face as the man paused for a second before returning the salute.

"I apologize, General. I did not realize you had a guest." The major general's accent was not as harsh as de Vernejout's, but had a sophisticated sound to it. "I only wish to convey that Major Laurens will recover. Lieutenant Colonel Hamilton is currently by his side, but wishes to let you know that he is available for any tasks or writing you require of him. I will return later."

"Thank you, Mr. Lafayette," Washington nodded sagely before gesturing to Tallmadge. "Before you leave, I'd like to introduce you to Major Benjamin Tallmadge, of the 2nd Continental Light Dragoons. It was he who led General Sullivan's forward advance. Major Tallmadge, this is-"

"Marie-Joseph-Paul-Yves-Roch-Gilbert du Montier, the Marquis de Lafayette and our esteemed General Washington's aide-de-camp. Please ignore the rank I hold, Major, for it is in title only until the General deems me learned enough to hold an actual command." The young man stretched out a hand and Tallmadge was surprised at the strength of the grip as he shook it. He was pulled into an unexpected two-cheek kiss, the French custom, and managed to compose himself as Lafayette pulled back.

"Sir," he said, before Lafayette glanced beyond his shoulder and nodded to General Washington. He left the tent just as quickly as he came, leaving a slightly smiling Major Tilghman, who had clearly seen the Marquis act this way before.

Tallmadge turned back, blinking a little in surprise as he gingerly sat back down. His leg ached from the movement he had inflicted on it. He pushed the pain away and looked at Washington who had a faint amused expression on his face. "The Marquis is...not what I expected of our French allies," Tallmadge commented lightly. It certainly was a world of a difference from the sour, arrogant disposition of Captain de

Vernejout. And the fact that the Marquis had said to ignore his rank and was not even a field commander and instead served as Washington's aide-de-camp, was telling. This was a foreigner who *wanted* to learn instead of demanding an army or command from Congress. Tallmadge's respect for Lafayette grew.

"The business with Captain de Vernejout," Washington commented, his tone light and Tallmadge nodded. True to his threat after Stoddard and de Vernejout's attempted duel, he had written a report regarding their conduct to Washington and Sheldon a few months earlier. "I recall Colonel Sheldon writing a request for Captain de Vernejout's recall to stand for a court martial?"

"Yes, though it seems that General Gates did not responded to Colonel Sheldon's request before the Colonel was dispatched to the Hudson Highlands, sir." One of the few instructions Tallmadge had been left with was to forward any correspondences from Gates about de Vernejout if they did not reach Sheldon at the Highlands first.

Washington made a small noise of understanding and Tallmadge sensed his commander was coming to the point of this meeting. He met Washington's square gaze with his own. "I will not dally you much longer, Major, as I am sure you have your men to attend to, but please convey my personal thanks and gratefulness for their bravery in trying to rally the men today. They have shown exceptional bravery and skill in light of reinforcements. I have already spoken to General Sullivan and he has commended your regiment for doing exactly as ordered as well as providing the necessary support."

Tallmadge smiled, the suffusion of praise that Washington had spoken warming him greatly. "I will convey your words to my men, sir. They will be grateful. I know that what had happened earlier will not dampened their ardor or spirits in this fight."

A faint smile of appreciation appeared on his commander's face as Tallmadge stood, sensing a dismissal in the words. "Major, I have asked each dragoon commander to please provide me with a requisition list of supplies that you require or have been without since mustering. Please have this list to me by tomorrow afternoon if possible along with the list of those the wounded, not wounded, and casualties."

"Sir," he replied. He sensed Washington did not quite see the recent action as a failure, but rather a missed opportunity. Tallmadge's normal reports on the status of the 2nd Light, compiled either by himself or Sheldon, consisted of the dragoons who were wounded by other means or had died. The fact that Washington was asking for the number of those not wounded meant he was already considering other plans for the 2nd, and possibly for the other three dragoon regiments in camp. And that in and of itself excited Tallmadge. The setbacks at Brandywine and Germantown would not prove to the British that they were losing this war, but rather prove they would fight to the bitter end even a seeming defeat.

He snapped off a salute and started to walk away, nodding to Tilghman, who helpfully opened the tent flap. He took slow deliberate steps so as not to limp or drag his wounded leg. He was about to step outside when Washington cleared his throat and spoke up again.

"Tallmadge, you've shown great initiative in your preparation of your men for tonight's action," Washington started. "I'd only ask that if you wish to continue this, please inform me so that future plans can be greatly enhanced. You have displayed a keen mind and sharp eyes for details that few have seen since our evacuation from New York. A good trait to have."

This time Tallmadge could not keep the wide, proud smile off of his face as he realized he had been paid one of the highest compliments any military officer could receive from his commanding officer. "Yes, sir," he replied before heading out of the tent. The flap closed behind him and Tallmadge stood for a few seconds, basking in the moment of high praise that had been heaped upon him.

He had hoped, but not exactly expected that General Washington had made use of his reports or anything he had sent to him by way of correspondence. It was not expected if only because he knew many of the other regimental commanders were doing the same, and he did not expect to have his reports stand out from those who were far more well-known, renowned in battle, or had connections he did not have. The fact that the general made mention of New York made him wonder if he had been watching him since then.

Spirits buoyed, he walked back to the part of camp that the 2nd Light inhabited. He was determined to rest for a few hours before rising with the light and starting on both the needed reports for Washington. He also looked forward to passing on his men the high praise that their Commander-in-Chief had given them.

11

Though the men cheered at the compliments Washington paid them for their efforts at Germantown, many of the men – especially those who had suffered injuries, however minor or major – realized it was the first time they had tasted actual combat. They had been assigned so many patrols, and had scraped by in many of the more serious battles that year without being much affected. Germantown was truly the first time they had come face to face with live musket fire and were expected to hold steady and push forth. Thus, the initial fervor and ardor at the fight had waned and the 2nd Light were not doing terribly well following their action at Germantown in early October.

A few of the men deserted in the weeks that followed. But the greatest toll was exacted on the commanding officers. One of the captains resigned and Tallmadge had promoted the man's lieutenant, John Shethar into his place. Tallmadge also put in a request for an adjutant to help with the reports and requisitions he needed to file, which was approved in short order. The adjutant that joined them was a young man by the name of Jeronimus Hoogland with the rank of lieutenant. He was from New York and was initially looked upon by the others with some mistrust due to his home city, but they soon accepted him as he proved he was competent at his job.

Colonel Sheldon, along with the two troops of the 2nd Light had returned from the Hudson Highlands after word of General

Gates' victory at Saratoga over General Burgoyne had quelled the threat of the British in the north. However, one troop of the 2nd Light still served under Gates in the Northern Army. It was still pleasant news as Tallmadge found out that on October 20th, de Vernejout had been cashiered and Lieutenant Seymour promoted to captain in his place. The young lieutenant had been writing a bulk of the reports that were sent to them as well as any troop updates and drills the men had run through, so the promotion was well deserved in his opinion.

However, with the return of the two troops from the Hudson Highlands, the mood of the regiment was disquieted and resentful. Tallmadge knew exactly why. The 2nd Light had been divided between those who had seen action at Germantown and those who had not. The ones wounded at Germantown proudly showed their battle scars and proclaimed they had been 'blooded' by the enemy. It was a bit of posturing that Tallmadge really did not need, as it created a hierarchy and sense superiority among those who had fought at Germantown. The two troops that had gone with Sheldon countered that their fight in the Westchester fronts was equally as important if not more so, dealing with the Tory 'cowboys' and their rampant devastation of the area. For the first time, Tallmadge was at a loss as to how to deal with this divide among the 2nd Light, but thankfully Blackden and – to his surprise – Stoddard intervened and set the men straight before things could truly escalate.

Stoddard, with his bloodthirsty reputation, told the men that under no circumstances were any of their postings not as honorable as fighting the British. He extolled them, like a deranged preacher who preached war sermons, saying that each British soldier or Tory traitor they killed, whether it be on the battlefield or on patrol, was one less that none of them had to worry about. The men took his words to heart and the conflict that had been brewing quieted as the 2nd Light troops got re-acquainted with one another during the month of November.

They were joined by the last of their detached troop in early December, as General Gates brought his troops down from the North to join Washington's encampment at White Marsh. Washington's army had made its move from Shippack to White Marsh to try to force General Howe into another engagement, as the army yearned for a battle and victory like that of Saratoga. Seymour was hailed by the 2nd Light like a hero, the men cheering at his arrival – though Tallmadge suspected it was because a lot of them detested de Vernejout and wished to make their support known to the recently promoted Seymour.

He had seen Seymour taken away by a few of the officers and later found them carousing around the tents singing in a slightly off-key manner. Tallmadge discreetly excused himself to avoid having to write up any of them for being drunk and disorderly, when they were clearly celebrating Seymour's good fortune.

Tallmadge's own injuries had healed within the two weeks the surgeon estimated, though his arm ached from time to time as the newly formed scar was settling. Adamson's arm, however, had not fully healed, though his friend had insisted upon returning to his duties. In the week after the battle at Germantown, Adamson had come down with chills and fever, which had passed, but hampered his arm's recovery. It was Belden who informed Tallmadge that Adamson wished to return to duty, but when he went to check up on his friend, he found him fighting Davenport who thought he should stay in bed. Pullings wisely stayed quiet through the whole thing, though his beady eyes jumped back and forth between the three of them as they argued on Adamson's health and capability to perform his duties.

In the end, Tallmadge relented and marked Adamson fit for duty, though it was with the strictest warning that no quarter would be given to him for his still-healing injury. He did not know why his friend was so stubborn to be fighting again, when he could clearly recover with no honor or status lost. But he had put the matter out of his mind and focused on their patrol orders they had been given since Washington had moved the army to White Marsh.

Since the news of Gates' victory at Saratoga had heartened the men and from the frequency with which he was called to Washington's tent for recent discussions on patrols and scouting maneuvers, he knew that his Commander-in-Chief desired a battle with Howe's forces before winter forced them to retire. He could feel it in the air too; the men who had not seen the action that Gates' army had hungered for a victory of their own, after being denied one at Germantown.

The 2nd Light spent the early days of December patrolling and skirmishing with the small forces Howe sent out to try to draw them in. One of the patrols resulted in the deaths of two privates from 1st Troop. It had also resulted in a strong reprimanding letter from Washington to Howe decrying the practice of deliberately targeting officers during such skirmishes. Tallmadge had been on patrol with Captain McLane of the Delaware Horse, and both of them had their men shot at – men who had been riding next to them. When he and McLane reported the incident to Washington, they did not say they had been deliberately targeted – a mutual understanding between them that they both led front-line troops and thus understood the inherent dangers of such a command – but only that they noted the presence of sharpshooters besides the usual British lines. But their attempt at concealing the matter did not go unnoticed by Washington – hence the letter to Howe.

The next patrol Tallmadge was assigned to was with Daniel Morgan's riflemen and Mordecai Gist's Maryland Continentals. Both regiments were posted to the left flank to counter any sweeping forces that would try to outflank them. It was an interesting and enlightening reunion between him and Morgan since they served earlier at the Battle of Short Hills. Tallmadge learned that it was not Horatio Gates who was the true hero of Saratoga, but rather Benedict Arnold, Enoch Poor, and Ebenezer Learned, who had deliberately ignored Gates' command to retreat and instead turned the near routes into a rally. Gates had come out of his command tent just as they were routing the enemy to claim his victory.

Tallmadge was heartened at the news since he knew from rumors in camp that Gates spoke with some openness against Washington and that he and some other officers were of the same mind set. The army could not be divided now, and he understood why Washington desired a battle against Howe. Washington wished to make his own statement, much like Gates had, to ensure that he had control of his army and it would not fracture into pieces. The information from Morgan would hopefully undercut the momentum of Gates and his cabal and curb any plots to have Washington removed as Commander-in-Chief.

The oddity was that Morgan spoke to him in free tones, instead of whispers. Tallmadge would expect such a story to be told in a hushed manner lest it be overheard by the aggrieved party. In an off-hand comment from Morgan, Tallmadge learned the reason why – not only did Morgan *wish* for him to spread the news, but he also commented that his usual troop of men, and by extension the 2ⁿᵈ Light, had the moniker among the other regiments of being Washington's eyes. There was always a 2ⁿᵈ Light troop, or part of a troop, posted with Washington constantly.

Tallmadge knew his men had a reputation, but had not been quite sure what that reputation was considering they had not served as a whole regiment since mustering back in January. There was always one troop detached somewhere and judging by internal conflicts and strife that had riddled the captains of the regiment, along with occasional unfavorable reports from generals they had been detached to, he had thought the 2ⁿᵈ Light had a reputation as unruly and average. Morgan's comments told him otherwise.

Still, even with the unruliness and internal strife, he was proudest of 1ˢᵗ Troop – his former command. Belden had proven himself a capable leader, even with Tallmadge's constant presence with 1ˢᵗ Troop. Belden was able to lead the men as well as follow Tallmadge's orders with minimal fuss unlike Stoddard or some of the other captains who occasionally voiced their questions at some of their orders. Such ability to lead and to follow was why Tallmadge kept picking 1ˢᵗ Troop for the duties he was assigned by Washington.

And so it was after Howe had retired to winter at Philadelphia that Tallmadge was given orders to take a small detachment, one troop, to patrol the area between the Delaware and Schuylkill Rivers. The rest of the Continental Army was to make its way to winter quarters at Valley Forge, and members of the 2ⁿᵈ Light that were not on detached duty were to winter at Chatham, New Jersey. It was on his first official detached duty command that Tallmadge would flourish as a battlefield commander.

December 14ᵗʰ, 1777

Analysis and anticipation of enemy movements were natural when planning a battle with several other officers, but as Tallmadge studied the map in front of him, it occurred to him that he was the lone soul who would shoulder such responsibilities if he and 1st Troop went into battle. His experience with detached duty was limited to leading more than one troop of dragoons on piquets or supply trains. He always wrote his reports addressed to Sheldon. This was the first time he would oversee a detachment of men and reported not directly to Sheldon, but to Washington himself. No one else were to receive his reports, not even General Pulaski, head of the cavalry of the Continental Army. Washington had specifically picked him to lead the patrols between the Schuylkill and Delaware Rivers, to report any enemy activity or movements, and most of all, to stymie the enemy's efforts in obtaining supplies going to Philadelphia, diverting them instead, to the main encampment at Valley Forge.

The weight of such a responsibility, especially since he knew full well the British cavalry counterparts were equally active at the moment, may have crushed a less experienced commander, but Tallmadge relished it. It was a chance to shine and prove his worth to General Washington, but also he was doing *something* to harass the British at every turn. He could also provide actionable intelligence for anything that Washington would be able to use to counter future plans General Howe might be plotting.

The risks were high since it was a large swath of ground to cover for just one troop of horse, and also due to the fact that if he did not anticipate or read his maps right, he could easily face capture or destruction of twenty-five good men and horses – much like his friend Colonel Samuel Webb had only a few days ago. Tallmadge had learned yesterday from the daily post rider that came and fetched his reports to Washington that Colonel Webb and his regiment had been captured on December 10th, trying to land for another attack on Long Island. The forces in Connecticut had been trying to capitalize on the gains made in their initial attack in August. Late fall storms on the Sound forced their boats into British hands. Sixty of Webb's men were also captured, among them his friend Captain Bulkley. There was no word on whether or not either of his friends had been given parole, but he knew they could have easily been killed by the churning waves of the Sound, or by British cannon fire. The news had tempered his enthusiasm and made him more aware of his own patrol area.

Since they began their patrol six days earlier, Tallmadge had not let his troop stop for longer than eight hours at most, one hour at the shortest. It was the only way to prevent the British from potentially ambushing them. Of the original thirty-six enlisted men, twenty-five remained after Germantown, and of the twenty-five, only eighteen had serviceable mounts. He transferred the other seven dismounted men to other troops, to repair at winter quarters in Chatham, while bringing seven men from the other troops to get 1st Troop up to nominal strength.

"Where to today, Major?" Adamson sat down with a heaviness of accouterments about him as Tallmadge studied the map he held on his lap. He was hunched over, a small piece of cooled firewood ember in his hand to make marks on the map if need be. The bright winter's sun was just about to rise over the tree tops and Tallmadge could hear the rest of the camp waking and preparing for the day's patrol. Due to the inconsistent nature of their patrols, Tallmadge had insisted that the men only bring bedrolls instead of tenting supplies. He made sure that whenever they stopped, there was a solid structure of sorts, be it a barn or shed or even a church in which they could have some shelter against the elements.

The men did not mind sleeping in close proximity to one another, and Tallmadge had seen the last six days of patrol tighten the bond between them. There was still the formality of respect from the enlisted to the officer ranks, but it was more casual as each man knew that winter was turning harsher with each day they and so sought to keep the man next to him warm and alert. Their patrols had also lent some camaraderie and good nature. They had raided two caravans of supplies and diverted one to Valley Forge, the other to Chatham. Spirits were high, even the midst of the daily dropping temperatures and Tallmadge was glad.

"I was thinking of circling around Germantown to the eastern side of Philadelphia to see if that supply wagon we heard about from one of the local farmers two days previous would be arriving," Tallmadge replied in an absent manner. They had made the day's camp just a mile or so back from Chestnut Hill at an abandoned barn that had been used previously by the Continentals as a campsite, before they had attacked Germantown.

"The corn fields there are still high enough to conceal the horses," Adamson commented, his words muffled. Tallmadge glanced up to see his friend chewing on a strip of dried salted pork. Adamson ripped part of it and offered it to him.

Tallmadge took it with a nod of thanks and let it soften in his mouth before chewing. Adamson had forgone the initial softening and instead was doing battle with the tough strip of meat.

"We'll have to dismount," he muttered as he stared at the map, but was not really seeing it. He remembered the cornstalks, starting to turn yellow and dry, but the farmer that lived there did not seem inclined to de-stalk his whole field now that winter's chill was in the air. "And probably circle wide to mask our footprints." A brief squall of snow had fallen yesterday, forcing them to stop their patrol early and find shelter at the barn, but the morning light had brought a stop to the snow, leaving the ground with at least an inch or two fresh powder.

"We could ride back and forth and into the cornstalks, sir," Belden's voice spoke up from behind. Tallmadge turned on the log where he sat and saw his captain walking up to them, holding a small tin that he poked his fork into. "Corn bread, sir. Would you like some?"

"No thank you," Tallmadge declined the offer of what looked like recently heated snowmelt with a still-pretty-solid cornbread soaking in it.

"Where's the snowmelt, sir?" Adamson stood up, the ragged ends of the salted meat hanging from his mouth as he gave up the battle.

"Right that way, Sergeant-Major." Belden was clearly suppressing a smile on his face at the sight. Tallmadge only shook his head as Adamson tossed him a casual salute and hurried away to where the snow was being melted over a small pot.

"Riding back and forth is a good idea," Tallmadge ripped the softened piece of salted meat and chewed it before swallowing, then stuck the next piece in his mouth. "But it would be obvious that an ambush is set up." An idea occurred to him. "There were four cornfields, right?"

"As far as I remember, yes." Belden frowned a little in thought.

"Okay, here's what we'll do-"

"Sir! Sir!" Davenport bellowed as he rode his horse hard into their encampment, startling some of the men who were in the midst of waking. He pulled up abruptly to him and Belden. Sweat poured down Davenport's face and his horse was breathing hard. "A large host of cavalry are crossing the banks of the Schuylkill. I didn't get a good count, but they definitely outnumber us, sir."

Tallmadge mouthed a curse under his breath as he stood up, hastily folding his map and shoving it into his jacket. He tore the piece of meat from his mouth and stuffed the rest into a small pouch he wore on his belt. "Belden, wake the men and get them ready with all haste," he ordered and his captain nodded quickly before hurrying to the barn to wake the others. He turned to the others. "The rest of you, boots and saddles! Let's go!"

He kicked some dirt and snow into the small fire, dousing it quickly before snatching his helmet and fitting it on his head. He hurried to Castor, who was tied to a nearby tree. None of the men had been allowed to unsaddle their horses for the last six days, and he was glad. He quickly mounted his horse as the others also did the same, some hastily throwing snowmelt on their fires first. He saw Belden in the distance, pushing a slightly sleep-addled private out of the barn towards the small house several feet away, more than likely warning the old man who had allowed them to stay the night. That was commendable on Belden's part and he hoped that the man had enough sense to either lock his door or flee if they were not able to hold the British off.

Heeling Castor, Tallmadge set a fast cantor down the road as Davenport rode alongside him. He could hear the others catching up behind him, but did not look back as he followed Davenport a short distance to where he had been posted as their lookout. He abruptly pulled his horse to a halt as he crested a hill and saw the host of red on horseback coming towards them. It looked like they were still gathering themselves on the banks of the Schuylkill, but some were already heading in their direction.

"Form up." Tallmadge turned in his saddle to address the handful of men who had accompanied him. "Single line, do not fire until I give the order. Then fire at will. All carbines loaded."

To his left he saw a cluster of trees followed by a line of fences. To his right was a sloping hill that ran downwards to the edges of Germantown. The original Hessian and British forces stationed at Germantown had retired to Philadelphia proper, officers boarded in stately manors and mansions while the soldiers camped out on the green.

He heard the acknowledgment of his command followed by a variety of clicks as carbines were half-cocked and primed before being holstered. Tallmadge glanced down at his two pistols, which were already primed and ready; he relied on them more than anything else. The one at his hip was also primed, but that would only be used if he was dismounted or Castor was shot out from underneath him. He swung his carbine around and pulled the hammer back full as he heard distant shouts of enemy horsemen who had spotted them on the ridge.

"Sir." Two more of his men joined him and he acknowledged their arrival with a curt nod, but did not look at them as they moved away to continue the line. He could hear Adamson telling them what the situation was.

"Ready," he called out as the horsemen started to charge up towards them, their sabres gleaming in the morning sunlight. "Aim." He sighted down his own carbine, taking a deep breath and letting it out as he estimated the distance. "Fire!" he called out and fired his carbine. His aim was true and the shot hit the horse of the soldier he had been targeting in the flank, sending the beast crashing into the ground as the others also found their marks.

The charge paused and the horsemen wheeled around, the narrow road and steepness of the hill making it hard for them to turn their beasts around without some difficulty. His men fired random shots at cavalry, sending a couple of men and animals to the ground as he pulled out one of his pistols. "Keep firing men!" he called out, firing his pistol at one who charged a little too close. The ball missed, but hit the ground near where the cavalryman had been charging, and he pulling his horse short. Tallmadge smiled at the incensed look upon the soldier's face before another shot made him flinch and the soldier wheeled his horse around to retreat to a safe distance.

"And stay there!" Tallmadge heard Davenport shout at the retreating horseman.

"Sir!" Adamson's shout down the line was followed by the discharge of several muskets to his left and he saw that most of the horsemen were being directed to climb up the steeper part of the hill where the fences were, to try to flank them.

He shook his head and turned Castor to the right. "Pull back! We'll circle around!" he called out, as he knew he could do no more to hold off the incoming cavalry; not without risking his men or his flank. He heeled his horse and rode down the shallow left side into the edges of Germantown, his men following behind him. The narrowness of the roads made it hard for Castor to find his footing. But Tallmadge managed to guide the beast around the edges of a wooded area as he heard the distant firings of muskets back up the hill. He knew the rest of his men who were at camp or had been coming up the road to join them had encountered the incoming British patrol.

He tried to get his horse to go faster, but Castor would not respond as he circled around the woods. Flashes of red in his periphery and above him alerted him that the British now had the high ground. The only things that stopped them from charging after him were the woods and the unknown terrain covered by fresh snow.

"Sir! Thank God, it's you sir!" He looked up as he heard the shout and sounds of hooves in front of him and saw Belden along with Webb, Pullings, and several others of 1st Troop coming down the opposite side of the road. "The farmhouse-" Belden took a deep breath, winded. "Sir, we couldn't stay. Three of the men-"

Tallmadge halted as they came level with the edges of the woods opposite the farmhouse. He could see the bright red barn across the thicket of bare trees, fallen logs, and large boulders that separated him from where their camp had been. The snow-covered ground of the woods was trampled and upturned, a clear indicator that Belden and the rest of the men had fled directly into the woods to escape the British forces.

However, he could see three blue-buff coated dragoons still left, holding their hands high in the air in a gesture of surrender as the British cavalry surrounded them. Even from a distance, Tallmadge recognized each of the three who had not been able to escape into the woods. One of them was Sergeant Mills and he watched with a dispassionate gaze as the sergeant was suddenly thrown to the ground by the butt of a musket to his head. The other two tried to leap to Mills' aide, but were held back by several bayonets pointed at their faces.

A British officer emerged from soldiers' ranks, sitting high on his black steed, decorated with the accouterments of a high rank. Tallmadge recognized the man as Lord Rawdon, one of the British officers who was assigned to patrol the Schuylkill. He had learned the name from one of the captured wagons which was supposed to be protected by Rawdon's cavalrymen.

"...Sir..." he heard Belden whisper behind him, but ignored his plea to do something as Mills was backhanded to the ground by the swing of a rifle to his face. There was a twitter of laughter from British cavalrymen that echoed through the woods.

Tallmadge knew they were visible to the British cavalry that surrounded the opposite edge of the woods and could see Rawdon directing cruel smiles towards him. They both knew that he could charge towards them, but it would also be suicidal and useless due to the sheer number of men he had with him. Rawdon was trying to goad him into attacking and was making sport of the fact that the three dragoons he had captured had surrendered.

"Just accept their surrender, you bastards," Webb muttered somewhere behind Tallmadge, and he heard the quiet murmur of agreement from others around them.

"Captain Belden," he said, drawing on the cold anger he was feeling to keep his voice calm and level.

"Sir." There was a hopefulness in Belden's voice that pleaded for him to order an attack, but Tallmadge ignored it.

"Take the men to the cornfield," he ordered. The men did not need to see this kind of atrocity being committed right in front of their eyes.

"But sir-"

"Do it," he said harshly, glaring at Belden, daring him to disobey his order.

"But...sir-"

"There is *nothing* we can do for the three now!" Tallmadge managed not to shout, not to lose his temper, but enunciated his words carefully. "They have surrendered and we can only continue our duties and wait for an exchange-"

The choking scream echoing across the woods cut off anything else Tallmadge was about to say. He turned back in time to see several of the horsemen descending upon Mills and the two others with their swords and bayonets. He tightened his grip on Castor's reins as his cold anger turned hot. He could see flecks of blood flying in the air as they hacked the men to pieces, their bodies prostrate on the ground. Rawdon drew a pistol from his side and pointed it at Sergeant Mills who was, by some miracle, still kneeling. Blood covered the man's visage, and Tallmadge was sickened at the sight. The lone report of a pistol was quickly followed by Mills' body falling to the ground.

"Sir-"

"Take the men and go," he turned back, his voice tight with anger. Belden and several others around him had stony looks on their faces.

Belden's jaw worked for a few seconds before he nodded curtly and gestured with a rough hand for the men to follow him. They did so with the utmost reluctance and Tallmadge saw some of them cover their mouths in an effort not to vomit at what they had just seen. There was truly nothing they could do for their fallen comrades now. As the last of the men joined the column headed towards the cornfields a hoarse pleading alerted Tallmadge that the soldiers had found the old man who owned the property and dragged him out.

He turned his horse, unable to look at what he knew would be the old man's fate. A heavy feeling engulfed him as he kicked Castor's flanks to follow behind the last of his men, the pleading from the old man filling the air before it turned to screams as the British horsemen hacked away at him. He heard the sounds of crackling wood behind him and knew Rawdon had set the barn and more than likely the rest of the old man's property on fire as a warning and for cruel sport. They had lost three good men today and Tallmadge was thankful that it was all they had lost.

The men were subdued as they made camp for the night deep in one of the cornfields they had chosen for their ambush. The wagon of supplies that was talked about two days earlier had not arrived, perhaps due to the poor fortune of the snow falling. But it allowed time for the men's tempers and moods to settle. Tallmadge was sure that if they had engaged in further action today, it would have been with reckless anger.

"Sir," a steaming cup of water was shoved in front of his face and Tallmadge glanced up to see Adamson holding. He accepted it just as Adamson nodded, a silent signal to him that Adamson had done his duty as the ranking non-commissioned officer and spoken to the men about why they had not been ordered to attack. The divide between an officer and an enlisted man sometimes necessitated an explanation that only one of their own could give and Tallmadge was grateful for Adamson's foresight.

"Thank you," he replied quietly.

"Get some rest, sir," Adamson added before walking away to join the rest of the men around the main fire that had been built for the night.

Tallmadge sipped the piping hot water, the taste a little bitter, but also with a hint of corn in it. It must have come from the stalks they had cut down to use as kindling. He took out the strip of pork from the morning and chewed on it absently, letting the hot water in his mouth melt the salted meat into something more palatable.

"Sir," Webb spoke up, his voice hesitant and confused, "if I may, ask, sir...why..." The young officer trailed off and fell silent, grimacing as he poked the fire with a stick. Belden, and Cornet Wadsworth were also sitting around the fire built for the officers.

"What would you have done, Lieutenant?" Tallmadge asked quietly, sipping more of the hot water. It warmed him, warding away the chill that nipped at them tonight. His cloak kept him somewhat warm, but it was not much against the occasional gusting wind.

"Have the men advance, and pick them off in the woods-"

"And what would have happened if say, one of your men's horses was lamed while in those woods, Jack?" Belden interrupted quietly. Tallmadge saw Webb shoot Belden a slightly wounded look, but he considered the question posed.

"Then..."

"We were fortuitous in the fact that the path we took from the barn across the woods was not littered with sharp rocks or stones covered by the snowfall," Belden pointed out. "There is also something else to consider, Jack. They outnumbered us. If we were to go into the woods and engage them, then what is to prevent them from circling us and trapping us with their lines?"

Tallmadge nodded in agreement; it was something he had considered and discarded just as quickly, but the fact that Belden had picked up on it pleased him. The captain had developed a sharp tactical mind. "There is also another aspect to consider, Lieutenant." He sipped some more of the corn-flavored water. "You may achieve the element of surprise and anger in your strike, but you must consider the consequence of such an action against a greater numbered force."

"The morale," Webb nodded before sighing heavily. "It's just that, sir, the men would have wanted a fight-"

"And they would have given them a good one, but against a force that they had seen slaughtering surrendering men? They would realize that there is only one option left to them, to die fighting. Surrendering would expose them to the cruelty of the treatment that had first incited them to fight, and fleeing without an explicit order would be seen as desertion and entail punishment if they are caught," Tallmadge finished and saw Webb sit back, his expression an unhappy grimace.

"I see, sir," Webb fidgeted for a moment before speaking up again. "Thank you sir, for parting with this knowledge."

"Take heart, Lieutenant, the men who lost their lives today will be avenged." He set the cup down and picked his quill back up to finish composing his report to General Washington. "It will be a day where they will not see us coming." The grimacing look disappeared from Webb's face as he nodded, pleased that they were to do something, if not at this very moment.

December 23rd, 1777

Their desire for revenge had to be tempered when they received an unexpected courier with a request from General Washington. The letter was short and succinct as Tallmadge read its contents. This was a mission of high import and Washington wished for him to be discreet. Discretion meant he was only to take one or two people with him that he absolutely trusted not to say anything to the others. That was the easy part, as he knew who he would already choose. The missive had come to him the night before by the last person Tallmadge would have expected to be a courier, Lieutenant Colonel Hamilton. The fact that the message was delivered by one of Washington's aide-de-camps spoke volumes as to its contents.

They had repaired to the outskirts of Germantown for the day and Hamilton said he would wait for him and his men to return with the necessary intelligence. Tallmadge had given the rest of the men a day of rest from constant patrolling, but had also ordered a watch to be set up. The men were curious about Hamilton's presence, but did not question it, having sensed it was a matter for officers and did not concern enlisted men such as themselves. Tallmadge had certainly seen unspoken questions on Belden's face when he told him the patrol would be left in his care for the day. But it seemed his captain was smart enough not to question the situation at hand.

Tallmadge folded the letter up and placed it, not inside his jacket, but rather deep into the pocket of his vest. He then sought out Adamson and Davenport and found the two sitting by several bales of hay that were stored in a large farmhouse that they occupied. It was owned by a Patriot family who had fled to Philadelphia to stay with relatives after Hessians occupied the village. The sprawling acreage made it ideal for them to stay out of sight of incoming patrols, but also have a vantage point from which they would be able to easily see any overt movements.

"Sir," Davenport greeted him with a nod. Adamson was stirring a small pot of something that actually smelled good.

"The sergeant-major here found a chicken that was half-frozen to death, but still alive, so we killed it and are cooking it for a feast tonight." Tallmadge could see that the men gathered around were already salivating, wanting to eat the stew being cooked. "The young pup of a lieutenant's got a salt box he carries around like a good luck charm and let us use some of it."

"Really," Tallmadge raised an eyebrow, surprised that Webb had that kind of luxury item on him. He supposed the lieutenant must have gotten it from his family and probably kept close it to him. It was rather generous of him to share the fresh salt anyone.

"Is it ready yet, Andrew?" Davenport gave Adamson a hard poke in the shoulder with his fork.

Adamson only frowned and absently waved the fork away from his side as he stirred the pot some more and lifted the small wooden spoon that he had. There was a bit of oily broth in it. Adamson tasted it stuck the spoon back into the pot and stirred some more. "Aye, it's ready, but remember what Webb said?"

"Aye," Davenport sounded put out. He took a large metal cup and gave it to Adamson who scooped a few large helpings of soup with chunks of meat and what looked like nibs of corn into the tin. He handed it back to Davenport who stood up and walked it over to Webb who was sitting on the opposite end of the barn, half asleep against a bale of hay that his horse was nibbling the edges of it. Webb seemingly woke up as Davenport approached and accepted his cup full of stew with a hearty smile and brief thanks.

Tallmadge watched the whole exchange in silence, his curiosity getting the better of him. Truth be told, it was good that Webb would get the first and best part of the stew since it was his salt they had used to flavor the meal; but to do receive the meal in front of all of the men seemed like a bit of pettiness and an overt abuse of rank and privilege. He did not comment, though, hoping Webb would learn the lesson on his own. The young man still seemed to have some trouble coping with the lesson he had learned a little over a week ago when Lord Rawdon had killed three of their own.

"Do you want some, Major?" Adamson offered and Tallmadge shook his head.

"Not at the moment, though it does smell good." He could not deny that his stomach rumbled a little at the smell filling the barn. "I'm actually here for you and Davenport."

"Sir?" Adamson frowned before looking around. "Forgive me, sir. Dole!" his friend called out to one of the men who was sitting and talking with several others. "Dole, the stew is ready. Can you take over?"

"Yes, sir," Sergeant James Dole stood up and moved to the pot with his cup in hand as the others started to crowd around. Adamson thrust an empty cup at Dole with the silent request to fill it while Adamson extricated himself from the crowd of men forming around the pot.

"Maybe I should go ask the lieutenant colonel and Captain Belden at the small house if they want any?" Davenport spoke up next to him, as they surveyed the scene before them.

"They didn't want any, I asked before while I was looking for salt," Adamson said coming over to them. "Sir, you wanted to see us?"

"Us?" Davenport looked confused for a moment before a wide smile appeared on his face. "Does this have to do with the lieutenant colonel being here, Ben?"

Tallmadge gave him a look to which Davenport coughed a little and muttered an apology for addressing him so familiarly in front of the men. "Yes and no. Unfortunately, I have to take you two away from the chicken stew here, but we're going to a slightly better place." He gestured for them to follow him out of the barn.

"What could be better than the chicken stew?" Davenport muttered, but it was cut short by a slight pained sound and Tallmadge saw the shadow of Adamson removing his elbow from Davenport's side.

"No helms," he said, ignoring Davenport's comments. Another person would have taken it as insubordination, but Tallmadge let it slide only because it was just the three of them outside and he knew Davenport meant no harm by his comments. He knew that he would have to eventually talk to him about it, as it seemed Davenport was picking up on a lot of Pullings' bad habits, but for now Adamson seemed to have kept him in check. "Cloaks are fine. Both of you have a pistol?" he asked.

"Yes," Adamson replied.

Davenport nodded, "Sir, what is this-" He was cut off again with a quick shushing sound from Adamson, who was realizing what kind of mission this was. Tallmadge was glad of his friend's quick uptake; Adamson was more than likely remembering the last time he had been detached on special assignment with him back in February to help Major Clark.

"No carbines," he stated. "Adamson, borrow Dole's sabre, Davenport I know you have your own."

"Sir," his friend acknowledged before he waved them to head into the barn to saddle up their horses with the necessary equipment.

As they disappeared back into the barn, Tallmadge walked over and untied Castor from the post where he was waiting, and mounted him. He hoped that with just the basic pistol and sabre, he, Adamson, and Davenport would be able to pass as either post couriers or regular cavalrymen instead of dragoons. Their blue and buff coats mimicked some of the Continental Army's officer uniforms, but in the darkness of night, he hoped they would only be identified with the familiar blue-white coat. Their plumed helms made them distinctively dragoons, so Tallmadge thought it prudent to leave them back at camp. He wished he had a couple of tricorns in order to look more realistically like basic infantryman.

The barn door opened once more as Adamson and Davenport led their horses out. They mounted their beasts without question and Tallmadge saw the initial jolly expression on Davenport's face had resolved itself into a more serious look. Adamson must have told something about the secretive nature of their business or perhaps he relayed something of his previous venture into such a world. Whatever it was, Davenport acknowledged him with a curt nod and Tallmadge heeled Castor to head into Philadelphia.

Though Philadelphia was nominally under British occupation, there were very few checkpoints and were easily spotted from afar. The cloaks they wore over their uniforms, to give them warmth against the frigid elements as well as to conceal their colors, provided some cover for them. Tallmadge guided them at a steady trot three miles to the edges of the city proper, using the back alleys and seldom patrolled roadways to reach his destination. They had been helpfully provided with the map of the area in the letter. It was crudely drawn, as if written in haste, but nonetheless, it was a great boon and help as he arrived in front of the tavern.

"Sir," Adamson whispered as they dismounted and he saw him gesture with a chin towards a British outpost that had been set up at least fifty yards from the tavern. There were at least four men on duty, two on one side of the road, another two on the opposite side. A small thatched hut of sorts was set up and Tallmadge suspected there was a British officer inside. The men huddled over their small fires, rubbing and warming their hands, more concerned about staying warm than of the coming and goings of those from the tavern.

"Let's head in," he murmured, tying Castor up to the hitching post. The tavern's name was the Rising Sun and a quick glance at the clientele upon entering told him it serviced mainly traders, farmers, and the like. A few men looked like soldiers, but the motley garb they wore spoke otherwise. He realized they were either Tory "cowboys" or Patriot "skinners" – men who raided and pillaged the countryside for coin, but had some leaning and loyalty to their respective causes. They were lawless men who answered to no one of authority and were usually a nuisance to deal with. Colonel Sheldon had said that a majority of his time in Westchester during the past year was spent dealing with the Tory 'cowboys' who were harassing local Patriot-leaning families as well as raiding their supply wagons.

Tallmadge discreetly drew his cloak closer to him as he signaled the barkeep and picked a table near the window, which gave him a good view of the road and outpost that led into the Philadelphia proper. Davenport and Adamson both sat down, Davenport across from him and Adamson adjacent to them.

"Three house ales and the stew if you will," he said with a grim smile to the woman that came over to take their order. If he had to guess, she was the matron of the tavern, judging by her dress and age. He reached into his pocket and pulled out some coinage, all British pounds and dropped what he thought was the appropriate amount, along with a small token he had received with the letter.

"Coming right up, sir," the woman nodded, finding the amount to her satisfaction and left.

"Sir-"

"Not here." He shook his head at Davenport's question and saw a slight frown appear on his friend's face. He looked confused for a moment, before realizing what Tallmadge had meant by his words and cleared his throat again.

"...Ben...why-"

"Information, Henry." It was Adamson who answered in a quiet tone as the matron of the tavern returned with three pints of ale and started to distribute them in an expert manner.

However, as she set his down in front of him, she quickly leaned towards him. "She should be arriving soon." Just as quickly, she stood back up and affected a cheery smile before heading away from them.

Tallmadge took a sip of the ale, letting the alcohol warm his throat on its way down. Davenport all but drank half of his in two gulps and set the tankard down with a wide smile.

"I can get used to this." The questioning mood had seemingly disappeared, but there was still something hooded in Davenport's eyes. Tallmadge knew his friend wanted answers, answers he could not and would not answer.

"Better than the chicken stew?" Adamson asked, a wry smile working across his lips.

"You're the one who cooked it," Davenport replied, taking another gulp of the ale.

"Aye, but this is better," Adamson agreed, just as the matron returned with three bowls of hearty stew and set them down in front of them. Tallmadge could not help the slight delight that rose up in him at the sight of not only meat, but potatoes and all sorts of root vegetables in the stew.

"Thank you," he said to the matron, who smiled and left them to their meal. Davenport did not bother with the pretense of eating in a polite manner and attacked the stew with some gusto. Tallmadge shook his head at his friend's antics, but also knew he would have done the same if he was not burdened by what he needed to do. Instead, he picked up his fork and ate in a restrained manner, as did Adamson, to his surprise, as he let his gaze roam around the tavern.

"Nothing yet," he heard Adamson murmur and saw his friend flick a look towards the windows.

He nodded, taking another bite of the delicious stew, glad that Adamson had picked up so much during his brief time with Major Clark in Setauket. His friend definitely had a head for intelligence gathering, something Tallmadge would never have expected from his former student. Adamson had been a rather vocal and distracted student, passionate in his debates, but did not have the wherewithal to twist and turn arguments into his favor by observation. Adamson had never spoken about nor made any indications that he wanted to gather intelligence – and only showed restraint and discretion when picked for such matters. It was invaluable and Tallmadge was beginning to realize that Adamson was truly someone he could trust.

They were about half way finished with their stews – Davenport having finished his in short order – when Tallmadge spotted movement outside of the window the tavern. The thick windows and darkness obscured the person who was approaching, but he could see the shape of a woman dressed in a cloak, her hood pulled up to protect her from the elements.

The door to the tavern opened and the woman stepped in, removing her hood. Tallmadge saw she was carrying a basket of eggs and knew it was the person he was supposed to make contact with.

"Ben?" Adamson had set his fork down and Tallmadge tilted his head in a slight nod.

"Ask her if we may purchase some of her eggs. We're looking for brown ones," he said. Adamson nodded, pushing his chair back with a quiet scrape and stood up. He flicked a look at Davenport who was staring between her and Adamson. "Davenport, check up on the horses."

"Ben, if you want me to leave because of the girl-"

"Check up on the *horses*," he emphasized, before gesturing with a chin towards the direction of the outpost. A frown appeared on Davenport's face, but he nodded, understanding his intentions.

"Got it," Davenport replied before he also stood up. He drew his cloak tighter around him and headed out of the tavern itself, waving a quick goodbye to the owner and his wife on his way out.

Tallmadge turned and resumed eating, though he discreetly watched Adamson approach the country girl who had set her basket of eggs on the table and was cheerfully talking to the tavern owner. She was rather plain-looking, with a button nose and brown hair tied in a simple style. Her skin was quite fair with a bit of ruddiness upon her face. She already had the curves of a woman in full bloom, though her hair was not covered to indicate she was married. She certainly was not skinny enough to indicate hardship, but neither was she dressed in the fashions that would indicate she was of the wealthier classes. From what he could see, her cloak was clean and had perhaps a single patch – which meant it was well cared for and used on a daily basis. He could only surmise that with Philadelphia taken, she and her parents were still allowed to keep their home and livelihood – and that livelihood was more than likely dealing with farmed goods.

He watched as Adamson shyly approached the girl, and saw him wring his hands as he talked. The girl had an open expression on her face as a small smile made its way up her lips, a rather pretty smile. She nodded and took the basket from the counter before gesturing to the eggs inside with an apologetic expression. From his vantage point, Tallmadge could see that they were all white-shelled eggs. Adamson shook his head and gesticulated before pointing at him and Tallmadge saw the brief moment in which the country girl set her eyes on him. The smile that had been on her face seemingly stilled for a second, before she nodded and headed towards the table where he sat.

He saw Adamson move towards the door, indicating with only a brief nod of his head towards him that he would join Davenport outside to keep an eye on the outpost, now that they had made contact with the agent General Washington wished for him to communicate with.

He stood up and pulled Davenport's chair back as the girl approached. She nodded and took the offered seat before he sat back down. "Would you like anything?" he offered, but she shook her head and set the basket of eggs down on Adamson's vacated seat.

"No thank you. I do apologize for not having the brown eggs

ready," she said and he shook his head.

"It is of no consequence," he replied, remembering the specific words he had to say to prove that he was her contact and she his. "The brown eggs would have tasted a bit sour I suppose."

"Aye," her smile dimmed a little. "Ann Darragh, good sir."

"Benjamin Tallmadge. That other man was one of my men, Andrew Adamson."

"I see," she replied, looking a little more at ease. "If I may ask, sir, what-"

"I wish to not give my rank, if you will." He shook his head a little and gestured with a darting look around the tavern. "We are in Philadelphia."

"I understand," Ann nodded as her smile became more hesitant. "Far better than you may know. Rank hath privileges, but can also be a hindrance when collecting information."

"There is truth in that," he nodded. She sounded like she was used to this business and he wondered if she had been a spy before the British had taken over Philadelphia. Her words indicated as much as she understood who could provide the best information – those who were of higher rank and gave away certain intelligence were to be far more trusted than those of lower rank who did not know as much.

"We normally would have transmitted this information to our contact in the army, but he has taken ill in recent days and this information could not wait. Our contact told us that he would try to get the matter out some other way, and it seems that you were sent." The smile disappeared from her face as she looked at him. Tallmadge was a little struck at how earnest and serious she looked, belying her age and the countenance he had expected from her.

"General Charles Lee has been giving information to the enemy." Though her voice was level, there was a certain hushed quality to it that made Tallmadge alert to any sort of eavesdropping or the like.

"Lee was captured just a little over a year ago," He was puzzled by her information. "If he was granted parole by the British before he was exchanged, he would have had the privilege of dining with them and the like."

"No," she shook her head, her eyes widening with alarm, "he was granted parole, but violated that parole by giving information and troop numbers to the enemy. He was telling them specifics about what he knew of the dragoon regiments that others had written to him about, about the strength of Washington's infantry, his artillery, and generals who may consider changing their loyalties or may be amenable to a change in the army's leadership with more sympathetic ties to the British."

Tallmadge stilled at the clarification. What she was saying amounted to treason of the highest level. And from one of the highest generals in the Continental Army too. "That's..."

She nodded solemnly. He could only gape at her for a few seconds before he found his voice again. "H-How...?"

"Major John Andre, adjutant-general of the British Army is quartered at my family's home. We were allowed to stay by the grace of God." Ann lifted a quick hand upwards towards Heaven. "He has guests over frequently and many times in the last two months it has been General Lee. He was exchanged back only a few days ago." Ann looked worried as a twisting fear that Tallmadge thought he could never feel cut deep into him.

Charles Lee was a traitor and here was proof. Washington and, by extension, the army were in grave danger if Lee was to be put in charge again. He had to warn him, had to return to Lieutenant Colonel Hamilton and give him the information Ann had just told him. He felt a little sick, the stew settling uncomfortably in his stomach. Just how much had Lee told the British about the Continentals? About the dragoons? Did they know about where the 2nd Light was wintering? No, no, he dismissed the thought. Lee only had information as recent as when he was captured, and that was a year ago. Anything else was in letters written to him by his compatriots. Any information about where each of the dragoons were wintering was not known to the British. He forced himself to remain calm.

"Thank you, for bringing this information-"

A sudden whoop and yell outside that sounded distinctly like Davenport followed by the unmistakable discharge of a pistol into the night startled him and Ann. They both looked out the window to see the blurred form of someone riding hard past the windows, waving a sabre in the air. Not even a second later, the door to the tavern slammed open and Adamson stuck his head in.

"Ben!" he hissed. "Patrol!"

Tallmadge cursed inwardly as he stood up, hand on the butt of his pistol as he saw the men that were sitting in the corner of the tavern look up with some interest. He ignored them and hurried out of the tavern, hearing a clatter of footsteps behind him. The cold air whipped at him as he stepped outside and saw that, indeed, several horses were riding hard down the road after Davenport, who was leading them on a merry chase.

A shout and distant whinny of a horse made him turn to see the guard post come alive with more horses bearing down at them, the British having spotted them. "Shite," Tallmadge muttered as he gestured for Adamson to mount and rushed over to Castor to untie him from his post. He quickly mounted him just as he saw a flash of color in the corner of his vision.

"Wait! Mr. Tallmadge, sir!" He glanced down to see Ann hurrying towards him. "Please, take me with you! The men- In the tavern, they're Tory cowboys! They know that I've been talking to you-"

"Ben-" Adamson's tone was low with warning.

Tallmadge gritted his teeth as he saw the horses coming closer, the men at the outpost furiously running towards them. He knew he could not leave Ann here; not after she was clearly seen talking and pleading with them. He shook his head and reached down to her. "Come on," he said as she grabbed his arm. He heaved with his strength to pull her behind him. As soon as she was settled, wrapping her arms around his waist, he heeled Castor hard, his horse responding with a quick jolt and burst of speed.

He expected her to cry out in fear, but she surprisingly stayed silent. He heard Adamson follow behind him and glanced to his left to see him hold up a hand with all five fingers spread out. They had five horsemen pursuing them. "Take the western road, meet back at camp," he shouted to Adamson, who nodded. He pulled away from them as they approached a fork in the road, Tallmadge riding hard towards the northeasterly direction while Adamson went on a more northwesterly track towards the Schuylkill. Both roads would eventually circle around to cross again, but as Tallmadge quickly glanced behind him, in the dim moonlight he saw the patrol that had been chasing them split apart. There were only three now that pursued him, hoping to catch him first with the extra weight on his horse.

"Come on, Castor," he slapped his horse's reins again, urging him to go faster as they galloped down the narrow road. The discharge of a gun being fired behind him followed by the sudden snap of leaves and branches to his left made him shy a little. He felt the girl's arms clench tighter around his waist, but she made no other sound. He dared not turn as the branches whipped by their faces, and felt her bury her head into his back as they continued along the narrow road. He could see a break in between the wooded groves and knew they were coming upon a series of farmlands that would give him better room to maneuver, but also give his pursuers the opportunity to flank him.

"Ann!" he called back, tapping one of her hands that clung to lapel the other grabbing his jacket near his waist. He felt her head move against his back and tapped the reins down to her hand. She apparently understood his intention as one of her hands released its white-knuckled grip on his lapel to take hold of the rein. As soon as she had done so, he reached down and drew out one of his pistols with his right hand. His left hand continued to guide Castor as they burst out of the woody section of the road and into the farmlands.

He heard the excited shout of the three British horsemen that pursued them as they too burst into the rolling farmlands. He shifted in his saddle, pulling a little on the reins as Ann did too, and Castor slowed down. He turned in time to see one of them direct the other two to flank him on opposite sides. Tallmadge knew he would not have time to reload; all three of his shots would have to count. He heeled Castor to charge forward, towards the one who had directed his comrades to the side and saw the British officer's eyes widen in surprise at his move before hastily reaching to the side to draw his pistol.

But Tallmadge was faster as he closed the distance between them and fired. His shot was true as the officer was thrown back, blood pouring from his mouth. The officer's half-drawn pistol fell from his limp hands as Tallmadge wheeled Castor around, holstering his pistol and taking the reins again. He felt Ann tighten her grip around his waist as he heeled Castor to charge forward, the shouts of dismay from the other two falling behind him as he continued.

He felt Ann shifting behind him before she shouted in his ear, "They've moved back, though one might be trying to cut through the corn fields to the left!"

He looked in that direction and through the dim moonlight saw that indeed someone seemed to be riding hard and fast through the high cornfields. He indicated for her to take part of the reins again as he reached over and pulled his other pistol from the saddle's holster and he nudged his horse closer to the edges of the cornfield. A quick glance to his right at the sound of a whinny told him that the other horseman was alerted to what he was trying to do, and was now racing back to warn his comrade.

Tallmadge pressed his lips into a thin line as he knew he could not make Castor go faster. His horse was clearly giving it his all, flecks of sweat were forming at his mouth and neck. Tallmadge pulled at the reins as they came to the end of the cornfield and saw the British soldier had just cleared it, his back towards him just up ahead. Tallmadge's timing could not have been more fortuitous. He pulled back on the hammer of his pistol and fired at point-blank range.

The British horsemen fell to the ground as flecks of blood, bone, and grey matter splashed across Tallmadge's face and clothes. He grimaced as he slotted his pistol back into its holster and took the reins back from Ann. Wiping a hand across his face he slowed Castor down looking for the remaining horseman. He received his answer a moment by way of a discharged pistol and Castor snorting in alarm as he reared. He fought to control Castor as the lone British horseman charged at him, sabre drawn in an effort to engage him.

"Stand and fight you coward!" the British officer shouted at him.

Tallmadge managed to control Castor enough for him to leap into a turn, and started to gallop away from the British officer. He heard the man curse behind him and fire another shot, but did not hear anything near him which meant that the shot went wide. He could hear the officer slap his horse's reins to chase him and felt Ann tighten her grip again. The fact that she had not voiced her fear at being shot at or being asked to take the reins twice now spoke well about her resolve and steadfastness to the Patriot cause. At the same time, he could not help but feel unnerved at the fact that she had not even flinched when he had killed the two British soldiers.

He could see the next thatch of woods now and set Castor to a steady gallop as he rode past the fields. The skies darkened around him as he rode into the narrow enclosed roads of the woods. He just needed to make it past these woods and into the next set of fields where the rest of the 2nd Light was encamped. A quick glance behind him revealed the British officer was foolishly following, and Tallmadge smiled grimly. The officer had not even bothered to reload his pistol and was holding his sabre aloft, urging his horse to go faster over the rough ground.

The officer would have the advantage soon enough, especially since he could feel Castor flagging, his horse's flanks heaving with heavy breaths. He had pushed him hard. Tallmadge had a single shot left from the pistol on his belt, but in the narrow confines of the woods it would be hard to get any type of shot off behind him. He knew he had the option of giving his pistol to Ann, but also knew that if she missed, there was no other way to defend themselves from an incoming attack.

"Come on, Castor," he urged his horse with a quiet whisper, focused on getting through the woods. "Come on..." His horse whickered as if trying to respond to his encouragement.

They rode the next half-mile in near silence save for the rhythmic hoofbeats and the harsh breaths of British officer's horse slowly gaining ground on them. Flashes of moonlight illuminated the narrow path through the woods, but Tallmadge was familiar with this trail, having ridden through it several times on his patrols. An idea occurred to him as he remembered a unique feature of these woods. There was a sharp ravine of sorts off the main road nearby. It had been an ideal place to set an ambush or for troops to rest for the night using the rocky overhang as shelter, but in darkness it was all but invisible unless one knew where to look.

He pulled Castor to a fast trot and pulled off the main road and onto what he knew was a very narrow path, but had been covered by leaves and bramble from recent storms. There was the risk of picking up a sharp stone or laming his horse from the narrowness of the path, but which Tallmadge knew that the British officer would catch up to them before they even cleared the woods. He had to act now before it was too late. Ann shifted behind him in response to his sudden deviation of the main road, but did not say anything.

"He's following," she called out after a few minutes and Tallmadge knew that he had made the right choice.

"I need you to hold tight. There will be an abrupt curve that I must take." He turned his head to look at her and saw her nod, her face set with grim determination.

Flashing her a quick confident smile, he turned back and slowed Castor down a little. It was literally a blind turn, as a wall of bramble and brush covered the edges of the ravine. The path was meant to be taken at a walk when going down, or from the opposite direction, skirting the edges to make it up to this part of the hill. But he knew that if he slowed down any further, it would give away his intention to the pursuing British officer. Another quick glance behind him briefly revealed the grim delight on the officer's face as he thought that they were slowing down due to the narrowness of the road and the added weight on his horse.

He took a deep breath and let it out quickly as they approached the brambled area. Tallmadge was already pulling Castor sharply to the left just as they burst through and for a moment, he thought he timed it wrong. He saw nothing but the dark pit of the ravine underneath him before his horse responded to his sharp command and gathered his legs underneath him, hitting the narrow path with bare inches to spare. Tallmadge could feel Ann tighten her grip a bit, but relaxed as they trotted down the narrow rocky pathway. He turned as the thunder of hooves echoed above them and looked up to see the the moment when the British officer burst through, a triumphant gleam in his eyes – only to have them widen in fear as he and his horse fell into the ravine.

Tallmadge turned away at the last moment, hearing the sickening crunch of horse, man and bones as he pulled Castor to a stop. "Don't look," he ordered Ann, lifting one of his hands to try to ward her away.

"I'm not," she replied, her voice muffled against his cloak. "Is...he-"

Tallmadge peered over the edge into the ravine and saw no signs of movement. Though the ravine was shallow, it had jagged rocks that were snow covered and he could see the slight glistening of something pooling from the fallen horse and soldier. Something else glistened too and a flash of moonlight revealed that the officer's sabre had pierced his horse, surely killing it even if the fall had not.

"Dead," he pronounced before he flicked the reins on Castor and his horse resumed its walk down the steep path. They reached the bottom in short order and Tallmadge turned them onto another path that would lead out of the woods. He set his horse into a light trot, the danger of pursuit not weighing on him anymore. He hoped that Adamson and Davenport had fared as well as he did in losing their pursuers.

They rode the rest of the way in silence, Ann relaxing her grip with the danger passed. He kept his own counsel as the rode back to where 1ˢᵗ Troop was encamped sensing that Ann did not want to talk nor was she asking for any sort of comfort after what had just happened. He thought that with the threat passed, Ann would have cried tears of relief, but there were no sniffles that he could hear nor any sort of movement that would indicate any sort of distress. It continued to puzzle him as well as fill him with a sense of admiration for her steadiness in the face of danger and death.

They exited the woods and rode into the open fields once more, Tallmadge clicking his tongue to urge Castor into a faster trot. His horse was tired, but obeyed his commands. As they rode up the small hill that led to the barn and a wide swath of fields, he felt Ann tap him on his shoulder and turned to see her pointing towards the distance. He looked at the direction she was pointing and saw the form of a rider galloping towards them. From his vantage point and the darkness of the night, he could not tell who it was, but it was no matter as they arrived at the camp.

"Sir!" Belden and Hamilton emerged from the house next to the barn, having heard his arrival. He pulled Castor short and reached down to pat him gently on his neck. He saw that a watch had been set up in his absence and those on watch stared at him with some curiosity as Hamilton and Belden approached him. He felt Ann remove her arms around him as she accepted a hand from Hamilton to dismount.

"Lieutenant Colonel Alexander Hamilton at your service, Miss..."

"Ann Darragh," she introduced herself just as the rider they had spotted in the distance raced in. Tallmadge automatically placed his hand on the butt of his pistol, but relaxed his grip as he realized it was Adamson. He had started to smile in greeting, but stopped when he saw a serious expression on his friend's face.

"Adamson?" he questioned.

"They got Davenport, captured." Adamson was out of breath as he shook his head. Tallmadge frowned, cursing quietly.

"Sir, should we move to another location?" Belden asked and Tallmadge glanced down at him as he saw Hamilton take off his cloak and offer it to Ann. She accepted it, shivering a little.

"Davenport won't talk, I know him," he reassured his captain, and the other officer nodded. It hurt to hear that Davenport had been captured, but he also knew he could do nothing for his friend. He could not wantonly risk his men to foolishly chase down and rescue one man. The only saving grace was that Davenport would hopefully be treated with civility and be transported to a prison where he would have the opportunity to be exchanged at a later date. He could only hope that as a non-commissioned officer, Davenport would be able to survive the prisons long enough for him to be exchanged. It was cruel and it hurt, but he forced himself to push past the hurt.

He dismounted as Hamilton led Ann into the house to rest and recover as well as to deliver the intelligence she had brought with her. She was in safe hands now. He led Castor to the barn to be watered and fed, patting his horse's neck for a job well done. Adamson joined him while Belden went to direct the curious men on watch to return to their duties. Though the gravity of the intelligence that Ann had shared regarding General Lee's traitorous actions weighed on him, he hoped that Lieutenant Colonel Hamilton would be able to convey the importance of it, and that Washington would take action to protect both himself and the army from Lee's machinations. Washington could not afford to let such a traitor continue to serve in the ranks of the Continental Army.

December 29th, 1777

Whatever became of Ann Darragh's intelligence was not known to Tallmadge, as Washington's replies to his reports provided no hint of what had happened. He filed the matter to the back of his mind as he continued his patrols, joined by Lieutenant Lewis' troop from the 1st Light whom they had encountered at Chestnut Hill just a couple of days earlier. The lieutenant was amenable to working with them, having lost a few men to skirmishes with the British. But it was clear that both detached dragoon troops had to retire soon due to diminishing supplies and lack of resources after some initial successful raids against the British, and the harshness of winter's cold grip as they settled deep into the season.

He planned for one more raid before sending off his final report to Washington and rejoining the rest of the 2nd Light at Chatham. They had received word from a local fur trader who complained about the lack of fair pricing he had received for his wares. The trader requested his monetary due for providing them with the information, but Tallmadge had replied only that he would consider it. He had no doubts that the trader would no sooner turn around and give the British patrols information about them in the same manner.

A couple of Lieutenant Lewis' men had been dismounted, so he effected his trap by setting them up with a broken axle on a covered wagon and two of their lamed horses. The rest of the men, along with his own, were hiding in the cornfields. To anyone who saw the broken wagon and horses alongside the road, it would seem obvious what had happened. Any patrol would seize the opportunity to claim whatever supplies were in the road and take the soldiers prisoner at the same time. This late in the winter, he knew that the British patrols, like his men, were in desperate need of supplies.

True to form, Pullings, who was stationed as one of the advance scouts in a cornfield about half a mile away, reported that at least thirteen British dragoons were approaching. They were also escorting a wagon from a recent raid. Tallmadge passed word to his men to hold until he gave the signal, all of them waiting deep in the snow-covered stalks of corn.

He had a few of his men dismount, using them as foot scouts stationed close to the edge of the fields, to relay when they should charge. That only left about sixteen of them mounted, but he hoped they would be enough in numbers to deter the British. He could hear the slow creak of wheels and noises of the approaching party and held himself still. With some luck, he and his men who were mounted were deep enough in the fields that they would not be noticed until it was too late.

"Ho there!" he heard a booming voice call out, and saw a flash of color as the rider who hailed the soldiers by the broken wagon rode by his place of concealment. "Surrender peacefully and you men will be treated fairly. You may now consider yourselves prisoner of the British crown and property." The voice had the ring of authority in it, and Tallmadge surmised it was the commanding officer of the group of dragoons.

"We heard of you," one of Lewis' men spoke up and Tallmadge frowned. This was not according to plan. "You one of Rawdon's men, aren't you?"

He could hear and feel the restless shift in his men around him as they recognized the name. They all still felt the sting and anger of what had happened last time they encountered Rawdon, and Tallmadge could feel the anticipatory mood turning hostile.

"Stop talking Phillips," he heard Lewis mutter next to him and glanced over at the junior officer who glared at nothing in particular.

"Lord Rawdon killed a few of my men days ago," Lieutenant Lewis murmured. "This is going to turn bad if we don't-"

The lone pistol shot firing into the air was all anyone needed as Tallmadge spurred Castor to leap from the cornfield. For a few precious seconds, he heard the noise of chaos before him before he burst out into the road at the same time sixteen of his men did so, instantly surrounding the thirteen other dragoons and the wagon. The men had their carbines pointed straight at the British, anger evident on their faces.

Tallmadge quickly identified the officer that had confronted the men at the broken wagon and pointed his pistol at him. He vaguely recognized him as one of the officers who had beat Sergeant Mills and his grip became a little tighter. The British officer, meanwhile, had already drawn his pistol, but it was pointed down towards the enlisted man who had identified him as part of Rawdon's command.

"Surrender," he said, marveling at the calm quality of his own voice. A quick glance around assured him the others were obeying his silent command not to fire, but more than one looked ready to kill the dragoons that served with Lord Rawdon. "Surrender and quarter will be given," he raised his voice, making sure that all his men as well as those under Lewis' command understood that not one of the British dragoons who surrendered would be harmed. They did not need to stoop to Rawdon's level, even if they all wanted some form of revenge.

"There are only sixteen-"

Lewis' whistle pierced the air and the rest of the two groups, about six more men who had dismounted walked out of the cornfields, pointing their carbines at the rest of the enemy dragoons. Tallmadge saw Webb reloading his pistol, having shot it into the air to alert them of the perfect instant to launch their ambush.

"Surrender, sir, and quarter will be given," he addressed the officer, a lieutenant colonel, once more. "You have my assurance and word that no harm will come to your men."

He could see the officer's eyes dart about, taking in the number of guns pointed at him and his men before he nodded curtly. He primed his pistol back to half-cock before holstering it, then drew out his sabre and handed it hilt-first to Tallmadge, who holstered his own pistol and took the proffered weapon. That was the signal to everyone, and the British dragoons held up their hands, holding their muskets upwards as they were taken away. He nodded to Lewis to herd the men into a semblance of a formation. They would be marched to the nearest Continental outpost to be processed as prisoners of war. The enlisted men would probably stay at the outpost while the two officers of the group would be forwarded to either the main camp or Philadelphia itself on parole. Tallmadge would have to write a letter to Washington asking if he wished to meet the officers or send them on their way – sans horses of course.

He tucked the officer's sabre under his arm as he saw Adamson suddenly gesture for him to come towards the wagon. As he approached, he could see Adamson frantically cutting away at something, and Tallmadge could not help the broad smile that appeared on his face. Henry Davenport had been tied to the back of the wagon, apparently part of a prisoner transport, and now had been freed.

"Sergeant Davenport!" he greeted. He wanted nothing more than to dismount and embrace his friend, but he knew with so many eyes on him and given the dignity of the surrender that had just occurred, he could not. Instead, he settled for a wide smile and a formal greeting.

"Major." Davenport's face was battered, one of his eyes swelled shut. He had clearly been beaten, but nonetheless, gave Tallmadge a knuckled salute and a grim smile. There was something distant in his eyes, something Tallmadge knew he would have to talk to his friend about in a more private setting, to find out its cause. But, they had freed Davenport from what could have been a miserable captivity and was happy that there was no need for a prisoner exchange.

Adamson placed a friendly arm around their mutual friend and led him away. Adamson would take care of Davenport in the mean time and Tallmadge could only hope that his friend had not suffered too greatly since his capture.

INTERLUDE VII

Washington did not need to look hard to see the weariness that hooded Major John Clark's eyes. The man sat hunched as he seemingly stared at the roaring fire in the house Washington had made his headquarters here in Valley Forge. Clark was thinner than the last time they talked, and an occasional hoarse cough emerged from his lips only to be muffled by his sleeve. The other man sitting in the room by the table fared no better, though he supposed Nathaniel Sackett always had a dour look about his face. Alexander Hamilton was attending to the mundane duties of an aide-de-camp as he poured a few glasses of wine and distributed them.

But Washington's concern was for Major Clark at the moment, as Hamilton offered the man a small glass of wine. Unlike the last time they met, Clark accepted the glass and sipped it gingerly, relief spreading across his face.

"I apologize, sir," Clark cleared his throat a little, "but I had to convey my resignation in person instead of writing a letter to you that might have gotten lost in this damnable weather."

"I see." Washington had anticipated that Clark would resign since the man reported his ill health in late November. But he had held out hope that it was just a lingering cold or minor sickness until Clark had arrived just yesterday. The man had been out of sorts, nearly frozen to death in the short trip from Philadelphia to Valley Forge. It was only on the intelligence

Hamilton had obtained via Major Tallmadge – along with a very interesting report from the major regarding how he had obtained his intelligence with a three-mile chase through the Philadelphia countryside with the female agent – that they had any idea Clark would be arriving. Hamilton had gone out in the snowy weather to make sure Clark made it to camp safely.

"If I may persuade you to stay your resignation and perhaps take a furlough until spring to see if your health improves?" he asked, shifting a little in his chair by the fire. Washington declined the offered drink from Hamilton who placed it on his desk instead to be drunk later that evening as a nightcap. Hamilton had proven himself indispensable since he had brought him onto his staff. He normally would have had Billy serve the drinks, but since Martha had arrived, he was attending to her needs per his request. His wife deserved every single comfort he could afford to give her during her stay.

Clark slowly shook his head as he sipped some more of the wine. "I will have to decline, sir, even though it is a very generous offer. I have been suffering from this ailment for a while now and it seems it may be doing me in. Come spring, I do not know if I will have the health to continue to serve in the army itself. It is why not only do I submit my resignation as the head of intelligence, but also my commission."

Washington blinked once, hard, and pressed his lips tightly together as he slowly nodded. He had no choice but to accept Clark's resignation. He knew that another plea, no matter what was offered, would not persuade the good Major to accept anything other than a full discharge of his duties and rank. Major John Clark was done with the war and Washington was disappointed and saddened to see him go.

"My agents will still report." A sad smile flitted across Clark's face as he took another sip, and this time, Washington could see a slight tremor in the man's hands. He truly was ill, but it seemed that whatever his illness was, it was not contagious. "God willing they're all a good bunch of men and women. Stubborn too. I've talked with them and they've set up their own system in the interim to get intelligence to you or the Lieutenant Colonel here for as long as you need them operating out of Philadelphia."

"I appreciate it," Washington nodded as Clark grimaced and coughed into his sleeve.

"There is a Lieutenant Charles Darragh serving in your army here who is related to one of my agents' families in Philadelphia. Lieutenant Colonel Hamilton is aware of him and Darragh has been appraised of the situation. He will receive intelligence from the sources in Philadelphia and pass it to you in that fashion," Clark explained and Washington glanced at his aide-de-camp who nodded once.

"Thank you for your foresight, Major," Washington said as Clark pushed himself up from the chair, having said what needed to be said. He too stood up and accepted a salute from the ailing major. "I will have the proper discharge orders drawn up by tomorrow morning, will that be satisfactory?"

"Yes, sir," Clark nodded, a smile of relief on his face. "Thank you again, sir, for the opportunity. I wish I could have done more, but..."

"No, Major, thank you for your service. The war will have lost one of its best, but you can rest assured that your efforts will not be forgotten," he replied, and Clark accepted his praise with some grace before he walked out of the room. Hamilton followed him out to escort the ailing man to one of the sturdier houses nearby to stay for the night, leaving only Washington and Sackett in the room.

"Well, Mr. Sackett..." he began without preamble and saw the other man adjust his spectacles.

"Based on what we know since General Clinton has been put in charge with Howe's return to England, there is a chance that Clinton would evacuate Philadelphia and return to New York to consolidate his position," Sackett speculated.

"But we do not know that for sure," he finished for the other man as he rounded the chairs and headed to his war table to study the maps. General Henry Clinton was a shrewd man, based on the various reports and intelligence he had gotten from Sackett's and John Jay's agents. He favored aggression and overt moves far more than Howe's defensive and laggard feints – which by the grace of God had preserved the Continental Army more often than not. Washington had already concluded since reviewing the reports from Gates' successful campaign in

Saratoga, that Philadelphia would eventually be abandoned by the British since they needed to reinforce New York. The loss of Burgoyne's forces in the North had put a serious strain on the British forces to hold two major cities.

Washington knew his own army could not conceivably fight for either city without incurring significant losses, but he also knew the British did not know of the Continentals' dismal lack of strength at the moment. Valley Forge had been a harsh mistress since they made camp with men dying from the elements or from rampant sickness in the wet, rancid cabins they had made for shelter. There was also the severe shortage of food and supplies. Washington had received reports that the picketing patrols between the Schuylkill and Delaware Rivers he had set up had gone to winter quarters. It was due to their own lack of supplies and the increasingly inclement weather which meant that whatever supplies they had bartered or taken from the raids would slow to a trickle now. Congress' Board of War was being intransigent and refusing a lot of his missives, even with the pleas he had Hamilton writing on his behalf. The only saving grace was that he had appointed his stalwart general, Nathaneal Greene, to the position of Quartermaster General to not only procure supplies, but also to stem the tide of discontent and calls for his removal as Commander-in-Chief. The cabal of generals and Congressional officials had grown since Gates' victory at Saratoga and Washington could only ask those who were loyal to him not to antagonize those who continued to talk behind his back.

It was a fine line of politicking, and the latest intelligence coup that Major Clark's agents had produced for him gave him another cause for worry. General Lee's return to camp had been hailed by Washington's detractors as a triumph and while Washington was glad that Lee had returned with renewed fervor, it had been tempered with the news that Lee had all but turned traitor in name. He had no proof to discredit Lee, whose popularity with the men, and especially with the officers of the cabal against him, was still strong. Washington knew he would have to bide his time and had all but ordered Hamilton not to say a word regarding what they both knew about Lee. The young man had taken his order with some frustration, but so far,

Washington knew his young aide-de-camp had adhered to it. He was touched by Hamilton's loyalty to him, and hoped that the responsibility of coordinating with Major Clark in obtaining intelligence had tempered some of the young man's impulsive behaviors.

"The year is young and the winter is still long, Mr. Sackett." He picked up a token absently, a silver one of a falconing bird with its wings folded and hood on its head. General Pulaski had been kind enough to part with it after their failed incursion into Germantown. Pulaski had only smiled when, after asking Washington to pick one of his unusual and mythical-looking tokens as a gift, he had chosen the only one that was not a mythical creature. Pulaski had explained in his broken English that the falconing bird token had denoted the spearhead dragoon vanguard – the likeness of a trained bird of prey.

"Aye, that it is," Sackett nodded. "We can only hope that the French would arrive soon, sir."

"Aye..." Washington nodded absently as he placed the token on New York. With the news that the French had agreed to send ships and men and were allying themselves with the United States of America and going to war against England, there was still hope yet. The only thing he knew was that, if Clinton decided to abandon Philadelphia come the spring, he needed eyes in New York. It seemed appropriate to leave the hooded predator token on New York itself until the hood could theoretically be removed.

12

The early days of 1778 had not brought much good fortune to the 2nd Light wintered at Chatham, New Jersey. When Tallmadge and 1st Troop arrived, he found himself readily placed in charge of the regiment that was stationed there, as Colonel Sheldon prepared to make an extended journey to outfit about one-third of the regiment that was posted under General Putnam on detached duty. After procuring supplies and weaponry for the detached troops, Sheldon would make his way to Hartford to plead his case for the four of six troops raised in Connecticut to be eligible for the same benefits as those of the Connecticut Continental Line infantry.

Lieutenant Colonel Blackden had been nominated, but not appointed, to the position of Quartermaster General of the cavalry as a whole by General Pulaski. Though Blackden did not get the position, he was ordered to head to Boston to procure clothes and equipment for the regiment and so was also away. Sheldon had barely left any instructions and Tallmadge had to contend with outfitting the rest of the regiment on his own. He had hoped for a day or two of leave or even plain rest since he and 1st Troop had conducted nearly non-stop patrols for the last month, but it was not to be.

Instead, he threw himself into now-seemingly regular duties as commander of the regiment, a little excited at the prospect of ensuring that at least part of the 2nd Light would be properly outfitted and that they would enter the renewed campaign with better discipline and fervor.

March 21ˢᵗ, 1778

Winter's grip still lingered late into March as a cold wind rattled the window panes and blew its draft into the small slave cabin he had commandeered as both his billeting quarters and office for the winter. He would have taken a bedroom and the parlor of the family's farm he was staying at, but relished the privacy and relative quiet of the single-room cabin. The family's slaves had been placed in another cabin that was previously used for variety of tools. A few the 2ⁿᵈ Light's junior officers were bunked at the farmhouse, thus made for slightly noisy and cramped conditions. Tallmadge joined them for nightly dinners, and the family's matron and servants did come out to clean the cabin and tend to his requests for firewood, food, when he could not join them for meals, or even to fetch him water to wash and shave his face.

The rest of the 2ⁿᵈ Light were scattered among the three barns this particular farmer owned. They lived in the upper areas while the horses stayed on the ground floor. Tallmadge learned that the farmer had been trading in bales of hay as his ware and during the early days of the war, had hid more than a few illicit goods along with people in his barns. The farmer had welcomed them, but expected them to take care of the barn if they wished to use it again as winter quarters if they were in the area next year. Tallmadge promised that his men would do their best and left it at that. It was the most ideal situation considering that the 2ⁿᵈ Light's initial winter quarters had been at Trenton billeted with a bunch of 'jacks' – their own derisive term for the drunken whalers who called themselves sailors of the Continental Army.

Each day the men were expected to report to the farmland for morning drills and today was no different. He could hear the clash of steel echoing through the area as the men practiced with their newly given swords. General Washington had authorized the issuing of sabres captured at Fort Bennington to the 2ⁿᵈ Light. They were broadswords that had been carried by the Brunswick Dragoons. Though they were heavier than normal sabres, they were much better than the bayonets that the men had carried last year. Now, the men were practicing with them, making sure the double-edged blades did neither their mounts nor their fellow soldiers harm.

The men were also in moderately good spirits since he had obtained, in early February, new leather breeches for them and two hundred fifty pairs of boots. Besides the procurement of supplies – for which he had taken to scouring the countryside of New Jersey, along with a plea to his friend Jeremiah Wadsworth to help give specie of credit – there were also recent promotions to be handed out.

When another of the captains from the 2nd Light's had resigned, Tallmadge proudly promoted Webb to the rank. Webb had colored a little in embarrassment, but seemed pleased to be commanding his own troop. He hoped that with the added responsibility and the lessons that Webb had learned under him and Belden, the newly minted captain would become the officer Tallmadge had first seen in him. He also promoted John Simonet de Valcour to lieutenant and placed him as Webb's second-in-command. The young Frenchman had worked hard to prove to the rest of the regiment that not all Frenchmen were like his former compatriot de Vernejout. He was a fast learner and Tallmadge hoped that with someone to guide, Webb would gain some of the maturity and spark he had seen when the lieutenant had first enlisted.

Elijah Wadsworth, 1st Troop's cornet, was also promoted to lieutenant, taking Webb's former position as second-in-command of 1st Troop. George Hurlbut, Captain Stoddard's cornet was promoted to lieutenant and second-in-command of Stoddard's troop after Lieutenant Hazard resigned. A few of the enlisted men were raised to cornet, though Andrew Adamson was not one of them. Tallmadge had offered his friend the position, but surprisingly Adamson refused, stating that he liked his position as sergeant-major and did not wish to join the officers' ranks. That had surprised Tallmadge, considering how much he relied on his good friend and how invaluable he had been to him all last year.

Adamson would not deign to give an explanation and Tallmadge had been ready to demand one, but something about his friend's tone and look during that private conversation made him decide to leave it alone. Out of the friendship between the two of them, however unconventional it was between officer and enlisted, he had let the matter drop. He knew it was a little petty of him, but he was disappointed that Adamson refused the promotion, and Tallmadge gave him the cold shoulder for a couple of weeks before coming to terms with it.

The next meeting he had was with Pullings, and he told his friend that under no circumstances, was he to refuse his promotion to corporal. He would be damned if at least one of his three friends did not get the recognition and rank he deserved after last year's campaign. Promotions aside, there was also the enlistment of new men to the regiment and outfitting them with horses and accouterments. Fifty-one men had deserted their ranks last year and ten had died. The fact that more had deserted than had died worried Tallmadge, and he had set about ensuring the discipline and morale of the men under his command were kept up.

He had received another piece of good news to pass along to the men regarding the day's general orders. Brigadier General Count Casmir Pulaski had resigned as Commander of the Horse, the overall commander of the cavalry forces in the army, and Colonel Moylan of the 1st Light had been placed in charge; though Tallmadge noted that Moylan still commanded his dragoons. How the man would be able to attend to the needs of all four dragoon regiments and also command his own was a momentous question and Tallmadge did not envy his position. Pulaski had sent each regiment missives about his plans and drills that should be conducted as well as made personal inspections and attempted to drill the men himself. Tallmadge had initially welcomed the man's tactical expertise and knowledge, until it had proven that Pulaski wanted tactics that were unsuited for the battlefields of continental America. He had also somewhat resented Pulaski's dismissal of his knowledge and advice on the 2nd Light, Pulaski labeling them as amateur 'tricks.' The other captains had been confused and misunderstood a lot of what Pulaski was trying to accomplish, due to the fact that the man did not really speak English and refused a translator.

Tallmadge had seen Stoddard up to his old habit of

antagonizing Pulaski and put a stop to it early, but even he himself had – this time – silently agreed with the volatile captain's sentiments about Pulaski and his grand plans for the dragoons. The plans were certainly much more suited for European cavalry, where open plains and charges were common. Here in the Continental states, plains were also common, but based on what they had learned last year, the dragoons were much better suited for flanking maneuvers and quick decisive routes or patrols. Pulaski had asked them to confront the enemy head-on which was suicide. Tallmadge hoped with Moylan as Commander of the Horse, there would be a new efficiency in communication and planning since Moylan understood what the dragoons needed.

"Sir?" Lieutenant Jeronimus Hoogland, the regiment's sorely-needed adjutant spoke up as he drew his cloak tighter around him. During the day, Tallmadge kept the fire going, but it was not so hot to make one comfortable enough to take one's cloak off. He liked it as it kept him awake and he forced himself to complete his duties before walking around to warm himself up.

"Post the General Orders of the day." He handed the missive to Hoogland who shivered a little and took it. "Spread the word to the captains that they will probably want to look at it. Seems like Pulaski resigned and Moylan is in."

One of Hoogland's thick eyebrows rose up in surprise before he nodded, his freckled-face breaking out into a wide smile. He had slightly crooked teeth from years of tearing strips of leather in his mouth as a tanner's apprentice. Hoogland was a bright and quick man and Tallmadge wondered why he had not graduated from his apprenticeship, but it seemed Hoogland was like Adamson in ways. He did not like to be noticed and preferred that others thought of him differently than what he truly was.

"Very good, sir," he said. "Anything else before I make my rounds for reports?"

"If you see Lieutenant Hurlbut, remind him that I need his troop's count on basic needs. Captain Stoddard should be expected back some time this morning so when he returns, check with him to make sure that he was able to procure some cordage for halters from the wagon he and his men were supposed to be escorting." Tallmadge said and Hoogland nodded. "Dismissed."

"Sir," the young adjutant nodded again and left, sending a gust of cold wind into the small cabin as he closed the door behind him. Tallmadge involuntarily shivered and considered putting another log into the fire, but a quick glance at the flames told him the temperature would settle once more.

Stoddard was among the handful of officers and enlisted men who were unable to drill on a daily basis with the men, because they served as escorts for supply wagons going to the various encampments including Valley Forge, where Washington and his army wintered. It made Tallmadge's command of the 2nd Light abbreviated, but he hoped that whatever training and discipline they received this winter would be enough to repel enemy forces and ensure that desertions were not as high as the past year. He pulled the next missive that the post rider had delivered and opened the seal, recognizing it as General Washington's. A small smile appeared on his lips as he opened it to read its contents.

Since Germantown, he had corresponded with Washington with far more frequency than before, normally about supplies or needs and wants of the 2nd Light. His picketing and reports had produced more information, especially about the location and numbers of enemy forces they encountered. He could tell that those reports had been most welcome to the general and so had striven to ensure that even in winter quarters, he was well aware of the immediate area he was in and anything that could be helpful to Washington.

Tallmadge, at first, had thought to send every piece of information he gathered, even a mundane story of the neighbors from the farmer and his family, but soon realized that first letter such information would be hearsay. He needed more than just rumor. Rumor was good, but sometimes it was misleading. But his plan to gather as much information as possible regarding Chatham and the immediate area was not to be. There was just nothing of consequence. He had written his first letter to Washington after billeting with an apologetic tone knowing he could not produce any concrete information.

That letter had received a quick reply stating that Washington understood his concerns but that he should put his energies into making sure his troops were prepared come the spring for the renewed campaign. When the snow lessened and the roads became somewhat passable, there was a flurry of letters requesting that wagons be escorted along with other important personnel and the like. Tallmadge took advantage of the orders by debriefing each of the officers who were assigned to the escorts. It was something he normally did, to ensure that the supplies had been delivered, but also to make note of any Patriot-allied family that perhaps they could take shelter with, or any routes that may be more safe than others. In each of these reports, he also made note of rumors they had heard or any enemy troops encountered.

It was not much, especially since the roads were still snow-covered and treacherous, but he could tell that Washington had been pleased with his foresight and efforts. Tallmadge unfolded the latest letter and read it. It was short and succinct; Washington requested that he personally check on supplies with General Putnam at Peekskill. It was an innocuous request along the lines of many he had received from the general for the past three months, but something about this letter seemed different than all of the others. He frowned and re-read it once more, slowly parsing the words until he realized what was different – Washington wanted him to *personally* go to Peekskill.

His interest was piqued as he realized there was someone, or perhaps some *thing* that Washington needed in Peekskill that was entrusted to him. The letter did not mention anything in terms of specifics. Tallmadge also noted that none of Washington's aide-de-camps were present, which suggested it was important, but perhaps unlike the situation with Ann Darragh back in December. That meant that the trip could take a few days to who knew how long.

Tallmadge set the letter down and rubbed his chin in thought. A lone officer riding through the countryside would attract some attention. Not a lot, since it was winter and many were on leave or furlough to go home to their families, but it would still be interesting for a lone officer to be traveling in such conditions. While he would never know the full details of Nathan's mission a year and a half ago that ended in his death, Tallmadge knew his best friend had been caught because he was just one man in a nest of vipers. No, he decided, he would have to employ the same cover he had when he met Ann at the Rising Sun. For one thing, it had taught him a valuable lesson, the benefit of having at least one other man present to watch his back and warn him of approaching patrols or enemy forces. He thought it to be somewhat like the company of friends out gallivanting around town – almost akin to having friends to drink with. Except it was not as gay as a harmless drink; Davenport's capture had proven that point and Tallmadge knew he would have to be careful about whom he picked to accompany him this time. He knew it had been divine providence that enabled him and his patrol to stumble upon Davenport just as he was being transferred to prison. It was perhaps His way of telling him that if he wished to proceed under such circumstances, he needed to be more aware and careful and not wantonly risk the life of his men in such endeavors.

Tallmadge folded Washington's letter up and placed it in between the folds of an orderly book. He would write his reply later. He would soon have Hoogland fetch Adamson and Davenport to see if they would readily accompany him again on this mission. None of the men nor officers made mention of what had happened with Ann late last year, which suggested his two friends could be trusted. It also told him they had not said anything to Pullings, even though he was their mutual friend. Pullings had developed a reputation as the center of rumors and gossip among the 2nd Light – a good person to go to for any particular concerns regarding the regiment, but also for stories of 1st Troop's heroics or any action that they had seen.

Tallmadge also needed an officer he could trust to carry on the 2nd Light's winter duties in his stead. Blackden was still in Boston procuring supplies for all four dragoon regiments and was not expected to return until spring. Sheldon was still in Connecticut petitioning the Assembly. That meant one of the remaining captains would have to take over while he conducted his mission. The prudent course was to let either Stoddard or Bull take charge of the 2nd Light – the two being the most-senior captains of the regiment. Except that Bull was part of the regiment that had been once again removed to Peekskill for the winter and Stoddard's actions last year did not instill confidence in the man's general leadership.

Tallmadge had no doubts that Stoddard was a capable

commander, but his increasingly excessive zeal in his treatment of Tories and other persons merited some worry. Each time he had sent Stoddard on foraging or escorting trips since January, the men that Stoddard served with had all quietly approached various sergeant-majors in the regiment to speak their concerns. Those reports made their way to him. While nothing serious had happened, Tallmadge had heard of Stoddard's threats with weapons to force civilians to comply with his orders, even threatening to brand them as Tories for not moving as fast as he liked. There was nothing to indicate violence against civilians, but the disturbing way Stoddard conducted himself on these trips made Tallmadge wary of putting the man in temporary charge of the regiment.

That left Belden. He supposed if he put Belden in command of the regiment, Stoddard would be somewhat mollified, since the two had served with each other at Fort Washington back in the early days of the war. But he had rarely seen Belden interact with Stoddard and thus wondered if the two's previous camaraderie had cooled. The other captains were too newly promoted still getting used to their new commands. Belden also provided an added benefit to Tallmadge; he would understand why he was leaving camp so suddenly and under quiet circumstances – having been witness to the whole Ann Darragh affair. Tallmadge rubbed his eyes as he reached over and drained the last bit of tea from his morning breakfast. Belden was his choice and it was something Stoddard would have to come to terms with. He could only hope that another wagon would need escort soon and Belden could send Stoddard out if there were any issues, so the two would not clash.

He sighed and set his cup down before pulling out a fresh sheet and starting a letter notifying Colonel Sheldon and General Putnam of his imminent arrival to the Hudson Highlands, on a mission from General Washington.

"I wish to decline the opportunity, sir."

Tallmadge blinked, surprise and shock flitting through him as he stared at Davenport, who was standing at attention in the one-room cabin. This was not the answer he had expected, but as his eyes flicked over to Adamson, he could see that his other friend had anticipated such an answer. A sudden burst of anger filled him as he realized Davenport's reluctance to go on the mission had been kept from him. He almost opened his mouth to make it an order, before he forced himself to push past the anger and keep calm.

"Would you care to explain your reason, Sergeant?" he asked, staring at Davenport with a flat look.

Davenport shifted, "Sir, permission to speak freely?"

"Granted."

Davenport flicked a look at Adamson before looking at Tallmadge, who understood the unspoken request. Whatever he wanted to say, it was for his ears only. Tallmadge jerked his head towards Adamson, indicating he should wait outside and the young man left, closing the door behind him. Tallmadge stared frankly at the older man who fidgeted a little before taking a deep breath. Davenport let it out slowly and cleared his throat. Tallmadge opened his mouth to tell him to stop stalling, when the man finally started to talk.

"Sir, I...am not at ease with this nature of going among the enemy and discerning their intentions." Davenport's voice was stilted, formal and tremored with something that Tallmadge could not identify. "I will fight them, sir. I am willing to face them in open combat and to take them down, but as far as being among them..." Davenport shook his head a little. "By the grace of God to have my neck stretched and hung up for all to see like a dog...no, sir. I...cannot."

Tallmadge was quiet for a moment as Davenport finished and folded his fingers together. He pursed his lips before he spoke up. "This is about what happened back in December-"

"No, it is not, sir," Davenport shook his head. "These are my feelings in general, sir. If you command me to, I will execute your orders to the best of my abilities and keep whatever secrets need be kept, but spying, sir? Spying among the enemy? I cannot willingly abide by that nor can I find any honor in such a despic- in such a dishonorable act, sir." Tallmadge caught the very moment where Davenport swallowed his true feelings as to spying and obtaining intelligence from the enemy, but he chose to ignore what his friend had almost said. Tallmadge knew if someone else, Stoddard for instance, had nearly said those words, he would not be feeling too charitable and would consider it an act of insubordination.

"You did not approve of the meeting at the Rising Sun tavern," he stated, and Davenport nodded.

"I did not," he echoed. "And of what happened afterwards, well, that is a matter of soldiers and duty sir. But to answer your question, I did not approve of the meeting at the Rising Sun tavern." Tallmadge saw Davenport look to the side before closing his mouth.

"You are free to speak your mind at the moment, Henry." Tallmadge realized that he really wanted to understand why one of his friends – whom he had known for three years before they had all joined the war and who had been one of his first friends after accepting his schoolmaster posting in Wethersfield – was so against what he was doing.

Davenport sagged a little in relief at his familiar address. "Ben," he licked his lips in nervousness, "I know you have your own reasons for skulking about, being all shadow-like and the sort with the enemy, but what if you're caught? You heard what happened to Captain Hale, sir-"

"Nathan- Captain Hale was out of uniform-"

"Aye, and that's the problem," Davenport shook his head. "Ben, if you're caught, even in uniform, they might not give you any quarter. Even if it is for military scouting purposes. What if someone like Rawdon caught you? He's shown that he doesn't give one whit about whether you are an officer or an enlisted man. You can bet that there are more lobsterbacks like him in the army. They want to *crush* us, sir. They don't want any rebellious tendencies and the first thing they'll do is kill people like you, sir, prisoner exchange not withstanding. Ben, spies are always caught and hung, even if they are officers. It's not honorable and it's something I don't want to be a part of. I'd rather fight the enemy and shoot them on the battlefield." He took a deep breath and released it, finished with his speech.

Tallmadge sighed quietly. He closed his eyes for a moment before opening them again. He could see that the initial nervousness in Davenport had returned, as if he doubted he should have spoken so frankly. These were Tallmadge's friends who followed him from Chester's Brigade to the 2nd Light. The past year had been trying on all of them as they adjusted from being in a militia regiment to being in the actual army. There were rules, regulations, and one could not readily be so lax without losing discipline. There was also the matter that their status as ranking officer and an enlisted man had widened the gulf between them.

"You are dismissed, Sergeant," Tallmadge said steadily, and saw a myriad of emotion flit across Davenport's face. Davenport saluted with a crisp nod as he spun on his heel and left the one-room cabin. As the door opened, Tallmadge gestured with a hand for Adamson to come back in and he did so, closing the door behind him as he huddled in his cloak.

"Sir." He could see that his friend wanted to know if Davenport had been merited with any form of punishment, but was not inclined to answer his unspoken question. Truth be told, Tallmadge did not trust himself at the moment to not rage or say something that was unbecoming of both an officer and as a friend. He belatedly realized he also needed to find another person to accompany him...maybe two if Adamson also declined this opportunity like Davenport.

"Do you wish to decline the opportunity?" he asked, marveling inwardly at how level he was keeping his voice and emotions in check.

"Is it not an order passed down from General Washington?" Adamson sounded genuinely confused.

"Yes," he replied, "and I have consented to it." He left the rest of the statement unspoken. He had not explicitly told Davenport and Adamson that it was spying among both enemy and allies, but merely a chance to gather intelligence and information regarding possible enemy movements. Yet the underlying meaning had been all but spelled out to his two friends. He briefly wondered if this was how Nathan felt when he had volunteered to go behind enemy lines. That the word 'spying' was implicit given the company. He knew he was doing the same, but he could not say such a word without giving weight to it. After all, they were not exactly going behind enemy lines, but rather reporting up to Peekskill and possibly waiting for an intelligence *source* to come to them instead.

"I believe that any advantage we can get over the enemy is an advantage well-worth examining and executing." Adamson gave a small shrug. "I have no opinion on this matter."

Tallmadge stared at his friend, scrutinizing him for any signs of deceit, of falsehood. He was tempted to demand a better answer out of his friend, to dig deep and have him state his unequivocal opinion on spying. But he resisted the temptation as he realized that he was angry at Davenport's answer, and was trying to take it out on Adamson instead. He was angry that Davenport had implied that Nathan's sacrifice was for nothing – that Nathan was a coward for stooping to the level of a spy, a gutter-rat that deserved to be hung; even though he knew full well that the man he considered a friend did not say those words. It ripped open the wound of Nathan's death that Tallmadge thought healed, and again turned that cold anger into a fiery one that was hard to control now.

He swallowed past the sudden painful lump in his throat as he sought to calm himself once more, to regain that cold anger at what the British had done to his best friend. Slowly, he managed to calm himself and finally nodded to Adamson's answer just as a knock came on the cabin door.

"Enter," he said, and the door opened to reveal Hoogland and Belden, the latter of the two rubbing his hands as they both stepped in. He surmised that Belden had been out checking with the guard posts, judging by how long it took for Hoogland to find him.

"Sir," the two of them nodded a greeting as Hoogland closed the door behind him.

"Belden, recommend me one of your men whom you would trust to be discreet," he said, resisting the urge to rub his eyes in frustration.

He saw his captain shoot a quick look at Adamson, opening his mouth before hesitating. Tallmadge could see the moment in which Belden realized there was a reason why Davenport was not here, and thus hesitate in his recommendation. He stared at Belden with a slight impatient expectation in his gaze, furiously quashing the temptation to tell the man to hurry up. He was deeply affected by Davenport's words and unspoken insinuations and valiantly tried not to take it out on his junior officers.

"Cornet Thomas Pool, sir," Belden spoke up after a moment of consideration. "He was appointed to the vacancy left by Wadsworth's promotion and has proven himself with discretion in regards to the men and their training." Belden gestured with a hand towards Adamson. "Sergeant-Major Adamson can attest to his strength of character."

"Sir," Adamson nodded, "Cornet Pool has proven himself to be adept in displacing rumors and hearsay."

Tallmadge stared at them, considering their words. What Adamson had said was that Pool did not spread any rumors around camp as the men were wont to do, nor was he considered a gossiping officer, unlike Webb, Stoddard, and a couple of the others. Wadsworth was a bit on the gossiping side, but he was not as bad as Webb or Stoddard when it came to rumors and stories. It was one of the reasons why Webb had been promoted, to curb his habit of such misinformation, but also to give him more responsibility so that he did not have time to pursue such activities.

He wondered though, about Pool. Were Belden's words indicative of the fact that because Pool had only just been appointed he was thus was afraid to speak his mind, or was he truly a man who really had no use for such rumor-mongering?

"Hoogland, please fetch Cornet Pool if you will." He decided to take the chance, especially since he did get a good recommendation from Adamson – and Adamson was astute enough to realize the situation he was in.

"Sir," Hoogland nodded once and left.

"Belden," he turned back to his captain and saw him straighten a little. "I'm placing you in temporary command of the regiment here for the next few weeks. I intend to be gone at most a month. You will continue your duties in assigning patrols for wagon supplies, along with fielding any correspondences and orders that may arise. General Washington has already been appraised of your temporary command here as have Colonel Sheldon and Lieutenant Colonel Blackden. Stoddard will report to you."

"Sir, Captain Stoddard-"

"Has no say in this." Tallmadge held up one of the letters he had sealed already. "You may give him this if he so wishes to contest the matter." He handed it over and Belden took it, looking a little nervous at the prospect of being in charge of the regiment that wintered here.

"Yes, sir," Belden replied as he pocketed the sealed letter. "Sir, I take it that the Sergeant-Major and Cornet Pool are to accompany you?"

"Yes." He left it at that and was slightly pleased when Belden did not ask for a reason and instead nodded.

"I understand, sir," Belden said and made to leave.

"Belden," he called back his captain again. "You'll do fine. Just keep the men drilling and continue your current activities and postings. General Washington will call for us when the British decide to leave Philadelphia, but it is still too soon with the rivers swollen for the next month and a half. If you need to write, send your missives to Peekskill."

"Sir," Belden knuckled his forehead before leaving, sending another gust of cold wind into the tiny cabin.

That left him and Adamson in the cabin and silence reigned in an almost uncomfortable manner. Tallmadge resolutely ignored it, hoping that Hoogland returned with Pool soon so that he could ascertain his character and, if it was to his liking, tell him of the assignment he was to undertake. He could feel his friend burning with the need to ask him what had happened, but the fact that he was being ignored and there was no hint of familiarity towards him, stayed his voice. A discreet look at Adamson told Tallmadge that his friend was keeping up the formality of officer and enlisted, and in a way he was glad that his friend had the mind to do so. He turned back to the roster book he had been compiling since the beginning of the 2nd Light's formation and looked it over, making some notations he had forgotten. The list needed more annotations and updates based on letters he received from Sheldon and Blackden in regards to their recruiting efforts, but it also listed the accouterments they needed and the one thing that bothered Tallmadge the most was the lack of usable horses.

With all of their patrols, especially with the men of 1st Troop who had accompanied him in the month-long patrol of the Schuylkill back in December, their own horses were either lamed or rehabilitated slowly. Even now, a lot of the men had worn their horses down so much that they were unusable.

The knock at the door made him look up and he closed the book and put it to the side. "Enter."

Hoogland entered once more with a man perhaps no older than he was. He had a weathered look about him, and Tallmadge saw that the man's hands were calloused from the years of working fishing boats in New London. In a way, he looked a little like Caleb Brewster, but somehow did not seem to have the vitality and playful sarcastic spark Tallmadge had come to associate with the whaler.

"Sir," Pool saluted as Tallmadge nodded to Hoogland for his dismissal. The young adjutant closed the door quickly behind him as he left, more than likely running to the farmhouse to get some warmth into himself.

"Cornet, your opinion in regards to going behind enemy lines," Tallmadge stated bluntly. "You may speak freely."

"Sir?" Pool's eyes bulged a little in surprise before he blinked and hastily composed himself. "Uh, sir, I...uh..." He flicked a quick look at Adamson and Tallmadge frowned. He looked at Adamson, but saw his friend with a very neutral expression on his face, indicating he would give no help whatsoever.

"Sergeant-Major Adamson has no bearing on your opinion, Cornet." He directed the young officer's gaze back to him. "And you may speak without fear of reprisal."

"Y-Yes sir," Pool stuttered before clearing his throat. "Sir, I believe it is shameful, but a necessary shame."

"Explain."

"Well, sir, it seems to me that if we send military scouts or patrols on the chance that they are looking for the enemy or ascertaining the movements of the enemy, then in effect, it is a form of spying. But to do it in civilian clothing, to disguise the efforts; there is treachery and shame in that. But it is necessary because what say that the enemy would not do the same," Pool replied.

"And honor?"

"Was it honorable for General Grey to attack in the night's silence at Paoli, sir? Like a wraith in the night? Honor has nothing to do with it, sir. When men kill each other, there is no honor in any of it. The British did not honor our requests for negotiation and representation and so we were forced to declare our independence." Pool quieted and looked down at his hands, wringing them together.

Tallmadge stared at Pool for a long moment before nodding once. Pool had his reservations about spying, but unlike Adamson who gave no voice to his opinion, his words were sound and reasonable. Belden's assessment was correct, Pool was a patriot, and impressively for a recently joined cornet, he understood the horrors that had been inflicted upon them in the last couple of years of the war.

"Pool, what did you do before you joined?"

"Fishing, sir," A wistful smile appeared on his weathered face before it sobered into a mournful expression. "My boats and my men were taken prisoner and killed by British privateers, sir. I had nothing left..."

Ah, so that solved the mystery of why Pool said those things. But he was still curious. "Why join up with the 2nd Light? Why not join up with a whaleboating crew or petition Congress for a privateer license?"

"I had hoped to be stationed with the regiment that is at Peekskill, sir, when I joined. They have been skirmishing against Governor Tryon's forces and it was he who authorized the raids against my boats and the like," he shook his head.

Tallmadge snorted quietly as he stood up. "Well, Pool, you might get your chance yet. You will be joining myself and Sergeant-Major Adamson here, on a excursion to Peekskill for the next few weeks."

A small smile appeared across the man's chapped lips as he nodded. "Thank you, sir. For the opportunity."

They arrived at Peekskill in a few days, to the surprise and obvious pleasure of Captains Bull and Seymour, who were stationed with their men up in the area. Tallmadge had hoped to catch Colonel Sheldon, but both had reported that Sheldon was still in Connecticut petitioning the Assembly. There was good news that Blackden was supposedly on his way back soon from Boston, having completed his requisition duties there, and wished to rejoin the regiment. There was no firm date on

Blackden's return, but he could tell that Bull and Seymour were hoping for a senior field officer to command the regiment stationed here instead of relying on the two of them to train, accouter, and field any patrols or requests for troops to be "on command" – the official term for detached duty.

He thanked both officers for their efforts, knowing that they and their seconds were curious as to his presence. He refused to say more as he presented himself to Generals Gates and Putnam. With the Congressional Board of War located somewhere in an undisclosed location in New York since the evacuation of Philadelphia, Gates essentially was in command of the Peekskill-Fishkill section of the Hudson Highlands, even though Putnam was overseeing a majority of the defenses there. He only made mention of his temporary stay to the two generals and said it was on the behest of Washington himself. Gates had frowned at that, but did not say anything more as he was dismissed.

Tallmadge returned to where Bull and Seymour's detachments were camped and waited for the next few days to see why Washington would order him up here for a vague purpose. In the meantime, he busied himself with checking up on the two troops and updating the roster lists that would be added to the orderly book when he returned to Chatham. He was glad that some of the Brunswick swords that were seized had also been distributed to the troops here, but also noted the lack of other needed accouterments and far more lamed horses than in the rest of the 2nd Light. It seemed that Gates had not been kind to Seymour's troop while were been at Saratoga and Bull had constant patrols throughout Westchester and in Northern New Jersey.

As he waited, he sent out Adamson to inquire with the locals and inhabitants as to anything amiss or anything that would be of interest. As for Cornet Pool, he had him inquire with the post-riders into any dispatches that seemed unusual or even had been delivered to the wrong camp or met some sort of delay. Both tasks were done with some discretion, but the two reported back with no news of any sort that would give Tallmadge a clue about the reason he was here.

About two weeks later, Tallmadge finally received his answer from of the last person he had ever expected to be a source or a contact – one of his very own 2nd Light officers, Lieutenant David Edgar.

April 3rd, 1778

Tallmadge studied the rather handsome lieutenant who stood in the room he had been furnished with for his temporary office and headquarters. Edgar stood rather self-assured and confident; every inch of a model officer. From what Tallmadge remembered, Edgar had been Bull's lieutenant before being transferred to serve under Captain Seymour since there was no lieutenant after de Vernejout's dismissal during the middle of Gates' campaign in Saratoga.

David Edgar was a little above average height, with a square jaw and a prominent nose. His hair was dark and thick when pulled back in its queue. Dressed in the accouterments of the 2nd Continental Light Dragoon, he was a dashing soldier who could easily walk into a ball and fill the gazes of every woman and man in the room with envy.

The lieutenant now stood silently in front of him after knocking on his door and requesting an audience. Tallmadge had sent Pool away, ostensibly to the quartermaster to continue to help outfit the regiment stationed here, but also to be on look-out for anyone who might interrupt their meeting. Adamson sat unobtrusively in the corner, seemingly busy with correspondences and reports. He saw Edgar flick a look to his sergeant-major, but made no comment or visual indication that he wished to speak to him and him alone.

"Sir, it is usually not my place and I humbly submit to any punishment you would deem fit, but I must confess that I was placed into this regiment at the personal behest of General Washington himself." Edgar kept his face neutral and did not fidget as Tallmadge stared at him.

Tallmadge knew he could not keep the surprise completely off his face, but he managed to school it so that it was perhaps not as noticeable. From what he remembered from Edgar's initial enlistment the man had resigned from the 4th New Jersey prior to being commissioned as a lieutenant of the 2nd Light back in late

January of 1777. It was not unheard of, since the 2nd Light had two captains from different states and two of the four troops raised as the 2nd Light were from out of state. He wondered if General Washington had recruited him then when his headquarters was in Middlebrook, New Jersey.

"Why tell me now?" he asked. Edgar implied that he was placed in the regiment as a personal spy for General Washington. Tallmadge knew that perhaps a year ago he would have demanded why Edgar was spying on the regiment itself, but more than a year of active service and detached duty for Washington changed his mindset. His only concern was why did Edgar tell him right now, when he could have easily just sent him a letter, anonymously or otherwise, relating whatever detail Washington wished for him to deliver. But Washington's letter had been succinct – he was to report to Peekskill and gather some mysterious intelligence. Edgar's confession piqued his curiosity.

"Because of this," the lieutenant stepped forward, pulling out a letter that had its seal broken and placing it on his desk.

Tallmadge took the letter and unfolded it gingerly, careful of the wax seal, and read the signature first. It was signed by James Wilkinson, General Gates' adjutant. He flipped the letter back over and read it carefully. It was almost nonsensical at first, but as he got deeper into the letter, the meaning became far clearer. It stood out towards the bottom of the letter, when Wilkinson quoted a line attributed to General Conway: 'Heaven has been determined to save your Country; or a weak General and bad Counsellors would have ruind it.' Tallmadge read the last few lines of Wilkinson's agreement with such words and pressed his lips together tightly.

The letter was disturbing at the very least and treasonous at the very most, in his opinion. It all but called for the ousting of Washington as Commander-in-Chief. He read the header – the letter was to General Horatio Gates. Judging by what Daniel Morgan had told him back in early December regarding what had really happened at Saratoga, Tallmadge felt a most unusual disquieting sensation in him. What Gates, Conway, and perhaps others of the senior leaders in Washington's army were planning made him feel a ill. It was not enough that he knew of General

Lee's supposed treachery from Ann, but now, here was written proof this cabal of sorts was plotting to oust Washington from command.

He glanced up at Edgar who had stood quietly while he read the letter. He noticed Adamson staring, having picked up on the fact that the letter had disturbed him. Adamson's posture indicated he was ready to take whatever action was needed if he wished it. Another thought occurred to Tallmadge – did Washington know of this cabal and their secret plot against him? Just as quickly he deduced that the answer was a negative. Washington's letter had only stated that he was to report to Peekskill and nothing more; which suggested that his general knew something was happening, but did not know the details.

"You signaled the general," he stated as he set the letter down.

"Aye, sir," Edgar replied, "through a pre-established signal that was communicated to me back in February of last year." Tallmadge saw Edgar was hedging on his words and gestured with a tilt of his head for him to continue. He had no doubts that the pre-establishment of a signal was probably Mr. Nathaniel Sackett's work – after all, the man had indicated that he and Major Clark were not the only ones who were part of the intelligence gathering agents Washington wished to field.

"I was notified that there was someone else of the 2nd Light, sir, that would be able to forward my...observations..." Edgar stumbled a little on what to call the letter he had given to him. "I...uh...did not realize it was you until your arrival."

"How did you realize it?" Tallmadge was rather curious as to how Edgar picked him out of all of the others of the 2nd Light.

"Observation, sir," Edgar confessed, "and rumors and reports, sir." He gestured a little to Adamson. "I had first thought it was the sergeant-major since he had joined the 2nd Light at its inception. I discarded Lieutenant Pool's consideration because I did not recognize him. But based on my...recruitment...I suppose, sir, I could only surmise that it would have been someone that the general would have had a chance to observe and know for a while now, sir. Not someone new..."

"And how are you so sure that I am not a part of, this?" Tallmadge picked up the damning letter with two of his fingers and waved it in the air before setting it back down.

"I do not know, sir," Edgar shook his head. "That was one of the reasons why I did not come forward immediately, sir. As I had said before, observation and rumors. All of us, well, those who are under Captain Seymour and Bull, know of what really happened at Saratoga courtesy of the good Captain Seymour himself and the stories told, but we also knew that the rest of the Army was not told and those who were sent to winter with us learned that there were two stories about what happened at Saratoga."

Edgar took a deep breath, "Sir, I am a lawyer and journalist by trade, a graduate of New Jersey College. Before the war broke out, I wrote for the local trade papers, recounting my observations and opinions. I am able to listen and ask questions that would shape people's opinions. As I had said, sir, I observed and I heard the rumors. The story that was prominently told was through Colonel Morgan's riflemen. They also told stories that said our regiment, the 2nd Light, was unofficially General Washington's eyes and ears. Sir, the only commander that I know of that was near Washington for a majority of all the previous year was yourself, sir."

Tallmadge resisted the urge to ask what sort of rumors had been spoken about him in regards to Washington, knowing it was a bout of vanity that stirred such questions. The other reason was that he was still unsure about Edgar, even with the man's apparent honesty. No sooner had the thought crossed his mind than he realized why it bothered him that the man was so openly honest. Edgar reminded him greatly of Nathan, with his jovial and open nature. Nathan had mentioned he would be sent to spy on the enemy, Tallmadge had had his doubts and reservations about his best friend's suitability as a spy. Nathan had been handsome, friendly, out-going, and the life of any party they had. He never been secretive by nature and that was what had drawn Tallmadge to him during their first year at Yale. Tallmadge had been friendless when he enrolled at Yale and Nathan's immediate exuberance had quashed the more cautious part of Tallmadge as they became friends. But in light of what he now knew and what he wished he should have done back then, he had kept his own counsel and only said platitudes and encouragement to his friend.

He had also acquiesced to Nathan's request not to dissuade him from his course of action in spying among the enemy as their mutual friend William Hull had done.

But this time would be different.

"Though I appreciate the vouchsafe of confidence and courage you have displayed to give me this, Lieutenant," Tallmadge started carefully as he folded the letter back up. He could see Edgar's slightly confused expression as he handed the letter back to him. "I would see that a modicum of discretion is observed next time a superior officer asks you for your reasons."

"S-Sir," Edgar blushed and ducked his head a little, "I-"

"Now we shall see to the problem of the letter," he interrupted whatever else Edgar was about to say and saw him look back up, surprise crossing his strong-jawed features.

"S-Sir..."

"How did you come about this?" he asked, staring at the lieutenant with a simple look.

"By chance, sir. General Gates enjoys either having an officers' dinner or parties every weekend. I happened to be at one of the parties, engaged in some discussion with the general's staff when the talk turned to General Washington's battlefield laurels and the like. Wilkinson happened to mention receiving a letter about General Conway's remarks and I wished to look for it. I found that," he gestured to the letter, "instead." Tallmadge realized that with Edgar's handsome looks and seemingly noble quality as well as his background as a scholar and writer, he must have been popular at the parties. It was with that thought that Tallmadge began to realize why Edgar had been chosen as Washington's personal spy. The man had the background and perfect cover to be asking such questions.

"How long ago was this?"

"Just a little over two weeks ago, sir." Edgar looked a little nervous. "I believe that Wilkinson might have thought it sent as he made no other mention of it."

"And might have already expected a reply," Tallmadge frowned as he rubbed his lip absently. "Though the Board of War has been recently busy with requisitions and with General Greene's recent appointment as Quartermaster General." Everyone had been hearing rumors and the gazettes had been speculating on Greene's loud presence, his initiatives to get the rusting machinery that was the Board of War to start moving and provide the army with its needed supplies. The letter was addressed to General Gates who sat on the Board of War. He made a small noise of thought. "This may work to our advantage..."

He gestured for Adamson to step forward. "Adamson, go find Pool and bring him back here. But before you do, how is your hand-writing?"

"Adequate, sir. I'll confess that I didn't really pay much attention to your attempts to further my penmanship in the year you taught me before I went to Yale," Adamson confessed with a sheepish smile, and Tallmadge silently shook his head.

"Mine is rather decent," Edgar spoke up.

"Enough to mimic most of Wilkinson's penmanship?" Tallmadge would have copied the letter on his own, except he knew that his hand was not as legible and compared to the other senior officers of the regiment, it was atrocious. He, himself, was able to read it, but he knew that some of the others were not on occasion, able to decipher his hand writing.

"I can try, sir." Edgar looked a little less sure, but unfolded the letter and stared at it. "I can try," his voice was more confident this time and Tallmadge met his glance with a firm nod.

"Do so." He stood up from his chair and gestured for Edgar to take the seat while waving Adamson to go fetch Pool. The other man did so without another word.

"You know, sir." Edgar flipped through a few stacks of paper he had on the desk and found one about the same size and shape as Wilkinson's damning letter, before dipping his quill into the inkwell and beginning to gingerly copy the contents. "I heard that Thomas Jefferson has a contraption of sorts that is able to mimic pen strokes and write duplicates without having to write the same of two letters."

As much as it interested Tallmadge to have such a contraption, he ignored the words and Edgar settled into his duties, having quieted when he realized that Tallmadge would not answer or reciprocate his conversation. Edgar was halfway through the letter when a knock came at the door. Tallmadge walked over and opened it a crack in case it was someone who was not privy to what was happening in his office. He nodded a greeting at Adamson and Pool's faces beyond the door and opened it to let them in before closing it behind them.

"I did not see anyone of interest, sir," Pool reported.

"Good." Tallmadge stepped to the other side of the room and his two junior officers followed. Adamson ignored Edgar while Pool only took one look at him, before focusing on Tallmadge, clearly realizing that whatever the lieutenant was doing was not for him to know. "Pool, has the post rider left yet?"

"Not yet, sir. The evening post-rider was still gathering letters from the tents on his rounds," Pool replied.

"After Lieutenant Edgar is finished, take the letter and discreetly place it in the post-rider's bag before he leaves if you will."

"Sir," Pool nodded solemnly.

"Edgar," he called out to the lieutenant sitting at his desk.

"Sir?" was the slightly distracted reply.

"Is there a party or officer's dinner any time soon?"

"In two days, sir. Officer's dinner. Captain Bull has been invited and officers are allowed to bring their lieutenants if they wish. Captain Seymour declined his invitation for his poor health," Edgar replied.

"I'll speak to Bull before I leave to have him bring you instead of Lieutenant Brown." Tallmadge nodded mostly to himself. "I want you to watch for any reply on Gates' part to Wilkinson. Do not take the letter, but report to me if he makes any mention of it."

"Yes, sir." There was a slight pause to Edgar's reply but it was punctuated as he lifted his quill off the paper and sat back, blinking, his face was overcome with sudden exhaustion. "Sir...I think I've finished."

Tallmadge walked over, Adamson and Pool following close behind. He peered over Edgar's shoulder to see that the lieutenant had indeed been true to his word. The penmanship was a little shaky and unsure in the beginning as Edgar had been carefully copying the letter, but by the end of it, Tallmadge could not quite tell which letter had Wilkinson's true handwriting and which was the copied one. "Good job, Lieutenant." He clapped the man on the shoulder and caught the watery smile on the man's face at the praise.

"Now for the signature-"

"Sir, I can do that, if you wish," Pool spoke up and Tallmadge glanced up to see him peering at the copied letter, which would have looked upside down from his vantage point.

"Cornet?" he questioned.

"Um, if you do not mind, sir," Pool gestured to Edgar for the quill and the lieutenant handed it to him. Tallmadge watched as Pool gingerly dipped the quill into the inkwell before scrawling Wilkinson's signature in a reasonable approximation all while the letter itself was upside down. "There..."

"Impressive," Tallmadge nodded absently as he stared at the forged signature on the letter. The only difference between the two was that the ink was still wet and shiny on the unfolded paper while Wilkinson's letter was folded with the wax seal still hanging off of it.

"I...uh...painted sea life whenever we were in port before enlisting, uh, sir..." Pool seemed a little embarrassed to be sharing such a thing. "There was no need to talk when my subjects were still life or landscapes. From here, it looked like a brush stroke of sorts..." The cornet quieted and took a step back. Tallmadge realized that was probably why Pool was quiet and observant, and why he conducted himself with some discretion and discipline that impressed Belden. The cornet was right; while painting, especially landscapes and still life, there was no need to talk and one could simply observe his surroundings and keep their own counsel.

He reached over and sprinkled some powder to dry the ink on the paper before taking the original letter and folding it back up. "Pool, stay here with Lieutenant Edgar in case he needs help. Adamson, you're coming with me to the Board of War," he said, as he ran the underside of the wafer of wax that had originally sealed the letter over the flame of a candle. The wax immediately began to bubble and Tallmadge lifted the letter away from the heat and re-sealed it, pressing firmly. He placed the letter back on top of the table and took the copied letter and folded it. He sealed it with a dollop of his own wax and set it in front of Edgar who picked up the quill again and began to copy the address even without his prompting.

He was finished in short order and looked up at him, waiting for more orders.

"Sir?" Adamson spoke up. "We're going to the Board of War?"

"This must get into the hands of General Washington. I intended to give this to General Greene so that it may be delivered to him." Based on what he had personally observed in the past year, as well as the rumors and politicking of General Washington's command staff that had reached his ears, there were perhaps only a handful of generals who were loyal to Washington. Greene was certainly one of them considering all the fuss he had made to the Board of War after his initial arrival just a couple of months ago. Tallmadge would rather have given the letter to Colonel Morgan, but he did not want to risk it being intercepted if he was wintering elsewhere. No, this letter had to be personally delivered to Greene, who would then more than likely deliver it to Washington in a discreet fashion.

Edgar's lips twitched in a small smile and Tallmadge knew the man was glad that his service as a spy was not for naught. Tallmadge still had his reservations about one of the members, of the 2nd Light, especially an officer, being Washington's personal spy. But it was on the behest of his general himself that he had responded to the vague inquiry to head to Peekskill. He was not about to make himself a hypocrite by not giving Edgar the benefit of doubt considering that he himself had spied and gathered intelligence under Washington's orders. He could only hope that this cabal would be put to rest before it jeopardized both the morale of the men and his general's credibility. This was especially troubling since he had not heard anything regarding Charles Lee's treachery, yet still read about the man in the General Orders of the day distributed among the men.

Tallmadge did not quite get to the northern outskirts of York City where the Board of War was convened before he crossed paths with a caravan of Continental officers headed to the city. To his surprise, he discovered that it was both Colonel Morgan and General Lord Stirling. Morgan had recognized him and in a rare moment of joviality, perhaps due to the home-brewed spirits he carried with him, had confessed that he and Lord Stirling were headed to the Board of War to petition General Greene the Quartermaster General for supplies for the soldier. at Valley Forge. Those were the official orders, but in actuality, Morgan said they were helping General Greene spread the true story of what had happened at Saratoga. It seemed Washington had been hearing more rumors about Gates' boldness sitting on Board of War attempting to counter Greene's efforts and thus had sent Morgan and Stirling.

Tallmadge realized it was another stroke of divine providence that he carried upon him the damning letter from Wilkinson to Gates, and handed it over to Morgan and Stirling with a warning of the content inside. Morgan smiled broadly and clapped him quite hard in the back, telling him that he would do the 'Old Man' proud, while Stirling only nodded solemnly and pocketed the letter. Stirling promised that it would be delivered in short order to Washington and Tallmadge left, returning back to Peekskill feeling confident that Gates' brazenness would be quelled soon enough.

He returned to a pleasing report from Lieutenant Edgar that the original letter had been placed in the post-rider's bag without incident, but that there was no mention of a reply during the subsequent party. Tallmadge collected Cornet Pool who had become fast friends with Edgar, and thanked the lieutenant for his efforts, but also advised him to be a little more discreet in the near future.

They arrived back to Chatham in the second week of April, the showers that were frequent in that time of year drenching them completely. However, Tallmadge's spirits were raised and thus he did not feel as miserable as one might under the constant soaking of rain.

But it appeared that the seemingly endless rain had dampened the mood of the regiment he had left at Chatham. As he arrived, the men looked rather morose, at their usual stations but not walking with the proud gait of dragoons that he had seen time and again while they were dismounted or mounted. He spotted Wadsworth hailing them with a wave of his hand from the barn, where he had been tending to his horse judging by the brush on his hand. After waving back to him, the young lieutenant ran to the main house to find Belden.

He did not see some of the officers he expected would be roaming around visible within camp, and surmised that some of them were sent on detached duty to escort more wagons or other things, now that the weather was warmer. The rivers would be swollen from snowmelt and drenching rain until late May, but with a majority of the roads in a passable state, there would be more calls for escorts or patrols.

Tallmadge dismounted and handed Castor's reins to one of the privates who had come up to brush and dry his horse down. He saw Adamson and Pool do the same, but waved them away, indicating he did not need them at the moment and they should tend to their mounts. They tipped their helms at him before following the young private to the large barn. Tallmadge pulled his sopping cloak around him and headed to his small cabin and stepped in, breathing in the dryness and feeling relieved to be out of the elements.

As he hung his cloak to dry by the well-tended fire – something that pleased him since he had not known when he would return – a knock came at the door. "Enter," he called out and Belden quickly came in and closed the door behind him. The young captain flicked rainwater off of his cloak and saluted him.

"Sir, welcome back," he greeted.

"Thank you Captain," he replied before nodding a little. "Pool was very discreet and helpful. Thank you for your recommendation."

"Yes, sir." Belden seemed pleased with this information, but the smile disappeared as he stepped forward and produced a letter and several pieces of folded paper from the inside of his jacket. "Sir, during your absence, Colonel Moylan stopped by unannounced for an inspection per his duties as head of the cavalry. This is a copy of his report that he sent to General Washington as well as the general's reply."

Tallmadge took the letter, noting that the seal was broken, and also that it was addressed in the vaguest manner, to the Officer Commanding the Second Continental Dragoons. It made sense considering that Belden was put in charge in his absence, but Tallmadge thought he had made that clear in his letter to

Washington before he left. He placed the letter down on his desk to read later and instead opened the report that Moylan had written.

The report was scathing.

Tallmadge had not discernible disagreement with the commander of the 4th Light, at least none he could remember in the times that they had worked together, but it seemed Moylan begged to differ. The colonel had painted the 2nd Light's conduct in last year's campaign in such a negative light, from the ill-advised skirmish near Perth Amboy that was led by Bland, to Paoli, Germantown, and even the picketing lines. Tallmadge did not remember any of Moylan's men joining them on the picketing lines between the Schuylkill and Delaware back in December. There was also mention of officers' being undisciplined and prone to fights among themselves, and Tallmadge had a feeling Moylan must have read a report regarding Stoddard and former Captain de Vernejout's aborted duel last year. Through all of it, Moylan blamed everything on the senior field officers and their shortcomings in procuring the necessary supplies and equipment for the coming year's campaign.

He frowned, anger filling him as he shot a quick look at Belden. Tallmadge would have expected the man to be angry at such a report, but instead, Belden looked morose and serious. He set Moylan's report to the side, wanting nothing more than to crumple it into a heap and throw it into the fire. Picking up the folded letter from General Washington, he opened it, still a little disturbed by the vague address it had been sent to.

And as soon as he started to read, he realized why it had been addressed the way it was addressed. He also realized why many of the men looked more miserable than the rain made necessary and why all the anger he expected from Belden had disappeared. If Moylan's report was scathing, General Washington's reply to the report was damning.

Tallmadge found his throat dry as he read the reply. Washington was furious at the report he had received and had all but blamed the officers for 'gallivanting across the country on personal matters.' He placed that blame on allowing the men to wear out their horses in such a fashion. The rest of the letter cut deeply into him, but it seemed almost seemed like a retread of the blame as Washington wrote his disapproval and reiterated that the 2nd Light would see to becoming respectable again before the spring campaign started. Tallmadge pressed his lips together as he set the letter down onto the table, next to Moylan's report.

"Who has been dispatched to command in my absence?" He could see that Belden wanted to ask him of his thoughts on the report and Washington's reply, but ignored it. He would be composing his reply, but it was something that Belden need not know about. He needed Belden and the rest of the 2nd Light to focus on drilling and preparations for the coming year's campaign.

"Webb, and Stoddard, sir. Several corporals and privates have also gone with them. There is a current escort of at least four wagons and I have placed two sergeants and Lieutenant Wadsworth in charge of patrols until they return." Belden glanced at his desk. "Sir-"

"You need not concern yourself with this matter, Captain," he sternly rebuked Belden who looked like he was about to protest for a moment before he nodded, receiving his unspoken message loud and clear.

"Sir," he knuckled his forehead, "is there any particular matter you wish to discuss with Cornet Pool and Sergeant-Major Adamson or may I bring them back into the fold of the 2nd Light?"

"None whatsoever." Belden was sharp enough to know Tallmadge was true to his word and would address the grievances leveled against the 2nd Light after Moylan's inspection, but wise enough not to inquire about it. "And Captain, thank you again for your recommendation. Cornet Pool's discretion was welcomed."

"Yes, sir, thank you sir." There was a hesitant smile on Belden's face as he left the cabin.

As soon as the door closed behind him, Tallmadge sagged, letting loose a sigh of frustration that had built inside him since he read the report and letter. He felt hurt by the scathing comments Washington had written. He could feel the disapproval and anger in the man's words even after all that he had communicated with his general over the last few months. The criticism seemed unwarranted considering that he had written to Washington multiple times regarding the lack of certain supplies, but the gaining of others. The comment about gallivanting across the country on personal business stung the most; he knew that 1st Troop's horses were in slightly bad shape after their month-long patrol of the no-man's land between the Schuylkill and Delaware. It so happened that 1st Troop was stationed here and Moylan must have taken in their worn down appearance which would have warranted that reprimand.

He unbuckled his sabre and pistol belt, throwing it onto his bed before he sitting heavily in his chair. He rubbed his eyes, hanging his head. He wanted to scream in frustration at the letter that he had received, the initial joyousness he had felt in warning his Commander-in-Chief of a plot against him in Peekskill rapidly plunging into dismay. This was not something he wished to return to. But he also knew that he needed to do something to politely let Washington know that his comments were unwarranted.

Breathing in and out several times, he forced himself to calm down. After a few minutes, he pulled a fresh piece of paper from his desk box, dipped his quill into the inkwell and began to write.

The next reply came by the way of courier a few days later and Tallmadge opened it with tentative apprehension in the comfort and privacy of his own cabin. It was personally addressed to him. Relief trickled like a soothing balm over him as he read Washington's reason for the reprimand. His general clearly understood that the criticism was unwarranted and was not directed at him in general, but he wished for him to understand why he had replied in such a way. Clearly, the general still believed in him, believed in the effectiveness of the 2nd Light, but wanted them to take more care in their activities – though they were important to the Continental Army itself – and to ensure that the rotation of men and horses sent out to such activities did not wear them out. The tone was mollifying and Tallmadge found himself smiling in relief at the fact that Washington understood that his initial letter was written in aggravated passion.

Just as he was about to fold the letter back up, he noticed a small strip of paper attached to the bottom, but not officially part of the letter. It was still in the general's handwriting, but the man clearly wished for him to disassociate this note from the letter. [*Thank you for bringing my attention to the matter regarding command.*] The smile on Tallmadge's face grew a little wider at the oblique mention of what Lieutenant Edgar had found in Peekskill and Tallmadge had copied and delivered to Lord Stirling at the Board of War. It helped soothe his frayed nerves that his general still considered him valuable and effective even with what had happened upon his return and that bolstered him. He folded the letter back up and set it on the table, leaning back against his chair as he considered what the renewed campaign would bring.

Rumors were flying that General Clinton would abandon Philadelphia and return to New York. The swollen rivers were slowly returning to their normal depths which meant that they would possibly be leaving soon. Even though the initial seizure of Philadelphia had been a blow to morale for the troops and the cause, Tallmadge knew that there was always a chance that the nation's capital would be abandoned given the perilous no-man's land between Philadelphia and York City. With Burgoyne's defeat up at Saratoga, Clinton had to split his army up between the two cities in order to garrison them effectively. Philadelphia was staunchly Patriot and thus Clinton would need to expend more troops to quell uprisings and uphold martial law. That left York City vulnerable to attack if there was a combined attack from Gates' army camped at Peekskill and Washington's camped at Valley Forge. Tallmadge had no doubts that the first skirmishes or battles of the upcoming campaign would involve both cities. The question now remained: Which one would his general order an attack on to cut off any hope of reinforcements for the British army?

INTERLUDE VIII

June 20ᵗʰ, 1778

Washington was not prone to any motion that would indicate nervousness, especially in front of his officers or even his aide-de-camps. But, with just his manservant, Billy Lee in the room, he felt free to allow himself the small gesture of tapping his chin. He studied the maps and letters splayed out in front of him, hunched over the war table in his tent at Middlebrook. The Marquis de Lafayette had delivered sorely welcomed news that the French had openly allied themselves with America and would start sending troops soon. The time and date of arrival of the needed French fleet had not been communicated to him, but Washington hoped it would be soon. He hoped to trap or even destroy Admiral Howe's British fleet if they were to sail to Clinton's aid. The French had also started sending more armaments and accouterments than the discreet ones shipped in by smugglers for the last two years. With Baron von Steuben's constant drilling along with that of the other European officers who were dedicated to the cause and not just there for glory, the Army had emerged from the darkness of a brutal winter at Valley Forge ready to give the British a fight.

 Washington had seen it in the men's eyes, had seen it in his officers' eyes. They were ready and all he needed to do was to point at a target and they would obey without hesitation. The only thing in question was the target itself.

His spies had heard rumors that the British were to evacuate Philadelphia soon, but did not know exactly when or how General Clinton and the others were to evacuate. He had sent word to some of the regiments wintering elsewhere to head to Fishkill to join Gates' forces and patrol the wide area in which Clinton could conceivably march his army into York City. All of his dragoon forces were sent to Gates so that he could utilize them in a wide area of influence that stretched from the borders of Connecticut down to the northern interior of New Jersey. It was a prudent measure and Washington knew that he would have assigned the 2nd Light to Gates if only for a certain major that had served him well in the wintering months – and before that – would be able to discreetly keep an eye on Gates. Gates had apologized for his role in the Conway affair and resigned his post from the Board of War. Washington had forgiven him and placed him in charge of the Hudson Highlands, owing to the fact that a lot of the soldiers under Israel Putnam had been vocal in their complaints about the man's abusive and gruff demeanor. He could not, in good sense, remove Putnam from command of their Hudson defenses, but instead placed Gates, since he was ranked higher than Putnam, in charge. He hoped it would curb some of Putnam's more...vocal tendencies.

At the same time, he knew his trust in Gates could never be fully realized after what he had discovered. His agent who was posted with the members of the 2nd Light and wintered at Peekskill was too low-ranked and would only be able to gather the most basic of information even if David Edgar had proven himself to be a useful spy. With Major Tallmadge now there, he hoped the young man would come to realize that not only was he to execute his duties, but he had been specifically posted under Gates to keep an eye on him. He had not said as much in his letter to Tallmadge regarding the 2nd Light's posting, but then again, the major had proven that he had an intuitive knack and knowledge regarding espionage that was growing day by day.

But even with Tallmadge's posting, it still did not solve Washington's more immediate problem. The lack of information regarding York City and Philadelphia. The agents that Nathaniel Sackett had procured were only effective to a certain degree;

giving him some troop numbers and locations of people of note. They could not tell him of future plans or even speculate about what the British were planning. He had one agent placed in a higher position, but that agent's viability was precarious due to the man's status as a paroled prisoner. He could not use that source unless it was dire or unavoidable. And now with the imminent evacuation of Philadelphia, Washington knew that he needed more eyes and ears in York City – now more than ever. The string of agents that Major Clark had produced in Philadelphia was coming to an end, and the time for new sources needed to be cultivated.

But Sackett had proven it was hard to get an agent in. Washington himself knew this; the few Sackett had sent him personally had either produced little useful intelligence or had been captured and executed. Washington tapped his chin again as he studied the war map. He would have asked one of his other officers to procure agents and establish an intelligence network, but after the political machinations Conway and his associates, he was re-evaluating the loyalty of some of his generals with a critical eye.

He knew he could trust Greene and Stirling, the latter of the two having forwarded him Gates' adjutant's damning letter. He could trust Morgan, and a few others, but all of them were men who had no taste for espionage. Short of outright asking one of them, he knew they all frowned upon the act of spying. It was not them who would have to go behind enemy lines, but they would not be able to pick people who would be effective at such a thing without showing their disdain and disgust at the person for the notion of being a spy.

No, whatever intelligence he needed to procure, it would have to be done after he dealt with the last of the political obstacles that had come to a head earlier this year – General Charles Lee. Lee was an outright traitor, a Judas who had betrayed the army. Letters written to him freely discussing banal military deployments or even locations were given straight to British command. Washington once thought he would be able to work with Lee, but with the man's return to camp earlier this year, it became strained and both had struggled to remain cordial. He had no doubts that Lee would make every attempt to oust him from his position, but instead of blundering like Conway, Gates, or any of the others, Lee would do it subtly; having learned from his comrades' failures.

Washington knew that his only recourse was to strike first, before Lee could make his move. And to that end, he studied his map, ignoring the knock on his door as Billy went over and opened it, his soft murmuring voice inquiring as to who was at the door.

"Sir, it's Lieutenant Colonel Hamilton," Billy said and Washington gestured with an absent hand for Billy to admit his aide-de-camp.

"Sir," Hamilton sounded a little giddy and he looked up from his map to see the young man holding out a ragged piece of paper. "From the Philadelphia network. Clinton is moving and has left the tail end of his heavy baggage train lightly defended."

Washington took the scrap of paper out from Hamilton's hand and read the abbreviated handwriting. It was succinct but told him everything he needed to know regarding Clinton's path out of Philadelphia. He looked back down at the map and placed a string of red tokens along the main road out of Philadelphia and up through several possible routes to the coast of New Jersey, near Perth Amboy.

He studied it for a few minutes before removing what were the least likely routes, owing to the fact that he and Clinton both knew it was contested territory. There was also the matter of *heavy* baggage that was mentioned in the scrap piece of paper. Washington knew that Clinton would want to take the most direct route, since it was his baggage train that would hold the British army escorting it and keep them from launching an all-out attack.

"Here," he murmured as he dropped a blue token along the line of red around Haddonfield, near Monmouth Courthouse. "We will strike here." All that was left was to draw up a battle plan, present it to his generals and find out where Charles Lee's allegiances were. If the man was truly a traitor, his colors would show during the battle and Washington would have his answer.

13

July 4ᵗʰ, 1778

Tallmadge had to admit he was readily impressed, and perhaps he was feeling the third cup of wine he was having, but General Horatio Gates could really throw a 4ᵗʰ of July party. Not only was Gates celebrating the second anniversary of the Declaration of Independence, but also of the victory at Monmouth Courthouse just days ago. Though the British gazettes and even the Patriot-leaning ones called it a stalemate, the fact that the British had all but retreated and Washington's army had prevailed until the waning light without giving an inch of ground looked like a victory in the rest of the army's eyes. The sobering news was that a lot of men had lost their lives due to the intense heat and humidity, but not as many as those on the British side.

Tallmadge even heard an amusing anecdote that Washington had ordered a majority of the army to strip down into their small clothes to stave off the intense heat. General Putnam's distinctive laugh and roaring voice had crowed that the British had fled purely at the sight of the army running all buck naked at them wielding only their guns and bayonets. He supposed there was some truth to that story given the casualty totals for both sides, but left it at that.

He took another sip of the wine he was holding as he took a moment from the festivities and small talk to simply observe everything around him. Wine was a luxury that was rarely afforded due to privateers and the soaring cost of supplies on the London Trade. Rum and all other spirits were somewhat easy to come by, but wine... Tallmadge intended to enjoy as much as he could and considering that there had been eight toasts already made and the night still relatively young – he expected there would be more opportunities to toast. However, he did indulge in a small private toast to the good fortune that had graced his Commander-in-Chief. The General Orders published in the aftermath of Monmouth stated that Charles Lee had been relieved of his command pending a court martial and dereliction of duty to be conducted by the Board of War and Congress. It seemed the traitorous general tried to effect a disastrous retreat from the initial attack at Monmouth Courthouse and had failed when Washington unexpectedly arrived sooner than anticipated. General Lafayette had been put in charge to rally the forces, and it had turned a near defeat into a victorious stalemate.

Tallmadge sipped another silent toast to what seemed to be another victory against Washington's detractors, not least the host of this wonderful lively party. It seemed General Gates had a change of heart soon after the whole of the 2nd Light was called to gather at Fishkill, just north of the defenses at Fort Westpoint and Peekskill back in June. Lieutenant Edgar had discreetly reported to him that it was but a week after his visit that he had, by chance as he returned from a patrol, overheard Gates sternly reprimanding Wilkinson, telling him that the whole Conway affair was not to be mentioned in any shape or form.

When Tallmadge and the rest of the 2nd Light had arrived back in early June, it seemed Gates was back in Washington's good graces. He heard nary a word of ill will towards their Commander-in-Chief at any of the meetings they had before they were sent to patrol the Westchester area of New York. After today, he knew he, Sheldon, and Blackden were to return to Westchester to resume their duties and so was determined to make the most of the good party that Gates was throwing for all of his general and field officers. He finished the rest of his glass and pushed himself up from where he had been leaning against the balcony, blinking a little as he felt the headiness of the alcohol coursing through him.

"Steady there, Major." The familiar gentle roll of a Virginian accent spoke up behind him and he turned to see Major William Washington walking up, holding a small glass of rum instead of the wine that was being served.

"Major Washington." Tallmadge nodded a greeting to the man, whom he had met once at the briefing tent of General Pulaski before their attack on Germantown. He noticed that another man trailed behind the major who bore the same rank. He had somewhat mousy, slightly bland features with light reddish-brown hair and wide blue eyes. His cheeks were suffused with the red of imbibed spirits and he held a full glass of wine.

"Tallmadge, this is John Jameson of the 1st Light," Washington said. "Jameson, this is Benjamin Tallmadge, 2nd Light."

"A pleasure." The dizziness that had briefly assaulted Tallmadge passed as he reached over and shook hands with the mousy-looking major.

"We were hoping you would join us while we also find Alexander Clough of the 3rd Light and get this debate started," Washington smiled, and Tallmadge raised an eyebrow.

"A debate on what?" He was always up for any type of debate, especially the ones he had engaged in with Nathan back during their college days. Though there were numerous women who had been invited to the party, the intrigue of debating his fellow majors of the dragoon regiments pushed aside his desire to converse with the ladies for now. The night was still young and if the debate proved not to his liking, he could always find a better conversation partner for the evening.

"The recent French alliance, foreign aid, all sorts of things that could affect the war's outcome," Washington smiled, "but most of all, how the British have turned tail at Monmouth."

Tallmadge laughed a little. "That is something worthy to debate. The cowardice of the British in their retreat.. He raised his empty glass. "If you gentlemen do not mind, I wish to at least have some more to whet my throat before engaging in such a manner of conversation."

"Certainly, though I suppose I could get some more wine to match you and Jameson here in case of extenuating circumstances." Washington's smile turned rueful. "I do really dislike that stuff, dreadful and thick."

Tallmadge only shook his head, a wide smile on his face. "Major-"

"Call me Washington- though I suppose that would be confusing. Call me William, then."

"William, aye, and you can call me Ben or Benjamin," he nodded. "As for what I was about to say, you must adhere to the rules of conduct in this forthcoming debate, good sir."

The other major nodded. "I suppose. Alas, my poor rum, what ever shall I do with you?"

"I'll drink it if you will not, William." Jameson made a move towards Washington's glass but the major was quicker and downed the whole glass with two gulps.

"Starting so soon are we?" Tallmadge could not resist the tease as he realized it was not exactly a formal debate, but rather a debate that involved imbibing sips of alcohol whenever things were not presented as exaggerations or falsehoods.

"Says the man who does not even have a full glass." Washington pushed his shoulder with a free hand before slinging a slightly drunken arm around him. "Come on Benjamin, let us fill our glasses and find Clough and get this debate started." Tallmadge let himself be pulled towards one of the servants that was holding a glass of wine, his mood lifting at the prospect of such company and debate.

His subsequent letter describing the event to his friends were met with amused replies. Colonel Webb, still a paroled prisoner in York City, had wondered how one could stay so sober and remember so much after thirteen toasts were rendered throughout the night. Jeremiah Wadsworth had an equally amused and heavily dry reply, stating that perhaps the commissary department should look into its stores of spirits and ration them so the army would not be so inclined to sleep off a whole day's worth of headache and drunkenness. Tallmadge had quickly penned his witty reply wondering if the commissary would celebrate or commiserate in far grander fashion now that they knew what was happening on the front lines.

Overall, it was a good break from the constant patrolling and duties that had engulfed most of Tallmadge's time since he had joined the 2nd Light. He was glad he could still enjoy such simple pleasures.

July 20th, 1778

Tallmadge covered his mouth and nose with a handkerchief he had produced from the inner folds of his jacket as he stepped into Captain Webb's tent. The young officer peered up with a miserable look from where he lay on his cot.

"S-Sir..." Webb made to salute, but Tallmadge waved at him to stop.

"Do you need anything?" he asked, resisting the urge to shake his head in pity. He had just come from Captain Shethar's tent with the same question. A summer malaise of sorts was going through camp and had hit two of the six captains, two cornets – James Wells and Jedidiah Rogers, along with Sergeant Dole, and sixteen privates.

"No, sir." Webb's voice sounded scratchy and hoarse and he looked no better. "I think the fever broke last night, though, was sweating a bunch. Felt like someone had run me over with several horses this morning though."

Tallmadge smiled behind his handkerchief, "Better tell those riding the horses to control their animals." It produced a small smile from Webb as he coughed once. It sounded like someone had run a sharpening stone over a worn blade.

"...Could use some more water, sir." Webb slowly glanced over to the small table set up next to his bed and Tallmadge nodded.

"I will let someone know. Get well soon, Webb, we need you," he stated before he stepped back out. He lowered the handkerchief from his face and glanced at Hoogland who was standing outside of the tent, waiting to write down what Webb needed. "Another pitcher of fresh water and probably some food. See if some of the cheese that was given to us has not hardened much and find someone to boil some bread and dried meat for him in a stew of sorts. He says his fever broke last night, so he might be able to join in a few days providing he gains his strength back."

"Sir," Hoogland scrawled his request with a blackened chalk on the paper and board he was holding.

Visiting the sick and ill was a task he could have easily left for Hoogland since he was adjutant, but since he was their immediate commanding officer and was not fielding paperwork at the moment with Sheldon and Blackden at camp, he had decided to visit. It was something he had been doing since joining Colonel Chester's regiment in the early days of the war. He hoped the visits had impressed upon the men that their commanding officers cared for them. He did, however, delegate the visitation and needs of the other sick men in the 2nd Light to their respective captains and lieutenants of the regiment. By doing so, he hoped to impart to the officers with a sense of responsibility towards those they commanded.

"Find the others and gather their notes. I want their needs, if they are within reason, for the quartermaster. They are to be fulfilled by no later than tonight. These men need to get better. We can ill afford the loss of their service," he stated, and Hoogland nodded before hurrying away to collect the reports of the others who had visited the sick.

It was not bravado or a rallying call to the men; rather it was a true need. Of the one-hundred forty-one men left, there were only three captains, five lieutenants, and three cornets that were on hand to officer them; not counting himself, Sheldon, or Blackden. Some of the lieutenants and cornets had just been promoted, and did not exactly have the veteran knowledge to officer the men in proper fashion, even though all of them had seen skirmishing patrols since their posting at the Westchester front back in June.

They were also short one captain, a lieutenant, two cornets, two sergeants, five corporals, a trumpeter and farrier, and forty-one privates. That group had been assigned a variety of detached duties from both General Washington and Gates. Since the stalemate at Monmouth, General Washington had brought the rest of the Continental Army up to the old headquarters at Middlebrook and distributed the army in a wide arc surrounding York City. Congress had gratefully returned to Philadelphia and the need for escorts and post-riders had risen considerably. Stoddard had been assigned to one such duty and Tallmadge was only regretted it had not come sooner.

Back in late June, Stoddard had been dispatched with a small group of men to take into custody a known Tory, Israel Underhill. Underhill had been accused of spying and dealing in the London Trade. Stoddard had not only taken Underhill, but also large quantities of sugar and supplies found at the house. He had blatantly reported his excessive and harsh treatment of other Tories who were Underhill's neighbors and those he suspected to be Tory sympathizers in the area.

Rumor spread like wildfire once that was written and sent to Gates. Gates had responded swiftly and stated that a court of inquiry was to be convened regarding Stoddard's conduct and excessive patriotism. The loud-mouthed ill-tempered captain had challenged the accusations, contending that one could not give an inch of mercy to any Tory or Tory sympathizer for the cause of patriotism and freedom for America. Sheldon had called Blackden and Tallmadge into a private meeting after Gates' 4th of July festivities to discuss Stoddard, and told them that one of the colonels in the area was to head up the court of inquiry. But that had been put aside in light of a request from Washington to send one of the 2nd Light's officers to Philadelphia to pick up and deliver five-hundred guineas for the army's use. Stoddard had been sent and Tallmadge was relieved that the troublesome man was gone from camp. He, and some of the other officers of the regiment, had considered Stoddard's actions embarrassing towards the regiment as a whole. It demoralized and confused the men.

But with the loss of Stoddard, two of his other captains sick, and only a handful of officers on hand to command the men, the hope that the regiment could serve as a whole had been lost since their posting to Westchester. It felt like what had happened last year, with so many of them attending to other duties. It made him wonder if the 2nd Light would ever serve as a whole in any future conflicts. Still, he did not let such thoughts linger and fester in his mind as he headed towards Sheldon's command tent. It was located on Kings Street in Westchester, and small outposts, manned by the captains of the regiment had been set up along the contested areas. Westchester and the surrounding area was plagued by the Tory cowboys and skirmishing British forces that forayed out of York City from time to time. Though the Continentals currently held the position, one had to be on alert at all times.

Lieutenant Colonel Blackden was conducting an inspection of the outposts and Tallmadge knew that when Blackden returned in a couple of days, he would take over the other man's duties. The two traded off every few days to give the other a chance to rest and recover from the long circular route of inspection and scouting of the outposts. It was something Tallmadge relished, but at the moment, it was quite dull, with little to no action by the British in recent days.

"Sir," he stopped outside of Sheldon's tent.

"Enter," was the swift reply, and Tallmadge stepped in.

He saw the colonel standing by his desk, in the midst of reading a letter that clearly had the scrawling signature of General Gates. Tallmadge felt his spirits brighten a little – hopefully whatever letter Gates had written meant they were to undertake action soon.

"Sir, is there to be action?" he asked.

"Yes," Sheldon nodded, the tail of his queue moving against the blue-buff of his jacket. When he had first seen Sheldon since the winter, he was surprised to see that the man had many more white and grey hairs than the last time. He seemed tired, but Tallmadge was willing to give him the benefit of the doubt as to his ability to command. "General Nixon is gathering the regiments of Hazen, Wyllys, Meigs, Greadon, Putnam, and his own for a sweep across Westchester and Eastchester. In two days time we are to confiscate Loyalist cattle, arrest anyone who resists and engage the enemy if they give us battle. At the same time, I have been informed that General Washington will establish headquarters in White Plains while we are doing this."

Tallmadge nodded, his initial unspoken question about why so many foot regiments were gathered answered with Sheldon's words. If they were to acquire that many supplies many men would be needed to move the supplies back to headquarters to be distributed among the regiments. "And our duties?" he asked.

"I'll command half of the regiment while Blackden takes the

other half and heads to Eastchester." Sheldon set the paper down and pulled out several sheaves of blank parchment and began to write. "I need you to give these personally to Captains Bull, Belden, and Seymour at the outposts and if you see Blackden on your way, send him back as soon as possible. Who is in Eastchester?"

"Bull, sir," he replied, and Sheldon nodded.

"Good," he replied. "Bull will be second to Blackden in his sweep since he is senior captain. Each outpost is to leave at least five men, all horsed, and three dismounted men for purposes of securing the post. The rest will join in the sweep."

"Very good sir," Tallmadge replied as he watched Sheldon finish scrawling the orders on the pieces of parchment and dry them with some haste before folding them. He did not bother sealing them and handed the three pieces of paper to him. Tallmadge took them and saluted Sheldon before leaving his commanding officer's tent. He headed straight to where Castor was tied up and quickly mounted him, setting him on a fast trot towards Eastchester and Bull's outpost. There were two more outposts set up before Bull's, technically commanded by Captain Shethar and Webb, but since both were ill, the outposts had fallen to their lieutenants to take care of. Sheldon had assigned the two additional lieutenants that had been promoted in late May to help the two smaller outposts.

Tallmadge was glad they were to take action soon, even if it was just a raid against Loyalist farms. With the arrival of the French fleet commanded by Admiral Charles, Count d'Estaing, there was talk of where the fleet would strike. It seemed prudent now with the forthcoming sweep of Eastchester and Westchester; it would not only be a show of force, but perhaps of further troop movement in an assault on York City itself. He was not privy to the number of British ships in York City's harbor, but considering that even the British gazettes were worried about the French fleet, he could easily assume that the French ships greatly outnumbered the British fleet. General Clinton had trapped himself in York City after his evacuation from Philadelphia.

After a short cautious ride of roughly half an hour, he arrived at the first outpost commanded by Lieutenant de Valcour. De Valcour was assisted by the newly promoted Lieutenant Pool.

Tallmadge had been proud to give the man his new rank and could see that Pool had been happy to receive it. He waved to de Valcour, who was on duty, and the Frenchman waved back as he slowed down to a walk.

"Lieutenant, has Colonel Blackden arrived yet?" he called out.

"Yes, sir. He is with Captain Bull at the forward outpost," de Valcour replied. "Is everything all right, sir?"

"Captain Bull will explain soon enough," he replied. Though he knew he could have explained what was to happen, he instead left it to Bull explain his orders since the senior captain more than likely had a preference on who went and who stayed in the three outposts they had in Eastchester.

"Yes sir," de Valcour nodded as he saw Pool emerge from the small outpost cabin he and de Valcour shared, with a curious look on his face. He nodded a greeting to Pool who tilted his head a bit, but nodded back without comment. Tallmadge heeled Castor back to a moderate trot as he rode past them. Some of the men on duty waved at him and he acknowledged their greeting with a curt nod.

The thickets of hilly woods and farmland engulfed him once more as he rode towards the second outpost, acutely aware of his surroundings. Even though they patrolled the area, the potential to ride right into an ambush by opportunistic Tory cowboys or roaming British patrols was great. Lieutenant Colonel John Graves Simcoe's Queen's Rangers, General Oliver Delancey's Tory brigades, and Emmerick's horsemen were known to patrol the same area as they did. Tallmadge remembered well what had happened in February of last year when he had encountered some of Delancey's Tories in Setauket with Major Clark. He relished the chance to face off against them now that he had his men with him.

Tallmadge arrived at the second outpost with little incident and waved to Lieutenant Jedidiah Rogers who was on duty. Rogers gave him a curious look, but did not question his presence or even issue a challenge. While a part of Tallmadge was glad, another part wondered if Rogers did the same for those who rode in the night. He sighed and pulled Castor to a halt, turning his horse to where Rogers was sitting at his outpost. This was a problem that needed to be remedied in immediate fashion. He would have thought that Blackden, on his way to Bull's outpost, would have noticed such a thing, but it seemed he had not.

"Lieutenant," he greeted and the fresh-faced young man saluted.

"Major Tallmadge, s-sir." Rogers had a slight stutter that was not quite noticeable unless certain words were spoken. He saluted crisply.

Tallmadge gestured for the lieutenant to step away from where he was as he nodded greetings to the rest of the men on duty. This was something that could be spoken about in relative privacy; he need not embarrass the young officer or demean him in front of his men. Rogers did so, with slight trepidation in his eyes. As soon as they were away from the prying eyes and ears of the men, Tallmadge gave a frank look at the young man.

"Lieutenant, I did not hear any challenge," he stated.

"But, sir, you were clearly on your way-"

"Rogers, there needs to be a challenge, even if it is just a simple inquiry as to my presence or a confirmation of sorts," he said quietly.

"But, sir-"

"We are in contested territory where any man may be captured by one of the cowboy bands or even a British patrol. They can easily have their uniform taken from them and worn by the enemy. They may use them to sneak past our patrols and gather intelligence," he pointed out. He knew from last year's reports that Sheldon had taken some of the men of the 2nd Light on such a patrol with stolen British uniforms in order to confuse the enemy. The fact that Moylan's 4th Light wore the dyed uniforms of British forces was not lost on him. To engage in such subterfuge meant that if one of their own was caught and stripped of their uniform – the consequences could be dire.

"Sir that's..."

"It may be seen as dishonorable, Lieutenant," he stressed quietly, "but it is something that the enemy is willing to engage in. You yourself have seen in the last two months of patrol duty how the Tories act here; not even a care in the world for the innocent men and women who live and tend to the farmlands here."

Rogers hung his head a little, shamed by the reprimand. "I...understand, sir."

"Take heart, Lieutenant," he smiled a little, hoping that the young officer would take his words with intention instead of being disheartened by them. "It is something that you were not aware of until it was pointed out, so there is no fault in that."

"Yes sir," the young man brightened a little, and Tallmadge patted him on the shoulder before stepping away to remount Castor. He swung onto his horse and tipped his helm at the lieutenant, who had a small smile on his face.

"Captain Bull will be by later with further orders, Lieutenant," he said and the young officer nodded before he continued on his way. A quick glance back made a rueful smile appear on his face as he saw some of the other men surround the young officer, more than likely asking him what was discussed. He turned back and continued on, riding through more fields and farmlands before he arrived at the last outpost that pushed deep into Eastchester.

It was fortified more than the last two outposts and Tallmadge could see two of the guards on duty shout down towards the others to signal an approaching rider as he rode in. Tallmadge smiled tightly; Epaphras Bull was an effective captain and commander. His detached duties over the past year and a half had taught him the skills needed to lead an independent group of soldiers since he was away from the regiment for so long. What was remarkable was Bull had also proven that he was willing to work with the regiment itself when integrated back into the fold. Detached command had both its drawbacks and advantages and Bull had proven to be one of those who worked well in all situations. It was why he was put in charge of a majority of the Eastchester section and was senior captain to the others posted in the area.

He saw Bull's lieutenant hurry towards him as he slowed Castor down and stopped short of the waiting lieutenant. Dismounting, he acknowledged the lieutenant's quick salute before the man gestured for him to follow, obviously assuming he was looking for Captain Bull and Lieutenant Colonel Blackden. The cabin that served as Bull's command post had two rooms, with a small bed in the far corner of the main room that was more than likely Lieutenant Brown's. Both Blackden and Bull sat at a small table that probably served as both a dining table and war map table, but there was a draughts board set up in front of them. It seemed the two had been playing a game when he had entered.

Tallmadge saluted Blackden and received a salute from Bull.

"Major?" Blackden looked at him with a curious gaze.

"Orders, sir," he addressed Blacken as he handed one of the three folded pieces of paper to Bull who unfolded it and read it over quickly. "Colonel Sheldon requests your presence back at headquarters as soon as possible. It seems General Nixon is preparing for a sweep of both East and Westchester. You are to lead the sweep down Eastchester with some of the men in camp and pick up the other troops along the way. Sheldon will be leading Westchester sweep."

Blackden clapped his hands onto his thighs. "Finally, something to do!"

"Five mounted men and three dismounted ones, is that correct Major?" Bull looked up from the orders that were written, and Tallmadge nodded.

"The soldiers from the other regiments will be taking cattle and supplies from the sweep." He could see Bull already thinking of who to leave behind as well as the logistics behind helping those would be burdened by the taking of the supplies. He opened his mouth to say something, but then closed it, lost in thought once more.

"Captain?" Bull was clearly thinking of something else, but a quick shake of the man's head told him he did not wish to voice his thoughts at the moment.

"You are headed to Westchester after this?" Blackden glanced at the other two folded letters in his hands as he pocketed them once more.

"Yes sir," Tallmadge replied.

"I have not completed my rounds of the outposts there, but if you would be so kind..." Blackden asked, and he nodded.

"It is of no consequence," He waved away the fact that Blackden had not even begun to check in with the Westchester outposts, and left it at that. It was not up to him how his senior officer conducted himself when doing such inspections. "If I may take my leave, sir?"

"Thank you, Tallmadge. I'll head back to the command post soon." Blackden waved an absent hand, indicating he wished to finish his game with Bull before leaving.

As he re-mounted Castor, Tallmadge nodded his thanks to Lieutenant Brown who had held his reins during the short time he was in the cabin. He galloped away, headed on a southwesterly path towards the nearest Westchester outpost.

This section of the road was the most treacherous, the southern part of Eastchester where it met Westchester's borders near Mamaroneck and New Rochelle. It was dangerous not only because it was more heavily frequented by Tory cowboys and British patrols due to its proximity to York City, but it was also along the coastline of the western end of Long Island Sound, where enemy privateers and their small boats lurked. He had received word from Caleb Brewster back in late May of General Oliver Delancey's plans to begin building a fort on the western edge of Lloyd's Neck, a small peninsula that jutted out into the Sound. It was the perfect spot for the British to set up an outpost to use as a safe harbor for their raiding ships, but also to launch attacks into southern New York in the Mamaroneck and New Rochelle areas.

The bright summer sun filtered through the leafy trees as he rode at a fast trot along the relatively flat coastline. It was a few hours since he had left Colonel Sheldon's command post and the afternoon sun, along with the slight rumble of his stomach, told him that supper would be served soon in the houses around the area as well as in the other outposts. He had timed his traveling well. Though there would still be patrols going back and forth through the woods, they would not be as numerous or active through this section as most would be concerned with the far more immediate care of feeding themselves and their men.

His initial elation was shattered when he heard the snort and whinny of several horses to his left and saw flashes of muted colors: browns, whites and blacks in a thicket of trees several meters away. He slowed Castor to a tentative walk as he heard loud, gruff laughter followed by a smattering of rough voices, trying to discern whether these were just traders and civilians or opportunistic Tory cowboys. He flicked his reins at Castor, urging him back into a fast trot as he rode past the intersection of the road, not quite turning his head to look at them. Perhaps they would not notice his presence. Instead, he tracked at them out of the corner of his eyes – they were all armed with a variety of muskets, but their clothing did not look quite Continental, nor was it militia.

He focused back on the road as he heard them take notice of his presence and he pressed his lips thinly together. It was only three men, but he had a feeling they were Tory cowboys. Judging by how free they were with their laughter, they were more than likely on their way home as he happened to run into them. He silently hoped and prayed that they would continue on their way home, to live another day, and ignore his presence.

His prayers were not answered.

He heard their horses' hooves beating an uneven sound on the ground behind him. They were following. Tallmadge cursed quietly as he flicked a quick look behind him to confirm what he had heard and saw the three cowboys pursuing him. They all had tight smiles on their faces as he turned back and urged Castor into a cantor. The wooded road was narrow and did not allow for much passage between trees; that was one advantage Tallmadge knew he had as he raced towards the first of the south-most Westchester outposts in northern New Rochelle.

He heard one of the cowboys' excited shouts as they gave chase and urged Castor to go faster. A few branches whipped at his face, one drawing a fast line across his nose and cheek, but he ignored the stinging pain as he continued out of the woods and into a small clearing. He could see the outpost already set up, in a dilapidated farmhouse that had been long abandoned and half-torched in a previous raid before they established an outpost there. The fields were withered and already growing with weeds that were half a horse's height. Tallmadge turned in his saddle to see the three still following, but not catching up to him. He stood on his stirrups and waved his arm towards the guards that were on duty, recognizing Seymour's troop, and saw one man racing towards the two guards. From that distance, he could not quite tell who it was, but thought it looked like Lieutenant Edgar. The men that were on duty all scrambled to grab their carbines.

Castor suddenly stumbled and whinnied as he went sideways, nearly unseating Tallmadge, who sat back down heavily in his saddle. The sound of a musket firing echoed not even a second later. He managed to control his horse and saw that Castor had received a graze from a musket ball, and turned to see that another one of the cowboys was now sighting down his musket, aiming at him.

Tallmadge immediately pulled his pistol out and fired an ineffective shot, but it startled the three cowboys, and he kicked Castor's flank to continue onward. His horse snorted in displeasure and some pain, but continued towards the outpost. The moment's pause given to him by his wild shot enabled him to charge into the relative safety of the outpost where he immediately turned Castor around – silently apologizing for the harsh treatment of his wounded horse – and pulled his carbine from where it hung over his shoulder.

He heard his name being called, but ignored it as he sighted downward at the charging cowboys who were beginning to slow as they realized they were coming upon a heavily guarded outpost. Tallmadge targeted the lead cowboy and fired. His shot was true and the man rocked back in his saddle, blood pouring from his mouth, and slid from it, dead even before he hit the ground. His horse continued on for a few feet, unaware that its rider was gone while the other two cowboys stopped.

The men at the outer edges of the outpost took it as their cue to fire. The smattering of carbines discharging into the air sent the other two cowboys retreating back into the safety of the woods.

"Sir. Should we pursue?!" he heard Edgar ask from behind, and turned to see him leading his horse by its bridle.

"No," he shook his head as he shouldered his carbine, watching the two cowboys disappear into the woods. One sergeant of the troop ran towards the men, waving his arms and shouting for them to stop firing. He pursed his lips for a moment, glancing at the dead body of the cowboy in the distance. The man's horse now stood looking rather docile, having stopped with no rider leading it. "Bury the dead. The horse can be used for one of the dismounted men."

"Yes sir," Edgar replied before quickly adding with a grim

smile, "a fine shot sir." Before Tallmadge could reply or even reprimand him for the unnecessary praise, Edgar handed the reins of his horse to one of the privates and hurried to help the sergeant direct the men to do as he ordered.

Tallmadge dismounted, holding onto Castor's bridle as he inspected the area where the musket ball had grazed his horse's rump. There was a noticeable gash, but it did not look too deep. He handed the reins to a sergeant who offered to clean and dress the wound, and headed to the half-burnt farmhouse that was Seymour's command post. Seymour stumbled out of the door, half-dressed as it was apparent that he had been sleeping when Tallmadge had arrived.

"Sir," Seymour threw a hasty and messy salute as he finished straightening his jacket and ran a hand through his hair.

"At ease, Captain." He waved him back and gestured for the two of them to enter the farmhouse.

"I'm sorry, sir, I was-"

"It is fine." Tallmadge stepped into the parlor room that Seymour had converted into both his office and bedroom, a straw bed shoved into the corner while the desk itself was wedged in the corner between the window and fireplace. Tallmadge surmised that the other rooms that had not burnt down served as quarters for Lieutenant Edgar and some of the other non-commissioned officers.

"I did not expect you here, though Lieutenant Colonel Blackden is currently, I think at Captain Bull's outpost-" Seymour seemed rather flustered, more so than Tallmadge had ever seen him. The source of Seymour's fluster made itself known as he noticed something he did not expect to see in any officer's quarters: a rather fine-looking lace fringe that seemed also to have a scrap of cloth attached to it. It was tangled into the straw mat on Seymour's bed. Tallmadge stared at it before turning to meet his captain's face which was slowly turning red.

"Uh, sir, I can explain-"

"Is she still here?" Tallmadge knew he had likely interrupted a private moment between the captain and whatever lady friend he had with him.

"Y-Yes sir," Seymour looked towards one of the doors that led deeper into the house. "Maria-"

Tallmadge shook his head, "No, no need to call for her." He turned towards the door, "Ma'am, my apologies for this interruption. I will be but a short stay." He did not wait for an answer as he turned back to Seymour and handed him the folded note, "If you need any resources or have any questions, I will be at Belden's outpost until the sweep commences."

Seymour colored further, clearly embarrassed that one of his senior officers was declining to stay with him due to the presence of his lady friend. "S-Sir..." The young man swallowed hard, pressed his lips tightly together and read the note. He glanced back up at him and nodded.

Seeing that his task was done, Tallmadge inclined his head sharply and left the house. He heard something odd and peered back to see a very pretty red-headed young woman with bright green eyes. Her hair was a little askew, and she muffled her laugh before ducking back into the room that was next to Seymour's. Tallmadge felt an involuntary smile appear on his face, though it quickly disappeared as he left the house. He had nothing against his officers or the men keeping the company of women as he understood that everyone, even himself, had needs. Such dalliances were allowed, so long as they did not interfere with their duties. In this case, he felt certain this would teach Seymour to be a little more discreet in entertaining a lady friend. He was technically on duty day in and out. He needed to be ready to advance with his men or even to pull back to safer ground if the enemy launched an attack. Such responsibilities left little time for visitors and he hoped Seymour had learned this lesson.

Tallmadge headed towards the stabling area and saw a few of the men already hard at work digging a grave for the fallen Tory cowboy. He could see Edgar and several of the men watching the surroundings with keen eyes, making sure no one else approached after what had happened. The dead man was already stripped of any useful weaponry and accouterments and someone had wrapped his body up in a spare canvas.

The sergeant that had offered to care for his horse had done an admirable job. As he mounted Castor once more, Tallmadge gave his compliments on a job well done as he received a small poultice he would be giving to Davenport once he arrived at

Belden's outpost. He had hoped to stay the night at Seymour's outpost, but due to the presence of the captain's lady friend, he though better of it. He headed out and arrived at the next outpost without further incident, though the sun had dipped low enough that a challenge was called to him as he entered the outpost's borders. Tallmadge was pleased with the necessary procedure, but he was a little concerned at the apparent skittishness of the men on duty, even after he replied with his rank and name and let the guards see him as he walked Castor in.

"Sorry about the men being so skittish, Ben-err, Major Tallmadge," Pullings greeted him as he dismounted and handed him the reins.

"Trouble?" he asked.

"Adamson's patrol ran into a few wandering Tories and they gave chase instead of giving ground. He thinks it might have been British regulars, maybe Queen's Rangers or Tarleton's men disguised as one of Delancey's Refugee Tories. He's currently supping with the captain and lieutenant," Pullings replied with jerk of his thumb.

"Is Davenport around?" he asked, looking around for his friend. Ever since Davenport had refused to go with him to Peekskill when they were encamped at Chatham, there had been a stilted sort of formality between the two of them. He had made no apologies nor even remotely considered an apology to the other man and instead continued to treat him both as a member of the 2nd Light and as a fellow sergeant. To him, the strained awkwardness seemed to come from Davenport's end. He obeyed Tallmadge's orders without comment and seemed more formal whenever he approached or even when talking with Pullings or Adamson in rare moments when rank and station could be discarded.

"Aye, need someone to fetch him?" Pullings asked and Tallmadge shrugged.

"No, I do not want to disturb him if he is busy, but if you could give him this poultice to heal Castor's wound over here." He pointed out the musket ball score which was now oozing and pussing, though his horse did not seemed bothered by it.

Pullings made a face. "Looks disgusting. This recent, Major?"

"Enterprising Tory cowboy," he shook his head and Pullings nodded.

"Use that trick I taught you?"

"It worked," Tallmadge smiled a little. Ever since Pullings developed a reputation as the regiment's sharpshooter on horseback, he had been freely teaching some of the men how to shoot. Tallmadge knew that it was improper for him to ask such a junior ranked non-commissioned officer for assistance in learning how to be more efficient with his carbine – even if Pullings was a good friend – so instead had pretended to oversee one of his friend's teaching moments, as an officer making sure the men learned how to shoot. They both knew he was also there as a student, but Pullings at least had learned some discretion in regards to that. "And it was not taught to me, *Corporal*," he emphasized as a slight jest, but also a warning for Pullings not to go spilling per his other habit of being the regiment's gossip.

"No it was not, sir." Pullings mimed slashing his own throat in a gesture of silence before knuckling his forehead. "I'll see that Davenport takes care of Castor for you, sir. You'll be staying long?"

"Probably the next few days. I need head up to Hurlbut's outpost before returning. You'll find out soon enough, Pullings."

"Yes, sir," his friend nodded before taking Castor away.

Tallmadge headed towards the mill house that had been converted into Captain Belden's outpost. It was on the side of a hill towards the valley area of the southern region of Westchester that led into New Rochelle. A creek ran through the area and while the creek bed itself was steep and wide, it seemed the flood of water only came during the thawing winter to spring months and dried into a trickle during the summer – the exception being summer's heavy rain showers. Unlike many of the other abandoned buildings that the 2nd Light had taken over and converted into outposts, the mill house itself was not burnt, but the surrounding trees and hillside were scorched and pockmarked; a sign of significant fighting before they had taken it over.

Pullings' report of possible British forces dressed up as Tories worried him, but did not hamper his excitement for the action to come in two days time. If Adamson was still at the mill house, it probably meant he was in the middle of giving his report and it would be a good place to start. He was fairly sure that what his friend had encountered was a probe of the outpost's defenses and strength. It made the men jumpy, but it also was good for them. If there was little to no action, the men were prone to making mistakes or being lax with their patrols and watchfulness.

Tallmadge entered, taking his helm off as he stepped into the mill house. It was a rather modest-sized house with narrow halls and small rooms. He could hear the sounds of utensils hitting plates and took a few steps forward to peer into the dining room to see Belden, Adamson and Wadsworth in the middle of eating. Belden was the first to spot him and hastily swallowed whatever was in his mouth as he stood up. His chair made a screeching sound across the wooden floor. The other two stopped and stared as he waved for them to continue to eat.

"Don't mind me, Captain-" he began.

"Sir. We weren't expecting-" Belden moved from the table and gestured for him to come in. "Please, come in sir. Would you care to join us for dinner? We were only-"

"It's fine," he nodded his acceptance of the food and saw Wadsworth run into a different room, coming back with a chair. He sat down on the fourth side of the square table as a plate, cup of ale, and bowl were procured and a stew of sorts was set in front of him. It smelled and looked rather familiar as he glanced up at Adamson who had served it to him.

"Yours?" he asked.

"You didn't get any last time I cooked, so here's some for now," Adamson seemed pleased that he remembered the last time he had cooked such a stew, in the dead of winter during their harried patrols around the Schuylkill.

"Many thanks." He accepted the bowl and ate some. It tasted rather bland, though he supposed that was because Adamson did not have Webb's salt box to flavor the stew. Even so it was not bad.

"Did you just get in, sir?" Belden looked a little concerned and Tallmadge shook his head as he reached into his pocket and pulled out the third of Sheldon's orders. He handed it over to Belden as he swallowed and wiped his mouth before speaking.

"We're seeing action in two days. Sheldon's dividing the

regiment into two. Blackden will lead half of the regiment with the infantry of Hazen, Wyllys, and Meigs into Eastchester. The Westchester half will be led by Sheldon and myself with infantry forces of Greadon's, Putnam's, and General Nixon's regiments. We are sweeping across the area down to probably Valentine's Hill – the final destination not confirmed, but are to confiscate all Loyalist cattle, supplies, and ammunition. If the Tories or British forces desire to give us a fight, we shall give it to them."

"If I may say so, sir, it is about time." Wadsworth thumped a fist onto the wooden table as Belden read the orders.

"Hear, hear," Adamson agreed, "and if I may add sir, my patrol encountered soldiers who might have been British regulars disguised as Delancey's Tories, sir. Though I do not know if this is the first time such things have happened, it seems that the British are aware of our presence here."

Tallmadge nodded, a smile gracing his lips as he took another bite of the stew. "I believe that with the retreat of General Clinton to New York, the British are no more than scouting our strength and defenses here. This sweep will discourage such action and serve to entrap his forces further in the city. With the French forces due to arrive, they will hopefully surround the bay to effect a surrender."

All three of his junior officers' eyes widened at his statement. "Do you really think that would happen, sir?" Belden asked, astonished.

Tallmadge shrugged, "While I do not know what General Washington's plans are, it is conceivable to think that this may be one scenario. I, however, would like to think that the further discouragement of the British forces here would do well for whatever overall battle plan the general conceives."

The surprised looks slowly turned into nods of understanding as they realized he was only voicing what might happen, not what would happen.

"Well, sir, we look forward to the action." Belden folded the letter back up, held up his cup of ale and toasted him. He returned the toast and continued to eat, feeling confident of what was to happen in two days' time.

It was not until a couple of weeks later that Tallmadge learned that their push deep into Westchester and Eastchester to challenge both the Tories and British forces was nothing more than a feint. It seemed that Washington had wanted Clinton to think he was to be surrounded by both American forces and the newly arrived French fleet. What really happened was that a force under General Sullivan and Greene was sent to attack Newport, Rhode Island, the other stronghold of the British fleet. Admiral d'Estaing was requested to bring his ships to Newport to help with the assault, but it seemed some kind of communication failed and the attack was deemed a failure.

Mistrust spread through the camp as those who did not really like foreign aid, like Gates and whomever was left of the Conway cabal, raised their voices again, and Tallmadge wondered if the alliance they had secured was the promised alliance of military aid against the British forces. In any event, routine patrols rued the day and the 2nd Light found itself back in its old haunts and patrols, disappointed in the lack of clear decisive action.

August 25th, 1778

It was not unusual for Tallmadge to find himself summoned to Washington's main encampment at White Plains at the behest of Colonel Sheldon to discuss patrols and coordinate with the infantry regiments at their established outposts. But a personal summon by General Washington himself – that was most unusual and piqued his curiosity. Tallmadge brought his horse up short as he approached the general's headquarters. It was the same house that had been used during their initial evacuation from New York almost two years ago. Tallmadge did not know what happened to Elijah Miller, but he hoped the man was able to find safe haven.

He dismounted and tied Castor to a post nearby. His horse's wound had healed nicely, leaving a noticeable scar where no hair grew. The good thing, in his mind, was that his horse was not lamed by the encounter. He knocked on the door to Miller's house nodding to two of Washington's life guards who stood at attention.

It opened to reveal a well-dressed black man in the uniform of the Continental Army. "Ah, Major Tallmadge, I presume?" the man asked, his English impeccable without a trace of any accent. "I am William Lee, General Washington's servant." The African introduced himself with a short bow and opened the door further, gesturing for him to enter. "If you will, sir, please follow me."

Though Tallmadge considered slavery wrong, he was not an abolitionist. He was rather surprised at how well spoken and mannered Lee was, his notions of how the south treated their slaves versus those in the north, crumbling a little. It seemed Washington did care for all of those in his charge, including his manservant, and Tallmadge's admiration for him grew. He followed William in and headed to the war room which was familiar sight to him. Tallmadge still remembered his harried ride from the front at Chatterton Hill to this very room, giving a quick report to Washington and the assembled generals on the British movements before leaving just as fast. There was only one general in the room now, and it was not Washington. "General Scott," he greeted with a salute that was returned with a brief nod.

"Major...Tallmadge, was it?" The general was an older man with grey-white hair and sharp beady eyes.

"Yes sir." Tallmadge was surprised that Brigadier General Charles Scott knew who he was. He only knew the man in passing and by reputation. Scott was a stubborn man and commander, bold to commit his forces, but easily set in his ways. The general led mainly Virginian forces and Tallmadge wondered why he and the general were in this very war room when Washington was not even there.

"General Washington will be here shortly. He is currently attending to other matters," William spoke up, staring at them with a polite gaze. "Is there any refreshment or things I may get for either one of you?"

"No, I am fine." Tallmadge waved his hand and shook his head a negative, while Scott just shrugged.

"A glass of any port if you will," he said, and William nodded before closing the door behind him.

A brief silence filled the room as Tallmadge walked over to the fireplace and stood near it. Maps were splayed out all over the war room table, but since General Scott was already studying it, Tallmadge did not want to intrude on a senior officer's perusal of it. However, near the fire, he had an angled vantage point and could sort of observe the maps without overtly studying it.

"If I may ask, sir, do you know what we have been summoned here for?" He started conversationally, hoping to maybe glean some information from the general. He had no idea what Washington wished of an infantry general nor a dragoon commander like himself when it was clear that the two of them had been summoned for a joint meeting.

Scott looked up at him with a slight flat look, "Something of import, I would suppose."

Tallmadge frowned a little, taken aback by the acerbic tone and the implication that he should have known not to ask such an inane question. But before he could say anything else, the general waved a hand in the air, more than likely realizing that he had spoken rather rudely.

"Forgive me, Major, but it was not communicated to me the nature of this meeting," the general apologized with a little more sincerity in his tone than before, "and it is something I find rather distressing at times."

"No offense was taken, General," Tallmadge was mollified by the general's words. He decided to take a step forward towards the war room table and saw Scott shift to the side to let him peer at the maps, a clear invitation for him to also study what was placed out in Washington's office.

He took particular note of the map that showed both Long Island and the Connecticut shoreline with Westchester, White Plains, and York Island mapped out to the western edges where the shoreline met the Hudson River. There were other maps that showed both New Jersey and the Hudson Highlands, along with one that looked like it was of the southern theatre, but Tallmadge studied the Long Island one. A slight wistful smile tugged at the corner of his lips as he recognized and remembered the names of the villages and towns he had visited while growing up in Setauket. He could easily imagine the cove and numerous inlets that made up the village, a sleepy little place where he and his brothers spent days fishing along the beaches or playing in the woods. There was a gigantic boulder near his father's church that they loved using as a fort. He still remembered the many times he and his brothers, along with a few others like Brewster and Woodhull, were disciplined for roughhousing and doing dangerous things on and around the gigantic boulder. Tallmadge remembered secretly relishing at Caleb and Abraham's misfortune of being punished more harshly because they were older than he was while he only received a more lenient punishment. He had a good childhood and seeing a map of his boyhood home sent a pang of unexpected nostalgia through him. His childhood home did not deserve to be under the yoke of their British oppressors.

The sound of the door opening brought Tallmadge out of his thoughts. He looked up to see Washington entering, and straightened.

"Sir," he greeted almost at the same time as Scott.

Washington merely nodded at them as he took his tricorn off and set it to the side. He was not alone; Lieutenant Colonel Hamilton and Major Laurens entered behind him. Tallmadge thought he saw the brief passing of French colors by a door deeper into the house followed quickly by Major Tilghman. He could not discern whether the colors belonged to the famed Marquis de Lafayette. He, like the others, had heard of General Lafayette's heroic actions in turning what could have been a route of the American forces into a strategic stalemate on the battlefield at Monmouth Courthouse. The men credited him with decisive action in the wake of General Lee's erratic call for retreat.

Hamilton briefly nodded at them as he hurried to a second desk in the far corner of the room and placed sheaves of paper and letters on the desk, clearly busy with other work. Laurens however, headed over to them and William also entered with a tray bearing General Scott's port.

"Major," Tallmadge greeted Laurens, stepping to the side to allow William to serve Scott.

Task done, Washington's manservant looked to Washington who waved a few fingers as he studied something on his desk. The manservant took it as a sign to leave, closing the door behind him.

"Major Tallmadge, good to see you again," Laurens greeted with a kind smile before turning to Scott. "General Scott, sir, thank you for coming."

Scott merely nodded as he sipped his port. Laurens walked to the war room table and pulled out the detailed map of Long Island, south-western Connecticut, and York Island. He spread it full over the other maps and arranged bits of rock and other tokens to flatten it as Washington came over with a small leather pouch which he poured out onto the table. They were similar to the red and blue tokens that Tallmadge had seen so many times. The most unusual was a silvery token that he instantly recognized as one of General Pulaski's – it was the hooded falcon that had denoted the 2nd Light during the planning of the Battle of Germantown.

Tallmadge noted that in Washington's other hand were a few opened letters that were folded back up and placed on the edges of the map; more than likely reference or scouting reports. He glanced over and saw Hamilton now sitting down at the table, furiously dipping his quill into an inkwell and writing with some urgency. It seemed that whatever Washington had summoned them for, it would not involve the energetic lieutenant colonel.

"Gentlemen, I have called both of you here for the purpose of discussing a singular problem that has been plaguing our army since the beginning of this war," Washington started without preamble or pleasantries. He picked up the silver hooded falcon token and dropped it directly onto York Island itself. "We are as blind to New York as we were when we left two years ago," he declared quietly staring at the map with a frown before looking up at the two of them. "I have called the two of you here for different reasons, but I believe that both of you would be able to come up with a solution to provide the needed intelligence regarding the British and their movements in and around New York."

Washington nodded to General Scott. "I am recalling General Gates from command of the Westchester line and giving command to you, General. Mr. Hamilton is currently writing up the orders that will be sent out soon enough."

"Sir," Scott straightened and nodded once. "I believe a viable solution is to send our scouts deeper into the lines and also to double our patrols."

"Very good," Washington nodded in approval to the plan, but Tallmadge frowned a little as he studied the map.

"Sir, if I may," he spoke up tentative as his eyes roamed the Westchester area. "We could cultivate civilian resources in the area to perhaps help our patrols." He was not sure of Captain Seymour's female acquaintance was a local of the area or perhaps a lady he was sweet on from his home, but it stood to reason that perhaps one or two friendly farmers or those of other professions in the contested area could help prevent ambushes or give them warning of patrols. There was the option of using Patriot 'skinners', the Tory cowboy equivalent, but since they were as ruthless as their counterparts, he had little inclination to enlist their help.

"Civilians?" Scott asked, dubiousness evident in his tone. "You wish to bring civilians into a military enterprise-"

"The area is a no-man's land of contested territory, sir." Tallmadge flicked a look up at Scott before looking back down at the map, and drew his finger across the Westchester region. "Our patrols are able to bring back intelligence and information, but we are not able to make any sort of successful incursion into the entrenched British and Tory forces around here."

"Neither are they if your regiment's reports are correct, Major." Scott pursed his lips. Tallmadge had a moment's confusion as to why Scott would already know of the situation in Westchester after only just getting promoted into Gates' position when he realized that the 2nd Light's reports were more than likely being distributed among all the senior commanders in an effort to plan further attacks.

"You speak true, but having a few of those friendly civilians act as a warning beacon or even just give us basic information on whether or not an enemy patrol has changed its normal routes would give us an advantage, sir," he reasoned. "We would be able to anticipate whether an attack would be coming or perhaps whether they are testing our defenses with new patrol routes and the like."

Scott shook his head a little, "I would suspect that they expect to be paid, Major."

Tallmadge nodded, conceding the general's point.

"And how would we pay them?" Washington spoke up, having not said a word during their slightly heated discussion. Tallmadge was suddenly aware of both his Commander-in-Chief's eyes and Major Laurens' eyes on him. He was also aware that Lieutenant Colonel Hamilton's quill had stopped scratching across the desk.

He chewed on his lower lip as he considered his general's question. His recent reports spoke of the status of payment and the disposition of confiscated goods from Loyalist homes and the like gave a very clear indication that inflation was working against the Continental dollar. British poundage was the norm and sought-after currency for any sort of trade. He had even dug into his own coffers to provide at least some payment for equipment that the men needed. He was tempted to first say British poundage, but the more he thought, the less appealing it became. For one thing, to pay someone with British poundage was a risk considering the shortage and value of the coin. Procurement of poundage would not be easy when Congress were trying to make Continental dollars the norm. Poundage was considered too British and identified many as Tories even though it was worth more.

"The payments would have to be small enough that an enterprising patrol would not see the sudden wealth," he murmured, mostly to himself, but thinking out loud. "But it would mark them as a spy..."

He glanced up as Scott snorted in an ungentlemanly fashion and shook his head. Tallmadge could clearly see that the general had no patience for spies, considering them beneath notice. While he did not blame Scott for such sentiments, as it was not gentleman-like to be engaged in such a fashion, he was not so willing to agree, having engaged in matters that could be considered spying in the last two years. He shook his head again and turned to Washington. "I do not have an answer that would be satisfactory, sir. The risk would be great to pay them in either fashion and we cannot ascertain the veracity of the information without doubling the patrols. And in that case, we may alert the enemy to our presence and change in patrols."

Washington nodded, and Tallmadge thought he caught the

hint of a smile underneath the solemness of his expression, but could not tell. "Very well then." His Commander-in-Chief turned back to Scott. "General, if you would be so kind as to coordinate with Colonel Sheldon and the others to double the patrols and extend our reach down into Mamaroneck and New Rochelle, it would be appreciated. My main concern at the moment is whether or not Admiral Howe's fleet will be moving towards Rhode Island or even to Boston to engage our French allies once more."

"Sir," Scott nodded once.

"Major," Washington turned to him, "please provide General Scott a list of men in the 2nd Light who would be of a friendly character to engaging with the civilians in the area."

"Sir?" Tallmadge was sorely confused and it seemed Scott was too, judging by the expression he wore.

Washington looked at them with a mild gaze. "The men will make inquiries of a discreet nature, polite conversation and the sorts as a part of their patrols. They will be ostensibly military scout, per General Scott's suggestion, but also engage with civilians without actually paying them as spies. However, in the course of their conversation, should they come across one or two that seemed disposed to such an agreement, then they would be entitled to some form of compensation for services rendered if need be."

Tallmadge nodded, "Yes sir." It was very shrewd thinking on his general's part and he realized that Washington did like both ideas, but also understood the risks. He was a little amazed at how sharp Washington's mind was in regards to employing the military forces they already had as military scouts, but also trying to forge contacts with any civilians one might become friendly with in their accustomed patrols. This was a further extension of utilizing resources and Tallmadge was glad that even though he could not come up with a viable solution, his general had taken his idea and turned it into something that worked.

Tallmadge already had a few of his men in mind who were especially personable. But he also knew that for some of the men he would have to couch their orders in a manner that did not give the indication that they were recruiting spies. It was a mindset that was still heavily frowned upon and Davenport's rejection of such an enterprise reminded him that he, Adamson, Lieutenant Edgar, and even Lieutenant Pool were in the minority when it came to spying.

"This solves hopefully at least one issue." Washington tapped the silver token, "But it does not solve our main problem."

Silence descended upon the small group as they studied the map for a moment before Tallmadge opened his mouth with some hesitation. "Sir, we could try another incursion into the tip of Long Island, similar to when Colonel Meigs launched a successful attack on the fish-tail-"

"The what?" Scott interrupted.

"Apologies, sir." Tallmadge realized that Scott and Washington would not have known that the end of the Long Island itself had the nickname of 'the fish-tail.' "This section, it's called 'fish-tail' ostensibly because it looks like one on maps by those who grew up on Long Island. Even though part of the fleet is located at Sag Harbor, the fish-tail section is the best way into Long Island itself-"

"Are you suggesting that we take Long Island, Tallmadge?" Scott's eyebrows rose, "I hope you do remember what happened with Colonel Webb's force when General Parsons tried to launch a far more ambitious attack-"

"Yes, sir." Tallmadge was a little put-off by the sudden rudeness in Scott's voice, as if he were a mere schoolboy. "One of my captains is Colonel Webb's younger brother and I have also been in correspondence with Samuel as he is a good friend of mine."

He frowned, daring Scott to say anything else about the failed raid on Long Island. Scott stared back at him with a flat look and Tallmadge took the opportunity to continue, stabbing a finger at the Hempstead area. "I understand perfectly where the raid failed." He drew a line east towards about where Huntington was, just a little under twenty miles northeast on the coast. "The plan was ambitious, but I know for a fact that this part of Long Island is known for its rockier coast and unexpected squalls and storms. It was what more than likely enabled the British to concentrate their boats and to unfortunately capture Colonel Webb. His previous raid to Setauket, which is here, worked, because there was a wider swath of the Sound to cover. Colonel Meigs' raid worked the best because the British could not, and still cannot patrol that swath of water without encountering our whaleboats or even the French fleet if it is agreeable."

"It is an ambitious plan," Washington cut in before Scott could say anything else. Tallmadge drew back, as he realized he was all but glaring at Scott – a senior officer no less. He forced himself to stand at a more proper attention after his impassioned explanation. "And it is something to consider." Out of the corner of his eyes, he could see Washington directing an unspoken reprimand at him with a look. Tallmadge cleared his throat quietly, chastised.

"Yes sir," he nodded once, acknowledging the reprimand.

"But it is something to be discussed at a later date. Thank you, gentlemen for your advice and counsel regarding this matter. General Scott, I expect you to be at your post by September 15th if everything is agreeable?"

"Sir," Scott nodded again.

"Major Tallmadge," Washington turned to him, "when you have compiled the list, please notify General Scott and also arrange the patrols in the manner that you think would benefit what we have discussed here today. I also wish a copy of the names that you would submit to the general."

"Sir," A very small part of Tallmadge was curious as to whether Washington would say anything about Lieutenant Edgar being a direct agent of his, but his Commander-in-Chief gave no indication that he knew of such a thing and so Tallmadge let the curiosity die. He saluted, sensing the dismissal. He gathered up his helm and departed, nodding to William who had been waiting outside the door.

As he headed to where Castor was hitched, he began to compile a mental list of the officers he had studied and known who would possibly be agreeable to such an endeavor. The only question left was if the patrols could be assured and effective enough. Any slip, any complacency or laxness among the men and the tentative network they were to form would die before it began.

He was also worried about the state of the men of the 2nd Light. The brief action seen a couple of weeks ago by General

Nixon had invigorated the men, but it had not produced anything that lasted. The men had been grumbling their boredom and dissatisfaction at their posts. Tallmadge knew the grumbling would only get louder as Stoddard was due to return any day now, having completed his assignment with apparent satisfaction in Philadelphia. He hoped that perhaps Sheldon would have another assignment for the captain, if only to curb some of the dissatisfaction before it spread across the whole of the 2nd Light. But he also hoped that this new assignment of doubling patrols, would invigorate the men a little more.

It felt like a start, but Tallmadge could not help feeling that something was about to happen; something that made him want to look over his shoulder and into the dark shadows, yet he dared not.

14

September 27th, 1778

September 27ᵗʰ, 1778

The 3ʳᵈ Continental Light Dragoons had been ambushed and massacred two nights ago in Old Tappan, New Jersey.

The news spread quickly through all of the outposts and camps of the 2ⁿᵈ Light. Tallmadge was already riding out to the first of four outposts even before the early sun had dried the morning dew. He could hear Blackden following behind him, then ride off opposite the direction he was going, to check in on the outpost in Eastchester while he checked on the one in Westchester. The original six outposts had been combined into two larger outposts, strung out like a clothes line, with the extension and doubling of patrols. It afforded a more vigilant opportunity to observe the enemy and interact with the local populace who were braving the no-man's land that Westchester and surrounding areas had become.

He and Blackden were riding out not only to check on the condition of the outposts, but also as a preventative measure, to reassure the men that all was still well. Meanwhile, Colonel Sheldon was in meetings with General Scott and the other officers stationed at the Westchester front, discussing to either take further measures or to distribute resources and men to make up for the loss of a whole dragoon regiment.

The 3ʳᵈ Light had been at a strength of a little over a hundred enlisted men and twelve officers. Though there were conflicting reports of casualty counts, Tallmadge had heard that it was perhaps fifteen or twenty dragoons killed, and a staggering fifty-four more wounded and captured. Colonel Baylor was one of those wounded and captured. The rest had fled across the Hudson and only arrived just yesterday with the frightening report. The 3rd Light had been posted on the New Jersey side, in a similar manner to the 2nd Light, and that worried Tallmadge the most.

Tallmadge choked a little on the bile threatening to rise up in him and swallowed it back down as he forced himself to concentrate on the road, riding with haste to the outpost. It was not fear that roiled of his stomach, but rather a dizzying combination of terrible admiration and worry. The reports from the survivors had said that the enemy had not fired a single musket shot, but rather had gone from house to house with a terrifying silent efficiency, like wraiths of the night, stabbing each man dead with bayonets. General Grey had been credited with the massacre and, in Tallmadge's mind, this cemented Grey's reputation for using brutal tactics, just as he had employed against those who fought at Paoli last year.

He could only imagine the horror if such tactics were used against the 2nd Light. He knew the men had to be reassured as well as disciplined to not let such wild stories spread, even if they were true. It was also one of the reasons why he and Blackden had been ordered to check on the outposts as soon as they received the news. Blackden had been explicitly sent to the Eastchester area. Stoddard and his men were stationed there with the troops of Shethar and Bull and since Blackden both knew Stoddard and grew up with him in the same town, he would hopefully be able to head off the biggest agitator in their regiment. Blackden hoped to appeal to Stoddard as a friend instead of as a senior officer, asking him not to spread more rumors than was necessary and demoralize the men. They could certainly order it, but Tallmadge had cautioned Sheldon that perhaps what the men needed at this moment was not only the discipline they had been drilled with, but also an understanding that the leaders of the regiment knew what needed to be done to calm everyone's fears.

And it was a lie that Tallmadge easily swallowed. During the brief meeting between himself, Blackden, Sheldon, with Adjutant Hoogland dutifully taking notes, Sheldon had seemed distracted, and unsure – more than Tallmadge had ever seen his commander. He and Blackden had prompted him a few times during the meeting, but had also finished his sentences and commands to at least come up with a tentative plan before riding out. Hoogland had not said anything in response to Tallmadge's inquiring gaze as they left, and so he left it at that. Perhaps there was something more that came down from General Scott or even General Washington that affected Sheldon, and he wished to be quiet about it before presenting it to them. At least he hoped that was the case – it made Tallmadge a little frustrated at the lack of command and presence from Sheldon.

As he rode into the large encampment he waved a greeting to the guards on duty, pleased that they were all alert and looking around. There had also been a rumor, but no report that Tallmadge could find – even with Hoogland's help – that a colonel of another regiment had found one of the 2nd Light's patrols unfit for duty a few days ago. Supposedly, they had been caught sleeping at their posts and had not paid much attention to movements on the road. He was glad to see that was not the case with these guards. He slowed his horse as he found the house that was the command post of the three troops stationed at Westchester.

"Major!" Adamson hailed him as he approached, having taken up the temporary duties of Lieutenant Pool who had abruptly resigned a little over two weeks ago.

Pool's resignation had been a shock to Tallmadge, having thought the man who had quickly earned his trust had found the opportunity to be part of what he and General Scott were planning to be worth his while. But it seemed that the man's ardor for such clandestine activities had either waned or something had changed his mind. Tallmadge had been forwarded his resignation from Belden, who appended his letter to him with some surprise and sadness; apologizing for recommending his character, to him when clearly he had not deserved such trust.

"Adamson," he greeted as he dismounted Castor and tied him to the hitching post. He could see the curious, but slightly worried of the men in the small camp. The news had already spread and he could tell the men were hoping for any sort of news that would soothe whatever fears and concern they had.

"Sir, is there-"

"Let's head in," he gestured for Adamson to precede him. "Belden and the others around?"

"Aye," Adamson replied as he opened the door and headed in. He gestured to his right. "I'll fetch them for you. Captain Belden is in his office, to your right."

"Thank you," Tallmadge replied, as he took his helm off and headed into Belden's office. It had been a lavish and large dining room, now converted into an office. He knocked on the door as he entered, but the two men had already risen – more than likely having heard his voice outside.

"Major, is there news-"

Tallmadge held up a hand to stop Belden's question as he gestured towards the upstairs. "I would prefer to wait until the others are here so not to repeat myself-"

"Of course, of course," Belden smiled, but there was some nervousness to in it. "Would you like something to drink, sir?"

"Yes please." He did not realize how parched his own throat was until Belden mentioned it. Wadsworth quickly moved to another small table and poured a glass of something that looked like Madeira. He accepted the glass and glanced to what Belden had been studying. It looked like roster sheets. "How are the doubling of patrols?" he asked as he heard some thumping upstairs. It was quickly followed by someone running down the stairs and out the door – more than likely Adamson to fetch either Webb or Seymour.

"It's been moderately effective, but it seems that the British forces have been reacting to our doubling of patrols now with their own. They have not raided as deeply as before, but I don't think that it will make a difference any time soon, sir," Belden frowned. "As for the other matter, Lieutenant Edgar has reported some success in the sections near our encampment, but Sergeant-Major Adamson and Sergeant Davenport have reported that people in the area have not responded well to the doubling of patrols along the coastal villages of Mamaroneck and New Rochelle."

"Might be a hub for the London Trade," Tallmadge frowned, as he walked a few steps over to study a map of the Westchester region. He was mildly surprised at the mention of Davenport's name, having thought that his friend wanted nothing to do with such clandestine ventures, but perhaps he had been wrong – or Davenport, given his sense of duty, had convinced himself that this was not a spying, but rather a military venture. Either way, Tallmadge was glad to hear that his friend had taken up the assignment with some aplomb.

The noise and thumping got louder as multiple footsteps came down the stairs and the door to Belden's office opened to reveal both Webb and Edgar. Both looked a little sleep-addled, but saluted him as they stepped into the room. He nodded at their gesture before Webb headed straight to the decanter and poured himself a rather large quantity of drink, while Edgar only poured himself a small amount.

"De Valcour's on patrol, sir." Webb gulped down his drink. "He's not to return for another couple of hours, I would think."

"Then please convey to him what is to be said," Tallmadge nodded as the door opened and Seymour appeared, some hay sticking out of his hair that was hastily plucked out by Adamson. He nodded once and was about to leave, seeing that all officers available were assembled, before Tallmadge gestured for him to stay.

"Sir?"

"You may help convey this to the men, Adamson," he said. Adamson nodded reluctantly and stayed, closing the door behind him. Tallmadge cleared his throat and clasped his hands behind him as he stood by Belden's war table. "I am sure you have all heard of what has befallen our comrades in the 3rd Light. The current facts we have are that there were fifteen to twenty men killed and at least fifty-four wounded and captured."

He paused for a moment to let the facts and numbers sink into his officers. They wore a variation of expressions, ranging from shock to stony looks of anger. But he could tell that underneath their expressions, they were all grateful for the confirmation of numbers and clarification of facts that he was presenting to them. It was simple efficiency that dictated his way of telling them things. There was no need to insert any more speculation than was necessary in his opinion.

"Colonel Baylor is a prisoner of the enemy and Major Clough has been killed. There are rumors of two officers that had been housed with the colonel either captured or killed, but we have not received any information regarding that," he said and could see Seymour chewing nervously on his lower lip. Of all of the captains of the regiment, Seymour and Bull were the most likely to have had correspondences with the other officers of the regiment. They had both served on extended detached duties far longer than any of the other captains and thus had contact and worked with the other dragoons.

"General Charles Grey has claimed credit for leading this despicable attack," he continued. "From the reports, it seems that the general directed his men to attack the 3rd Light while they slept and attacked with only bayonets." Angry frowns appeared on the men's faces. Some crossed their arms while Webb muttered something too soft for Tallmadge to hear, but he thought the young man said 'coward.'

"Our current orders are as stands," he met each one of their gazes. "We will continue the patrol routes laid out, but Colonel Sheldon has requested that we have nightly ones too to counter any possible attack that may come from General Delancey's Tories or even the Queen's Rangers."

"The colonel thought of that?" Webb muttered and Tallmadge stared at him, wondering why he would make such a comment. Webb was roughly elbowed by Seymour who stood next to him. "What?" the younger man grumbled, but shook his head and fell silent.

"I am sure it was suggested to him under your advisement, right Major?" Seymour spoke up, and Tallmadge frowned, wondering what the captain was implying.

"Yes..." He shot a quick look at the others gathered, but they only shifted their feet a little and did not provide any sort of answer. Even Adamson shrugged as if he did not know what was implied. "Captain Seymour, is there something you wish to add?"

"No, nothing sir," Seymour shook his head. "I just wished to make sure the facts are facts instead of the rumors we have been hearing."

Tallmadge was puzzled, but decided to let the comment go as he continued. "Please convey this to the men. I am sure that we will have further orders in the next few days as General Washington determines the course the dragoons may take in retaliation to what has happened to our comrades. But for now, we will continue our regular duties."

The hint of potential future revenge was always a good thing for the men, and he saw their angry frowns give way more agreeable nods and tight smiles. Even though as a regiment, the 2nd Light was fiercely proud of their accomplishments and duties, they also had a bond like no other infantry or artillery regiment – they were all horsemen, picked to join one of four regiments in the Continental Army and thus were united in fraternity.

"You are dismissed," he said and his officers all nodded, saluting him before heading out, or in the case of Edgar and Webb, more than likely heading back upstairs to sleep. He caught a glimpse of Seymour following Webb, their heads together in quiet conversation. He could briefly make out an angry, almost defiant expression on Webb's face. Tallmadge wondered what sort of mood had overtaken the young promising captain in recent months; his disposition had soured and sometimes was almost insubordinate. Tallmadge's own letters from Webb's brother, Samuel who was still a paroled prisoner, indicated no distress on Samuel's part; he had been treated with respect and kindness befitting his rank and command. Still, perhaps the younger Webb was feeling the strain of a family member being held prisoner. Tallmadge thought that he should talk to Webb and counsel him on anything that may be wrong, but it was something he could do later.

Turning his attention elsewhere, he was more puzzled to see the tail end of a gesture by Edgar towards Adamson before the two disappeared from his view, Edgar's footsteps echoing up the stairs. "Belden," he turned and stopped the captain of 1st Troop from sitting back down at his desk.

"Sir?"

"Are the men all right?" he asked, gesturing towards the door where the others left.

"Sir?" Belden looked confused. "I believe that they were worried when we received the news regarding the 3rd Light-"

"No, not that," he shook his head. "Was there anything said or done recently, maybe a patrol that encountered more soldiers than anticipated or perhaps one of the men had been wounded-"

"Oh," Belden's face turned up in a slight grimace. "Well, nothing but the usual, sir."

"The usual," Tallmadge stated flatly.

Belden nodded once. "The usual...with a certain captain returning and his...zeal...of sorts..."

Tallmadge refused the urge to pinch the bridge of his nose. "There have been no duels..." He meant the statement as a question and saw his captain shake his head a negative.

"Lieutenant de Valcour has also given Captain Stoddard a wide berth," Belden reassured him. "We hold your wishes in the highest regard, sir," he said, "and understand the consequences."

"And nothing else of import has happened?" he asked. While he was proud that the men upheld his order not to participate in any duels while he was with the 2nd Light and if they wished to, to resign or be transferred elsewhere – he could not help but think that Belden was hiding something. Whatever he was hiding, Tallmadge was sure it was not directed at him; but they mystery of whom it was directed at bothered him.

"No, sir," Belden shook his head again, "though some of the men are disappointed at the fact that we will not be getting any new horses."

"General Washington's directive was to take steps to correct the abuse of the horses. The patrols must be conducted in a manner that saves both horse and man and cannot be gallivanting across Westchester." Tallmadge had not been too happy to forward such a reply, but he understood where his Commander-in-Chief was coming from. It was the same problem that plagued the initial meeting that he had with General Scott and General Washington regarding the potential of cultivating contacts. They currently did not have the money to authorize the purchase of remounts for the men and the horses lamed in recent weeks of constant patrols would have to be spared usage until they could be rehabilitated for future use. "I cannot go against it, Belden."

"I understand, sir," Belden nodded, as he took the paper he had been writing on. "Would you like to amend any of the patrols, sir?"

"No, I will leave that to your discretion." Tallmadge was reassured by his calm confidence that Belden had the whole thing in hand and glanced at Wadsworth, who was already back at work at his desk. His task was done and he felt better now that his officers had been reassured. "Please inform Colonel Sheldon or myself if the situation changes, especially overnight."

"I will sir," Belden replied. "And thank you sir, for coming out here and letting us know of the situation."

"Be vigilant, Captain. The British may think we are vulnerable now that the 3rd Light is but a shell of itself," he cautioned, as he opened the door and headed out. He would be damned if his own regiment was caught in such an ambush, like Baylor's men. As he sent a silent prayer up to the dead and wounded men, he could not help but worry about the comments said by Webb and Seymour. It troubled him, but what exactly their comments portend, he did not know.

October 7th, 1778

The reassurance he gave to the men after they learned the fate of the 3rd Light was shattered a little over a week later. Night had long fallen by the time Tallmadge arrived at Washington's main encampment in White Plains. He knew the general would not be pleased by such a late summons, but he had spent the whole day scouring the Westchester countryside for the raiding party that killed nine of his men and eleven horses. It had been a patrol led by one of the lieutenants and when word reached Colonel Sheldon's outpost at Bedford a few miles northeast, Tallmadge was leading a secondary patrol with Stoddard. He had been trying to discern whether or not Stoddard was the cause of the recent unease he felt after Webb and Seymour's uncharacteristic behaviors just a week and a half ago.

His attempt had proven inconclusive, and soon they were hailed by Hoogland acting as an express rider from Sheldon with the news of the ambushed patrol. Tallmadge had immediately reacted, and Stoddard responded with typical zeal, and the two of them along with the men who were with them had set out to find the interlopers. They scoured the area in which the attack had taken place, and sent alerts out to the two outposts for any sign of the attackers, but by the time night fell, they had not found the British patrol that had ambushed the men.

Tallmadge and the others returned to the encampment, disappointed, and still angry that such carelessness could have happened to one of their own. Blackden told Tallmadge that he intended to look into why the patrol had been ambushed in broad daylight in such a fashion. Hoogland, who had remained at camp after delivering the express message, then informed him that General Washington had requested his presence while he had been out. So after a hasty dinner, he rode out from Bedford once more, down to White Plains to answer the summons. He knew any other officer would have sent apologies and arrived the next day, but Tallmadge did not want to abide by such complacency and formality. He he hoped it would not reflect ill on him to answer the summons at such a late hour.

He arrived at the Miller house once more and dismounted, tying Castor up before heading to the door. The two lifeguards outside the door stared at him as he knocked and he removed his helm as he heard the door being unlocked. William's coal black face peered out, mildly surprised to see him at this hour.

"My apologies for disturbing the general at this late hour, but if you could tell him that Major Tallmadge is reporting as requested," he said, wondering if William remembered him.

"I will, sir, please wait." The door shut once more as William did as he asked. He did not have to wait long as the door opened again, this time with a gesture from Washington's manservant to proceed in. "It's good to see you again, Major. Will you be needing anything to drink?"

"Any port would do, thank you, William." He could see the hint of a smile on the Negro's face at the mention of his name, and he handed his helm and cloak over to him.

"Very good, sir." William left, taking his cloak and helm with him as Tallmadge proceeded into the war room where Washington was sitting at his desk. There was no one else in the room and Tallmadge assumed that Lieutenant Colonel Hamilton, Major Laurens and Tilghman were elsewhere, or perhaps asleep.

"Sir," he greeted with a crisp salute, and Washington looked up to give him a small nod of acknowledgment.

"Major, the lateness of the hours does you credit." Though the statement sounded like praise, Tallmadge could hear the slight disapproval in his Commander-in-Chief's voice.

"I apologize, sir." He held himself at attention. "Nine of my men were ambushed and killed this morning while on patrol and we spent the day looking for the enemy forces that committed such a heinous act."

"And what did you find, Major?" Washington asked.

"It was not a prelude to any sort of attack, sir." His continued correspondences with his general since the previous year had given him some insight into what his commander wanted, and he had his answer ready. If he had not had such insight into Washington's needs, he would have answered that they did not find the patrol. In this case, he knew that with this latest attack coming so soon after the ambush of the 3rd Light, it was an effort to either draw out Washington to attack or commit his forces in a place of the British's choosing. "We were not fortunate enough to come across the British force that attacked my men."

"Would there have been a breach in the ranks to have such a thing happen?" Washington asked and Tallmadge knew he was asking about his and General Scott's recent initiative to cultivate contacts in the region.

"It is still too soon to know, but it may be a possibility." He acknowledged the wisdom in Washington's words. "I will ask Lieutenant Edgar to look into it."

If he hoped to draw a reaction out of Washington, Tallmadge was disappointed; he saw no hint of acknowledgment of the fact that he knew Lieutenant Edgar was one of General Washington's personal spies. Instead, Washington folded his hands together and sat back a little. "Major, I have called you here, because of your comments during our last meeting."

"Sir-" Tallmadge was alarmed that his comments had been contemplated for such a long time. He stopped when his Commander-in-Chief held up a hand for silence.

"You graduated Yale, did you not, Major?"

"Yes sir, class of seventy-three, sir." He was a little confused by this new line of questioning. "I spent three years teaching at Wethersfield before answering the martial duty that we were given as God's children on this green earth, sir."

"With General Wadsworth's brigade, if I remember correctly?" Washington asked, not looking at him, but instead, shuffling a few papers around, as if he were looking for something.

"Yes sir, Colonel John Chester of the 6th Connecticut Battalion," he replied.

"Based on what you were saying in regards to Long Island, I take it you were not born in Connecticut?"

"No sir." Tallmadge could feel his confusion growing, but he did not sense any type of deception nor anger in his commander's voice, and so answered in kind. "Setauket, Long Island."

"Ah," it seemed Washington had found what he was looking for. He pulled out a single piece of paper and set it down in front of him. From his vantage point, Tallmadge could only make out the scribbles of notes jotted down, but could not read what was written. "Yes, Setauket, on the Sound side..."

"...Sir?" he asked, but received only a mild look in return.

"Your friend, the late Captain Hale, had nothing but praise for you when I interviewed him just a little over two years ago," Washington started, and Tallmadge felt his breath catch in his throat at the mention of his dearly departed friend.

"S-Sir-" he barely whispered, a sudden unexpected lump forming in his throat as he realized that everything Nathan had said about being chosen by Washington himself to undertake his mission had been true. Tallmadge had believed his friend when he said those words, but he had not truly *believed* until now.

"He said that his friend, a Lieutenant Tallmadge, had been the one to call him to action, to join when at the time he could not and fight for the cause because of his obligations. Though the interview was brief, his character was sound and he was of a disposition that I could not deny him the opportunity." Washington stared at him, his eyes holding his own with an intensity that Tallmadge had not thought him capable of. "Captain Hale mentioned that this same lieutenant had also apparently talked of his childhood home on Long Island, describing the roads and village to him, but rather on the chance for him to visit during times of peace.

"This lieutenant, who became a captain, was also a man of integrity, who refused to denigrate or spread rumors about his friend's death when he had been notified. One might have even said it was cold, that he did not care, but there was a measured care in the lack of words. That care was spoken in action, in a willingness to honor his friend's memory by undertaking what many consider to be deplorable and dishonorable. But he kept his counsel and silence, and thus was tested when a Major John Clark was sent to enlist his aid in exploring opportunities to seek out intelligence against the enemy.

"This was also a man, who then became a Major, who clearly rose to the challenges of command, rallying his men not to fight each other in meaningless duels, but to instead, fight the enemy. To be the vanguard and spearhead of a hooded bird of prey, a falconing bird, to rally the men and drive the enemy back." Washington's voice was warm with pride. "And this was a man who has continuously executed his duties with resources much more limited than I have wished for him. Who harassed the enemy, but understood the value of discretion and of few words. Who is decided, energetic, and who speaks always to purpose and never to flatter."

Tallmadge could only stand there, stunned by what was coming out of Washington's mouth. He had been watched and observed by his Commander-in-Chief for *that* long? That each assignment, each missive or command that had come to him until his very moment had been a test of sorts? Or perhaps not even a test as he did not know what to call it anymore. He opened his mouth a little, but closed it again. He did not know what to say.

"This was a man who caught my eye the first time he was mentioned to have gone back for his *horse*, his horse of all things, when we evacuated Brooklyn, and who returned with a measure of actionable intelligence," Washington finished and inclined his head at him. "Major Benjamin Tallmadge of Setauket, Long Island."

"S-Sir..."

The knock at the door saved Tallmadge from saying anything. It opened to reveal William holding a small glass of port that he had requested. The negro stepped in and handed him the glass, but Tallmadge quickly set it down, his hands shaking in sheer incredulity and nervousness. William left just as quickly as he entered, closing the door behind him. Tallmadge shot a quick glance at the glass of port, his throat suddenly parched as he swallowed again.

"S-Sir...I...I...don't know what-"

"I learned my mistake in sending Captain Hale out woefully unprepared on his mission and vowed to not do the same in the future," Washington interrupted him with a gentle look on his face. "And so I have given it much thought since our last meeting, Major." He gestured towards the war table. "Though the idea of using our men as scouts is an assured resource, along with the idea of using civilians as beacons and information sources, it is only a temporary measure. I wish to establish a more permanent venture in New York."

Tallmadge shot a quick look at the war table, noting that the silvery hooded-falcon that had been placed on York Island was still there, standing tall and proud, the only token on the map. He had originally thought that Washington having the token was pure coincidence, but knowing what he knew now, he wondered if it had been intentional on his general's part. Considering how shrewd he now knew Washington could be, he would not put it past the general to have taken the object as a calculation of sorts.

"Permanent venture?" he asked and received a nod of confirmation from Washington.

"New York has always been closed to us," he started, "and now with Philadelphia back in our possession and our new allies openly supporting us, it is imperative that we are able to anticipate the enemy's movements."

"We will have to employ civilians as spies, sir." Tallmadge forced himself to move past what Washington had said about him, and instead focused his thoughts on this new puzzle laid out before him. "Though like you had said, compensation may be an issue." He absently rubbed his chin as he looked to the side and thought. "If they are openly paid, then the money can be traced so it would put them at risk. But they will need some form of compensation whether it is any expenses occurred or otherwise." He quickly thought back to Nathan's death and what had precipitated it. "They will have to be native to the area, sir..."

And with that thought, he realized why Washington had chosen him, and he saw him nod in affirmation to his unspoken realization. Since he had grown up in Setauket, he would know the area the best. It was why he had been chosen as Major Clark's contact over a year and a half ago when the major was trying to gather intelligence on Long Island. And with that, he also knew whom he was going to ask to possibly spy on the enemy. A small smile spread across his face as he looked back at General Washington. "Sir, I will need permission to leave the regiment on detached duty to Fairfield. There is a person there who may help me get in contact with a man I know who would be agreeable to helping us."

"Who is this man?" Washington asked and Tallmadge winced.

"I'd rather not say at this moment, sir, in case he is not agreeable to my persuasions." He shook his head, hoping that his Commander-in-Chief was not disappointed. To his mild surprise, Washington smiled at his answer.

"A very wise answer, and one to keep note of, Major," the general said as he drew out a blank piece of paper and started to write his orders. "While you search out your man, I will be creating an alias for our hopefully new agent. This is one of the lessons I have learned since the death of Captain Hale."

"Sir," Tallmadge nodded once, watching as Washington finished writing the quick orders and dried the ink before folding them up and sealing them. After he had finished writing the address, he handed the paper over to him.

"Report directly back to me when you've established your man on Long Island and have explained what needs to be done," Washington said and Tallmadge nodded, pocketing the orders that were addressed to Colonel Sheldon. He knew that Sheldon would not be too happy, but it was an order that would not be countermanded, especially since it came directly from Washington.

"Sir," he saluted.

October 10th, 1778

Tallmadge was relieved to see numerous whaling boats along the docks as he rode into Fairfield, Connecticut, roughly a year and a half since he had been there last. There was hope that Caleb Brewster had not gone off on another privateering venture and was still in town. Though his letters to Brewster had been few and far between since their last meeting, it had been nice to hear of his childhood home on occasion. He dared not write and send a letter ahead about his arrival, knowing that absolute secrecy was key in this tentative venture he was undertaking.

He stopped by Whitehall's Tavern and hitched Castor to the post, setting his helm on the saddle horn. He pulled his cloak closer to him at the cold sea breeze blowing in from the nearby docks. It seemed much colder here than in Westchester, though it was typical of the Sound's unpredictable weather patterns that sent gusts of mid autumnal wind into the seaport town. Stepping into the tavern, he noted few soldiers, and he wondered if General Silliman's 4th Brigade was still stationed here. He knew Silliman kept his home in Fairfield and had served with Gates in the Burgoyne campaign last year, but he did not know where the 4th had been posted after Gates and his army rejoined the main army.

Still, the tavern was crowded for this time of day and he moved past bodies that smelled of sea and salt to reach the bar. He signaled for a glass of ale and it was promptly given to him. "Sir, I'm looking for one Caleb Brewster," he asked the owner as he served him. "Is he still in port?"

"Aye," the owner nodded with a toothy smile on his face, as he discerned he was not a Tory or a British from the flash of blue and buff facings on his uniform under his cloak. "The lieutenant's probably drinking some of his men under the table over there. They just came back with a recent successful haul."

"Explains why it's so crowded in here," Tallmadge commented and the tavern owner just laughed before accepting his coin for the ale. Tallmadge took the glass and started to push through the crowds of rowdy sailors and women who were carousing with them. A few had started singing bawdy sea shanties that would make anyone in polite company blush. Tallmadge only smiled at their good fortune, and also the fact that it was a pretty jaunty tune, he had to admit.

It took him a good ten minutes moving about the tavern before he heard Brewster's boisterous voice over the din.

Seconds later, the crowd parted enough for him to see his friend's familiar bushy beard and wide smile as he successfully out-drank another one of his comrades. The poor sod of a man collapsed and was promptly hauled away by two of his compatriots as Tallmadge pushed himself through, catching Brewster's eye.

"Well, well! Look at the Tall-boy!" Brewster crowed and stood up, swaying just bit to the laughter of those around him. He took it with some good grace and staggered over before engulfing Tallmadge in a rather crushing hug.

"Caleb," he greeted, spilling a little of his ale as Caleb pounded him hard on his back. Two other men had already taken his chair and the other formerly occupied by the fallen drunkard and were continuing the festivities.

"So, what brings you here, Benny-boy?" Brewster threw a sloppy arm around his neck as they walked away for a bit more peace and quiet.

"Was wondering if you are able to bring me over to the home?" he asked. He kept his voice moderately low, but loud enough for his friend to hear over the bawdy shanty about the jacks themselves that was now taken up in roaring force by a majority of those in the tavern. The tune suddenly changed into a version of 'Spanish Ladies' that was definitely not for delicate souls.

"Home, eh?" Brewster nodded once. "This way of speaking..."

"Caleb-"

"I know, I know," Brewster waved an absent hand as he turned his head this way and that, before making a grab for the ale in Tallmadge's hand. "Can I-"

Tallmadge sighed as he relinquished his ale to Brewster. "Yes." He had rather liked the sour taste, but if it would help Brewster settle down and talk with him, he'd rather part with it. To his surprise, the whaler did none of that and instead led him to a table in the corner occupied by those who had already fallen asleep from the festivities. He placed the untouched ale in the middle of the table with an aplomb that told Tallmadge Brewster was definitely not as drunk as he initially seemed.

"So where's the kidlet?" was the next question out of Brewster's mouth.

"Kid-oh, Adamson." He had forgotten that Brewster had taken a shine to Adamson seemingly wanting to adopt him and teach him the ways of the sea, much to Adamson's chagrin. "On patrol duty at camp."

"Would have thought he'd come with you," Brewster grinned, curling his thick fingers around the mug of ale, but he did not sip it. "He was definitely a burr to your side, Tall-boy; can't find loyalty like that in a lot of people."

"I'll tell him that you send your regards and offer," Tallmadge replied and Brewster laughed, pleased with his humorous comment.

"Knowing the kidlet, he'd probably find some creative way of impaling me on a fishing harpoon for that," his friend smiled widely. "Kid's got a mouth and an imagination that's a mite frightening, Tall-boy, when he wants to plan a revenge or something. Sending him over on that boat was rather interesting."

"Really?" It was something that Tallmadge never knew about his friend and was surprised to find out.

"Aye," Brewster nodded. "God help anyone who decides to betray the Patriot cause in front of him." He shook his head a little, fingers still curled around the mug of ale. "So, nostalgic for home again, Tall-boy?"

"Wanted to meet another one of our old friends," he answered in a vague manner and saw Brewster frown.

"Then you didn't hear yet, though I suppose none of the gazettes publish it since it's barely worth a mention. But, I tend to hear it since it involves my detached duties here," Brewster finally took a sip of the ale and squint into the mug. "Aw, shite Tall-boy, you got that other piss."

"Caleb-"

"Never mind," Brewster took another sip and looked at him. "Woody's got himself arrested. Jailed right here in Fairfield for illegal services on the London Trade."

"What," Tallmadge stated flatly.

"One of the sloops we actually have patrolling the Sound caught him a week ago, plying his harvest with known British traders in Norwalk. It was just the basic, corn, wheat, potatoes, you know, but he was caught," Brewster shrugged, "and sent up here. I've been trying to plead with General Silliman and the local authorities that he's a Patriot just trying to make some money, but they're not listening."

"Well...shite," Tallmadge cursed under his breath, as he rubbed his eyebrow and shook his head. Stoddard and his men had been sent on foraging trips since late August in an effort to curb the man's toxic zeal, and Norwalk was one of the towns where he had been sent to requisition supplies or feed for the horses. Everyone knew that it was a hub for the London Trade, but also controlled by Patriot forces at the moment. It seemed that Abraham Woodhull was caught up in a net cast by zealous Patriot forces that wished to punish those who traded with the British instead of the Patriots.

He rubbed his eyebrow again as he considered his options. Caleb had confirmed that General Silliman was more than likely in town, but he did not want to go through Silliman to possibly free Woodhull, since Washington had made it explicit that this be a secret venture. He knew Caleb would keep quiet, having discerned his intentions without him outright stating it, as well as having assisted him and Major Clark last year. Going through General Silliman meant that freeing Woodhull would be noted on Silliman's record, subjected to perusal by Congress and the Board of War. No, this had to be kept quiet.

Another thought occurred to him and he sat up a little as he pondered it. It would be asking a rather large favor from one of his friends at the Commissary Department, but if it was achievable, Woodhull's release would still be on permanent record, but a civilian one instead – and utterly benign as a result. He reached over and plucked the mug of ale from Brewster's fingers, ignoring his yelp of protest as he downed a mouthful and set the mug back down. He stood up, intent on heading out.

"Where are you going now, Tall-boy?" Brewster asked.

"Wethersfield," he called back before he pushed his way through the crowd and back outside. He hoped his friend would not mind him stopping by unannounced for an introduction to Governor Jonathan Trumbull of Connecticut, whom he would ask to pardon Abraham Woodhull.

October 13ᵗʰ, 1778

Three days later Tallmadge found himself riding back to Fairfield, Abraham Woodhull's pardon secure upon his person. Jeremiah Wadsworth had been overjoyed to see him, and had not asked a single question as to why he wished to be introduced to Governor Trumbull. Tallmadge suspected that Wadsworth and Deane, whom he had met at the initial party hosted by General Wadsworth at the Webb house were also deft at the craft of espionage.

Now, as Tallmadge arrived back in Fairfield, he could still see Brewster's whaleboats docked, but there was far more activity on them which meant his friend would soon embark on another raid. A few of the sailors absently waved as he rode by towards the town's local jail, and he waved back. He vaguely recognized a few of them from his last time on one of their boats crossing the Sound, but also from seeing them at the tavern. He supposed the men were curious as to how their captain and leader was familiar with a cavalry officer such as himself. Tallmadge trusted Brewster to be discreet, but it seemed that given the friendly greeting, he had been accepted by Brewster's whalemen.

"Tallmadge, is that you?" A familiar voice brought him out of his thoughts as he pulled his horse up short to see General Silliman exiting the local general store with an adjutant carrying several packages and sacks. Silliman waved a hand for the adjutant to continue on as he walked over.

"General Silliman, sir!" Tallmadge greeted with a quick salute as he dismounted and shook the general's hand.

"Major, good to see you." Silliman looked a little older and perhaps more worn by his time on the front lines, but he seemed well. "What brings you here to Fairfield?"

"One of my friends was caught on the London Trade, so I asked for a pardon from Governor Trumbull, sir." Tallmadge decided to hedge a little on the truth.

"Trumbull? You need not have gone all the way up to Hartford, son," the man shook his head. "I could have helped. The 4ᵗʰ is currently stationed here to watch for any incursions along the Sound."

"I know, sir, but this was a civilian matter, not one for the military and so I did not want to bend such regulations in a manner that would have benefited myself," he shrugged, and saw his friend shake his head, a smile on his face.

"It is honorable of you to think in such a manner, but the next time it happens, please, do not hesitate to call upon me to help you." Silliman patted him on the arm, "It would not be an inconvenience to myself, nor would it be going outside regulations. Your friend was on the Trade?"

"It seems so, sir." He had hoped Silliman would not ask about Woodhull, but it seemed that the man was curious enough, and so Tallmadge indulged him. "From Long Island, sir. I have yet to ask him why he would consider the British a better trading partner, but I suppose that with the occupation of the area..."

"Aye," the general nodded sagely. "I would think you heard about Colonel Webb?"

"Yes," Tallmadge shook his head, "it was a pity that the plan was ambitious enough, yet the unpredictable weather patterns caught him in such a manner."

"Has his brother been doing well?" Silliman asked and Tallmadge thought it an odd question, but nodded.

"As far as I know, but it seems that there has been some strain on Captain Webb lately. I was thinking of asking Colonel Sheldon if he could be given leave to visit his brother to perhaps reassure him of his good health and treatment." Tallmadge had been wondering if Webb's recent comments and perhaps his sickness back in July had been a result of the strain of having his older brother as a prisoner of war. While they had been moderately assured that all officers were treated with respect, he knew that the latest report of the massacre of the 3rd Light had not cast the British capture of prisoners in a good light. Between what Rawdon had done while they picketed last in December and what Grey had done to the 3rd Light, it stood that Captain Webb had every right to be worried about the state of his beloved older brother.

"It would be a good plan, Tallmadge," Silliman agreed, and it reassured Tallmadge that the idea was a solid one. He saw Silliman look towards the docks and shake his head. "It's about time the jacks get on with their activities."

"Have they been causing trouble, sir? I know their leader and can speak to Lieutenant Brewster on your behalf if you wish." He was a little concerned, but Silliman only shook his head, a wistful smile on his face.

"No, they tend to make a bit of a ruckus whenever they arrive, but they are respectful of the area. Many of the sailors I know having lived here, so we have an agreement of sorts." Silliman shook his head before gesturing in the opposite direction than he was headed in. "After you are finished with freeing your friend, would you care to dine with myself and my wife tonight before you are to return to camp?"

"If it will not be too much trouble, sir." Tallmadge could not help but leap at the opportunity to not only catch up with an old friend, a person he considered a mentor of sorts, but also for another home-cooked meal that he knew he would miss for a long time. "I do not wish to impose upon your generous hospitality."

"Nonsense," Silliman smiled, before he bent over a little and whispered loudly. "I will tell you all about Gates and the brave charge he effected at Saratoga."

"Or lack thereof." Tallmadge could hear the derision in Silliman's mock whisper and saw the general's face crinkle further in delight before he pulled back. He had guessed correctly that like many of the others who had served at Saratoga, like Colonel Morgan, and Captain Seymour, Silliman was one of the generals who disliked the fact that Gates had received credit for winning the battle. "I'd be happy to join you tonight. Thank you for your invitation, sir."

"Then I shall make my farewells and see you later." The older man tipped his tricorn at him and Tallmadge did the same with his helm before mounting Castor again and starting off to the jail.

He arrived in short order, dismounting again before tying Castor up and knocking on the door. It opened to reveal the warden, a craggy old man with yellowing teeth and a weathered face. "I have a pardon here from Governor Trumbull for the prisoner, Abraham Woodhull," he said, handing the sealed paper over, which the warden broke open and quickly read before handing it back to him without even an acknowledgment. The man silently pulled the door open further and gestured for him to come in.

Tallmadge stepped into the jail, wrinkling his nose at the stench that wafted around the enclosed area. It smelled sour and dank, with the faint odor of excretions and unwashed bodies. He resisted the urge to put his arm up against his nose and mouth and instead followed the warden as he led him to one of the cells at the farthest end of the dark building. Oil lamps hung sporadically and Tallmadge could see many of the prisoners huddling in corners, some wearing only rags while others lay in puddles of their own filth.

The warden stopped, and in the faint sunlight that filtered into the cell along with the glow of a lantern he was handed, he could make out his childhood friend's narrow face, covered in a fair amount of dirt and dried blood. Woodhull had started when the clanging noise of keys unlocked the door, and peered out at them, his eyes wide with fright.

"Abraham," Tallmadge greeted as the warden swung the door open.

"Ben? Tallmadge, is that you?" Woodhull's voice was raspier than normal and he coughed once, a little hoarse, but otherwise made no other sound.

"Warden, please give us a minute here." He turned back to the warden who had approached, intent on unlocking Woodhull's chains. The man stopped and shrugged in a silent manner as he ambled on out and moved away from them.

"He's mute," Woodhull groused in a slightly sour manner. "Apparently his tongue got cut out. Only writes for communication."

Tallmadge filed that information away and crouched next to his friend who was blinking his eyes slowly to adjust for the brightness of the lantern set near him.

"What are you doing here, Tallmadge?" Woodhull flicked a look at him.

"Freeing you," he replied and heard a quiet snort of disbelief from his friend. "I'm serious. I have a pardon here from Governor Trumbull, absolving you of any and all wrongdoing from participating in the London Trade. Since it was your first offense, I told him that you would never do such a thing again since you could not know the differences between the Patriot ones and the British ones and only so happened to get caught up in a sweep of sorts."

Woodhull made another noise of disbelief and Tallmadge shook his head as he stood up and headed out to where the mute warden stood. He gestured for the man to give him the keys, and the man did so. Taking the keys with him as he stepped back in, he bent down and started to unlock Woodhull's manacles.

"Seriously, Tallmadge, what *are* you doing here?" Woodhull asked, his voice a hissing whisper.

"Freeing you-"

"That is a load of horse shite, Tallmadge. Don't think that I don't remember what you were really doing the last time I saw you." His friend suddenly grabbed his wrist in a painful vise-like grip. Tallmadge was a little surprised at the strength considering that his friend had been in jail for over a week now. "Did you know what Hewlett and Simcoe did to Setauket after you left?! They beat the families that had stayed and were suspected to be Patriot sympathizers, Ben. All because they couldn't get you or your friend there."

Tallmadge frowned and pressed his lips together flatly. "I'm sorry," he apologized before continuing to unlock the manacles, "but I speak true. I do have a pardon from Governor Trumbull for your release."

"Out of the generosity of your heart, I suppose," Woodhull groused, releasing his wrist and sitting back.

"And some curiosity, I suppose," Tallmadge said, keeping his voice light and conversational as he finished unlocking the leg manacles and helped his friend remove them from his raw and flayed skin. Woodhull winced, but shook his head at any assistance that Tallmadge wanted to provide to him. Woodhull gingerly stood up, flexing his legs and shaking them. "Why trade with the British? We could use the corn and wheat you grow at your farm, Woodhull."

"Why put myself more at risk in either losing my property or perhaps even my own farm by not trading with the British, Tallmadge," Woodhull arched an eyebrow at him. "They trust me. I provide them with food and provisions and I get a modicum of reassurance that my property stays my own."

"They trust you." Tallmadge stared at him as Woodhull held his wrists out for him to release the shackles there.

"They trust me-" Woodhull repeated, but stopped short as his eyes widened and his narrow face became narrower, a frown pulling it downward. "No, oh no, Ben. No way...there is no way I am-"

Tallmadge tilted his head in earnest. "Abraham, you said so yourself, you have their *trust-*"

"And I have my neck, *intact*, Tallmadge," his friend hissed back at him, clearly angry with what he was insinuating. "I'd like to keep it that way."

"Then why help?" he asked. "Don't think for one second I believed that you were helping out Adamson because he paid in coin. I know you Abraham, I know how much your cousin meant to you when he was killed evacuating Long Island! I know that another one of your cousins serves as a captain and that you certainly don't want to see him captured or worse."

Woodhull was stonily silent as he glared at him, but Tallmadge was not finished. "You want to know why I think you trade with the British and got caught? It's because you want to *do* something, but you don't know how to do it. I only know you were here because Caleb Brewster knew you were here, and I'm suspecting that you tried to tell Caleb something, but the warden here, well, he doesn't let anyone see the prisoners unless they have an official pardon or have served their time."

Tallmadge reached out and grabbed his friend by the shoulder, squeezing it gently. "Come on, Woodhull, I know this. I know *you*." He shook his shoulder a little, "And I know you well enough that when you walk out of here, even if you don't decide to agree to this, you'll find yourself back in the same exact spot. You knew what my man was doing there and you wanted to help. Why warn me away? Why would you and Roe warn me in such a fashion when, if you are as neutral as you claim, you could easily have let them capture me and try me as-"

"A spy," Woodhull hissed, his word barely catching across his breath as he pulled his shoulder away and held his wrists up to be released. Tallmadge sighed and unlocked the manacles, letting them fall away as Woodhull rubbed his raw wrists a little. The narrow-faced man looked away for a long moment, his face giving away none of his internal thoughts. Tallmadge secretly marveled at how well Woodhull could school his expression, but when his friend turned back to face him, he saw the fear that was evident in his eyes.

"All right, Tallmadge. I'll do this," Woodhull reluctantly agreed, his voice quiet, "But there has to be safeguards."

Tallmadge smiled tightly, overjoyed that his childhood friend had agreed to do such a thing. "There will be. No one but myself and General Washington would know about this."

That statement certainly got Woodhull's attention and he blinked, rubbing his wrists again. "Washington?" he hissed quietly and Tallmadge's smile grew a little wider as he nodded.

"We need a man on Long Island who is willing to go into New York. I recommended you," he said and saw Woodhull scoff nervously before holding out a hand to him. Tallmadge deposited the pardon into his hands. "I'll send a mutual friend to find you in a week or so and we will proceed from there, all right?"

Woodhull looked away, snorting slightly as his sour disposition returned. "I think I know this mutual friend, Ben. He's not exactly subtle, you know."

"No, he's not, but do you know any other who knows the Sound like the back of his hand?" he asked. Tallmadge had no doubts that Brewster would be more than happy to volunteer, or at least ferry letters from Woodhull to Fairfield. The only thing was that he would have to set up an express of sorts in order to convey the letters to Washington. That was something he would have to discuss with the general once he returned to White Plains.

Woodhull shook his head as he flexed his legs out once more. He took a few steps towards the open cell door before turning around. "Petticoats and handkerchiefs," he called out, and Tallmadge frowned at him before realizing what he was saying. He nodded and watched his friend walk out of the cell, a newly freed man.

Tallmadge followed him a few minutes later, handing the keys back to the warden who locked up behind him. He exited the jail, wondering if he would see Abraham walking down the road to the docks, but there was no sign of his friend anywhere.

He smiled to himself as he knew he had chosen the right person to become his agent and spy. Woodhull's caution and instincts had already taken a hold of him and he did not want to be seen fraternizing with a Continental officer, lest he be associated with the Patriots instead of maintaining both his neutrality and Tory leanings in the eyes of the British.

Tallmadge untied Castor from his post, mounted him and headed back to the docks. He arrived to see Brewster helping his men lift what looked like barrels of powder and small-arms ammunition onto one of the whaleboats. He caught Brewster's eye with a wave of his hand and saw his friend whistle to one of his fellow sailors to take over, as he walked off of the docks towards him.

"Found Woody, Tall-boy?" Brewster asked and Tallmadge shrugged, a non-committal answer to anyone watching, but the whaler caught onto his gesture and chuckled lightly.

"Do you mind making a visit home in about a week or less?" he asked and Brewster glanced around before shrugging.

"If you say so," his friend smiled tightly. "Though the reception we received last time wasn't so pleasant."

"Petticoats and handkerchiefs," he answered and saw his friend puzzle out what he meant before he laughed long and hard, slapping his thighs and nodding.

"All right then," his friend nodded. "Clever."

"His idea," Tallmadge replied evasively and saw Brewster snort a little.

"Clever little rat-faced bastard."

Tallmadge hoped that Woodhull was not hiding anywhere near the docks and did not hear the amended compliment. Though he had grown up with the two of them, Woodhull and Brewster were closer in age than he was to them – only a year apart by his reckoning. The two were cordial with each other, but there was always an edge of rough teasing between them, especially since both lived bachelor lives but were of complete opposite disposition. He had always wondered how the two got along as neighbors, but supposed that it was likely due to the calming presence of their mutual neighbor, Nancy Strong and her husband Selah, who kept the peace. Tallmadge knew that Selah was a Patriot through and through and Woodhull's idea of using a clothesline with petticoats and handkerchiefs to signal Brewster had come from Nancy: it was an old form of communication they had come up with during those adolescent years. When they would sneak out at night, Nancy would help them avoid their parents by hanging a petticoat and a number of handkerchiefs to signal what cove was safest to enter to avoid their parents' wrath after spending a whole day out on the Sound or skipping chores.

"This isn't going to be a single trip, is it?" Brewster asked and Tallmadge shook his head, wondering if his friend would consent to what he was trying to form.

"Well, then," Brewster shrugged. "I'll keep an eye on the petticoats then. Going to get someone here?"

"Yes," he said, proud and happy that Brewster had counted himself in. "You know-"

"They're never going to catch me, Ben," his friend interrupted. "You don't need to worry your plumed head about me hanging off of a rope. You send the kid, though to be the courier, I can't guarantee that I'm not going to adopt him and turn him into a whaler, impalement on a fish hook or not."

"Good luck with that," he replied and Brewster laughed. He had a feeling that even with Adamson's willingness to skulk in the shadows and be a spy, his friend would probably feel betrayed if he was sent to be one of the couriers for Woodhull's correspondences. He supposed he could use Adamson in some other capacity so not to aggravate his loyal friend. "I'll be back soon, more instructions and the sort," he said and Brewster nodded as he tossed him a jaunty salute.

"See you soon, Tall-boy," his friend said.

Tallmadge wheeled Castor around and set him off at a pace towards General Silliman's house. As he rode away, he could not help the warm feeling of pride that engulfed him at his success. He had two agents who were willing to provide intelligence about Long Island and New York. The next step was to let General Washington know of his success and begin the process of ensuring that his agents would not be caught by the British and suffer the same fate as his best friend. Like General Washington, Tallmadge was determined to learn from the mistakes that Nathan had made, in order to honor his friend's memory and not send anymore of his own friends up to Heaven with him.

Tallmadge returned to camp a day later, having spent the night as Silliman's guest. He had been prepared to spend the night at a local inn, but the general had insisted that he stay after evening meal and Tallmadge had reluctantly agreed – a little embarrassed that as a junior officer, he was staying at the house of a senior officer. He had left in the morning and arrived back at Bedford in the late afternoon. He first considered riding directly to White Plains, but Tallmadge wanted to report to Sheldon before making his way to White Plains later in the evening for his successful report to Washington.

"Blackden," he greeted as he saw the lieutenant colonel step out of Sheldon's tent, two pieces of paper in his hand. He dismounted and tied Castor up to the post just as the lieutenant colonel thrust the two sheets into his face.

"We've a serious problem, Tallmadge." Blackden's voice was strained and Tallmadge frowned, taking the letter into his hands and started to read it. He vaguely recognized the hand writing as Stoddard's.

"What..." he began, but trailed off as he continued to read. The letter made no sense and was laying out a series of accusations and events that Tallmadge could not discern. "Blackden, what is-"

"The last page, Benjamin." In the whole time they had served with each other, Tallmadge had never heard such trepidation in Blackden's voice, nor had he ever heard the man call him by his first name.

Tallmadge quickly turned to the last page and shock filled him. All six captains, six of the seven lieutenants, and two cornets of the regiment – a total of fourteen of the eighteen officers – had signed the letter. A letter addressed to Colonel Sheldon, judging by the post script at the bottom, beneath the signatures. "B-Blackden...what..." His eyes scanned the last paragraph, which all but called for Sheldon to retire from command.

"We've got a mutiny on our hands," Blackden pronounced

gravely.

SOURCES

Primary sources in the writing of this material are not limited to the following:

"Connecticut's Revolutionary Cavalry: Sheldon's Horse" by John T. Hayes (1975, Pequot Press)

"General Washington's Commando: Benjamin Tallmadge in the Revolutionary War" by Richard F. Welch (2014, McFarland and Company, Inc.)

"Memoir of Colonel Benjamin Tallmadge (1858)" by Benjamin Tallmadge & F.A. Tallmadge (reprinted 2016, original 1858, Thomas Holman)

"General Washington's Spies: On Long Island and in New York" by Morton Pennypacker (1939, Long Island Historical Society)

"Revolutionary Spies: Intelligence and Espionage in America's First War" by Tim McNeese (2015, Fall River Press)

"Battles of the American Revolution – 1775-1781: Including Battle Maps & Charts of the American Revolution" by Henry B. Carrington (1881, Promontory Press, NY)

Library of Congress – The Washington Papers (1776-1783)

Silas Deane Papers (1776-1783) – Connecticut Historical Society

"Record of Service of Connecticut Men in the: I. War of the Revolution, II. War of 1812, III. Mexican War" - from the enlistment records compiled by Major Benjamin Tallmadge

"Nathan Hale – The Life and Death of America's First Spy" by M. William Phelps (2008, Thomas Dunne Books)

The Benjamin Tallmadge Papers Collection (1775-1825) -

Litchfield Historical Society

Secondary sources:

"Washington's Eyes: The Continental Light Dragoons" by Burt Garfield Loescher (1977, The Old Army Press

"A Proper Sense of Honor: Service and Sacrifice in George Washington's Army" by Caroline Cox (2004, The University of North Carolina Press)

"Westchester Gamble: The Encampment on the Hudson & the Trapping of Cornwallis" by Richard Borkow (2011, The History Press)

"The Glourious Cause" by Jeff Shaara (2002, Ballantine Books)

"Washington's Spies: The Story of America's First Spy Ring" by Alexander Rose (2006, Bantam Dell)

"George Washington, Spymaster: How the Americans Outspied the British and Won the Revolutionary War" by Thomas B. Allen (2004, National Geographic)

"Tri-Spy Walking Tour" as presented by Margo Arceri of the Tri-Village Historical Society

The New York Historical Society Revolutionary War Maps Collection

The Third New Jersey Regiment "The Jersey Blues"

"The Life of a Revolutionary Soldier" as presented by the Deane-Webb-Stevens House

ACKNOWLEDGMENTS

This story would not have been possible without my editor Dorian Fox. Thank you for cutting down the unwieldy dialogue, formatting issues, use of tense and Oxford commas.

Thank you to Kerry Hynds of Aero Gallerie for the cover art.

Thank you to the curators of the Connecticut Historical Society, Litchfield Historical Society, New York Historical Society, and Colonial Williamsburg for allowing me access to the actual letters of various people in this story.

Thank you to the following people: Mr. McGrath for piquing and keeping my interest in history; the late and great Professor Coffee for turning history from dry lectures to interesting stories. Joy, thank you for pointing me in the right direction when I first started this ambitious project. Elina, thank you for being one of the first to read and edit this story. Thank you also to Jaclyn for your constant support and story recommendations to open my eyes to different worlds.

Lastly, thank you to my parents. I have and will always cherish your support.

ABOUT THE AUTHOR

Sandra is a lifetime member of the Connecticut Historical Society and a former long-time resident of the state. She currently resides in California. *Patriots* is her first published work.

Printed in Great Britain
by Amazon

45687781R00280